BLOOD HEAT

DOCTOR WHO – THE NEW ADVENTURES

Also available:

BLOOD HEAT

Jim Mortimore

First published in Great Britain in 1993 by
Doctor Who Books
an imprint of Virgin Publishing Ltd
332 Ladbroke Grove
London W10 5AH

Copyright © Jim Mortimore 1993
'Doctor Who' series copyright © British Broadcasting
Corporation 1993

ISBN 0 426 20399 2

Cover illustration by Jeff Cummins
Phototypeset by Intype, London
Printed and bound in Great Britain by
Cox & Wyman Ltd, Reading, Berks

For Brian

Who planned to write but was unable to complete his work, and whose memory will remain in every book, most especially in this one.

JM

'Fear is the parent of cruelty.'

J. A. Froud

INVOLUTION

It remembered feeding. Now it knew only hunger. That and the pain, invading it like a parasite, controlling, consuming, relentless and inviolable.

–kill– the pain told it.

It struggled to understand but this space, this . . . single universe with its shortage of physical dimensions was not enough to contain its thoughts, let alone its body.

–kill!–

A hatchway opened in reality, offering it a tiny glimpse of its own universe. A reward. A promise.

–!kill!–

It framed questions. What did the pain want? Why would the pain not let it feed? What is 'kill'?

–!do not question. Obey!–

What is 'obey'?

–!!kill!!–

What is 'question'?

–!!KILL!!–

Alone, it was paralysed. Starving, it could only die; with the experience, finally, came the understanding that it must obey.

It began to scream.

PART ONE

FUTURE PAST

In the part of the TARDIS which she used as a laboratory Bernice Summerfield sighed with frustration. She carefully placed the Alexandrian scroll she was trying to preserve back in the small airtight safe, capped the bottle of preserving fluid and racked it neatly alongside the other jars and bottles on the bench.

'This is a bit of a switch for you, isn't it?'

Bernice jumped at the sound of Ace's voice so close behind her. 'Are you sure you don't get your jollies creeping up on people?'

Ace shrugged. 'That's Spacefleet service for you. Anyway, I thought you were into digging stuff up. Archaeology. All that. Not sloshing around with paintbrushes.'

'Sometimes archaeology *is* sloshing around with paintbrushes.' She handed the items in question to the younger woman. 'Here. Make yourself useful.'

Ace took the brushes across the lab to a sink unit where Bernice had set up a tank of cleaning fluid. She dumped them into the fluid to soak while Bernice relocked the safe. 'Anyway, why use all this prehistoric stuff? There's gear in the TARDIS even Spacefleet has never heard of.'

'Stasis fields? Preserving equipment? Translation and interpretive software? Nah.' Bernice ran her fingers through her cropped hair, then frowned when she remembered she hadn't washed her hands yet. 'Sod it. Anyway, I'm just a twenty-sixth-century girl. The old-fashioned approach has always appealed.' She crossed to the sink unit and began to wash her hands.

'The quiet life getting to you, is it?' Ace said.

Bernice grinned. 'I'm sure I don't know what you mean.'

Ace moved back across the lab and leaned against a filing cabinet. She plucked the last of her redesigned marble-sized nitro nine smartbombs from her pocket and began to flip it casually from hand to hand. A tiny red LED glowed steadily on the nonreflective casing. 'It's getting to me alright.'

Bernice towelled her hands dry. 'I'd never have guessed.'

Ace looked up, while continuing to juggle the bomb. 'It's okay. It's not armed.' She grinned. 'Disarm.' The LED turned black and she pocketed the device.

Bernice threw the towel at Ace. 'Sometimes you really scare me.'

Ace laughed. Her fist snapped out to catch the towel. She twisted it into a long, damp rope, curled it around both fists and pulled it taut with a wet slapping sound. 'You should have known me before.'

Bernice reached for her hip flask and unscrewed the cap. She offered the flask to Ace, who shook her head. 'I hardly need to,' Bernice said. 'Your sense of humour alone's enough to put me in an early grave.'

Ace's smile flattened. 'It's nothing the booze won't do first.'

Bernice paused with her hip flask halfway to her mouth. 'Is there a point to this conversation?'

'It's just my way of saying I like you, Benny.' There was a hard edge to Ace's voice which belied her words.

Bernice took a gulp from the flask, re-capped it, and slipped it back into the hip pocket of her overalls. 'Perhaps it'd be better if you didn't. Comment, I mean,' she added pointedly.

Ace chewed her lower lip thoughtfully. 'We could be friends, you know. We don't have to keep sniping at each other like this.'

'You seem to be doing enough sniping for both of us.' Bernice paused. 'You've been out of Spacefleet for months now, and you weren't even happy when you were in it. Why do you still wear the armour?'

Ace shrugged. 'I like it.'

'Rubbish. It's more than that. You depend on it.'

Ace absently kicked the side of the lab bench. 'Think you know everything, don't you?'

'Ace, that's not what I meant and you know it.'

Ace was readying an angry reply when a third voice boomed out behind them. 'I can understand the attraction.'

Both women looked towards the wide doors which led off the lab into other parts of the TARDIS. The Doctor stood framed in the doorway. 'But that doesn't lessen the danger.'

Ace looked away. 'You're a fine one to talk.'

The Doctor frowned. 'Don't be like that, Ace. It's not polite. Especially not when I've come here to warn you both.'

'Warn us?' Bernice said sharply. 'About what?'

'Something's happening to the TARDIS.'

Ace laughed humourlessly. 'Just when I was beginning to enjoy the peace and quiet.' Pushing past the Doctor, she headed towards the lab doors. 'I'm going to change,' she said in reply to his pointed look.

The Doctor rubbed his eyes tiredly as Ace left the lab.

Bernice caught his eye and shrugged. 'So what's up with the ship?' she asked.

The Doctor began to prowl around the lab, talking rapidly all the while. 'Basically,' he explained, 'the fault seems to lie within the time rotor itself, which is a little worrying, especially when you consider the personality schism the old girl suffered not so very long ago – ' The Doctor paused in mid sentence to mop his brow with a silk handkerchief. 'Yes. Very worrying indeed.' He stuffed his handkerchief absently back into his top pocket.

Bernice reached out to straighten the triangle of silk projecting from the edge of the pocket. 'With you, what isn't?' She gave the handkerchief a last satisfied pat and stepped back to admire her handiwork. 'Now. What was that about a schism?'

Without warning, the Doctor suddenly charged out of the lab. Bernice gave a start of surprise, then followed him into the corridor.

'What I was referring to,' he called back without looking round, 'was the personality schism the old girl suffered as a result of your recent adventure in Edwardian England,

5

although, I must confess, what's happening now seems to be more of a physical effect. In fact one might almost say it's taking the form of a rather complicated – ah.' He skidded to a halt.

Bernice caught up with him as he began to poke at a glowing roundel with his umbrella. 'What's up? Is it serious?'

The Doctor straightened from his examination of the roundel. 'I'm rather afraid it is.'

Suddenly Bernice became aware that the Doctor was looking over her shoulder with a worried expression. She turned, following his gaze. Behind them the corridor walls were beginning to glow.

And dissolve.

'Ah,' said the Doctor again. 'Oh dear. Ah. Hm.' He began to run along the corridor, away from the glow, towards the console room. 'Come on!'

But Bernice didn't move. She felt an odd calmness steal over her. She moved closer to the phenomenon, studying it. The effect was fascinating; obviously it was some kind of high-energy transformation resulting in scintillant particle emission – but transformation of what? And into what? Captivated, she watched as large, irregular sections of the corridor walls slid quietly away into a kind of iridescent murk. She reached out to touch the nearest patch.

Her fingers vanished.

'No! Benny, *no*!' The Doctor started back towards Bernice, a panic-stricken look on his face.

Startled, Bernice moved away from the area of the discontinuity. Or rather tried to. Her arm wouldn't move; wouldn't come free of the curious area of grey sparkle.

And now her hand was missing from the wrist forward.

The Doctor slid to a halt beside her.

Bernice laughed nervously. 'Give me a hand, would you, Doctor? I seem to be one short.'

The Doctor's expression was serious. 'Don't move.'

'Staying still doesn't seem to be the problem.'

The Doctor scowled grimly. He poked the area of sparkling grey with the end of his umbrella. It stuck fast.

'Oh dear.'

'What?'

'I was afraid of that. It is a physical schism. A rift.'

'What's that?'

'A rip in the fabric of the TARDIS leading into the Vortex. Something that theoretically impossible.'

'Why is it theoretically impossible?'

'Because theoretically, it's impossible for an outside agency to destroy a TARDIS.'

Bernice swallowed. 'Ah.' Her arm had now vanished as far as the elbow. 'And what's going to happen when it reaches the rest of me?'

The Doctor licked his lips. 'It would take so long to explain that I might not have time to rescue you.' Leaving his umbrella hanging suspended in midair, half of its length vanishing slowly into the rift, the Doctor turned and hopscotched quickly back up the remaining solid areas of the corridor towards the console room.

'Might not?' Bernice said worriedly, as another six inches of arm quietly vanished. 'Doctor!'

The Doctor dashed into the console room, skidding to a halt at the sight which greeted him.

'Oh dear,' he said softly.

Where the hexagonal central console had been was a swirling area of luminescent grey.

From the corridor, Bernice's voice echoed, *'Hey, Doctor, whatever you're going to do, you'd better hurry up and –'*

There was a long silence.

The Doctor took off his hat and lowered his gaze to the floor.

The floor, too, was beginning to dissolve.

He hopscotched to the door and was just in time to see another section of corridor, that containing the last few inches of his umbrella, vanish into the rift.

There was no sign of Bernice.

Ace had been asleep. The scream brought her awake fast. Without even opening her eyes, she flung aside the covers

7

of her bed, grabbed the first clothes to hand and headed out of her room at a dead run.

Ace did not call out as she ran through the endless, dimly lit corridors of the TARDIS. Silence was one part of Spacefleet she hadn't left behind. Before long she had reached the console room. She burst in through the door. 'Doctor, what – ' She broke off.

The room wasn't there. Just a swirling, iridescent grey fog.

The scream stopped.

Ace scrambled backwards as the grey area surged towards her. Now she became aware that the whole corridor behind her was coming apart as well, something she had seen and reacted to, but not consciously registered while running.

Certain the console room was empty, Ace turned to continue her search in the eerie silence which now seemed to envelop the TARDIS.

The Doctor was standing directly behind her, his face in shadow. Only his eyes were visible, wild and burning in the darkness. His normally spotless cream safari jacket and precisely creased trousers looked as if he'd been sleeping in them. Ace let out a startled cry before quickly recovering. 'Doctor! Are you okay? I heard – '

Without the slightest acknowledgement of her concern, the Doctor pushed past Ace and hopscotched along the disintegrating corridor.

Ace followed, yelling questions all the way. 'Doctor, what's happening? Are we in danger? Where's Benny? Doctor! *Where's Bernice!*'

The Doctor said nothing. His pace accelerated until she was scarcely able to keep up. Eventually the patches of greyness infecting the corridors became more intermittent, finally vanishing altogether. As if they had been concentrating around the console room and the more frequently inhabited areas of the ship, Ace thought with a shiver. As if they were searching for something. For us.

The Doctor abruptly slowed and dashed through a large, wood-panelled doorway. Ace followed him into a chamber she recognized as the secondary console room; a Victorian-style analogue of the main console room, panelled with circles of mahogany and complete with brass-railinged central console, arched viewscreen, and brightly coloured indicator boards positioned against the chamber's six walls.

Registering his presence, the TARDIS tried to bring up the ambient lighting to an operational norm. The Doctor's hands blurred across the banks of instrumentation encrusting the central console. Lights flashed. The brass mechanism adorning the centre of the console began to describe complex movements, like a tiny orrery. The engines began to hum somewhat uncertainly.

The Doctor prowled around the room and settled on an Edwardian chaise longue which Ace knew for a fact hadn't been present only minutes before. He placed his head in his hands.

Hesitantly, she moved across the room and sat beside him.

'Listen, Ace,' the Doctor whispered before she could speak. 'I've set the TARDIS controls to fight the invader. . . . not sure if it'll work. . . . might be . . . too powerful for the old girl to . . .' The Doctor's face creased in pain. 'To . . . stop. I . . .' He swallowed. Ace could tell he was suffering badly. 'I couldn't help . . . Benny. She's . . . she's . . .' The Doctor threw back his head with a cry of utter despair. Ace recoiled back up the chaise longue with the force of it.

The scream faded. Ace realized the Doctor was trying to call her name. She reached out to touch his arm. The muscles in it were rigid. His fingers were pressing hard against his temples.

His eyes fixed upon Ace's with terrible certainty.

'Remember me – ' The words were being squeezed out, pinched between teeth clenched in fear. 'Then I can't . . . really . . . die.'

'Don't be stupid,' Ace said too loudly. 'You can't die!'

The Doctor forced a smile which didn't come anywhere near his eyes. 'Time Lords live a long time, Ace, but we're not immortal.'

9

Ace stood up and yelled angrily. 'You don't know what you're talking about!'

The TARDIS lights began to dim. Local gravity fluctuated.

'Doctor!'

'Symbiosis, Ace. I suffer, the old girl reacts.'

Ace began struggling for breath. The air in the console room was getting dusty and foul. She became aware that the constant hum of the engines was faltering. She gasped with sudden realization. The ship was responding to the Doctor's belief that he was dying! That was why it was disintegrating. That was why –

Her eyes flickered around the room, her attention caught by something ... something different ... She blinked. The dimensions seems to be shrinking. A minute passed. The room was definitely smaller.

Ace felt near to panic. She controlled her fear with an effort. By this time the oscillating brass time rotor was scraping the ceiling on its upward sweep, and the air tasted as thin and dry as that on a mountain top. Grey patches began to appear on the interior doorway.

'Snap out of it, Doctor! Something's wrong with the TARDIS. You're making something happen to the TARDIS!'

The Doctor simply stared. There was a cold, black light behind his eyes, as if they looked out from nothing but an empty shell. Ace shook the Doctor to get his attention, but he just slumped sideways on the chaise longue and curled up into a foetal ball, knees and elbows tucked into his chest, his body language clear enough to need no translation.

Ace moved to the Doctor's side. She took his hand. The skin was icy cold and waxy to the touch. She tried to bring back some warmth to his body by chafing the limb, but no matter how she searched for a response, however slight, there was none.

Ice began to form on his skin.

Ace didn't know what to do. Her gun was in her room. In any case, how could you shoot a grey splotch? She stood nervously. There was a sharp pain above her eyes.

Her senses reeled with the lack of air. Had her head really cracked against the ceiling? That was impossible! The console room was . . . was as big as . . .

The inside of a police telephone call box.

Ace let out a frightened yell. There were no echoes. Her effort used up the last air in the cupboard-sized space in which she was trapped. Ace clutched at her throat as she fell to the floor, squashed into a ball in one tiny corner by the collapsing dimensions of the TARDIS. Her lips became numb. Her eyes began to glaze. Her chest heaved with the unsuppressible compulsion to draw oxygen into her burning lungs.

And then the last breath was gone. There was no air, only silence and dust.

It was the end.

No! She wouldn't accept it! There was no way she was going to . . .

' *– do it before this stuff swallows me up completely*!'

' *– pletely*!'

' *– tely*!'

. . . she remembered colour; here there was none.

She remembered sensation; here she could feel nothing.

'*Hey, Doctor, whatever you're going to do, you'd better hurry up and –* '

' *– and –* '

. . . okay, then. She'd start from first principles. Where was she? Who was she? Was she even really a 'she'?

Questions.

She knew that *questions* were patterns of *ideas*; that ideas formed consciousness and consciousness defined intelligence.

Here she was only intelligence.

Except that there were no . . . *questions* here . . . no *patterns* and therefore no possibility of –

. . . opened her eyes. The TARDIS lights were bright and cheerful. The console room was humming with its usual, eerie vibrations. The central console ticked and whirred with steady efficiency. The time rotor was still and dark;

the TARDIS had landed. A glance around the room confirmed her suspicions. Beyond two flat steps, the exterior doors were wide open. The light shining from the room made a bright rectangle on the ground. Ace saw ferns growing from black, mulchy earth. A patchy ground mist began to creep into the ship.

Beyond the rectangle of light everything was in darkness.

Ace shakily regained her feet. She moved unsteadily to the doors and leaned against them for support. Eerie cries echoed distantly, along with a soft rustle of wind moving through the ferns and the tiny sucking noises of the mud.

Ace scratched her head in puzzlement. Had she been asleep and dreaming? Her fingers traced the outline of a large bruise on the top of her head. She stared wonderingly up at the ceiling. High above her head there was a barely discernible red smear on the wooden panelling.

Blood.

So much for the dream-theory.

Ace wondered where the Doctor's body was. She glanced back over to the chaise longue, half expecting to see the dead Time Lord draped across it. The item of furniture was no longer present. There was no sign of the Doctor.

A large rectangle of paper was lightly blu-tacked to the nearest side of the time rotor: a note from the Doctor. Ace tore the paper off and squinted in order to read the handwriting:

Ace. I'm fine. I'll be back soon.

The note was signed with an unintelligible scrawl.

Ace scowled irritably. She opened a roundelled cupboard and rummaged inside for a coat. It took her a moment to find one; the cupboard was bigger than an average-sized room. As an afterthought she grabbed her old satchel from a nearby hatrack.

When she re-entered the console room there was another note tacked to the time rotor:

Ace. Take your coat off. It's dangerous out here.

Ace frowned. She crossed the console room and stepped out of the TARDIS. Mud squelched underfoot. She moved cautiously to the edge of the patch of light projected from the ship. Her eyes tried to pierce the murk beyond, but could make nothing out beside the ambiguous shapes of vegetation. Branches and bushes slashed the umber sky into jagged shapes. The eerie sounds were more pronounced than ever; they drifted like smoke through the soggy air.

Something made Ace glance back at the TARDIS. She could make out the impossible geometry of the console room through the open doors of the ship's police-box exterior. But the view was narrowing: the doors were closing! She began to splash back towards the ship but she was too late. Just as she reached them, the doors glided shut, first thinning to a knife edge, then sealing off the light from inside completely. Ace thumped a clenched fist in frustration against the simulated wooden exterior.

As the darkness closed in around her, Ace wished she'd brought a torch. She groped around in the pockets of her jacket, wondering if the Doctor had ever had the common sense to place a torch there. She found a stale bar of chocolate, a crumpled paperback book and three missing pieces from a jigsaw she'd tried to complete a month before. Buried deep in the fluff lining the last pocket she tried, Ace's fingers closed on something small and square. She drew it out. A box of matches! Ace grinned. She pulled out a match.

'I wouldn't do that if I were you.' The Doctor appeared beside her, hat jammed jauntily onto his head, umbrella draped casually across one arm, clothes miraculously clean and neat.

'Doctor! You were – '

'Never mind that now. Did you see my note?'

Ace nodded.

'And my other note?'

'Yeah. So what? It's not exactly the front line here, you know.'

The Doctor sighed. 'Have a sniff. Recognize the smell?'

Ace wrinkled her nose. 'Spacefleet toilets.'

'Methane. Marsh gas.' The Doctor leaned a little closer to emphasize his words. 'Highly inflammable.'

Ace glanced down at the matchbox. A hint of a grin touched the corners of her mouth. 'You know,' she said slowly, 'I thought you were dead.'

Avoiding her question, the Doctor glanced at the TARDIS. 'Did you close the doors?'

Ace shrugged. She shook her head.

'Must be something to do with the HADS then.'

Ace gazed nervously into the darkness. The Hostile Action Displacement System only ever came on line when the integrity of the ship was threatened in some way. Because it had the ability to travel through time as well as space, the TARDIS's defence system was designed to predict incipient danger before it actually happened. All of which meant that lurking somewhere nearby, perhaps as near as the next few minutes, was a threat which the telepathic mind of the TARDIS had decided was worth preparing for.

'Are we in danger?'

The Doctor shrugged.

'Shall we go back to the ship then?'

The Doctor blinked with indecision. Something was compelling him to stay outside when it was quite apparent that an undisclosed danger was lurking nearby.

Ace sighed impatiently. 'In that case, perhaps now you'll tell me exactly what last night was all about? I mean, if the HADS are operational, why didn't they warn you about those splotchy things?'

The Doctor took a deep breath. 'Well, you see, it's difficult for the TARDIS to anticipate a danger coming from within herself. Her interior is supposed to exist in a state of temporal grace, you know.'

'That means no weapons work inside the TARDIS, right? Well if that's the case, how come the grey splotches managed to virtually destroy it? And where is Benny? is she inside, or dead, or what?'

'I'm sure she'll be fine.' The Doctor glanced narrowly at Ace. 'Anyway, I thought you didn't care too much for Bernice?'

Ace immediately opened her mouth to reply, hesitated, then closed it without speaking. She turned away.

She was on the point of turning back when a foul-smelling, reptilian, armour-plated nightmare erupted from the surrounding foliage with a chilling scream and charged directly at them.

Ace recovered her balance and spun round. 'It's a dinosaur!'

They leaped in opposite directions. The TARDIS lurched as four tons of heavily armoured reptile crashed into its side.

The Doctor's voice echoed out of the darkness. 'Get back, Ace! As far as you can. Quickly!' He then went on in slightly awe-struck tones, 'Ornithischia nodosauridae. Genus: *Edmontonia*. Fantastic, isn't it?'

'Fantastic? It's trying to eat the TARDIS!'

The dinosaur churned the ground as it began another powerful charge, its dome-armoured twenty-foot length moving with unbelievable speed upon four short but muscular legs. This time there was a loud crack as the animal smashed the impressive bulk of its forward-projecting shoulder horns into the flank of the ship.

'Oy!' Ace ran at the dinosaur, waving her arms. 'Just you stop that right now!' The huge armour-plated reptile ignored her. She groped in her pocket for the smartbomb she'd demonstrated earlier to Bernice.

At last the reptile seemed to notice her presence. It ripped up a small bush from the ground in its powerful jaws and began stamping the ground with its front limbs.

More impressed than she cared to admit, Ace backed warily away from the creature. Its glassy eyes followed her every step. Slowly she brought the smartbomb to her lips. 'Target input: reptile, mass four tons, metric range five metres. Arm. Standby,' she whispered.

The little red LED on the bomb began to glow innocuously.

Ace was about to launch the smartbomb when the Doctor's voice echoed distantly from the mist. 'I should think the edmontonia's got at least as much right to live as either of us, wouldn't you?'

Ace shrugged. 'How did you – '

'Don't forget to disarm it,' the Doctor's disembodied

voice said pleasantly, ignoring her question. 'Save it for a rainy day.'

Ace looked down at her hand. 'Disarm.' she muttered irritably.

The LED winked out and she pocketed the device. She stared at the edmontonia, which was stamping and huffing loudly. 'Phew,' she said, sniffing disdainfully. 'Got to take more care of those teeth.' She ducked into the under-growth and began to make her way towards the place from which she estimated the Doctor's voice had originated.

The edmontonia charged the TARDIS again. This time it moved.

Glancing back through the undergrowth, Ace saw the TARDIS tip over and begin to slide towards a sticky pool of black tar some yards away.

'Doctor!' Ace yelled above the tremendous din of the creature.

The Doctor's voice drifted distractedly out of the sur-rounding mist. 'Don't worry, Ace. It can't possibly regard the ship as a threat. It's probably just observing territorial rights. I don't suppose the old girl smells very familiar, that's all.'

'But last night, the TARDIS was dying. You said there was no power. Are you sure it'll be okay?'

'Ace, trust me. The old girl knows how to look after herself.'

The edmontonia gave one last violent heave. The TARDIS toppled over the lip of the depression and sank quickly into the glutinous tar. In moments it was gone.

Ace said, 'I'll take your word for that, then.'

The edmontonia gave a little snort, flipped its muscular tail in the mud and ambled away into the misty dawn.

Ace watched the creature's oval footprints slowly fill in with mud. 'Doctor!' she called indignantly into the murk.

'It's alright, Ace, there's no need to shout.' Standing quietly beside Ace, the Doctor regarded her with the somewhat spaced-out look of one who has misplaced his spectacles, or possibly his mind. 'Is there a problem?'

Ace sighed and pointed.

First the Doctor's eyes and then his whole head swivelled tortoise-like, to follow Ace's finger to its inevitable, glutinous, terminus. The Time Lord scratched his head. He crossed to the tar pit, dipped a finger into the muck, held it up to the light, kneaded it into a little ball, sniffed it, stopped short of tasting it, and instead flipped the mass away into the primitive, non-flowering vegetation bordering the mud in which they stood.

'A colloidal deposit of vegetable fibre, mineral salts in solution and indeterminate trace chemical constituents,' he said succinctly. 'In short: tar.'

Ace was beginning to feel that the Doctor's ability to miss the point bordered upon the sublime. 'Why didn't the TARDIS dematerialize if the HADS were operational?'

The Doctor thought for a moment. 'I expect she realized we weren't on board. She's not stupid, you know.' He paused in thought. 'Of course it is just possible, what with the damage inflicted on her last night, that the old girl might have felt there was more danger involved in dematerializing than there was in being buried.'

'Danger?' Ace said worriedly. 'In what way?'

The Doctor did not reply.

'Doctor! Our ride home just got itself turned into a million-year-old fossil!'

Incredibly, the Doctor grinned. 'I've had worse starts to the day,' he assured her confidently. 'And anyway, look on the bright side: it could make some palaeontologist's life really interesting.'

Dismissing the disaster as if this sort of thing happened to him as regularly as breakfast time, the Doctor held out some oval objects for Ace's perusal. 'What do you make of these?'

'I expect they're just giant chicken's eggs. I hear they have them in cloud-cuckoo-land.'

The Doctor began juggling the objects. 'Close,' he said. 'But no cigar, I'm afraid. They're gizzard stones, although from the species seismosaurus rather than Avionix giganticus.'

'So?' Ace prompted impatiently.

'Well. On the one hand – ' The Doctor gestured with one hand, juggling the gizzard stones with the other. ' –

Seismosaurus existed in the upper Jurassic times, concurrently with all the vegetation you see around us. Our old friend edmontonia there, on the other hand – ' The Doctor gestured with his other hand, then looked faintly surprised when the gizzard stones tumbled to the ground. ' – didn't evolve until almost fifty million years later, during the end of the Cretaceous Period. He dusted his hands. 'Which leaves us with a rather alarming puzzle.'

'Not to mention some muddy gizzard stones.'

'Hm.' The Doctor bent to recover the stones, changed his mind, lost his balance, and whirled his umbrella madly until he managed to regain it.

'The instruments couldn't be mistaken about where we are?'

The Doctor shook his head, then made a grab for his hat. 'Even if we were in another geological era, that still wouldn't explain the simultaneous appearance of two creatures over fifty million years apart in evolutionary terms.'

Ace thought hard. 'But if someone was mucking about with time?'

'Then it's possible, yes. But the power necessary to maintain the simultaneous existence of species that lived that far apart would be enormous. I've seen it done with individual animals, but the effect was temporary and localized to a few hundred yards, and even that required almost the entire output of the national grid. Look around us. Cycads and ginkgos. Tar. Dinosaurs. Gizzard stones. We're talking about simultaneous ecosystem overlap over a relative period of at least a couple of hours, and a spacial distance of ... well, how far can you see? Well, anyway, it'll be more when the sun rises. No. The power required to adjust the timeflow and overcome temporal inertia on that scale would be ... well.' The Doctor balanced precariously in the mud on one foot, grimaced, took off his other shoe and proceeded to scoop mud out of it. 'It simply couldn't exist on something as small as a single planet.'

'Then how . . .?'

The Doctor shook his head, then his shoe, then put his

shoe back on his foot, holding onto Ace's outstretched hand for balance as he did so. 'There are a few individuals who might have the power, the know-how or the inclination. The Guardians; Rassilon; myself, for that matter. The Master could probably have wrangled it with a bit of jiggery-pokery. Not to mention the alien species which could have – '

'Yes, but I don't understand why,' Ace interrupted. 'Nobody would expend that much time and effort just to mess up the lives of a few dinosaurs, right? They'd have to have a reason, wouldn't they? And how does it tie in with the attack on the TARDIS? Have we even decided if there was an attack on the TARDIS yet? And what about Benny?'

'Frankly, my dear, I haven't a clue. Still, time enough for that another time. Yesterday's another day, as they say.' The Doctor shrugged, put his foot down and promptly sank up to his ankles in the mud. 'Oh dear.'

'Here.' Ace grabbed hold of the Doctor's umbrella and pulled him clear of the mud. 'I'm not very happy about all this.'

'You're not very happy! Ace, if I'm right,' the Doctor hesitated, 'or even if I'm wrong, the whole causal fabric of the universe could be under threat!'

Ace smiled slightly. 'I knew I should have blown up that dinosaur.'

The Doctor tut-tutted and moved off into the undergrowth.

'Now where are you going?' Not receiving a reply, Ace ran after the Doctor. After a few minutes he stopped abruptly, and Ace ran into him. She smoothed a handful of damp hair out of her face and stared questioningly at him. He placed one finger on his lips.

She peered into the light mist, trying to see or hear what had caught his attention.

As she watched and waited, the temperature rose some degrees and Ace felt a fresh layer of sweat start out upon her face. Without comment the Doctor fished a brand-new tennis headband from one of his pockets, stripped away and discarded the cellophane wrapping and pressed the cloth in her hand.

Ace stared pointedly at the discarded packaging. 'I hope that's biodegradable.'

Smiling sheepishly, the Doctor retrieved the wrapper, shook it clear of the mud and crammed it back into a pocket.

Grinning, Ace secured the sweatband around her forehead and once again peered into the middle distance. As she watched, the sun rose and the mist began to boil away, shifting and melting to reveal the sky.

As the last shreds of mist faded into the bright early morning, Ace could make out more and more of their surroundings. Bowl-shaped cycads on slender trunks no wider at their base than her waist swayed in the heat-generated convection currents like a forest of ninety-foot-high inverted pendulums. Nearer the ground, ginkgos, ferns, shrubs and smaller trees fought for possession of the sunlight. There were no flowers here to introduce colour into the scenery, but the many different shades of green, grey, brown and cream brought a sombre beauty to the land which Ace found quite breathtaking. Far away, chalky mountains shimmered beneath a thin layer of cloud.

Insects droned loudly. A hot wind slithered between the tall cycads, rustling the undergrowth and rippling the mud in which they stood. Ace found herself overwhelmed by the primitive beauty of the land. For a few minutes she forgot the fate of Bernice, and the TARDIS, and the possibility of their being marooned here, and just drank in the perfection, the cleanness of this younger Earth.

From the foliage to Ace's right came a sudden sharp hiss. A reptile measuring up to Ace's shoulder in height burst from the nearest patch of vegetation and ran towards her with comical strides. Mottled brown and grey with a pattern of dark orange tiger stripes across its back, it looked a bit like an elongated, featherless ostrich, except it was more sinister than that. In place of wings it had two spindly forelimbs. Hooded glassy eyes and sharp teeth were set in a pointed skull, which was connected to

20

a compact body by a sinuous neck. The animal propelled itself by digging thrusts of two powerful hind legs. Ace saw all this before it vanished into the vegetation on the other side of the clearing, leaving her with no more than a fleeting glimpse of a whiplike tail flicking the mud in its wake.

Ace jerked a thumb after the reptile. 'What was that one?'

'An ornithomimus, Ace, a Cretaceous theropod. Its diet consisted of insects and fruit. Nothing to be scared of. And nothing like what we're looking for.'

Ace paused a moment. Something the Doctor had said didn't seem to add up. 'Hang on. I thought you said that ornithomimus ate fruit?'

'And so it did. Probably in copious quantities. Why do you ask?'

'Well do you see any fruit trees? We've walked a couple of miles now; in this heat they ought to be growing all over the place.'

The Doctor paused, tipped his hat back, gazed up at the sky, raked his umbrella through the nearest patch of foliage and turned to regard his companion with a gimlet eye. 'You're half right, Ace. Look here.'

Ace peered closer. As the Doctor poked at a shrunken tree with his umbrella. She could see several gnarled pods, shaped like walnuts, hanging from its branches.

'Yeah, so?'

The Doctor plucked one, sniffed it, took a bite.

'How do you know it's – '

' – safe?' The Doctor smiled as he munched. 'The joy of life lies in the taking of risks. Here.' He offered another of the strange pods to Ace. She took it hesitantly.

'Go on, take a bite.'

Ace glanced suspiciously at the Doctor, then handed the fruit back. 'There's a little too much joy in my life at the moment,' she said dryly. 'Thanks all the same.'

As the Doctor took the fruit, the ground trembled, spreading lazy ripples through the mud beneath their feet. Sudden panicky whistles and strident hoots sounded as more variations on the ornithomimus began to move with increasing swiftness through the vegetation.

The Doctor's body straightened into an attitude of acute concentration. 'This is it,' he hissed. He hooked Ace's arm with his umbrella handle and, ignoring her irritated expression, struck off at an oblique angle to their previous direction of travel. 'We're going to need a vantage point.'

A few minutes later, from the top of a nearby outcropping of rock, Ace found that she could see over the tops of the cycads to the distant horizon. The Doctor settled comfortably on the gritty surface of the rock; she did so as well.

The vibrations and noises of alarm from below increased.

'It's a volcanic eruption, isn't it?' Ace shivered with anticipation.

The Doctor glanced at her. 'Don't get your hopes up.'

Ace quickly ran through the acceptable alternatives in her mind. 'An earthquake then?'

'You could say that, Ace. Yes.'

'Well hard!'

The Doctor merely smiled at his companion's enthusiasm. He pointed towards the direction of the sunrise. Ace let her gaze follow his pointing finger and her eyes widened with awe.

'Aren't they *absolutely magnificent?*' cried the Doctor.

Facing into the prevailing wind, Ace shielded her eyes from the sun, squinting to make out details in the undulating carpet of muscular flesh ambling towards them as if nothing short of a medium-sized mountain might stop it. For a moment she looked back at the Doctor and saw that he was grinning wildly, one hand clutching his hat tightly to the top of his head as if the strength of his vision might blast it into the air.

'Simply magnificent . . .'

Over one hundred and twenty foot from nose to tail. Weight averaging in excess of one hundred and forty tons. A living, breathing army of reptilian flesh.

Seismosaurus.

'There are hundreds of them, Doctor!' Ace wrinkled her nose as the wind strengthened. 'And they stink!'

Ace was reminded of the day she'd visited the City Farm with her class from school. She'd thought the smell was bad then but this was a hundred times worse and the herd was still miles away.

The Doctor merely regarded the approaching animals with something like rapture. Ace stood up to get a better view.

In appearance the seismosaurus was a thing to behold. A grey and brown fleshy body bigger than an articulated truck was supported by four legs of stupendous proportions which sank inches into the ground with every step. The front of the tremendous body supported a huge, sinuous neck topped by a ridiculously small head, while the rear anchored the base of an equally long and sinuous tail, most of which the reptile somehow managed to keep off the ground as it walked. The ground shook when these creatures moved but Ace was charmed to note that, because of their small strides, hovering tails and necks, and heads delicately questing for food over seventy feet from the ground, they took on the appearance of almost comically monstrous ballerinas.

After several moments had passed, Ace thought to glance at her companion. The steadily increasing wind whistling around the high rock seemed hardly to touch him, even though Ace was finding it difficult to keep her balance.

'Look at them, Ace. Feel the ground shake as they walk. No cares, no worries, for what can touch them? Not even the great meat eaters could get close. What does it do for your sense of wonder, Ace, tell me that!'

Ace did not reply. The Doctor fell silent and together the two time travellers watched the herd amble closer and closer.

After half an hour or so she sat down again. 'How long are we going to stay here?'

'Oh they'll come a lot closer to us yet, if my calculations are accurate.'

'Oh yeah?'

'Don't be so skeptical. They might take a while, but they'll be here.'

'And then what?'

'Then? Why we shoot them of course!'

'Oh?' Ace peered at the Doctor interestedly. 'What with?'

The Doctor pulled a Polaroid Instamatic camera from his pocket and waved it under Ace's nose. 'What do *you* think? I'm not the Brigadier, you know.'

Mentally, Ace compared the Doctor with the portly, genial, grey-haired gentleman she'd met while visiting Earth a couple of years ago. 'You're not wrong there.'

Ace felt her stomach rumble and realized it had been a number of hours since her last visit to the food machine in the now submerged TARDIS. 'Anyway, talking of cameras – which I'm not – I don't suppose you've got anything to eat? I'm starving.'

'That'll be the prospect of never seeing a West-End cafe again,' observed the Doctor, handing her two rounds of hot bacon sandwiches, a Mars Bar and a litre carton of chilled fresh orange juice. Ace accepted the food, compared it to the apparent volume of the pockets from which it had been produced and simply decided not to ask unnecessary questions.

Unwrapping the sandwiches, she began to eat. But as she began to chew, Ace shivered: she had a sudden feeling that something was going on just out of sight. Maybe even as close as the next hill.

Something terrible.

– the pain of loss blood on her bare feet sweat in her hair a fierce ragged tearing sensation in her chest –

The day was hot, almost too hot to walk unprotected, let alone run. Nevertheless, running was just what she had to do if she hoped to elude those who wished to capture or kill her.

Nimbly, the woman scrambled over great shattered blocks of stone, split by years of encroaching vegetation, instinct moving her legs to find the places where the ground was safest. As she moved, she clutched a tiny

24

bundle of charred cloth to her breast. Something indistinct was wrapped in the cloth. It jarred against her as she moved. Her mind was filled with a sharply defined fear. The sensation existed in contrast to the sluggish flow of indistinct emotion which normally lived there. The fear was of the unspeakable things that would happen to her if she was caught. It stimulated responses within her brain, pulling precisely focused memories from the fog of her moment-by-moment existence, driving her body beyond its limits in the need for escape.

Memories of hunger and the search for food.

Memories of the big stone things you could go inside, and of what delights you might find there. Things you could put over you to keep you warm in the darktime. Things you could put in your mouth that tasted bad but made the pain in your belly go away for a while.

There was nothing irrational about her fear.

The hunters were coming.

The herd took another hour to reach them. When it came the noise was incredible, but so slowly had the decibel level increased that Ace only became aware of it when she realized that her conversation with the Doctor was now being conducted at the kind of pitch normally reserved for competing with a Wembly Cup Final crowd during the course of the winning goal.

'You what?' the Doctor yelled.

'I said: it's just a thought, but we could go and work out how to retrieve the TARDIS from that tar pit!'

'A place for everything and everything in its place, Ace,' quipped the Doctor. 'We must do something about your attention span.'

'We've just spent five hours on the trail of the largest, loudest, smelliest land-travelling animal ever to inhabit the planet! I'd think that'd be good going for a world-class athlete with the unswerving determination of Sherlock Holmes.'

'Nonsense! Take these magnificent specimens here, for example.' The Doctor gestured towards a nearby group of seismosaurs. The smallest adult in the group would have outweighed three double decker buses. 'The immense size and feeding habits of these sauropods combine to stabilize and control their internal temperature. If they stopped grazing for too long, they'd die. And think how long a creature of their average size must live to reach its optimum conditions for survival. Twenty or thirty years at least. Now do you think perhaps your span of concentration is just a tad limited?'

Ace had to laugh. 'Blimey, where have you been, Sherlock? Gizzard stones make eating more efficient. These things are probably only ten or fifteen years old.'

'Hmm,' the doctor mumbled. 'I see you've been availing yourself of the TARDIS library.'

'You bet.' Ace smiled at a sudden thought. 'Imagine what it'd be like to have constipation. You'd probably explode!'

The Doctor sat next to Ace. 'Ace, one day you'll learn the meaning of sobriety,' he said pointedly.

'Hah!' Jumping up, Ace grabbed the camera from the Doctor's hands and bounded towards the edge of the rock. But before she could begin the descent she heard the sharp breathing and scrabbling sounds of someone climbing up the rock towards them.

Before the travellers could do anything more than exchange incredulous glances, a wild-eyed face was thrust into theirs, then immediately withdrawn with a despairing wail.

The Doctor reacted with blinding speed, but even then he only just managed to grab the woman's wrist before she toppled back off the rock to certain death amongst the seething mass of animal life below.

'I didn't think there were any human beings in the Jurassic era?' Ace said. The Doctor did not reply. He was studying the woman's face. She was struggling to get away, but was not quite strong enough to break the Doctor's grip on her arm. She was clutching a ragged bundle of cloth in her other hand which, presumably, was the only reason she was not actively attacking him. She seemed absolutely terrified. The Doctor muttered a few soothing words under his breath. After a few moments, the initial panic died away, and the woman became quiescent.

The Doctor turned to Ace. 'Look at the structure of her skull. The brows are flattened, not protruding. The brain case isn't as large as australopithecus. I think we're looking at Homo sapiens here.'

'So she's not the missing link?' Ace said.

'The only thing that's missing here is a liberal dose of civilization.'

Ace wrinkled her nose. 'And soap, by the smell of her.' She peered more closely at the woman. Her face was a mask of scratches, bruises and dirt, but her eyes were clear. Clear enough to see that the light of humanity was no longer there, if it ever had been. She was making indistinct noises. A low keening seemed to come from somewhere down in her chest. It was such a plaintive sound that Ace couldn't help reaching out to touch the woman's face in sympathy. She pulled her fingers away for a moment and studied them incredulously. 'Doctor, look – she's wearing make-up!'

Ace held out her fingers for the Doctor to inspect.

He nodded sagely. 'I'm beginning to think I may have made a terrible mistake,' he whispered.

As Ace was about to query the Doctor's remark, the woman tentatively stretched out her other hand and touched Ace's cheek with one trembling finger. Incredibly, she spoke. 'Warm bloods,' she whispered. Her voice was cultured but she spoke only a corrupted English. 'Warm bloods no kill warm bloods no kill me.'

The Doctor's reaction to her voice was electric. From the moment the mysterious woman had appeared until that point in the confrontation, he had worn a kind of puzzled look on his face, as if trying to remember something which persisted in eluding him. Now it was as if he had suddenly remembered what he had forgotten.

He took a clean handkerchief from his pocket and began gently to wipe away the grime from the woman's face. Eventually he let out a soft sigh of recognition. He sat down on the rock and put his head in his hands, waving away Ace's attention distractedly.

Understanding his need for isolation, Ace turned to the newcomer. 'Is that your baby?' she asked in a gentle voice. The woman looked too old to have a baby, but perhaps hardship and not age had lined her face. 'Can I see?'

The woman clutched the bundle of rags fiercely to her chest. 'Cold bloods come cold bloods come kill me kill . . . my . . . baby.' Racking sobs began to shake the woman.

Ace shivered. The woman had obviously suffered some kind of emotional shock. 'Do you want to explain what's going on now Doctor?' she asked pointedly.

'I don't think we're going to have time.' The Doctor turned his attention back to the woman. Under his gaze her sobs gradually quietened. He began to speak, slowly and clearly, so there could be no misunderstanding. 'The cold bloods come. The cold bloods come to kill. We must run from the cold bloods.'

At every pause in his voice, the woman nodded and her expression grew more and more stricken with panic. At the end it was only the Doctor's enormous willpower, embodied in his mesmeric gaze, which stopped her from bolting like a startled rabbit.

'Where must we run to hide from the cold bloods?'

The woman stared at him in blank incomprehension.

Ace ventured. 'She doesn't understand what a question is. Let me try.' Ace turned to the woman. 'The cold bloods come. Kill your baby. Hide your baby. Then cold bloods no kill. Hide your baby. Hide her!'

The woman shifted from foot to foot in obvious agitation.

The Doctor stared at Ace proudly. 'That's brilliant,' he said.

'Do you think she's got it?'

The woman's agitated movements increased.

They became aware of a howling in the distance, a fast-approaching roar of anger and hunger, easily audible even above the noise of the herd of seismosaurs.

Ace gazed out across the plain. About two miles away she could make out about half-a-dozen reptiles, which although considerably smaller, resembled picture-book illustrations she had seen of *Tyrannosaurus rex*. They were covering the ground between them at a rate of speed that was scarcely believable. Following closely behind them were a set of larger reptiles, three in number, which were of a sleeker appearance, with longer necks and arms, double crests on their heads, and tails held out horizontally for balance. Ace squinted in amazement. There appeared to be still a third set of creatures, also reptiles, riding upon the backs of these dinosaurs, for all the world as if they were riders out on a hunt.

Following the direction of Ace's gaze, the Doctor said grimly, 'I think we're in for some unwelcome company.'

'You could be right. What are they?'

'The ones in front are herrerasaurus. Vicious little carnivores. Rip you to bits as soon as look at you.'

'And the others?'

The Doctor huffed quietly to himself. Things were beginning to seem a lot clearer now. 'Well. The larger ones are called dilophosaurus. They're meat eaters too.'

'And the riders? They look like men.'

The Doctor's face hardened.

'Not men, Ace, psionosauropodomorpha. *Silurians*. The original rulers of the Earth.'

Hello? Is anyone there?

Who is that? It's my eyes, you see. I can't –

Hello? Oh come on, stop messing around! Doctor? Ace? Is that you? Are you –

Hey! Hey, someone touched me! Who was it? Who touched –

What? What do you mean, can I move? Of course I can't! Do you think I'd just be sitting here if I –

Sitting? Am I sitting? Standing? Lying down?

Oh God, what if I'm –

Hey! You touch me again and I'll –

Hey, what are you doing? That really –

No!

Stop it!

STOP IT!

... *please* ... tell me what you want ... Can't you just ... tell me what you want ... Why do you have to

keep . . . no . . . oh . . . not again . . . I don't think I can . . .
not again notagainnot*AGAINPLEASENOTAGAIN*
NOTAGAIN!
   . . . open . . .
   . . . open my eyes . . . yeah . . . sure . . . easy as blinking.
Easy as . . .
   Hey. Hey, I can do it. I think I can –
   I can see. God, what have you done, I can see.
   I can see!
   Oh. That's strange. I feel –
   What's happening to –
   M . . . m . . . me? What's –
   Ha . . . h . . . m . . . ma? Mama –
   Mama?
   Mama!
   MAMA!

Still clutching her pathetic bundle of rags, the woman
scrambled back down the rock face towards the edge of
the herd, all the while making little moaning noises of fear
in the back of her throat.

Ace turned to the Doctor, but he had already started
down the rock face crying, 'No, Jo! Wait!'

Without a pause to wonder how the Doctor had
deduced the woman's name, Ace began her own descent.
Halfway down she slipped on some loose, gravelly stones
and began to slide. As she dipped beneath the level of
the swaying cycads, Ace's view of the hunters was abruptly
cut off. Somehow she didn't find that the slightest bit
comforting.

When Ace finally hit the ground, her fall was broken
by a mat of crushed vegetation and mud. She struggled
to her feet. Avoiding the flank of a curious sauropod, Ace
began to wipe the muck from her jacket and trousers. She
thought for a moment and then yelled, 'These things hunt
by smell, right, Doctor?'

'Actually, most of the great carnivores had very sharp
eyesight and good hearing, although under present circumstances, I would concede that the olfactory senses
would have an advantage.'

Ace considered. This seemed to be the Doctor's round-about way of saying that he thought she was right. The sight of him rubbing mud and flattened plant matter into his clothes only served to confirm her supposition. She started smearing the mud into her own clothes, hoping it would smell as bad to the hunters as it did to her.

'Where's Jo?'

'She's here with me.'

'How do you know her?'

'I don't.'

'But you know her name.'

'That's right, Ace. I know her name. Throw me your jacket.'

Ace complied.

'And don't forget your face.'

'Just as well I never wanted to be an actress, isn't it?' Ace began to work the gooey slime into her skin.

The Doctor took Jo by the shoulders and gently removed the top half of her clothing, replacing it efficiently and unselfconsciously with Ace's jacket. Leaving the dazed woman to figure out the zip fastenings for herself, the Time Lord raced through the mud and grabbed hold of a nearby ornithomimus which was about the size of a Shetland pony. Swiftly tying the ragged sleeves of the smelly garment round the animal's slender neck, the Doctor slapped his open palm against its leathery rump. With an indignant squeal the creature leaped between the massive flanks of the milling sauropods and vanished from sight. The Doctor yelped and sucked his knuckles: the dinosaur's hide was *hard*.

The Doctor suddenly reached out with one impossibly long arm and snagged Jo, who was beginning to show signs of impatience. 'And you can stop champing at the bit,' he said firmly. 'We'll have you out of here in two shakes of whatever passes for a lamb's tail.'

Not responding in the slightest to the tone of his voice, the woman began to edge towards the outside of the herd.

'How long before the hunters get here?' asked Ace.

The Doctor produced a glass bottle from his pocket. 'Not long. High-metabolism dinosaurs like that could move like lightning when they wanted to.' He began to sprinkle the contents of the bottle around the area on which they had been standing. Ace could smell the distinctive aroma of aniseed. 'Or when they were compelled to,' he finished. A small seismosaurus began to investigate the new smell, but was quickly shuffled away by an adult.

'What are you doing?' Ace yelped as she dodged the huge infant.

'Disguising our smell with one that's even stronger.' The Doctor shrugged. 'It works for fox-hunt saboteurs, perhaps we'll be lucky.'

The Time Lord grabbed Jo by the hand and began to lead her towards the centre of the mass of sauropods. 'Come on, Ace. We'll use the herd to conceal us while we get away.'

Ace nodded in admiration. 'Smart.'

'Thanks.' The Doctor pointed out the flaw in his own plan. 'Just try not to get stepped on. I'd hate to have to take you home in an envelope.'

For Ace, moving through the herd proved to be no problem. Although masssive enough to crush a Spacefleet landing boat by gently leaning on it, the average seismosaurus was a very slow-moving creature.

Even though none of the creatures seemed to be travelling any faster than about two and a half miles per hour, it still took them forty minutes to reach the middle of the herd, which Ace thought might be three miles wide in some places. The only difficulty they encountered was making themselves heard above the din of several thousand tons of dinosaurs all busily champing, squealing, thudding and slithering through the mud.

The fleshy horizon was a little lower in the centre of the herd, since this space was mostly occupied by younger creatures weighing, she guessed, around thirty to fifty tons. Ace gazed around herself in wonder. She was just starting to get used to the smell and now she had plenty of time to study the surrounding creatures. They snuffled and snorted in contentment as they nibbled at the ground with astonishingly mobile lips. What they didn't manage to scoop into their mouths they trampled absolutely flat, and

Ace reminded herself not to get too close even to one of the very small ones. All in all, she thought, it was rather like picking a careful path between a moving series of gigantic, living cliffs.

Once Ace reached out to touch the nearest sauropod – she had to stretch hard even to come up as far as the thing's knee – and was surprised to find the skin was actually warm, with a rough, knuckle-like texture. Until then, Ace realized, she had fallen into the trap of regarding cold-blooded animals as actually cold. Now she realized her mistake with a kind of soft-edged wonder.

As she followed the Doctor and Jo through the herd, the fascination she felt was slowly replaced by a sense of unease. Ace felt the situation getting away from her. The loss of Bernice, the TARDIS, the Doctor's premonition, the arrival of Jo – it just wouldn't add up. Something about this whole business was making her feel really edgy, but she just couldn't put her finger on it.

The hunters raced along a short length of the perimeter of the herd, slapping their mounts in frustration and glaring angrily at the contentedly milling sauropods. They knew they were less than half a mile from their prey. But it was here, at the very threshold of their desire, that the hunting beasts balked.

Not one of them would get within fifty feet of the herd.

The fact that this distance was the average length of a sauropod's tail merely angered the hunters all the more.

The youngest hunter, Imorkal, reined in his dilophosaurus and carefully considered the slowly moving herd of sauropods.

Though following a generally bipedal form, his body was definitely not human. Standing seven feet tall, Imorkal would tower over any human counterpart. His hands were long-boned and sensitive. His feet showed the evolutionary hallmarks of his ancestors: three toes, ribbed, curved and linked by supple webbing. All musculature on the powerful frame was of the hunting type; the tendons long, elastic, firmly anchored to the bone structure. The bones themselves were of hollow construction, which meant that although big, Imorkal could move extremely fast when he needed to.

But the most striking thing about Imorkal was his face. It was leathery, mottled dark green and brown, containing mobile features and a third eye, situated at the crown of the skull, in a smooth fluting of the bone-structure around which the scaly flesh was tightly wrapped. The nostrils were forward facing, rather than downward facing, and the ears projected laterally from the skull. Both organs were highly sensitive, the ears particularly so; a curious evolutionary twist had positioned several small holes in the veined pinna, so he could determine the distance and direction of a sound as accurately if it came from behind as in front.

His eyes were glistening pools of intelligence.

Like most of his race, Imorkal's emotional state was transient and highly excitable. At the moment, his third eye was gleaming faintly with a mixture of frustration and anger. Imorkal was not a being to whom patience came easily.

How will you proceed? Chtorba, the shortest, oldest and arguably the most intelligent of the group, was watching his charge intently. What would his student do now?

I am considering.

When the hunters conversed they did not only use words. Body language was incorporated into it, and more. It was a very thorough means of communication, able to describe complex functions elegantly and handle multiple conversations succinctly.

I shall link with one of the hunting beasts. Send it into the herd. I will be able to control its fear of the sauropods.

Vronim, charged with the protection of Imorkal by his father, the Silurian Leader, made known his fears: *I think it would be prudent to return to the Capital. The climate is cold here, even with full control of the atmospheric blanketing. Our blood has not yet acclimatized, our reactions will be sluggish.*

Return to the Capital sporting no prize! Allow our

quarry to escape within this herd of slow-minded animals! We would be held in less esteem than the lowliest mammals!

'Imorkal.' Chtorba's voice was deep and rich, resonating with the tensions in long vocal chords. The fact that he used purely spoken language added a certain extra emphasis to his words. 'We will not dispute your wisdom in leading the hunt; you have gained trophies enough to decorate the Capital walls themselves. But I tell you, Imorkal, you have not yet learned enough to become Leader in your father's place.'

Imorkal's fury was boundless. His third eye blazed a livid crimson and his face trembled with the effort to control his expression. *I will not be beaten by a mammal because of some whimpering teacher!*

Chtorba sighed. It was typical of his pupil that he respected none of the etiquette of language exchange, let alone acknowledged the respect due both to an excellent tutor and a personal friend of his father's.

'The Leader has seen fit to place you in my charge for the duration of this hunt.' Chtorba felt a hint of anger glimmering in his third eye. 'And by the Egg, I will make good on that promise.' He moved his own dilophosaurus in nearer to that of his pupil. '*Do you understand?*'

Imorkal looked away without replying.

The glimmer faded from Chtorba's third eye. He glanced at Vronim. The warrior was smiling placidly. Idiot.

After a moment's silence, Imorkal pulled out a fluted horn from his leather pouch and began to play a complex melody upon it. One of the hunting beasts obediently moved level with Imorkal's dilophosaurus. The beast – a herrerasaurus – was small, standing only five feet at the shoulder, but it massed around three-hundred pounds and was very, very fast. Careful training had made it fearless when at the hunters' command.

Imorkal linked with the reptile.

He motioned it into the herd.

It was only with the greatest effort that Ace controlled a rapidly developing feeling of panic. She had developed a sudden, overwhelming sense of . . . well, intrusion was

35

the only way she could describe it. Mental intrusion. A sense that she was being sought out. Hunted.

'Stay together, Ace,' whispered the Doctor. 'Something odd is going on here.'

He held tightly onto Jo's arm. The woman was straining and muttering a string of incomprehensible words beneath her rasping breath. She obviously wanted to run. Something was making her increasingly nervous.

She wasn't the only one. Ace, too, was finding it difficult to hold onto her rationality. The towering flanks of the sauropods seemed to press in around her with claustrophobic suddenness. She felt disoriented. Something was definitely affecting her mind.

Ace felt her slow steps increase in speed to become headlong flight. She began to run between the great walls of reptilian flesh, a prisoner in a huge, living maze.

Time seemed to twist crazily. Her ears were filled with the thump of her own heartbeat. Her chest pounded with the ragged, lung-tearing pain of flight.

Then Ace heard another sound: the pattering of light footfalls behind her. She turned, narrowly avoiding the sequoia-like forelimb of a massive sauropod.

Running towards her was a reptile; one of the carnivorous herrerasauruses the Doctor had pointed out to her earlier. It had powerful hind legs, cruelly hooked teeth, grasping claws, savage jaws; everything about it was sharp and violent. The reptile was less than fifteen feet away and its bone-yellow teeth were bright in the narrow shafts of sunlight snaking between the necks of the sauropods.

For a fraction of a second, Ace didn't move.

Perversely, it was not a loud roar so much as the soft *hssssssss* of the reptile and the *plishplishplish* of its footfalls in the mud which shocked her into flight. But as Ace tried to manoeuvre, her foot turned in the slippery ooze and she fell flat on her face.

Before she could move, a scalding pain ran diagonally across her back, immediately followed by a trickling warmth. Ace gasped; her mouth filled with mud.

The ground shuddered.

Fear of suffocation momentarily overcame her fear of

being savaged. Ace sat bolt upright, frantically scooping great handfuls of the sticky slime from her face and ears. She opened her eyes; realized she was practically nose to nose with the reptile. She shuffled rapidly backwards, gasping at the foul stench from its claws and teeth.

The reptile stayed exactly where it was, its glassy eyes regarding her with frozen hatred. After a few moments, Ace became aware of the reason why the thing was not attacking her again. From the neck back it had been crushed into the ground by the tremendous hind limb of one of the grazing sauropods.

The limb had missed her head by less than a foot.

There was something wrong with Jo. She couldn't walk upright any more. Her back looped forward in an obvious attempt to alleviate an abdominal pain. The Doctor touched the side of her ribs. Her eyes flicked briefly towards him and he caught a hint of her suffering. Her complexion was pale, even through the dirt smearing her face. She was sweating. He was worried about that. The smell of sweat would carry, perhaps as far as the hunters.

'Try to relax,' he told her.

Jo pointed with her free hand to her stomach, then to her mouth, making nibbling noises and a pained expression.

'Are you hungry? Do you want food?' The Doctor produced a Mars Bar from one pocket and carefully unwrapped it before handing it to the woman. She sniffed it, made an effort to smile, and tucked it into Ace's jacket. Then she pointed to her mouth again, and repeated the chewing and swallowing gestures.

'I'm sorry. I don't have what you need.'

Jo's face fell. She pointed to her stomach, rubbing it gently through Ace's jacket. 'Cold bloods come kill my baby.'

And suddenly it all made sense. The Doctor stared with horror at the woman, realizing abruptly why she was so ill. Even as he wondered what she was actually clutching in those filthy rags, Jo said again, 'Cold bloods come kill my baby.'

There was only *need*.

Even here, surrounded by the soft billow of the amniotic sac, warm and nurtured by her mother's body, even here safety was not enough. Not nearly enough. And ... there was something else. Something beyond the distant thrumming of her mother's heart. A thought where there should have been none.

Mother did not equal safety.

Mother equalled pain. Pain and burning.

And guilt.

All around Ace, the sauropods stomped and chewed, shaking the ground with their movements and adding to her disorientation. Great ropelike shadows drifted across her from time to time, cast by the serpentine necks of the vast beasts. The sun flashed repeatedly into her eyes. Ace found both sides of her face were aching badly because she was squinting constantly into the relentless glare. Her headband was gone, lost somewhere in the mud. After a moment's thought, she took off her pullover, ripped off a strip of her shirt and tied it around the top of her head, letting the filmy material form a semitransparent shield across her eyes. Almost immediately the ache in her cheek muscles vanished as the glare was reduced.

She struggled back into her pullover, cursing the herrerasaurus when her efforts caused her to moan aloud at the pain in her back.

Somehow the sight of the reptile, smashed flat into the ground, did nothing to alleviate the anger she felt, or the burning sensation spreading rapidly through her body.

The Doctor lifted Jo gently onto the back of an ornithomimus. The woman was near death. If there was to be any hope for her, he had to get clear of the herd. What he would do then, he didn't know. The hunters were still out there somewhere. Perhaps he could appeal to them; they were, after all, intelligent –

He paused, sensing a change in the herd around him. The ornithomimus bucked gently beneath his grip. The Doctor looked up. The larger sauropods were changing direction around them, moving away, leaving them exposed in a vast area of flattened vegetation.

Exposed, but not alone.

Panic. Movement. Change.

Amniotic fluid bubbled, muscles flexed, contracted.

There was *light*.

And *sound*.

And *fear*.

And *pain*.

Things for which she had no words; unrefined experiences which burst from her in a fluid scream.

And she drew deep, shuddering breaths.

Exhausted, Ace reached out to lean against a nearby wall. She felt metal. The metal was smooth, and had once been flat, though now it was buckled and bent out of shape. There was a smooth-edged hole in the metal. Rotting rubber sealed the edges of the hole. Ace pushed harder against the cool surface; it moved beneath her weight, creaking rustily in the silence.

There was writing on the metal:

Clifton Wholefood Bakery and Delicatessen
Best bread in Bristol

Ace ran her fingers lightly, wonderingly, across the writing on the side of the van before moving on. At the end of the road, more of the metal walls were piled up into a bizarre, nightmarish sculpture, her intended route almost completely blocked. Ace scrambled over the precariously balanced pile and lurched down the other side.

She was out of the bushes at last, standing upon the lip of a vast rocky chasm cut into the earth. A freezing wind whistled around her face, whipping her hair into her eyes, blasting the shreds of delusion from her mind. She gathered a double handful of hair and knotted it back out of her face. She looked around.

Up river, a ruddy, swollen sun glinted off the twin masonry towers and curving metal supportwork of a suspension bridge. Ace wandered towards the bridge and out across its cracked tarmac surface. She peered through the double rows of metal railings. A long way down in the darkness, water glinted. The soft, low-frequency hooting noises of amphibious dinosaurs drifted upwards. As the edge of the sun hit the distant horizon, its light sparkled on the remains of a big city, about a mile up river. The city was overgrown with jungle and seemed completely devoid of any human life.

Looking back at the nearest of the bridge support towers, Ace saw there were two metal plaques fastened to the masonry. One read:

Clifton Suspension Bridge
Commenced 1836
Isambard Kingdom Brunel, F.R.S., Engineer
Completed 1864

The other was less decorative, although equally didactic.

The Samaritans: We Care

She wondered if they'd send an ambulance or just want to talk.

She swayed dizzily, nausea, fear, pain and hysterical laughter combining to completely ruin her sense of balance.

Whoops! Her gaze raked across the Portway hundreds of feet below. *Watch that first step, it's a killer!*

Ace tried and failed to regain her balance. She staggered towards the nearest support and grabbed hold of the double railings which separated her from two hundred and fifty feet of thin air. Rotten with rust, the metal began to crumble beneath her fingers.

Ace found herself holding nothing but oxidized powder. She began to fall.

Green.
Everything was green.

She struggled to form words. 'My nuh . . . my *name* . . . is . . . *Benny*! My name is Benny! Hah! Did it!'

The three eyes watching her blinked with slow, considered intelligence.

'Actually, my name's Bernice. Bernice Summerfield. I'm thirty-two years old, and I'm a human.'

Something tickled in her mind.

'What?'

Three eyes blinked in sequence. The fluted skull tipped to one side, studying her. 'Where do you come from?'

'From twenty-sixth-century Earth.'

A hiss of cold breath. 'How is that possible?'

'By time machine of course. Well, time and space machine, actually. It's called the TARDIS. Can I have some food?'

The food was green too.

When she had eaten, Bernice began to feel a little better. 'You're helping me, aren't you? Helping me adjust to your world, your way of thinking. I'd go mad otherwise, wouldn't I? I'm still frightened when you come into the room.'

'Why?'

'I don't know. Why are some people scared of spiders? It's a phobia. No – it's more than just a phobia, isn't it?' Bernice wished she could control her shivering.

'You are right. The fear is . . . built in . . . to all humans.'

'But you're not human.'

A hissing laugh. 'If I were of your race, I would – ' A breath. 'I am sorry. I am being inconsiderate.'

Bernice shrugged. 'It's okay. But I have some questions. What have you done to me? What do you want from me? Why are you helping me? What planet is this? And who are you? To name but a few.'

'I am the Leader of this City. This is my home planet, Earth. By the human calendar the year is 1993.' A thoughtful pause. 'I will answer the rest of your questions after the experiment.'

'Experiment?' Bernice went cold. 'No-one mentioned any experiment!'

41

'Well naturally, since you are the subject. If I had mentioned it to you before you would have tried to escape.'

'Subject? Escape? Mentioned it before what?'

Bernice had the first of her answers as the cold feeling spread suddenly throughout her body. She fell over as her legs collapsed. She tried to rise, couldn't. Tried to speak, couldn't.

Before I ate the drugged –

PART TWO

WORLD OF NO TOMORROWS

Liz Shaw gasped for breath as she climbed the stone steps of Jacob's Ladder towards the top of the Cheddar Gorge. Six hundred and twenty three steps; more than three hundred feet of near-vertical ascent. Inside the Complex was a low-power elevator which would have taken her to the lookout point in minutes, but Liz liked to climb. She liked to feel the air, clean as springwater in her lungs, liked to feel the tired pressure of the muscles in her calves and feet. These and other sensations, though painful, told her she was still alive. Alive and sane in a world where the simple act of continuing to draw breath was a miracle in itself.

Liz paused for breath where the steps widened into a stone platform at the second rest-point. Twenty years ago, children would have stopped here, laughing gleefully as their exhausted parents struggled to take just one more step before stopping to rest. The children would have turned apple-turnovers on the steel railings which bordered the edge of the platform while their parents yelled angrily at them to desist, and then read aloud from the large, steel-framed information board.

You are now approaching the Cretaceous Period. Eighty-five million years have passed since the fossil soil at this level was deposited. Species you might have seen in the Cretaceous Period include: Triceratops, Brontosaurus and Tyrannosaurus rex.

Liz ran her hand along the ragged stump of the support pole where the poster had once stood. A falling stegosaurus had carried away the pole, the low brick wall and the steel railing, not six months ago. It was a tribute to the workmanship of some long-dead builder that the information board had survived so many years at all.

Liz looked up. Trees looped overhead, obscuring the dark sky. Branches and the upturned bowls of cycads hissed softly in the wind. Even after nearly two decades, Liz climbed the Ladder every second or third evening, stopping here, where the trees were thickest, to listen for birds.

A futile hope; the world had forgotten birds.

By the time she had regained control of her breathing, Liz decided tonight was going to be no different from any other, and continued upwards. Another couple of minutes' effort and she had reached the top of the Ladder. Here the trees thinned somewhat and a rocky path, overgrown with ferns, gingkos and shrunken conifers, ran along the top of the gorge. The ferns glowed with a dim light as they moved gently in the night air. A lot of different types of plant life were starting to do that lately. Just last month, Alan Tomson had come back from a food gathering expedition with a basket full of palely glimmering oranges. He'd found the fruit trees growing wild on the heath at Upton Cheyney and thought he'd stumbled on a vitamin gold mine. Liz had explained how the breakdown of the photosynthesis exchange in some plants produced chemical impurities which accreted in the leaf and stem cells, and that some of the impurities were phosphorescent, causing the ghostly glow she now saw. Once he found out the oranges were inedible, Alan had shrugged and suggested the fruit be used as night-lights for the children's dorm, preserved in glass jars and hung beyond the reach of inquisitive little fingers. The idea was quickly taken up over much of the base and soon considered perfectly normal.

Liz briefly scanned the surrounding area. The concealed hatchway which marked the upper exit to the Complex lay to her right, buried in the ruined foundations of an old tourist lookout tower. The tower itself had long since been demolished. It had been too conspicuous a landmark for curious Silurian eyes. Liz took another moment to gather her breath then, waving to the sentry she knew was hidden there, turned left, away from the tower, and continued back upwards along the spine of the ridge.

As she walked she plucked a handful of stems from the surrounding foliage, something to place on the grave. A gesture, nothing more, and a wasted gesture at that, if she believed the Brigadier. Then again, it wasn't his husband buried there, was it? Wasn't his hopes and dreams lying cold and impotent beneath the damp limestone hill.

Not for the first time, Liz wished there were still flowers, any kind of flowers, a splash of colour amongst the cool greens and browns and greys. Something to give pleasure to her eyes and hope to her mind. Liz shook her head. The thought was stupid, even maudlin. This world held no place for tradition, for remorse, or, some thought, even for hope. The Earth was changing, had already changed; for a moment Liz wondered briefly how much longer she would be able to survive in it. Then she put the thoughts from her mind. Volition did not enter the equation. The animal drive to live, to eat, to draw breath and perhaps, again, to love, would sustain her until she died.

In this world there could be little more.

Alan Tomson ushered the Doctor along innumerable rocky passages deep in the heart of the Complex. His legs ached abominably and his mouth felt dry and hot; this was all he needed on top of a day's foraging.

An hour had passed since he had brought the two strangers into the Complex. Jo had been unconscious when they'd pulled her from the ornithomimus and taken her to the sickbay; unfortunately, the other stranger, the Doctor, as he called himself, was anything but. Although Alan was sure he'd *meant* to take the Doctor straight to the administration centre to make his report, somehow what actually seemed to have happened was that he had agreed to give the Doctor a quick overview of the Complex and then organize some people to help look for his friend Ace, still lost outside.

The Complex was honeycombed with passages, long and winding, interconnected with other passages and chambers. The passages were mostly bare rock with poured concrete floors, warmer than they looked, and dimly lit by jars of phosphorescent vegetation or mutated fruit. He explained to the Doctor that, while the Complex used electricity as a power source, the supply of irreplaceable light bulbs was carefully conserved, being used only for the most important areas – the administration centre, the labs and the infirmary.

For his part the Doctor expressed a polite, though distant, interest in everything Alan showed him. He seemed distracted. Alan thought he was probably worrying about Ace. He was about to mention this when a fair-haired little boy of about eight years of age came charging down the passage towards them.

'Hey, Alan!'

'Hey, Tom-o. How you doing?' He swept the boy into his arms and hoisted him into the air.

'Okay. The orange in my night-light's gone out though.'

'We'll have to get you another one then, won't we?'

'From outside?' The little boy's eyes opened in wonder.

'Yep.'

'When can I go outside to get oranges?'

'When you're old enough.'

'But when will that be?'

'All I can say is: you'll be old enough when you are.' He put Tommy back onto the ground as the boy made a playful grab for his beard. 'What did you learn at school today, Tom-o?'

'Applied maths. It was neat. I know what a 'quation is!'

'You mean an *equation*. Now off you go and do your homework, so you don't forget.'

'Okay. See you!' Tommy raced off along the rocky passage.

'Applied maths?' questioned the Doctor.

Alan watched him go. 'He's eight years old. Weapons training starts when they're ten. They need background for that. Ballistics. You know. The maths is couched in terms the kids can understand, of course, but nonetheless – ' He broke off, aware that the Doctor had turned away. 'Something wrong?' he asked sharply.

The Doctor did not reply.

Alan's voice hardened. 'We're not breeding a race of monsters, if that's what you think. We're preparing them

48

for survival. It's not their world out there anymore, in case you hadn't noticed.'

'I've noticed.'

'Yeah, well . . . We'll have to get a move on if we're to stand any chance of finding your friend. You can ride, I take it?'

'Elephant or unicycle?'

Alan frowned. 'Horse actually.'

The Doctor turned to gaze directly at him. 'Actually, there are some things I have to attend to here,' he said abruptly. 'I'd be very grateful if you could organize the search without me.'

Alan hesitated.

'Of course, if that's a problem . . .'

'No. Of course not. I'll let you know if we turn anything up.'

'When you turn anything up, you mean.'

'Er, yes, okay. When we turn anything up.'

Liz laid the stems of fern against what she privately thought of as their rock. No – just her rock now. For a moment Liz felt hot tears prickle in her eyes. She muttered angrily, 'Elizabeth Shaw, don't you dare cry!'

'Sad thoughts?'

Liz turned in surprise. Standing not more than a few yards away, silhouetted by the fernlight, was a smallish man carrying a crook-handled umbrella and wearing, of all things, a cream safari suit and matching hat. The small man doffed the hat politely.

Liz stared. 'Who the hell are you?'

'Don't you know me, Liz?' Was that a faint note of hurt she could hear in the man's voice?

'If the Brigadier sent you to keep an eye on me, you can just go and tell him to . . . well. He'll know what he can do. I've told him enough times in the past. Now please leave me alone!'

The man stepped closer. His feet made no sound among the ferns.

'Look, just get lost, okay? I work hard enough for the Complex as it is. This is my time.'

49

'Some would argue that the time of Man is gone.'

'Yes, well, I'm not a man, am I?' Liz said pointedly.

The newcomer laughed. It had been a number of years since Liz had heard a laugh as soft, as ironic, or as infectious. Despite herself, she found she was smiling.

'Look, who are you? I haven't seen you around the Complex.'

'Perhaps I'm from another Complex.'

'There aren't any since we lost Moscow. Everybody knows that.'

'I can see I'm going to have to do some catching up if I'm to alleviate the situation here.' The man smiled. 'You can help me if you'd like.'

'Help you!' Liz's voice held more surprise than anger.

'Why yes. Just as you did twenty years ago against the Autons and the Nestene Consciousness.'

Liz blinked in absolute astonishment. Her heart was racing now, but with excitement, not anger. A huge belly laugh bubbled up from her stomach, after which she was silent for a long while, just grinning insanely. 'The Brigadier told me you could – what was the word he used? Yes, that was it. *Regenerate.* I never believed him,' she said finally. 'But it's you, isn't it? It's really you.'

The man smiled modestly. He held out his hand.

Liz found herself clutching the hand, gripping the cool skin and hanging on for dear life while tears of joy poured down her cheeks. 'God help me, Doctor. You always were a presumptuous bastard. Yes, I'll help you, of course I will. Just try not to get yourself killed this time, you hear me? Try not to get yourself killed!'

The Doctor's eyes narrowed at Liz's words. 'What do you mean, "This time"?'

'Don't you know?' Liz rubbed her chin thoughtfully.

The Doctor smiled a charming smile. 'Why don't you tell me all about it?'

The search for Ace had taken Alan, together with Julia Adams, along the remains of the A37 towards Bristol. Darkness had found them scouting through the ruins of Woodspring, travelling east towards the suspension bridge.

In the countryside, it had been almost possible to imagine there was nothing wrong. The roads were a mess, of course, and there was still the occasional unsalvageable car smashed into the verge and rusting into oblivion, but the horses knew almost instinctively to avoid these. The suburbs, however, were a different matter. Here the evidence of civilization was still present, if you could bear to look hard enough: a toppled milk float, its freezer compartment vandalized; a child's blood-stained bicycle, rusting in the outskirts of a fifty-foot patch of elephant grass. By the time they had picked their way through the wreckage of the seventeenth house, Alan was filthy, thirsty and near exhaustion.

The last house he'd explored had been the worst so far. He'd tracked a low creaking noise to an upstairs room. In one corner, a child's crib was rocking gently in the draft from a shattered window. Moving closer, he'd been horrified to discover a near perfect set of baby clothes. Little blue bootees and mittens, one still attached to a tiny plastic comforter, Sooty-and-Sweep bib in blue and white, fading as the years had leached all colour from the material.

Inside the set of clothes had been a huddle of tiny white bones.

The baby's had been the first actual body he'd seen for several years. He knew that the disease everyone still thought of as the Nightmare accelerated the decay of the organisms it killed; the presence of a skeleton indicated that the disease hadn't claimed this tiny victim. He'd found himself imagining a long ago night: the city in flames, panic ruling the streets. Downstairs the parents would have barricaded themselves in their house, perhaps already dying. Upstairs, the baby was crying in fear and hunger. Had they tried to reach the poor thing, he wondered, before the inevitable claimed them? Had they died hearing their child's uncomprehending cries, unable to reach or comfort it? Tears sprang from his eyes as he imagined the baby starving to death inside the prison of its crib . . .

Alan had run for the bathroom, then, making it just in

time. Somehow it had seemed irreverent to throw up in the baby's room.

Liz sat with her back to the cool rock and gazed up to where the moon flickered hesitantly through thick umber clouds.

'You know, I'm almost scared to close my eyes. In case you're gone when I open them.'

The Doctor touched the inscription in the rock by Liz's side with the tip of his umbrella. 'Is this for . . .?'

'My husband.'

'Ah. Of course. You married.'

The Doctor wedged his umbrella into a crack in the rock and leaned casually against it.

'I can hardly call you "Miss Shaw" any more then, can I?'

'His name was Lester. James Lester. We had two years together. He died while looking for food. Tripped and hit his head on a tree.' Liz hesitated. 'I took my own name back.'

The Doctor nodded.

Liz continued, 'You know, it's like being a kid. You do something wrong, or there's an accident . . . it all gets out of your control. You stand terrified and shout for help. Then the grown-ups come and everything's alright again.'

The Doctor nodded sagely. 'But this time you are the grown-ups. This time there's no-one to hear your shouts of fear.'

'Yes . . .' Liz fell silent for a moment. 'And then you arrive.'

'Yes.'

'Why? Why now, after so long?'

The Doctor was silent.

'Dammit, *why make us wait so long!*'

The Doctor licked his lips. 'You said I died here?'

Liz tried to calm her breathing. 'We all thought you'd died at Wenley Moor. True we never found a body, but what with the Nightmare breaking loose . . .'

The Doctor looked away.

'Damn you, don't condemn us for not looking for you.

52

We couldn't help it! We were trying to survive!' Liz wiped her cardigan sleeve across her face. 'You could have come back, helped us. Why didn't you?'

The Doctor whispered, 'I'm here now, Liz. The one the monsters have nightmares about.'

'What?'

The Doctor pursed his lips thoughtfully. 'Just something I said once, in my arrogance.'

Liz stood, reaching out to touch the Doctor's shoulder. He turned before she could complete the movement.

'There's just one fatal flaw in my reasoning.'

Liz drew her hand back, shivering at the expression on the Doctor's face.

'The Silurians aren't monsters, are they?' he said.

Darkness had found Alan and Julia on high ground a little over a mile from the town centre. The partly burnt remains of a country home told Alan the land through which they were riding had once been an estate, but, like everything else he had seen, time had wrought an incredible sea change on it. New seeds had germinated, pushing aside and strangling all but the hardiest of the normal vegetation. Strange smells and stranger noises drifted from the branches and tangled boles of the forest. In places the vegetation glowed with varying degrees of brilliance.

And looming up through the forest were two dark towers made of crumbling brick: a bridge.

Julia set a course towards the nearer of the towers, her rifle unholstered, glancing suspiciously to either side. Alan spurred his horse forward to draw level. 'I don't know about you, but it doesn't look as if anyone's come through here recently.'

'It's a big city and Ace is just one woman.' Julia shrugged. 'Still . . .' She urged her horse forwards.

Liz touched the Doctor's arm briefly as they stopped before the door marked:

'He probably isn't the man you remember,' she warned him quietly.

'That seems to be a growing malaise,' the Doctor replied enigmatically. Reversing his umbrella, he used the handle to rap smartly on the door.

A moment later a gruff voice proclaimed: 'Come in. Door's open.'

Liz pushed open the door and ushered the Doctor into the room.

Sitting behind a large desk was the Brigadier. He was studying the information contained in a buff folder.

Liz tried to see him the way the Doctor would. A tall man with thinning, iron-grey hair, the Brigadier retained an upright posture. A fit man for his sixty-three years, he worked out every morning, eating sparingly from a carefully planned diet. His face still retained the angular planes which, she remembered, had once made him a classic example of the handsome military man. The mustache was as carefully tended as it ever was. But something was different, and Liz realized with surprise what it was: twenty years ago the Brigadier's eyes had sparkled with life and humour. That light was gone now, replaced by a kind of . . . indifference.

'Miss Shaw.' The voice was exactly as she thought the Doctor would remember it. A deep, rather fruity baritone, with a touch of upperclassmanship about it.

The Brigadier replaced the sheets of paper in the buff folder and stood, crossing to a small but heavy safe in one corner of the room. He nodded politely, but distantly, to the Doctor. He replaced the file in the safe and withdrew an oblong package. He placed the package on the desk and unwrapped it. Revealed was a small book with a plain grey cover. The book was damaged. At least half of it was missing. The Brigadier sat heavily. He steepled his fingers above the book and studied the Doctor's face. Liz noticed that something he saw there gave him reason to blink curiously, as if he half remembered something from long ago. But then he appeared to dismiss the feeling, or memory, or whatever it was, pushing it to the back of his mind for later analysis. Liz sighed inwardly. Sometime over the last twenty years the Brigadier had become a perfect example of the kind of man who knew there was a place for everything and therefore insisted on finding places for both things and people which patently didn't need them.

The Doctor peered sideways at the book on the desk.

'Not a Mills & Boon, the cover's all wrong.' At the Brigadier's expression, the Doctor smiled gently. 'Hardly your cup of tea, anyway, I suppose. A Hemingway, perhaps? First edition, plain cover – *The Old Man and the Sea*?'

The Brigadier frowned.

'That book is the reason you invited us here, isn't it?'

With a visible effort, the Brigadier controlled his impatience.

'This book – this part of a book – was found by my medical officer, Sam Meredith, wrapped in a shawl carried by your friend, Jo. I happen to know that it was entrusted to her by her uncle, General Hobson, twenty years ago. Why has it taken her so long to bring it to me? Where on Earth has she been all that time? *And where's the other half?*'

'You could always ask her.'

'I'm afraid that is impossible. Jo has rather extensive internal injuries and is suffering from septicaemia. She is in a coma.'

'Ah. I can see you may have a problem then.'

The Brigadier took a breath. 'Don't you care about your friend? About what happens to her?'

'With so many people better qualified to care, I hardly think I need worry, do you?' The Doctor clasped his hands behind his back and turned to study the gilt-framed Turner hanging from a picture rail on one wall. 'It's a fake, you know. A good one – but you can tell by the direction of the brushstrokes that whoever painted it was right-handed.'

'Turner *was* right-handed.'

'Ah. But when I met him he'd sprained his right wrist

falling down a flight of stairs. He painted this picture with his *left* hand.' The Doctor turned back to face the Brigadier, adding pleasantly, 'It's a mistake anyone who didn't know the man could've made.'

The Brigadier's eyes suddenly snapped wide open. An expression of recognition spread across his face, but if Liz expected a smile, she was to be disappointed.

'Why, Doctor. How exactly like you to come back from the dead.'

The nearest of the bridge's two towers emerged from the thinning, ghostly ranks of vegetation.

Julia dismounted. 'We'll cross one at a time. Just in case.'

Alan swung his leg across her horse's back and dropped to the ground. He swayed dizzily as he thought about how high the bridge was.

Julia led her horse out onto the bridge. Her torch glimmered faintly. Shortly her voice drifted back across the bridge. 'Okay, come on. And take it easy, the safety railings aren't worth a damn.'

'I'll be careful.'

The horse shied nervously as Alan led it between the rusted tollbooths and out onto the bridge proper. He gripped the reins more tightly, as much through nervousness as through concern for the horse's safety.

As he left the shelter of the forest edge, a warm wind, laced with the damp, earthy smell of the forest, caused the bridge to sway. The horse nickered. Alan drew the animal closer, stroking its muzzle and whispering comforting nonsense words. Absurdly, he found himself responding to the words slightly better than the horse.

Alan shone his torch about him as he moved out onto the bridge. Underfoot, the tarmac was cracked and partly melted. The bridge was liberally scattered with flakes of rusting metal and thick twists of wire. Alan glanced along one of these to the edge and realized it was a snapped support cable. He glanced upwards. Other cables rose into the darkness beyond the reach of his torchlight. Far overhead, twin curves of metal arched into the darkness before him. He tried to estimate the number of support cables left intact. The figure he arrived at was not in the least reassuring.

He continued walking slowly forwards. As his eyes became adjusted to the darkness prevailing beyond the forest, he began to make out more details. To the right, low on the horizon, the moon was slowly rising to cast a silvery light on the ruins of Bristol, and on the river which snaked beneath the bridge. To the left, the gorge deepened and dark cliffs rose, intermittently lit by faintly glowing patches of vegetation. Ahead, one lane of the bridge was blocked by the rusting hulk of a motor vehicle. His boots began to crunch on pieces of broken glass, partly embedded in the tarmac. As he led the horse around the hulk, another strong gust of wind struck the bridge and caused it to sway. The movement caused another momentary wave of dizziness to flood over him. He reached out to the car for support, but as his fingers closed around the door frame, the metal crumbled into powder, and he lost his balance. Overcompensating, he stumbled backwards into the horse, which reared, nostrils flaring. The animal bolted forwards, knocking him aside as it galloped across the bridge.

He fell with a shout, rolling across the ridged tarmac while broken glass bit into his clothing, and found himself clinging to the concrete lip which had once supported a section of safety railing. Three feet from his face, the edge of the bridge was a broken mess of concrete and metal. Beyond that was darkness broken by the faint glimmer of moonlight on water far below.

And something else.

Or rather, some*one* else.

Hooked to a T-shaped metal girder by her satchel strap and one leg was the woman who must be the Doctor's friend.

'Hey,' said Ace somewhat blearily. 'Do you know I can see right up your nose?'

'I suppose it's no good asking where you've been all these

57

years?' The Brigadier gazed at the Doctor. 'I suppose not. Still, now that you're back you can begin by helping me.'

The Doctor said quietly, 'To restore Mankind to its position of supremacy on this planet?'

'That's correct.'

'And the Silurians?'

'They can be – '

There was an urgent knock on the office door, which opened to admit a tall, well-built man in a sergeant's uniform.

'Sorry to barge in on you, Brigadier, but a Silurian hunting-party has been spotted in the gorge, by the corral. They've got carnivores with them. They look as if they mean business, sir.'

'Very well, Sergeant Benton. You know we can't let them get away with knowledge of the Complex.'

'I know, sir. Measures are already in hand.'

'Very good, Sergeant. Carry on.'

Benton saluted and left the room.

The Doctor rounded on the Brigadier. He took a pace nearer and gazed contemptuously up into the taller man's lined face. ' "Measures are already in hand"? Nothing changes, does it, Brigadier?' He turned away in disgust. 'The arrival here of these Silurians has given you a second chance to make peace. And what do you do about it? Talk? Try to negotiate a common ground for understanding? No! That would be much too easy, wouldn't it!' The Doctor almost spat the final words from his mouth. 'I don't know why I don't just leave now.'

Throughout the Doctor's tirade, the Brigadier had remained calm, his face blank, his hands clasped stiffly behind his back. When the Doctor had finally finished, he said quietly, 'You won't leave because you can't leave. Something is preventing you, though I don't know what it is. I need your help, Doctor. Provide it, and I'll help you, in whatever you want, in any way I can.'

The Brigadier extended his hand towards the Doctor's back.

The Doctor turned to gaze at the offered hand. 'We're going to need drugs for Jo. Antibiotics, clear fluids, surgical equipment and facilities. You have trained medical staff, I presume?'

'Janice Martin is surgically trained. Obtaining the equipment she needs to operate on Jo is going to be harder. According to intelligence reports, the only hospital with the facilities you need intact is in London. Even on horseback that's two days away.'

Billy Wilson crept silently through the deep undergrowth surrounding the corral. The knife in his hand was twenty years old and honed to a fine point, carefully dulled to present no telltale gleam or reflection in the darkness. His head echoed with the sound of burning, and screams. Twenty years of pain and anguish and terror welled up inside him. He felt an almost overpowering urge to scream aloud, above the sound of the voices in his head. To let the world know he was still here. Still *here*, not lost in some nightmare interior landscape. With an effort, he held the impulse in check, and instead he began to whisper, soft words, lost in the darkness, over and over again. 'Teach you to cry for me . . .'

Between him and the reps, the horses were jostling in the corral, whinnying and making nervous little half jumps at the barred fence. Carefully, Billy climbed the fence and lowered himself into the corral. He slid like a shadow between the horses, using their sounds and smells to disguise his own movements. Oh, there was nothing stupid about Billy. They all thought he was mad, and maybe he was. But if he was, he knew who was responsible.

And who would pay.

Leaping from the corral fence with a hideous screech, Billy threw himself upon the nearest Silurian mount. The dilophosaurus took a few seconds to register the extra weight on its back.

The rider did not.

In the time it took to draw a single breath, Billy found himself face to face with a twenty-year-old vision from the burning ruins of Glasgow. Somehow the Silurian had twisted on its mount. Now its face was inches from his own, the mottled skin pebbly smooth like a lizard's, its eyes glowing with revulsion and hatred.

Billy's arm came up in a reflex movement as the Silurian's third eye began to shine sullenly. The knife slammed into the creature's neck even as pain filled his body.

Billy and the Silurian screamed together. Immediately there was pandemonium. The hunting dinosaurs broke loose from their control as the remaining Silurians brought their minds to bear on the attacker. The horses suddenly ran wild as the hunting dinosaurs slammed into the corral fence, smashing it down. The warm night air was filled with screams from the horses, the hissing of the dinosaurs breath and the hideous sound of animal flesh tearing like paper.

Billy felt every muscle in his body spasm as the Silurians brought their killing force to bear on him. In his mind the voices of his brother and parents rose imploringly. Blood cascaded down his body as his knife was wrenched from the dying Silurian's neck by his own spasming arm.

'Teach you to cry,' Billy sobbed. 'Cry the red tears for me . . .'

The two glowing third eyes hung before him like great bloody lamps in the darkness. A third rose, weaving unsteadily, to join them. With a supreme effort, Billy lurched forward and buried his knife up to the hilt in the nearest.

'Christ on a stick!'

Julia leaped to her feet and charged forward towards the pandemonium within and beyond the corral. A stampeding horse hurtled past within three feet of her; foam splashed from its muzzle onto her face. Julia sidestepped, bringing her gun to bear in the darkness, hunting desperately for a target. A mass of reptiles and mammals formed a living barrier between her and Billy. The screams were like a wall before her.

She shook her head, trying to clear it, unable to shake loose the clinging, maddening itching.

A horse slammed to the ground in front of her, two reptiles clinging to its chest and back, snapping and hissing, and a gap in the barrier opened momentarily. Trying not to fire indiscriminately, Julia loosed two shots into the darkness. There was a high-pitched squeal and the light from one of the glowing third eyes dimmed as it sank towards the ground. Breathing a prayer, Julia ran forward, her feet slipping in the muck of the corral. Now the second eye vanished too, as the Silurian wheeled its mount and charged away into the darkness.

Julia fired twice more into the night, unable to see what effect her shots had on the fleeing Silurian. Behind her came the sound of more shots as Benton led a few UNIT soldiers to mop up the other reps.

'Billy? Billy!' she called.

Julia peered into the darkness, feeling dizzy, almost drunk. She remembered a day when, as a teenager, she had gone midnight swimming with her friends while on holiday on the Scilly Isles. She'd swum too far out in the darkness and had lost her sense of direction. Panic had set in quickly and terror had grown from that. She could only stay afloat in the darkness so long. Where was the shore? She could hear her friends, but their voices suddenly seemed very far away, and she couldn't tell which direction they were coming from. That was how she felt now: trapped in an alien environment, only yards from light and warmth, but unable to reach it, while out here with her was . . . Julia shuddered and gripped her gun tighter. Somewhere in the darkness, not far from her, was a Silurian hunter. Maybe it was dead, like the beached whale she'd swum into that night so long ago. Yeah. Maybe it was dead – but maybe, just maybe, it was only injured and was waiting for the chance to –

Not two yards from her a tall shape suddenly rose and lurched forward. Julia whirled with a startled yell, her finger tightening reflexively on the trigger of her gun.

'No! Julia, *no!*'

Alan knocked her gun arm upwards and the bullet flew wild into the darkness.

'Alan, what are you playing at? I told you to stay put!'

Alan grabbed hold of Julia and shook her. 'Julia, calm down, calm down! It's over. It's over.'

The figure lurched forward to collapse at their feet. Caked with blood and excrement and juddering wildly, the whispering voice was recognizable, even if the face and body weren't. 'Teach them to cry ... cry the red tears ...'

Julia drew a shuddering breath. 'Christ on a stick, Billy, I almost shot you!'

Ten minutes later the Brigadier gazed coldly down at two Silurians lying prone in the churned muck of the corral. One was dead, a ragged wound in his neck testifying to Billy's bloodthirsty determination; the other was unconscious, although breathing shallowly; one of the bullets fired from Julia's gun had grazed his skull. Behind a face he kept carefully blank, the Brigadier's thoughts were churning wildly. Things were getting out of hand. Measures needed to be taken, and the responsibility was his. He drew his pistol and weighed it thoughtfully in his hand before lowering the muzzle to point at the unconscious Silurian's closed third eye.

There was a noise behind him. Sergeant Benton cleared his throat, pointedly ignoring the Brigadier's very clear intention.

'There were three reps altogether, sir. One got away.'

'I see.' The Brigadier frowned thoughtfully. 'You know what it will mean for us if the existence of the Complex is revealed?'

Benton nodded.

'Then I leave it to you to see that it isn't, Sergeant.'

'Sir!' Benton saluted and hurried away into the darkness.

When the Sergeant had gone, the Brigadier returned his attention to the prone figure. He aimed his pistol for a second time. A second time he was interrupted, this time by a quiet presence beside him.

'Just thought I'd get an idea of the managerial policy involved here,' said the Doctor. 'Don't mind if I watch, do you, Brigadier?'

The Brigadier said angrily, 'Why do you find it so hard to understand, Doctor? It's a war; we're at war with these . . .' The Brigadier gestured with his gun at the unconscious Silurian.

'People?' the Doctor suggested gently.

'. . . things.' The Brigadier spat the word out in disgust. 'We are at war with these *things*.'

The Doctor leaned casually against his umbrella. 'The cause of war can be identified and a solution devised you know, almost always.'

The Brigadier's voice hardened. 'The cause has been identified.' He kicked the Silurian with the toe of his boot, grimacing in disgust as the creature hissed in a pain reflex.

He raised his gun. 'As has the solution.'

Ignoring the ragged pain from his wounded neck, Imorkal gazed up at the moon with thinly disguised loathing. He hated the moon. It had come to symbolize the mammal dominance of the world. Their one-time dominance, he corrected himself grimly. His lips twitched. No Human would ever have called the expression which flitted across Imorkal's face a smile, but he laughed nonetheless, a soft, hissing laugh, which held more pain than humour.

Imorkal had never known the Silurian civilization at its peak. He had been hatched into the mammal-infested world less than twenty years ago. His life had been spent idolizing the suffering of Humans and longing for a return to the golden age when the world was younger, cleaner, hotter than it was now.

Beneath him, the dilophosaurus shuddered. Imorkal strengthened his link with the reptile, urging it on to greater speed.

In his short life Imorkal had never really experienced fear, although he had observed the suffering of others as part of his education. Now he was beginning to know the sensation intimately: the yawning gulf within signifying loss and the potential end of self and, worst of all, showing that he was not the infallible hunter he had thought.

He touched the makeshift bandage around his neck nervously. It was soaked with blood, though at least that was beginning to clot now. If he was lucky he might make it far enough to be able to rest in safety for an hour or so. Then he might risk taking the time needed to concentrate on communicating with his father, the Leader, half a world away.

Imorkal was not lucky.

Less than ten miles from the gorge his dilophosaurus collapsed with a wheeze. Imorkal let out a high-pitched squeal of surprise and alarm. When he attempted to disentangle himself from the fallen animal he almost screamed again, this time with pain, as the broken ends of the bones in his forearm grated together.

Imorkal shuddered and emptied the contents of his stomach into the surrounding foliage. A few minutes passed as he tried to control his body functions. Gradually, as his own agony diminished into a dull wash, he became aware of the sharp, nagging pain of the dilophosaurus, filtering through the link. Imorkal struggled to rise. He stumbled along the sixteen-foot length of the dilophosaurus, past the shuddering limbs and heaving belly, to the twin-crested skull and eyes glassy with fear. Imorkal rested one pebbly hand across the side of the animal's face. He had seen the worst: a long shallow mark was raked across the animal's flank: a bullet wound inflicted during the fight. No doubt the wound had been bleeding copiously ever since. The faster he had driven the dilophosaurus to flight, the more the animal's exertions had pumped the life-giving blood from its body. Now there was a trail which would lead the mammals straight to him, not to mention any carnivores which happened to be hunting. Imorkal was faced with the very real possibility of his own death. Already he thought he could hear noises in the night; shouting, the baying of dogs.

In a last gesture towards the loyal dilophosaurus, Imorkal opened his third eye and concentrated on the animal's mind. The least he could do was end its pain and fear. To leave it as it was, in pain, would be less than civilized.

A moment passed and Imorkal sighed with confusion. The dilophosaurus was still breathing. He closed his primary eyes and concentrated on what he could perceive through his third eye alone. The confusion changed into fear and horror when he realized there was nothing to perceive. The mind fog which he had detected earlier had closed down around him completely. He was totally cut off.

And the sound of dogs was getting closer.

Benton and the three UNIT soldiers pushed through the foliage into the clearing in which the dilophosaurus lay. Benton wrinkled his nose in disgust. The rep had obviously died within the hour. Its bowels had loosened and the stench was abominable. Steam rose from its innards, and from a long wound on its flank, from which entrails and a bloody mess of organs spilled. Benton motioned the tracker forward. Holding the three dogs at arms length the woman moved towards the corpse. The dogs began to mill in confusion.

'Well?'

'Sorry, Sarge. The dogs can't seem to pick up a trail. I dunno, it must be due to all this carnage. God.' She swallowed. 'It's a mess, isn't it?'

Benton shrugged. 'I suppose we're not the only hunters abroad tonight. Ironic really. That a rep should be killed by a dinosaur. Oh well. Better get back and report, I suppose.'

'Right-o.'

Benton scratched his ear idly as he followed the tracker past the stinking corpse and into the night.

After the Humans had gone, the flank of the dilophosaurus heaved. A roughly textured hand covered in gore emerged from a deep slit in the skin. The hand was followed by an arm and then the rest of Imorkal's body. Grabbing handfuls of vegetation, the Silurian began to wipe the worst of the dilophosaurus's insides off himself. Silently, he congratulated himself. Even with a broken arm and a damaged third eye he was more than a match for these mammals.

Imorkal's humour did not last long. He knew he was not strong enough to reach the fortress in the northern part of this country – Glasgow, they called it – where his airship was moored, before his wounds caused him to collapse. Then he remembered an old story his father had told him when he'd been smaller. About the place in Derbyshire called Wenley Moor, where his father had first awoken so many years ago. About the original deep shelter built there to enable many thousands of his people to survive the arrival of the moon in Earth's orbit. Now Imorkal's humour returned. There would be power there, a vast reactor, laboratories, communication amplifiers. And Wenley Moor was less than a quarter of the distance of the fortress.

His mind made up, Imorkal lost no time in trudging off into the night, pausing only once to rip creepers from a high tree which he used to make a sling for his broken arm.

As he trudged onwards, Imorkal began to form a plan. If luck was with him, the Wenley Moor shelter systems would be intact. From there he could contact his father and tell him what had happened to Chtorba and Vronim, and about the humans massing in the caves at Cheddar. And if the mammals followed him there and tried to kill him again – well then, the power source was enough, when detonated, to wipe out this wretched island and its entire mammal population . . .

Right at this moment, Imorkal could not think of a better way for a warrior prince to die.

Liz slept badly, jerking awake from a formless, cloying nightmare at daybreak the next morning. Sunlight – reflected along polished rocky 'chimneys' leading from the top of the gorge – slanted in through the ceiling of her room and dried the sweat on her face. Not for the first time Liz felt the warmth and thought of brighter days, long ago, in Cambridge, where she'd taken her degree. Liz splashed cold water from a bucket onto her face to dispel both the bad dreams and the good memories alike. One was as out of place in this world as the other.

Disinclined to have breakfast, Liz set off along the rocky tunnels towards the labs where she worked; a small mountain of culture plates awaited her analysis there, the latest of many attempts to analyse and control the mutation rate in edible plant fibre. As she walked, Liz felt a familiar sensation of despair rise within her: it was frustratingly difficult to do any effective work when, for example, it was next to impossible to maintain even the most basic sterile environment. Brains the Complex had aplenty – it was equipment which had dwindled over the years now that industry had ground to a halt in the outside world. Liz couldn't count the amount of glassware which had been broken in accidents over the years, all irreplaceable now, of course. The Petri dishes had only survived because they were made of plastic. Last week the bearings had finally worn out on the big centrifuge. The mech department were cannibalizing a whole load of apparently unrelated mechanical spares to fix it. She imagined the centrifuge wobbling like an old washing machine as it spun and shuddered.

Liz's thoughts rolled on in an early morning muddle. She could have done with a strong cup of coffee to wake herself up, but real coffee was rationed like everything else in the Complex. Twenty years was a long time to survive without trade or industry to provide the things you needed for day-to-day existence, let alone any kind of real work.

A quiet voice from the corridor ahead made her stop, and Liz was suddenly aware that her feet had been wandering as much as her mind.

'Sorry, Miss Shaw. This passage is off limits.'

'Sergeant Benton, you poor man, have you had any sleep?'

Benton shrugged in the gloom. 'Needs must when duty calls.'

'Very philosophical. You're guarding the Silurian Julia shot?'

'The rep? Yes.'

Liz suddenly felt her temper rise. 'This is patently ridiculous!'

There were more footsteps along the passage. Heavy, military footsteps. The Brigadier's voice, fresh from a sound sleep, asked: 'And what, precisely, is so "patently ridiculous", Miss Shaw?'

Liz rounded on the Brigadier. 'Brigadier, for a start, your prisoner isn't a "rep" he's a Silurian. He's a person like you or I and judging by your normal behaviour, at least as intelligent. Keeping him under lock and key is inhumane and unnecessary. How would you like to be stabbed, shot at and then imprisoned when you were in need of medical attention? I bet you haven't given him any food either.'

The Brigadier said calmly, 'Miss Shaw, the rep is a prisoner of war. Any concessions shown to it may end up being used against us – '

Liz laughed with contempt. 'Rubbish. Brigadier, I know you too well for that to wash. I watched you last night. You were going to kill him. Only the Doctor prevented you. So you locked him up in this cell hoping that he would die during the night from his injuries and conveniently clear up what you perceive to be an unwanted problem. Look me in the eye and tell me that's not true.'

The Brigadier had begun to tap his swagger stick impatiently against his thigh. 'If you've quite finished, Miss Shaw – '

'Not by a long shot, Brigadier. In case you haven't read my reports for the last six months, I'll recap the situation for you: mutation rates are causing the food supply to become unviable. I no longer have the technical facilities necessary to carry out essential control experiments or analyse potential new sources of food.'

The Brigadier sighed impatiently. 'Your point being?'

'My point is this: inside that cell is a member of an intelligent species who may be able to help us.'

The Brigadier was silent.

'Well?'

'I am fully aware of the situation within the Complex. However, I do have certain priorities to which I must adhere – '

'Brigadier, that is the most patronizing example of – '

'Miss Shaw! May I remind you that, temper notwithstanding, you are still a member of UNIT and as such – '

'From the day I signed that blasted contract you've assumed the air of a kindly dictator. Well, I'm not an impersonal resource and I'm most definitely not a puppet of the military!' Liz drew a breath to continue, but the Brigadier raised his hands tiredly.

'Miss Shaw, please, this is all old ground. You're right, of course. Both UNIT and humanity need your expertise. *I* need your expertise.' With an obvious effort the Brigadier lowered his voice. 'Sergeant Benton, please arrange to have the prisoner transferred to sickbay immediately. Under guard.'

'Sir!'

The Brigadier caught Liz's eye. 'And make sure it gets something to eat.'

'Right away, sir!'

'There you are, Miss Shaw. Happy now?'

'If he's not already dead!' Liz turned on her heel and marched away, more upset by the exchange than she cared to acknowledge.

During the night, a dapper figure had come into the sickbay and kept silent vigil by Ace's bedside. As the hours drew by the figure neither moved not spoke, merely watched as the young woman tossed and turned in feverish sleep. Eventually, the figure laid a cool hand upon her brow. Gradually her fever receded, her brow smoothed out, and she slept more peacefully.

The figure withdrew its hand after a moment, smiled sadly, turned and left the sickbay.

When morning came, Ace struggled upright in her bed, surprised to find she could manage it with only minimal pain from her back. She stared around herself curiously. She was in a small ward. There were three beds. One was empty. A screen had been placed around the third.

She reached for the glass of water on a nearby bedside table and became aware that someone was standing beside the bed.

'Doctor?'

The figure neither moved nor spoke.

Ace blinked. No. The figure was taller than her companion. Stockier. And his eyes –

A slender woman with a pleasant smile came over to

the bed. 'You'll have to go now, Brigadier. I have tests for young Ace here.'

Did the figure shake his head slightly at Ace before he left the ward? Ace frowned and turned her attention to the second newcomer. 'Who're you then?'

'Actually I'm a doctor. Jan Martin, at your service.' She assumed an expression unique to the medical service, part frown, part smile. She took Ace's pulse and placed a thermometer under her tongue. 'We don't often see anyone your age in here.' Jan reached under Ace's armpits to examine the lymph glands there. After a moment she lowered Ace's arms, withdrew the thermometer from Ace's mouth and studied it. 'Well,' she said seriously, 'I'm sorry to have to tell you that your temperature and pulse rate are perfectly normal, and that there are no signs of infection whatsoever.'

Ace grinned. 'Smart bugs know better than to mess with me.'

Jan pointed across the ward. 'Your clothes are in the locker there. And there's a message from the Doctor. He says to have a large breakfast, you're going to need it. Whatever that means.'

Ace frowned. 'It's his call to arms.'

'Yes, well his "call to arms" better not be too strenuous, that's all. You've just had a nasty experience. If he wants you to go gallivanting around outside, he'll have me to answer to!'

'I'll bear that in mind.' Despite Jan's disapproving look, Ace jumped out of bed, grabbed her clothes and began to dress.

An hour later she stood with the Doctor beside a chestnut stallion at the head of the gorge and tried to work out what it was about being outside that made her feel light-headed and dizzy. It wasn't the fact that she was once again seeing something other than the inside of a dingy cave system, and it certainly wasn't the comforting appearance of the fields and trees sloping down to the shores of the small inland sea where the towns of the Somerset Levels had once stood. This world wasn't her world any more – hadn't been for years, if what the Doctor had told her was true – and yet there was something about it . . . Maybe it was the air which made her feel fresh and alive, air filled with exotic smells instead of the faint but ineradicable taint of human sweat and fear. Yes, Ace thought that was probably it. That and the sun. Hot and yellow, burning down from a cloudless blue sky, the sun was no longer the familiar sight she remembered from her childhood. It was fiercer, wilder, somehow untamed. Like the world upon which it shone.

Ace took a small, chromed Hillman Avenger vanity plate from her satchel and pinned it to the horse's bridle. Sunlight glittered from the single word.

'Avenger,' the Doctor smiled very gently. 'I think the Brigadier would approve.'

'Y'know, Doctor, there's something about this place . . . I think I like it here.'

Beside her, the Doctor shielded his eyes from the harsh sunlight and gazed in surprise at the young woman's face. 'I thought you'd hate it.'

'Because of the way I remember it?' Ace frowned. 'When you come right down to it, what did England ever have for me? School? My mum?' Ace snorted. 'This place, it's well – it's more like me.'

'Is that a touch of optimism I hear? And I thought you were the confirmed cynic.'

'Pragmatist.' Ace flipped her hair back from her eyes with one hand, the other keeping a firm hold on the horse's reins. 'Anyway, that's the whole point of it, isn't it?'

The Doctor looked puzzled. 'What's the whole point of what?'

'Oh, I don't know.' Ace waved expansively at the fantastic surroundings. 'Being an adult. Learning what you're all about. Deciding what's right for you and where you fit in.'

'Planetary invasions, attacks by carnivorous dinosaurs and the odd tumble from a high bridge notwithstanding?'

Ace stretched her shoulders, feeling the scars in her back sting as the skin tightened around the stitches. 'The pain reminds you you're alive.' She rested her head against

71

the horse's neck, inhaling the smell of the animal, lost in memories of other times and planets.

There was the sound of other hoofbeats as five more riders drew nearer. The Doctor looked around. 'Time to go, Ace. Are you up to it?'

Ace lifted her head. 'So soon. Don't I even get a chance to meet the Brigadier again?'

The Doctor frowned. 'No time, I'm afraid. And I don't think this Brigadier is the man you remember. You've got your itinerary?' he finished briskly.

'You should know! You stuck it in my head.'

The Doctor pretended embarrassment. 'It's important, you know. Vitally important.'

Ace swung herself easily into the saddle. 'As important as getting the medical gear for Jo?'

The Doctor hesitated.

Without waiting for a reply, Ace turned her horse and followed the other riders slowly up the gorge, past the place where Billy Wilson and a few others were working with rakes and spades to clear the stinking remains of the previous night's violence, through strange and twisted trees and into the morning haze.

Benton set a course north-easterly across country. At first this didn't make any sense to Ace; London was almost due east from Bristol. Then she realized Benton must be planning to intersect the M4 motorway somewhere beyond Bath. She wondered if he realized the horses would make poorer time on the hard tarmac of the motorway, and be more inclined to throw a shoe, than they would on open countryside. Then again, she supposed, it was all swings and roundabouts. There appeared to be very little open countryside left. Ace rubbed her horse's neck reassuringly. 'Don't you worry,' she whispered, 'I won't let them take you anywhere daft.' The horse nickered softly, responding to the tone of her voice, and the tiny fragment of Mars Bar she managed to dredge up from one pocket.

As the morning progressed, the heat intensified. The noise level increased as animals stirred and began to hunt. Before very long the forest of cycads through which they rode echoed to the sound of eerie cries, mournful hoots, and the occasional coughing roar, chilling animal scream and long silence following a successful kill. On these occasions Ace peered around curiously, but her view was restricted by the thick undergrowth.

Several times Jan peered around at her, as if Ace's status as a former patient was reason enough to show concern. Ace swallowed her irritation, instead urging her horse forward to draw level with Jan's. 'So what's the story, here?' she asked. 'It never used to be like this, did it?' She waved one hand at the thick vegetation.

'Of course not. There are theories, some pretty wild, some just plain stupid. There's been talk of everything from time travel, to a Malthusian control, to the divine retribution of God. Me, I think it's just the Silurians. I think they can clone things, force breed the result. They want the world the way it was; we're incidental.'

Ace let out a breath. 'And the water levels are rising, right? In the cities and the low-lying areas?'

'That's right.' Benton had slowed his horse to match their speed. 'The reps have bases everywhere, but their main city is in east Africa, on the equator. They get their power by induction, without the use of wires. It's geothermal power and it comes from installations at the polar caps. Meltwater is an inevitable by-product.'

'Blimey. They don't like us much, do they?'

Benton scowled. Ace thought his face was too naturally good-humoured to scowl quite that much. 'Of course they don't like us. They're reps,' Benton said, as if that explained everything. 'They've made war on us ever since we discovered their first shelter under Wenley Moor.' His voice lowered. 'You'd think they'd have been grateful. If it weren't for us mammals, they'd have been snoring quietly till the crack of doom.' Benton urged his horse forward into the lead position once again without waiting for a reply.

Ace shrugged. 'Pushed his button, didn't I?'

Jan said quietly, 'A great many people think that way, Ace. It's inevitable when you consider the events of the past twenty years.'

Julia added, 'We've been invaded. I don't suppose there are enough civilized people left alive to make a good football crowd. There's probably no more than a million people left in the whole world. Most of those live like animals.'

Jan nodded. 'It's not our world any more. Whatever the Brigadier says about fighting back, whether we win or lose, that much will always be true.'

'So we really are at war, then,' Ace said.

'Yes. We really are at war.'

Ace's eyes shone.

The Doctor and Liz were in sickbay studying the recumbent form of the captured Silurian. Or rather the Doctor was studying the Silurian, while Liz studied the Doctor.

Though his face and body were that of a completely different man, his attitude seemed to derive from the person she remembered. He rushed about as busily as he had ever done, perhaps more so, fussing here and there, checking the surgical proceedings, laying a hand on the Silurian's brow from time to time as if to reassure himself the creature was still alive. Somehow, if anything was needed during the proceedings, the Doctor was able to anticipate the need. He was there, whether it was with an encouraging word to Doctor Meredith, a tray of instruments, or a pot of genuine Darjeeling tea when surgery was over and monitoring had commenced.

Liz tried to sort out her own feelings now that the Doctor had turned up again. When she'd known him before he'd had the air of a kindly schoolteacher, an old-fashioned politeness combined with a childish petulance which was almost endearing. This new Doctor was more of an enigma. He rarely spoke and when he did the sentences were frequently unclear in their meaning. He was very much the picture of a man with some tremendous problem on his mind. It was almost as if helping herself and the Complex staff was merely a means to an end of his own, instead of an end in itself.

At some point during the proceedings, the Doctor had vanished, presumably to say goodbye to Ace and the medical team. Now he was back just in time to observe the Silurian's recovery from surgery.

Using a portion of their limited supply of gut, Meredith had performed a neat piece of suturing on the flesh around the Silurian's third eye, damaged in the fracas the night before. At other places the pebble-textured skin was swollen and discoloured a deep reddish-brown. Taking a best guess, he'd set what appeared to be a broken humerus. From what Liz had seen of the musculature beneath the skin, and having a rough idea of how the tendons would be attached to the bone, she wondered at the force Billy must have used to break the arm.

Her gaze travelled back along the grainy torso and shoulders, to the head. The face was moving, muscles beneath the skin twitching slightly. Liz knew the creature must be feeling pain; they knew so little about its metabolism that Meredith had decided that to administer pain suppressants might prove highly dangerous. Liz felt a pang of sympathy for the creature. He had not made a sound during the whole procedure, though he'd lost consciousness when the arm was set.

As a couple of medical orderlies bundled up the blood-stained masking sheets and began to clean the surgery, Liz felt a familiar distant tickle begin deep within her ears.

The Silurian opened its primary eyes.

The Doctor moved forward. There was no hint of a smile in his face. Liz wasn't sure the Silurian would have appreciated it anyway. Behind them, Meredith was ushering the orderlies from the sickbay.

The Doctor said, 'I know you're scared. There's no need to be. But it's very important we talk. Do you understand?'

The Silurian made no sound. Only the quiet hissing of its breath and the thudding of her own heartbeat broke the silence.

The tickling sensation increased.

'You have to vocalize. Humans can't link.'

The leathery lips quivered. 'I am Chtorba.'

Now the Doctor smiled. 'I'm the Doctor.'

Chtorba looked around himself, somewhat nervously, Liz thought. 'I am alone.'

'I'm afraid one of your party is dead. The other is still free.'

Chtorba blinked. Liz saw the play of muscles around the fluted crest framing the third eye. He winced. 'No. I am *alone*.'

'You mean you cannot link?'

Chtorba managed a stiff nod.

Liz moved a little closer. 'Is that because the other Silurians are out of range, or because your eye is damaged?'

Chtorba was silent.

'Do you understand the question?'

The eyes regarded Liz impassively. 'I understand the question.'

'We don't doubt your intelligence, Chtorba.' The Doctor turned to Liz. 'But, Liz, you have to understand that Chtorba is alone, injured and scared. In his situation it's easy to misinterpret genuine scientific interest for the gathering of military intelligence.'

Liz blushed, aware of how her question must have sounded. 'I didn't start the war,' she said bitterly. 'I don't *want* a war.'

Chtorba seemed about to respond to Liz's comments when the Brigadier entered the sickbay. He strode to the bed, tapping his swagger stick against his thigh.

'Has it said anything useful yet?'

Liz glared pointedly at the Brigadier. 'His name is Chtorba.'

The Brigadier favoured Liz with a cold glance. 'We know Silurians can communicate telepathically, and that this sense is linked to their third eye. The rep is a security risk.'

Liz scowled. 'What are you trying to say, Brigadier? That we should kill Chtorba? That would be okay, I suppose, except for the information you'd lose. Perhaps we should mutilate his third eye; stop him from communicating at all until he's well enough to interrogate?'

The Brigadier appeared to consider Liz's suggestion seriously.

'Good grief, Brigadier, I can't believe you would actually – '

The Doctor said quietly, 'Are there any electrical supply shops with their stocks intact left in Bristol?'

Both Liz and the Brigadier gazed in surprise at the Doctor, who added impatiently, 'TV repair and hi-fi shops, places like that?'

'I expect so, but why – '

The Doctor did not reply, merely took an old-fashioned quill pen from an inner pocket and began to scribble on a corner of a bedsheet. He tore the linen and handed it to the Brigadier. 'That's a list of components I'll need to build a telepathic emission dampener.'

'A what?'

The Doctor sighed. 'It has been a long time, hasn't it, Brigadier? A telepathic emission dampener is a device for dampening telepathic emissions. Without lobotomizing the patient,' he added pointedly.

Liz said, 'Chtorba will be unable to link with other Silurians.'

The Brigadier considered. 'Could it be used to treat those suffering from the race memory malaise?'

The Doctor frowned. 'Maybe.'

The Brigadier studied the list thoughtfully. 'Good show, Doctor. I'll have someone arrange to fetch these items for you A.S.A.P.'

'Most kind.'

As the Brigadier turned to leave, Liz said pointedly, 'Now perhaps we can start behaving sensibly towards these people!'

The Brigadier turned back into the room with a chilling expression on his face. He indicated the far end of the sickbay, where Jo Grant tossed and turned feverishly in her bed. 'Look at Jo,' he said quietly, when he was sure he had Liz's full attention. 'You know what's happened to her, don't you? Stillbirth? Haemorrhage? *Septic shock*?' When Liz made no reply, the Brigadier went on, 'Your

77

friend here caused that to happen by hunting her as if she was an animal.'

Liz stared at her shoes.

The Brigadier continued, 'Yes, they're intelligent. Yes, they're civilized. But they still hunt us. From choice. Because they enjoy it.' He paused again to allow his words to sink in. 'Now you tell me what special consideration we would allow anyone who did that to Jo, or to someone like her, who was unable to defend themselves?'

The Brigadier waited for a reply, but Liz had none.

In the silence, only the Doctor noticed that Chtorba was studying the two arguing humans with a look of deep concentration.

The motorway, when they joined it about five miles east of Bath, was choked with wrecked cars. The tarmac had obviously melted and reformed a hundred times or more since the days of the Nightmare. Most of the cars had sunk several inches into the gooey black surface.

Ace was quite relieved when Benton did not actually lead the group onto the surface, but guided his horse along a thin strip of grass at the very edge of the tarmac. In some places the vegetation had completely overrun the motorway, exploding up through the cracked tarmac and engulfing everything on its surface in a uniform carpet of green-grey foliage. To Ace these areas had the look of surreal gardens, with hedge ornaments shaped like cars and trucks and the occasional toppled motorcycle: the planet's way of celebrating life, even amongst death on such a monumental scale.

Jan noticed Ace's blank gaze and misinterpreted it. 'You okay?'

Ace blinked. 'Yeah. No problem. Why d'you ask?'

'Thought you looked a little green around the gills, that's all.'

'No.' She shrugged off Jan's concern. 'I'm starving,' she added and the older woman turned away, frowning.

Alan Tomson caught her eye as she said this, and his lips twitched in a half smile. Ace smiled right back.

The smile froze on her face as she saw the dense foliage beyond his shoulder stir unnaturally.

'Alan, watch it! There's something in the –'

There was a shattering roar and something heavy and muscular with snapping jaws and grasping claws pushed easily out of the foliage.

Someone yelled: 'Christ, it's a baryonix! Get out of the way!'

Ace was moving even as the horses began to panic. She was vaguely aware of Jan Martin being flung from her saddle to lie still upon the ground as her horse bolted.

Ace flung herself from her horse at Alan in the precise moment she saw the jaws descend for a killing bite. Alan was frozen, half turned in his saddle; the horse was screaming, about to bolt. By comparison with the speed of those jaws, everything else seemed to be crawling at a snail's pace. Ace was momentarily aware of another body hurtling towards them before her shoulder slammed into Alan's chest and all three of them tumbled to the ground.

The horse's scream ended as the jaws continued downwards to fasten upon its neck. There was a sticklike *crunch* and a horrible tearing sound. Ace was aware of the horse's body, headless, crashing to the ground beside her face. Grabbing Alan by the hair and shoulders she scrambled backwards, avoiding the gush of blood by a handbreadth.

There was a volley of gunfire. Benton had his horse under control and was firing round after round over their heads.

Ignoring the bullets, the baryonix vanished into the foliage, its prize impaled on huge claws.

She became aware that Alan was yelling. 'Ace! It's okay, you can let got now. Thanks. I'm too young for a toupee.'

'Toupee?' She glanced sideways at the decapitated horse. 'Jesus.'

Ace realized she was sitting on Alan's chest. Julia was sitting on his legs. Only Benton was still in his saddle; the other four horses had vanished. Jan and Rod were sprawled on the ground.

Ace allowed herself to be pushed backwards as Alan began to disentangle himself. He grinned, a slightly stunned look on his face. 'If I thought I'd have women fighting over me all the way from here to London I'd have suggested we leave yesterday.'

Abruptly, he sagged to the ground in a dead faint.

Ace exchanged looks with Julia, who began quietly to laugh.

As the Brigadier stood in the clearing so recently vacated by Ace, hands behind his back, swagger stick clasped loosely in a trembling fist, his thoughts returned again and again to the Silurian in the sickbay. Every fibre of his being, every bit of experience he'd ever had, as a soldier, as a civilian, as a human in a world of aliens, screamed out to him to kill the invader. Forget about studying it, forget about talking to it, just bury it as quickly as possible.

Unable to work out how much of his immediate response was due to animal instinct and how much stemmed from other factors, he had climbed Jacob's Ladder to the top of the gorge and then walked back to the clear part of the ridge in the hope of finding some resolution within himself. Now he lifted one hand to shield his eyes from the hot late-afternoon sun and gazed out across the sea which covered the Somerset Levels, hoping, almost, that sight of the calm waters would soothe his troubled mind.

'Saluting the dead?'

The Brigadier turned in time to see the Doctor perch cross-legged on a mossy rock a short distance away, looking, he thought, rather like a precocious imp dressed for summer safari.

'What do you mean?'

The Doctor swept his umbrella out in a generous arc across the glittering water to where a number of crested hadrosaurs were scooping up vast mouthfuls of weed and munching contentedly in the hot sunshine. 'Twenty years ago the streets of Somerset were filled with people. There were couples with mortgages, children on bicycles, pensioners ... A mobile library stopped in Glastonbury for three hours every Wednesday afternoon. In Ilsford there were ducks in the pond on the village green. You could hear them all through the village on a quiet day.'

The Brigadier took off his cap, wiped his brow with a handkerchief, and replaced his cap. 'You paint a vivid picture, Doctor. I'm just not sure of its relevance.'

'Like the Turner on your office wall, then.' The Doctor smiled. 'What I meant was: assuming responsibility for the human race is like trying to control the sea. You plan, build, anticipate – like the people of Somerset, perhaps, with their mortgages and library books, safe in their assumptions about what life was about.' His voice took on a deeper timbre. 'But when the water level began to rise . . .'

'. . . there was nothing they could do about it. I see. You're saying mankind is helpless in the face of his own destiny. That despite anyone's best efforts nobody knows for certain what's around the next corner.' He paused. 'I'm an old man, Doctor. And I'm scared of the day I won't have the strength to fight any more. Sometimes, you know, I think we shouldn't even try; that perhaps our time is at an end, and yet . . . something inside tells me giving up equals suicide; that it's my duty to fight, so long as I can draw breath, or aim a gun, or conceive a tactic.'

Wearily, the Brigadier sat next to the Doctor on the mossy rock. He placed his swagger stick across his knees and sighed.

'The fight's been so long and mostly it hasn't been like a fight at all. They just do what they do, changing the planet, our planet, and we can't do a blasted thing about it. Sometimes it seems all we can really do is die. But every time I even consider throwing in the towel, I think of the children. Of how they'll die or, more likely, how they'll live – and I have to fight on.' For a moment the quiet was punctuated only by the distant, mournful hoots of the duckbills, and closer, the rush and sigh of the undergrowth moving restlessly in the hot breeze.

'Hobson's choice, I suppose.' He stood, brushing ineffectually at his precisely creased trousers. 'Blast. Now I've got moss on my uniform.'

The Doctor stood too, and they began to walk along

the ridge, paralleling the edge. After a moment the Doctor said, 'You wanted to ask me something.'

'How on Earth did you – ' Abruptly the Brigadier broke off. 'Actually there was something, but . . .'

'Don't you trust me?'

The Brigadier hesitated. 'It's odd. I know you can change appearance,' he said slowly. 'You're the same man, and yet you're not.'

'And you're worried in case my affiliations can change as easily as my face?' the Doctor suggested gently.

'Well, yes, in a word. You see, in this world trust is not an easy thing to come by. I have to know you're on my side.'

'Brigadier, the only thing you have to know about me is that I'm always on the side of the good guys.'

The Brigadier did not return the Doctor's ingenuous smile. 'That's right,' he said slowly. 'But who do *you* think *are* the good guys?'

The Doctor did not reply.

Ace wrapped her arms around her knees and made herself comfortable against the gnarled bark of the fruit tree beneath which they rested. Benton was handing out dried hadrosaur steaks. When she received her piece, Ace found the meat was tough and stringy, but had a strong flavour, much like salted beef. She tucked in with gusto.

In the six hours since the baryonix had attacked, and the horses had scattered, they had walked, stopping to rest only once. Benton had driven them hard, but they had covered a lot of ground. More than thirty miles, she estimated.

It wasn't enough.

'Why don't we get one of the cars going?' she asked through mouthfuls of food.

Benton handed out the last piece of meat and looked at her. 'Even if we could get a car going, using it would alert any reps in the vicinity to our presence. The reps regard all humans as dumb animals. The Brigadier wants it to stay that way until the time comes to strike back.'

'But there aren't any Silurians, are there?' Ace mused

thoughtfully. 'I mean, we'd know about it, right? Because of the race memory thing.'

Benton stared hard at her as he began to repack his satchel. Ace gained the distinct impression he wanted her to shut up, but she was damned if she was going to do that. 'I mean, come on, we can all do the maths. It'll be tomorrow night at least before we get back from London, and that's if we're lucky. What chance has Jo got if we take that long? I know these cars look a mess but I'm sure I can get one running fast enough to make it worth –'

'Forget it,' Benton said warningly.

'No, I won't forget it!'

'I have my reasons.'

'So do I!'

Benton closed his eyes for a moment, as if trying to draw upon an inner strength, or perhaps come to some decision. Ace realized she'd made a fundamental mistake when her gaze dropped from his face to see his pistol, now clasped lightly but firmly in his hand. It rested across his knee, facing generally in her direction. The safety catch was off, she noticed.

'Good psychology, Sergeant,' she said dryly. 'Make friends with the troops. Take them into your confidence, get them on your side.'

Though she remained perfectly still, all her muscles were tensing for action. It had been a fair while since she'd fought in Spacefleet, and she no longer wore the armour which might have saved her from a bullet wound, but still, if push came to shove, they'd see who gave the best account of themselves.

'I have my reasons, and I have my orders,' Benton repeated coldly. He held the gun out butt first to Ace, who stared at it in surprise. 'Take it. You'll need protection if you want to travel alone.' He paused meaningfully. 'Or even if you don't.'

Ace blinked.

'Leave or lead. Your choice.'

Ace made no move towards the gun. 'Keep it. I only hope when Jo recovers nobody tells her your decision about the cars.'

Benton holstered the gun. 'Congratulations,' he said neutrally. 'That was the hardest choice of all.'

'I'm not sure I know exactly what you mean by that, Sergeant, but thank you anyway.'

Still without showing any sign of movement, Ace allowed her thumb to move an eighth of an inch, disarming the smartbomb she had cradled in her left hand throughout the entire exchange.

The Doctor rubbed his hands together with an expression of childlike delight as a couple of lab technicians carried a number of large plastic boxes into the laboratory and set them down on the largest bench.

Liz watched with some amusement as the Doctor began to ferret about inside the boxes, occasionally holding aloft items and crowing with delight, finally upending the boxes and tipping their entire contents out across the bench, for all the world like a child with a new set of Lego.

'Oh my word,' he said softly. 'An inverse ratio multistage storage and discharge capacitor. Wherever did you find that? I didn't think they'd been invented yet.'

Liz smiled at the technicians as they filed out of the lab. 'Thanks, Mike, Carol. He'll be happy for hours now.'

'Yes . . .' the Doctor was muttering as Liz closed the laboratory door. 'Yes, yes, yes, yes, yes . . . Now then.' He looked up. 'Do you have such a thing as a soldering iron?'

Liz started to answer, but the Doctor himself cut off her reply by patting his pockets. 'Never mind,' he mumbled, briefly pulling up his trousers to investigate the inside of his socks, before shaking his head and once more returning to his pockets. 'I'm sure I have one here somewhere – ah! Here we are.' Triumphantly he withdrew his hand from an inside jacket pocket and waved it about in the air. Liz laughed when she saw the Doctor was clutching a thick, old-fashioned biro, the kind you sometimes used to win at seaside amusement arcades, containing about twenty different coloured cartridges of ink.

'Now I don't think you're going to do much soldering with that,' she observed humorously.

The Doctor peered owlishly at the biro, swirling it

around, as if writing words in thin air. 'Do you know, Liz, I rather think you're right! Perhaps if I might use yours after all?'

Liz pointed to a large metal cabinet. 'Second shelf.'

'The rubbish I keep in these old pockets of mine...' The Doctor jammed the biro back into his jacket as he wandered distractedly towards the cabinet. He retrieved the soldering iron from the correct shelf and glanced up at Liz. 'The old team, back together again, eh?'

Liz moved forward across the lab, taking a seat beside the Doctor at the bench. She cast a critical eye across the stacks of equipment, old radio and TV spares, resistors, bits of this and that. Most of it she couldn't even identify, that which she could was just, well, just junk, really.

'Doctor, what on Earth do you hope to accomplish with all this, all this rubbish?'

The Doctor waggled an admonishing finger in her face. 'Ah. It may look like muck to you, my dear, but remember: where there's muck, there's brass.'

Liz laughed. 'It's good to see you behaving like yourself again.'

The Doctor suddenly froze. 'Behaving like myself? What do you mean *behaving like myself*?'

'Well, you know – like your old self, I mean.'

'Old self? My *old* self?' Abruptly the Doctor passed a hand across his eyes, as if to clear his vision. Liz thought she saw a look of absolute terror pass momentarily across his face.

'What's the matter?'

'I ... nothing. Nothing.'

'Come on, Doctor, you can't fool me. Something's the matter, isn't it? Is it to do with the Silurians?'

'No, most definitely not. At least...' He paused. 'They haven't got time-travel technology, have they?'

Liz shrugged. 'Not so far as we know.'

'Someone else, then.'

'Someone else is what?' asked Liz with some exasperation.

'Manipulating me. Creating incredible coincidences like my meeting with Jo. Mucking about with time.' The

Doctor shivered. 'My time, my personal history . . . Mmn, pass me that box of resistors, would you please, Liz? We've got a lot of work to do.'

After the argument with Ace, Benton announced that the group would press on until dark. Ghostly light from the surrounding vegetation added to the silvery sheen of moonlight already glinting through the trees. According to his estimate, which Ace privately agreed with, they should be able to cover between five and ten more miles between now and full night.

There were groans of complaint from Jan and Rod as Benton began to strike the camp. Jan, particularly, felt justified because, as she said, she'd spent most of the previous night tending to Ace's and Billy's wounds. Ace could see there was another row brewing, this time between the medical staff and Benton, and had just decided to set an example by leading the way into the jungle, when the undergrowth parted and a small dinosaur, a compsognathus, no bigger than a fully grown turkey, strutted into the clearing.

Glassy eyes bright and beady, its head jerked this way and that in search of food. Then, bold as brass, the reptile strutted right past where Benton was arguing with Jan, tucked its head into his rucksack, emerged gripping a chunk of meat in its jaws, and retired to the edge of the clearing, where it tilted back its head and began to gulp down its prize.

All this happened in less than half a minute. Benton gaped in silent astonishment, gun drawn in a reflex action. Unaware of the ridiculous picture he made, he aimed the gun at the reptile, which ignored him completely and continued eating.

It was as much his expression as the audacity of the little scavenger which caused Ace to smile. Within moments the clearing rang with laughter. Even Benton was forced to smile wryly as he holstered his gun and continued to pack, the argument with Jan forgotten.

At the sound of the laughter, the compsognathus

paused for just long enough to regard the humans with an unblinking stare, then resumed its meal.

Moments later they were walking again, moving into the deepening shadows, as night drew close around them. Ace, taking the rearward position, was aware of the tiny pattering footsteps of the scavenger as it followed them, just out of sight, obviously hoping for more scraps. It seemed their party had adopted an unofficial mascot. She wondered how Benton would take it if she named the reptile after him.

Pulling a set of watch-maker's tools from his pocket and placing a tiny pair of horn-rimmed glasses on the very tip of his nose, the Doctor began to restructure components and fit them together as if nothing alarming had ever occurred. After about an hour had passed more or less in silence, Liz went to fetch two trays of food from the kitchens. The Doctor ate his food distractedly, while soldering, then piled components on the empty tray to form a kind of huge circuit board, into which he quickly integrated the metal parts of his cutlery.

'I bet you didn't enjoy that one bit, did you?' Liz said, with an accusing stare at the tray and cutlery.

'Mmm? Sorry, Liz. Enjoy? Oh yes – it was delicious. My compliments to the chef.' The Doctor looked around, snagged a set of valves and added them to the rapidly expanding device.

'What was it then?'

'I beg your pardon?'

'I said, what was it you ate?'

'Oh, er . . . turkey, wasn't it? Pass me the phase inverter would you, Liz? Thanks.'

'There hasn't been a turkey cooked inside the Complex for more than a decade. Now come on, Doctor. You've been hunched up there for hours like one of Santa's little helpers and the most intelligent comment I've had out of you in all that time is "Pass me the phase inverter"!'

The Doctor carefully put down a complex component he was delicately adjusting with a tiny screwdriver. 'Mm. Sorry. Been concentrating. Things on my mind.'

'Such as?'

The Doctor took off his glasses, polished them and slipped them back into their case. 'It's the Brigadier,' he said slowly. 'I can't help thinking there's more to him than meets the eye.'

'He's a stiff-necked old coot, if that's what you mean, but then he always was. He does have tremendous responsibility. You have to respect him for shouldering that burden at least.'

'I suppose you do. But I think it's more than that. He told me about the Silurian fortress, you know. In Glasgow.'

'That old thing? It's been abandoned for years.'

'Not according to the Brigadier. He seems to think it's active – a control point for the Silurians' Arctic power base.'

Liz huffed in astonishment. 'He played that one close to his chest.'

'Mm. Thing is, he has plans to attack it. Control that, he says, and you control half the Silurians' power supply.'

Liz thumped the bench angrily, causing the Doctor to make a grab for his device in order to stop it overbalancing. 'The Brigadier thinks he's Errol bloody Flynn! If he messes it up, the Complex will be discovered, and then . . . He's risking all our lives when he ought to be negotiating for peace!' Liz sighed and put her head in her hands. 'I'm really not at all certain I can take any more of this military bullshit.'

She raised her eyes uncertainly to the Doctor. 'It's got to end sometime, hasn't it? In peace, I mean?' She hesitated. 'Or are we all going to die?'

'Everyone dies, Liz.'

The Doctor took out his glasses again and picked up a component from the stack in front of him. He fiddled distractedly with it for a moment, before placing it back on the bench. He replaced his glasses in their case.

'Er, look, Liz. You can carry on with this now, can't you?'

'Of course. I'm not just a pretty face you know.'

'Thanks. It's just that I've got some things I need to do.'

Liz reached out to touch the Doctor's hand. She was

hard put to say who was the most surprised when he didn't turn away. 'If you want to talk about it, whatever it is . . .'

The Doctor patted her hand. His skin was curiously cool, she noticed. 'Thanks, Liz. Maybe later. I just need to be alone for a bit.'

'I understand.'

The Doctor eased himself off the lab stool, as though even that slight effort was too much for him. He stopped in the doorway of the lab as Liz called hesitantly after him, 'You will be coming back, won't you?'

He smiled. 'The amplitude threshold compressor may turn out a bit tricky. If you get stuck I'll be in the sickbay with Jo.'

'Sure.'

An hour passed with only a smattering of conversation, before Ace became aware she could no longer hear the footsteps of the compsognathus following them. She'd become attached to the little reptile, with its endearing habit of peering through the vegetation at them, and had taken pleasure in throwing the odd piece of fruit to it.

She felt oddly disturbed by its absence.

Feeling confident enough to risk a little side-trip of her own, she slipped away into the undergrowth. She'd travelled no more than a hundred yards when she came across the little reptile plucking at the remains of a dead animal about the size of a horse. The compsognathus looked up as she approached, before resuming its meal.

'You eat a lot for a small fellow, don't you?'

Ace moved closer, suddenly aware that the dead animal *was* in fact a horse. She reached out to touch its flank. The flesh was cool. Part of the hindquarters was missing. There was a lot of blood. Ace hoped its death had been quick. She looked towards the head, hoping the eyes would be closed, and that was when she saw the bridle, and the Avenger vanity plate pinned to it.

Ace ran at the compsognathus, waving her arms and shouting. The reptile backed warily away and hid in the undergrowth.

She examined the ground, but soon realized any attempt to bury the horse would be futile. She had nothing to dig with, and besides, it would take too long and she'd never find the rest of the group in the darkness afterwards. Finally, she turned and ran after the others.

As soon as she had gone, the compsognathus emerged from the undergrowth, the smell of fresh meat drawing it back to feed.

Lost in thought, the Doctor wandered along the rocky passages of the Complex. As he walked, the same fair-haired child he'd seen yesterday bounded down the corridor towards him. The little boy looked considerably more lively than the Doctor felt at that moment. As soon as the child drew level with the Doctor, he stopped, staring upwards with big, solemn eyes.

'Hello, mister. You look sad.'

The Doctor crouched down beside the child. 'I suppose you could say I am sad. I've been thinking about how gloomy the Complex is sometimes. About how it might be brighter with some flowers around. What do you think?'

The child looked puzzled. 'What's a flower?'

The Doctor sighed. 'Never mind.' He straightened up. 'Where are you off to?'

'B'listics class. See you!'

The Doctor forced a smile as the child vanished along the passage. The smile faded quickly once he was alone. In human terms it had been centuries since he had thought like a child, seen the world as a child would see it. He wondered if he was guilty of leaving the most precious part of himself behind. Then again, he thought, if I have, I'd never know, would I? Ipso facto.

He resumed walking, nodding politely, if a little distantly, to people who passed him, dark thoughts swelling desperately in his mind.

It was the first time he'd really had an opportunity to think since arriving on this parallel Earth. The first chance to really consider the implications of the destruction of the TARDIS. Well – its partial destruction anyway. Oh, getting knocked into a tar pit was inconvenient, to say the least, but that problem could be solved relatively easily at any time. What worried him far more than he cared to admit was in what condition the ship was likely to be when he finally brought it back to dry land. And what it might be likely to do.

Something had invaded the TARDIS. That same something had dragged both himself and his companions from the safety of the Ship and flung them for an unmeasurable time into the Vortex. Both actions were impossible.

At least, they always had been.

And now Bernice was missing – flung out of the Vortex to some other part of the planet, he assumed – while he and Ace had arrived on a world in which he had apparently died: killed by the Silurians before they had emerged to take control of the planet.

Murdered.

That too he had, until now, considered impossible.

The Doctor took the cream silk handkerchief from his top pocket and mopped a thin sheen of sweat from his brow. He had wanted to give it all up; the adventuring, the manipulating, the meddling. He'd promised himself he would and he really had meant it, hadn't he? As a member of a long-lived race even he matured, it just took more time that was all. A change had been on the cards for some while, was long overdue, in fact. All he'd wanted was a rest. A change of scenery. A change of pace.

And now this.

The doors to the sickbay loomed ahead of him and he pushed them open. He nodded to Doctor Meredith as he made his way slowly past the office, the sectioned-off part of the ward which now housed a sleeping Chtorba and, finally, towards the bed in which lay the slight form of Jo Grant.

An orderly was sitting in a chair beside the bed, watching the few pieces of equipment the sickbay boasted, which in turn monitored Jo's sleep, making sure it did not quietly turn into something deeper. The orderly glanced up as the Doctor approached, and smiled. He moved away, drawing the screen behind him as he did so.

Now the sounds from the rest of the sickbay receded

into the distance, and even the gentle ticking of the monitors faded into silence as the Doctor looked down at the pale and bruised too-old face, framed by its dirty blond hair, and wondered if he had ever really looked at anyone before.

There was a swishing sound behind him. Liz stepped into the aisle beside the bed and drew the screen shut behind her.

'I came to ask how you want to modulate the effect of the negative feedback circuit.' Liz fell silent, her attention captured by the pale, trembling form dwarfed by the hospital bed. 'She was very beautiful when she was younger, wasn't she?'

The Doctor blinked. 'I suppose so. I always say the beauty of a person is on the inside. Jo was luckier than most. She was honest, forthright, loyal, charming . . .' He hesitated, smiled sadly. 'Stubborn as a mule when it suited her. I once heard Sergeant Benton say in confidence that Jo rushed in where agents feared to tread. I think he was trying to make a joke. To show how much he liked her.'

'Benton knew her? She worked for UNIT?'

'Yes. She was General Hobson's niece, you see. He gave her part of that book the Brigadier seems so pleased with. And even when everything that was human about her had been destroyed by years of living rough, being hunted like a wild animal by Silurians, even then something inside her wouldn't give in to the Nightmare, and she remembered that she had to bring the book here, to him. She must have thought it was the most important thing in the world.' The Doctor trailed off into a thoughtful silence.

'You were close to her too, weren't you?' Liz said softly.

'She was my assistant when you left to continue your research at Cambridge.'

'But I didn't – that is, I mean, I – um. Parallel universes, right?'

The Doctor nodded. 'The beauty was on the inside, and now there's only an echo of death.'

Liz sat on the chair. 'For what it's worth, I am sorry. You see this sort of thing all the time. Kids who've grown up in the Nightmare, or been, you know, mentally affected by it. They . . . they don't understand about protection. Don't understand the implications. They aren't really human any more – and there are so many. The Silurians, they hunt them for sport, perhaps just because they're bored, I don't know. And Jo, in a way she was lucky. If they'd caught her, before the, you know, the birth, then . . . Well. I, hear they take . . . trophies. You know? From those they hunt.'

Liz paused as Jo's eyes fluttered alarmingly behind pale, clammy lids. Her mouth opened in a sigh. She stirred, muttered something unintelligible, and then lapsed back into an uneasy sleep.

'She knows, doesn't she, on some animal level? That she isn't pregnant any more? I can't begin to imagine her pain.' For a moment Liz was silent. 'I can't imagine how I thought the Brigadier was wrong. I can't imagine talking, *negotiating*, with people who would do this to another intelligent being. I know she's nearly my age, really, but God, inside she's just a child!'

The Doctor perched beside Jo on the bed, being careful not to touch her hands, resting lightly on the bedsheets, hardly even rumpling them.

'It's all a matter of values, isn't it?' he mused quietly. 'In this world values must be altered. Should I help the humans to change what has now become their destiny? Are the Silurians really the rightful inhabitants of the Earth? Or is there some third alternative?' He paused. 'Perhaps I've been guilty of interfering in history too much. Perhaps . . . Perhaps if my universe is this universe, I did do the wrong thing. Perhaps my personal destiny was to die, in 1973, here on Earth.'

Liz now shifted her attention to the Doctor, but he seemed not to be aware of her presence. She kept silent, aware that he needed to speak, knowing the best thing she could do was listen. Listen and try to understand.

'Yes – that makes sense. I was supposed to die. But somehow I managed to trick my way out of it, and in so doing created a parallel universe – one containing Ace's Earth and all its subsequently crystallized points of future history – in which I could still remain alive.' The Doctor stood abruptly. 'Could I have been that arrogant? Abused my power so much?'

Liz felt now was as good a time as any to speak up. 'You're just feeling guilty. God knows, enough of us have done that over the last twenty years. What if I had noted down the antidote formula correctly, as you asked me to that time in Wenley Moor? What if I had worked harder, been more insightful, done this, or that? Would it have made a difference in the long run?' She sighed. 'The answer is, we'll never know.'

The Doctor fixed her with a cold stare. 'But I'm not like you, Liz. The joy and the curse of every Time Lord is that he *can* know. And if all this pain, all this destruction is my fault then that would explain everything. The threat to the TARDIS, Bernice being flung off into the Vortex, Ace and myself arriving here.' He hesitated. 'The only force capable of invading a TARDIS is the primal force of the universe itself, the entropy of time. If I have created a paradox in my arrogance, then the paradox must be resolved. If I am to die, then I must die. The real universe must prevail, and it holds no place for me.'

Liz struggled to understand the Doctor's words. She was about to ask for clarification when he continued, 'On second thought, that's not right either. Only one universe can exist, the laws of matter and energy dictate that inescapably. I have travelled into the future of the universe, crystallized moments of it, from a point in my personal timeline *before* I was apparently killed. If that happened then Ace's universe, the universe in which I am alive *is* the real one, ergo *this* one cannot be, therefore I was not meant to die, and . . . hmm. Suddenly I'm very confused.'

Liz blinked. The Doctor continued, 'On third thought, no, I'm not. Confused that is. The Brigadier was right: what's real is real – and what isn't can be dealt with.' He turned to Liz and beamed. 'Thank you, Liz. You've helped tremendously!' And he patted Jo's bedsheets gently, turned and left the sickbay.

Liz stared after him and wondered why she suddenly felt so scared.

Ace looked around, curiosity mingling with horror, as she and the other members of the medical team walked carefully through the ruined outskirts of London, towards the long-dead heart of the city.

Surrounding them on all sides, stark in the early morning sunlight, were the hollow shells of buildings, overrun with luxuriant foliage and seething with animal life. Even from the end of the M4, only a couple of miles beyond Hammersmith, the city had appeared to be little more than a grassy bulge on an otherwise flat horizon. The tall buildings she remembered were gone, breached and finally demolished by the relentless onslaught of the jungle. Only the Post Office Tower, which she had visited on a school trip when she was ten, remained, and even that was less than half the height she remembered: the restaurant section had completely vanished and a fine growth of young trees now replaced the jungle of masts and dishes which had once sprouted from the upper levels. Ace shuddered, imagining what she might see if she climbed the tower and gazed out across the city: the view would be wildly different from that of her schooldays.

From conversations with Julia and Alan, she already knew that the botanical gardens, parks and squares of the West End had erupted out into the drab grey streets which had previously hemmed them in on all sides. She pictured them flowing together to form a living carpet of green, undulating across the skyline, filling and covering terraced ranks of houses, softening and blurring the blocky shapes of factories, cinemas and shopping centres.

All along the route into London, smashed and burned cars filled the roads like toys thrown carelessly aside by a spoilt child. In the ruins of the Hammersmith flyover a school bus lay on its side, its walls and tyres burst. There were no bodies, just old bloodstains smeared across the peeling paintwork.

Gardens had exploded from their borders, flattening fences and demolishing walls. Trees arched overhead to fill the road and cover the ruined vehicles with shadows. Ace noticed there was something strange about the trees. They weren't just mutated, they were *warped*, melded together in a disturbing genetic potpourri; tropical fruit hanging from the branches of holly trees, segmented towers of palms emerging randomly from the trunks of conifers.

Colonies of monkeys fed from the fruit which clustered there instead of coconuts.

'I suppose the monkeys came from the zoos, right?'

Julia followed Ace's gaze into the trees. 'They feed on the trees; the dogs and smaller dinosaurs feed on them. They thrive in this climate.'

'Yeah? What about the bigger animals?'

'Bagged a tiger this summer, while I was hunting for food.'

'You're kidding.'

'Straight up.' Julia rolled back her sleeves so that Ace could see a parallel set of deep scars running between her wrist and elbow, above and below her forearm. 'I was nearly its dinner.'

Ace whistled. 'Teeth or claws?'

'Teeth. Almost lost the arm.'

Alan said quietly, 'Actually the damn thing did eat her. She just tastes so bad it threw her back up and promptly died of internal haemorrhaging.'

Ace raised one eyebrow. 'I bet. Here, check this out.' She rolled up her shirt to show an oval area of ridged and puckered skin crossing her stomach. 'Plasma burn from a Special Weapons Dalek.'

Julia shook her head in amazement as she looked at the scar. 'Why aren't you dead?'

'And what's a Dalek?'

'Let's just say it makes a starving tiger look like a furry toy.'

'Well you're all a bunch of wet blankets. None of you can beat this.' Alan stretched the collar of his jacket, and Ace saw a deep purple bruise spreading across one side of his neck. 'Little present from Kyla Parker, down in technical.'

'Cut yourself shaving more like,' said Julia.

Ace grinned. 'Looks terminal to me. We may have to amputate.'

Julia shook her head in mock seriousness. 'Ah, there'd be no point to that. His IQ would just get bigger.'

Alan affected a look of hurt surprise. 'Ganging up on me, huh?' He was about to expound further when, with a great sigh of disturbed branches, the monkeys sprang from their perches and vanished into the jungle. There was a light pattering as a shower of nuts, berries and half-eaten pieces of fruit fell all around them.

Ace had time to exchange puzzled looks with Julia and Alan before a man stepped warily from the undergrowth in front of them.

Beneath a tangled growth of beard and hair, the man's face was darkened by a vicious set of bruises. He was dressed in the damp rags of a Saville Row suit, and clutched a mouldy leather briefcase and an umbrella which wouldn't have protected him from a water pistol.

Jan immediately unsealed her medical kit. 'Hello? My name's Jan. Can you hear me?'

The man did not reply.

Benton placed a restraining hand on Jan's arm. She shrugged him off. 'It's okay. He doesn't look as bad as the others we've seen,' she said.

'He may be able to help us.'

Benton frowned. 'Leave him.'

'I can't do that.' Jan raised her voice. 'Can you *understand me*? I *want to help*.' Jan pulled a syringe from her medical kit. 'I'm going to give you an *antibiotic injection*.'

The man listened carefully as Jan spoke, his head cocked to one side. He stared curiously as she filled the syringe from a glass bottle, standing quite still as she approached.

'Right then, the first thing to do is roll up this sleeve . . .' Jan reached out for the mouldy fabric. 'Now, this might hurt just a little bit.'

The man backed away as Jan pressed the needle of the syringe to the skin of one filthy arm. He lifted the mouldy briefcase in front of him, and gestured violently with it. Ace found the gesture pathetic rather than threatening.

Jan hesitated, then moved closer. 'It's okay. I'm not going to hurt you. I want to help you. Do you understand?'

The man thrust his face forward into Jan's and screamed like an animal. His teeth were black and uneven. Ace was glad she couldn't smell his breath.

Shocked, Jan dropped her medical kit and backed away.

Benton moved in front of her but did not draw his gun. 'Go away!' he said in a loud, firm voice. 'Go on! Get out of here!'

The man's face crumpled in fear and he turned and ran, his aggression vanishing as quickly as it had begun.

Two hundred yards away a group of teenagers jumped him from the undergrowth, grabbed his briefcase and carried it off, crowing in triumph over their prize. The man first of all looked astonished, then sank to his haunches and began to rock backwards and forwards, clutching his knees to his chest and sobbing.

Jan glared indignantly at Benton. 'How dare you do that,' she hissed angrily. 'We're all the same. All of us.'

'You're wrong. Where's his dignity? His intelligence?' Benton scowled. 'The animals communicate better than he does.'

He picked up the medical kit, turning it over thoughtfully in his hands. Bitterly, he said, 'The reps've put animals above us. Never forget it. Never forget what they've done to us.'

He wiped the kit free of soil, closed the lid and handed it back to Jan. She took it without speaking.

'We have to stop them. At any cost.' He turned and continued walking in the direction of central London.

Liz rubbed her eyes tiredly and stared at the breadboard rig on the lab bench in front of her. Together with Carol Jeffries and Mike Roqos, Liz had worked through the night to complete the device. At the Brigadier's orders, Sam Meredith was keeping Chtorba sedated until the device was ready for use. This worried Liz: nobody knew what long-term effects the sedatives would have on Chtorba's metabolism. She wanted to have the device up and running as soon as possible.

'That's it, Liz.' Carol stacked the last empty cardboard box in one corner of the lab. 'It must be pretty much finished now – there's only this left.' She held up a black metal box fitted with a row of SCART sockets.

'Uh huh.' Liz blinked sleep from her eyes and struggled to focus on the item Carol held. 'What's that then?'

Carol turned the thing over in her hands and shrugged. 'Er . . . I dunno.'

Liz laughed. 'Don't be dozy, it must fit somewhere.' She took the item from Carol and peered at it, holding it up to the stack of components wired together on the breadboard – tea tray! a tired voice in her mind said far too loudly – first one way, then the other. No matter how she tried, she couldn't work out either what it was supposed to do or how it fitted into the device. She sighed.

'Coffee?' offered Carol.

'Please.'

'Mike! Kettle.'

'Oh, thank you very much.'

'Shut up and boil. Can't you see Liz is flummoxed?'

'I'm not flummoxed. I'm just really tired.' Liz pushed herself away from the device and slid her hips onto the flat surface of a clear bench. She ran a tap into a lab sink for a few seconds and splashed cold water onto her face. As she dried off, Mike announced the arrival of three chipped mugs of coffee.

'Cheers.' She sipped. 'And full marks for being able to make this bilge taste vaguely useful.'

'All compliments gratefully received, boss, thank you very much.'

'What now?' asked Carol.

'Well, finish your coffee and then you two can slope off if you like. You've put more hours in on this overblown TV set than I have.'

'Sure?'

'Yes. Go on, before I change my mind.'

When Mike and Carol had gone, Liz settled back against the wall and sighed. For most of the night, as well as struggling with the components of the device, Liz had also struggled with recurring memories of the Doctor's strange and frightening monologue at Jo's bedside. For the last couple of hours she had managed to keep her

99

thoughts upon the work at hand. Now they turned to the Doctor's words, and the fear she'd felt last night began once again to fill her mind.

Ace jumped as a fearful scream ripped out of the shadows, together with the vicious hissing of reptiles.

Further down the high street the sound of falling shelving came from the smashed front of a grocery store. A writhing mass of animals burst through the shop window and onto the street.

Benton halted the group with a word, and drew his gun. Ace peered closer. The mass of fighting animals seemed to be composed mostly of small dinosaurs. That wasn't all though. There were also furry shapes mixed up with the reptiles. Rats? No, Julia had said there were no rats any more. Dogs, then. And somewhere in there was the dark grey hide of ... Ace peered closer, shuddering when she realized the dark grey she could see wasn't animal hide, it was a suit. A tattered, mouldy, Saville Row suit.

The scream became muffled and then stopped abruptly. A dog leaped clear of the pack, something wet and dripping clamped between its jaws. The man inside the coat continued thrashing in silence as the animals tore viciously through the material, foam and blood mixing to lie upon the street in sticky puddles. Pieces of flesh and suit were eagerly snapped up by the other snarling animals.

'Back.' Benton signalled the group to retreat. 'We'll find another way.'

Jan hesitated. 'I could help – '

'You tried that before and look where it got you.' Benton scowled, aimed carefully into the writhing mass and fired. There was a splash of red, the suited figure jerked once and was still. The animals were not. One, a three-foot long deinonychus, turned from its meal to stare directly at them with coal-black eyes.

'Now get going!'

As the group warily backed away, the deinonychus returned its attention to the now unmoving body, ripping through flesh and fabric alike with cruelly sharp hind claws.

Jan marched up to Benton and slapped him. 'That wasn't necessary!'

Benton lifted one hand to his cheek. He did not speak. The others stopped, waiting to see what he would do.

'What's the matter, got nothing to say? Or would you rather speak with your gun?'

Benton refused to be provoked. This annoyed Jan even more. She stared up at the Sergeant, searching for some clue as to his motivation. As her eyes met his, she recoiled abruptly.

Ace was watching Jan as she looked into Benton's eyes. Whatever the woman saw there was evidently enough to kill any further argument.

In his dream, Alastair stood on the beach at Margate and stared out at the sea. A chill wind had risen, blowing in from the north, whipping the sea water into swirling grey shapes, topped with foam. Fifty yards from the shore a tiny black dot rose and fell with the waves. A yell of panic, thinned by distance, rose above the wind. Alastair squinted into the wintry sun. The black dot resolved itself into a head of hair, a woman's face, a screaming mouth.

The face slipped beneath the water.

Alastair began to run.

Emerging from the grip of his dream, the Brigadier swung himself out of his bunk. He sat on the hard mattress and shivered, hugging himself, searching in the semidarkness for his talisman, the watch she'd given him in gratitude, the watch whose hands had not moved for . . . how many years now? He slipped the watch onto his wrist. Doris had survived that cold day in Margate and they'd grown closer together, drawn at first by laughter and ice cream, and later, by tears and gentle, unforced explanations. They'd had ten good years together before –

The Brigadier shook his head. Let go of the sadness, he thought. Let go of the regret. He was too old and had too much responsibility for such distractions. Doris was dead. His duty was to the living.

Feeling his back click with age, the Brigadier stretched,

101

yawned, and tried to decide whether a fake coffee or a real brandy would dispel the dream most effectively.

That was when he noticed the safe door was open.

His heart lurched in his chest and a cold shiver raced through his limbs. 'Damn,' he muttered, then, 'Sorry Doris.'

He felt under his pillow, breathing a sigh of relief when he was able to withdraw a small, oblong, canvas-wrapped package. He pulled his uniform on quickly, his heart trembling painfully in his chest.

'Damn,' he said again, feeling a sudden sharp pain in his chest. 'I really am too old for this.'

Twenty yards back up the high street there was a small side turning. Benton moved back past the group to take the lead again, and Ace followed him into it. Jan and Rod followed her and Julia and Alan brought up the rear, glancing backwards even as the noises of the feeding pack faded into the undergrowth.

Slowly, they moved forward. Here the undergrowth was thicker, undisturbed by larger animals. Hybrid trees with waxy, pear-shaped trunks and clusters of great triangular yellow leaves arched overhead, casting thick, aromatic shadows across the road.

Soon, Ace realized the only sounds she could hear were their own footfalls. She frowned. Surely it shouldn't be *this* quiet?

Before Ace could comment on this oddity, Benton stopped.

From somewhere in front of them came a low growling sound.

Ace peered past him into the undergrowth. A pair of luminous eyes hung there, unblinking. Ace looked closer. The eyes belonged to a mangy black dog – she thought it might have been a Labrador – its fur knotted over stringy muscles and crawling with lice. The eyes were rheumy and swollen, though they focused without any difficulty upon the group of humans. Ace seemed to see herself reflected in those flat, staring eyes. She shivered. Here was something that knew no reason. That you couldn't trick, or fool.

Benton spoke quietly. 'Move backwards. Slowly.'

But before anyone could move there came the sound of soft footfalls behind them. Ace turned.

The street was full of dogs.

Silently they came, more and more of them. Padding from shadowy doorways, hopping crippled from window sills, creeping from piles of rubble which had once been garages, slinking from the rusted hulks of cars; some looked like Alsatians, others might have been Labradors, Setters, Jack Russells – one could have been an old, threadbare Afghan, its muzzle flecked with foam, one eye closed by weeping scabs; the entire pack driven wild by time and pain and hunger. Ace felt herself grow cold at the stink of them, sickened by the stench of old meals coming from beneath clicking, scratching claws; hissing warm from behind jagged teeth and panting tongues.

She jumped at a touch upon her shoulder. Beside her, Julia and Alan had drawn their guns and were backing together, forming a circle with Benton, Jan and Rod.

'I said this was a bad idea,' Alan muttered.

'You did not.' Julia flipped off the safety catch of her gun.

'Well I would've done if I'd known.'

'Sshh!' Benton clicked back the hammer of his service revolver.

Ace grabbed her smartbomb from her pocket and set it to accept voice commands. Then she stopped. How was one bomb going to help them against dozens of dogs?

The dogs formed a ring, encircling them completely.

The rheumy-eyed Labrador began to bark. Benton shot it between the eyes and it fell over without another sound. In the silence that followed it was possible to hear the thin stream of blood pattering from its muzzle onto the dusty tarmac. A Jack Russell padded forward to lap eagerly at the patch of wetness.

Ace licked her lips nervously.

There was a sound. It began as a sigh but grew quickly into a terrifying howl, the baying and snarling of thirty or forty starving animals. The circle began to close. Benton fired again. A second dog fell; two more immediately began to tear at the corpse. Julia and Alan began to squeeze off well placed shots.

A scrawny mongrel hurled itself towards Rod. Julia picked it off with a single round. Another snapped its jaws shut around her calf and she swore loudly. Alan shot it through the chest. It fell away with a howl, trailing scarlet from jaws and stomach, and was itself quickly silenced in the mass of suddenly moving animals.

As one the dogs leaped towards them.

Ace cupped her hand around the smartbomb and began to whisper instructions. Then the Afghan hit her at waist height and the weapon fell to lie motionless on the ground between them.

Liz had turned up the lights in the lab. She had pillowed her head on her arms and was struggling against the desire to sleep. She knew the moment she did that the terror would come back. The device she had almost completed lay before her on the bench, its single remaining component resting beside it, square and black and enigmatic.

Liz yawned and eased the cramp in one arm.

With a shockingly loud crash her coffee mug fell off the bench and shattered on the floor.

That did it. There'd be no more hanging about, not if she had to slap the Doctor awake herself. She deserved an explanation; in plain English too, not one that was so solipsistic it vanished up its own –

The door to the lab burst open and the Brigadier strode in, swagger stick at half mast, an angry expression on his face.

'Alright, Miss Shaw, where is he?'

Liz eased herself upright, yawning and rubbing her eyes. 'If you mean the Doctor, I don't know. As a matter of fact I have something I need to discuss with him myself.'

The Brigadier huffed angrily. 'It's completely outrageous! The man thinks he can come and go like a, like a – who's in charge around here, anyway?' He marched out of the lab without looking back.

Liz groaned. She splashed cold water on her face, snatched the curious black component off the bench and set off determinedly after the Brigadier.

Ace rolled on her back on the ground, her hands locked around the Afghan's throat. Foam and saliva dripped onto her face and neck. She closed her eyes and tried not to swallow. Someone was screaming. Something coughed repeatedly and Ace realized she was still hearing gunfire. Not everyone was down, then. Beside her head the smart-bomb lay unmoving, its LED blinking red.

Ace felt the Afghan tense, its muscles like hydraulic cables, its body slamming violently from side to side as it snapped and snarled. In a distant part of her mind, Ace wondered what it would be like to feel those sharp, dirty teeth rip into her face or stomach. She tried to remember how long it took to die of rabies. Was it days? Weeks? In this world it was more likely to take shorter than longer.

Ace sucked in a deep breath.

'*Altercomtargetsmultimammalcanineskulloccipitalpene-trateretcomradunitsfiftyvelunitsmaxdetnegEXECUTE*!' she screamed desperately and clamped her mouth shut again.

There was a gentle breeze beside her face, a wet *crunch* and a gush of blood. The Afghan convulsed, stiffened, fell on top of her, its body a dead weight. Ace pushed it off and wiped her face thoroughly before opening her eyes. She looked around; the dogs were dropping like dominoes, blood spurting from their heads.

Benton, Julia and Alan had stopped firing and were staring in amazement as the animals convulsed and fell in quick succession. Jan and Rod were huddled on the ground, clutching each other in terror. Rod was also struggling to free his pistol from a holster which was still buttoned shut.

'Don't waste your ammunition,' Ace told him.

A moment later the last animal lay still upon the ground, a neat hole drilled through the back of its skull, most of its face gone.

Benton looked at her questioningly.

There was a harsh whine and something blurred through the air to hover above her outstretched palm.

Ace patted the smartbomb affectionately, deactivated it and shoved it back in her pocket.

'What now?' Jan asked, her voice trembling.

Ace slapped the back of her neck. 'Anyone got any flea spray?'

The Brigadier charged into the sickbay, rather like a human tank, Liz thought with a smile. 'Where are you, Doctor?' he boomed impatiently.

There was no reply.

'Doctor Meredith! Doctor – '

'Brigadier, listen.' Liz could hear something, a knocking sound coming from inside the linen cupboard.

The Brigadier wrenched the doors open and was faced with the incredible sight of Sam Meredith bound to a chair and gagged with his own sheets. He tore the material from the doctor's mouth.

'Bundled me in here, he did,' spluttered Meredith furiously. 'Like a pile of old washing!'

'The Doctor?'

'Yes of course the Doctor! Who else?'

With Liz's help the Brigadier soon freed the irate medic.

'The man should be restrained! Expelled! I insist – '

'Doctor Meredith,' the Brigadier said gently, 'I should think there are more important matters to consider.'

Meredith ran his sleeve across his face. 'I . . . Of course. I'm overreacting. I'm sorry. It's just . . .' Angrily he shrugged off the last clinging folds of sheets. 'I must check on the patients.'

Liz glanced at the Brigadier as Meredith bustled away into the ward area. His face was dark and brooding. For the first time, Liz noticed he carried a canvas-wrapped package under one arm.

'He's really done it this time,' the Brigadier announced, to no-one in particular.

Liz couldn't bring herself to ask the question uppermost in her mind. She turned away from the Brigadier as Meredith returned, not quite knowing if she should be grateful for the interruption.

'It's rather bad news I'm afraid.'

Liz went cold. 'Not Jo?'

The Brigadier pushed through into the ward area as Meredith shook his head. 'If anything, her condition has improved slightly.'

'Chtorba, then?' The Brigadier pulled away the screens from the Silurian's bed. 'Well. Now we know what else he was up to last night.'

The bed was empty.

A flaked crystalline spear, the Silurian fortress rose in the night above the ruins of Glasgow. Dominating the tumbled blocks of city and suburbs, the fortress was streaked dark green and black with knife-edged shadows. Though perfectly still, it somehow maintained a disturbing appearance of movement. Moonlight glimmering from the ridged surface lent it the appearance of being carved from mottled black and green ice, as if huge blocks of sea water had been frozen solid, ripped free of the ocean and transported onto dry land.

Approaching the tower from the south came a flapping speck of life; a pterosaur. Moonlight glittered across the blue and grey tiger-striped hide, the forty-foot wingspan. Eyes and powerful claws that were no more than tiny chips of ice lost in the distance grew rapidly until the reptile hovered above the fortress, circling in order to allow its riders to select a suitable landing site.

Clutching his hat, the Doctor stepped unsteadily from the improvised harness lashed to the pterosaur onto the topmost level of the fortress. Beside him, Chtorba ran his hands along the side of the jutting skull and began to dissolve his link with the reptile.

Realizing he had a free moment, the Doctor stared curiously around, adding a closer inspection of his surroundings to the general impressions he had gained from the air.

The top levels of the fortress were scalloped, with a hollow in the centre forming a shallow well. Oval holes spaced around the inside of the well formed what the Doctor assumed were entrances to and exits from the interior. They had landed on the edge of the well: a broad, flat area broken only by irregular incrustations, like ramparts. The surface was cool and dry, like snake skin. On closer examination, he noticed the surface was shot through with thin silver lines which sparkled in the moonlight as if dusted with frost.

The air was heavy with a sweet, unfamiliar odour.

He straightened, leaning casually on his umbrella as the pterosaur pulled itself towards the edge of the fortress with muscular spurts of its huge, leathery wings. As the Doctor watched, it launched itself into the air, falling, banking, climbing, its abrupt transformation from awkward ground dweller to elegant flier more startling than that of caterpillar to butterfly.

The Doctor became aware that Chtorba was observing him closely. 'Your affinity with other reptiles, it's quite impressive.'

Chtorba appeared to consider the Doctor's words. 'For Silurians the ability to link is as natural as breathing.' Without discernible pause, the Silurian added, 'Why did you help me escape?'

The Doctor returned Chtorba's gaze steadily, his eyes flicking between all three of the Silurian's. 'Ask me again someday.'

'You will not explain your motives, yet you ask for my trust.'

'I give you my own as collateral,' the Doctor said sharply.

'Indeed.' Chtorba was silent for a moment. 'But then you do seem to have left yourself little choice.'

'Yes, I do, don't I?' The Doctor spun his umbrella thoughtfully by the handle. 'Bit of an unclear situation, wouldn't you say?'

'The Brigadier would find the situation very clearly defined.'

The Doctor deftly halted the movement of his umbrella. 'I'm afraid you're right.' He gazed upwards. 'The moon is very beautiful tonight, isn't it?'

Chtorba followed the Doctor's gaze upwards, past the fortress ramparts to the inky sky, and did not speak.

'It's a hard sight to get used to, isn't it?' said the Doctor.

'I remember when there was no moon in the night sky.' Chtorba cupped his hand and allowed a few stray moonbeams to pool in the palm. 'In certain phases I have noticed the pattern of craters on its surface forms the shape of a face. A face with only two eyes.' Chtorba's breath hissed gently between his teeth, the equivalent of a human shiver, perhaps. 'I find its presence disturbing, and ... sometimes frightening.'

The Doctor lowered his gaze, patted his hat more securely onto his head, slipped his umbrella into the crook of one elbow, and said abruptly, 'A man without fear is a fool to himself, Chtorba. Shall we go inside? I expect you'll be wanting to contact your people.'

The Brigadier allowed the screen to fall back in front of the bed. 'If I'm right, the Silurians will know our position within hours and will in all probability launch an offensive against us.' He rubbed his eyes tiredly. 'So much for the Doctor being on our side.'

'That's quite ridiculous, Brigadier. The Doctor would never – '

'I simply report facts, Miss Shaw. Unlike people they do not lie. Chtorba is missing. The Doctor has obviously helped him escape. He also made an attempt to steal this – ' the Brigadier gestured with his package ' – from my safe last night.'

Liz found her gaze captured by the pain and betrayal in the Brigadier's eyes. 'I can't believe it. I just can't.'

'He was my friend too, Miss Shaw. Perhaps we're both guilty of looking too long and too hard for a miracle that was never there. But now we have to face up to the truth.' He hesitated, almost as if afraid to speak the words of condemnation. 'The Doctor has betrayed us to the enemy. His actions could bring about the death of every man woman and child in the Complex!'

PART THREE

CALL TO COLOURS

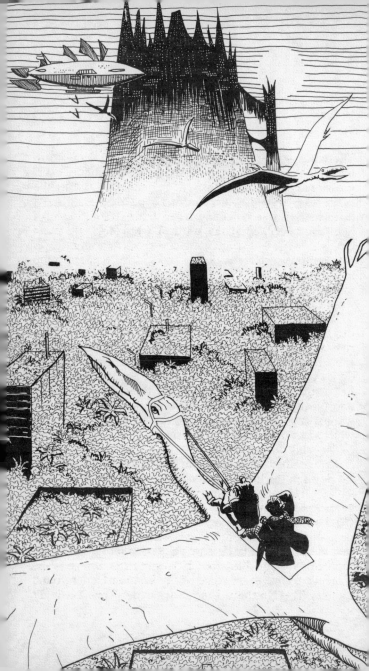

There was a triceratops skeleton partly buried in the north bank of the Thames, upriver from the crumbling, overgrown remains of the Houses of Parliament. Looking the other way, beyond a curve in the river, Ace could see a huge banyan tree emerging from the shattered dome of Saint Paul's Cathedral, one of the few buildings still intact enough to rise above the jungle. Ace took a moment to wonder how such an obviously ancient tree had grown up in such a few years. Unable to come up with an answer to her question, she promptly forgot about it. It probably wasn't important anyway.

The approach to the river had been hard going, precarious at best, in some places highly dangerous. Though the river was currently at low tide, there was evidence aplenty – in the mud and silt clogging the roads, and the abundance of swamp plants in Parliament Square and Whitehall – to suggest extensive annual flooding. Hadrosaurs and other duckbills swam elegantly through the muddy waters, munching serenely on the willows and cycads which lined both banks of the river.

The stink was appalling.

Ace climbed onto the parapet of the north bank and sat down in the lotus position. 'Guys is on the south side, isn't it? Has anyone thought about how we're going to get across the river?'

Julia heaved herself onto the wall beside Ace with a deep sigh. She rubbed her calf where she'd been bitten that morning. 'The bridges we've seen so far have all been too badly damaged to cross. If Westminster Bridge is the same we'll have to try some of the London Underground tunnels. The Northern Line crossed the Thames, didn't it?'

'Sounds like a lot of work.' Ace considered. 'What about a boat? There's plenty of raw materials here; building one should be easy.'

In reply, Benton pointed out into the river. A bow wave of muddy water was spreading in a V-shape from the middle of the river towards the far bank. The water between the halves of the wave humped massively. 'Plesiosaurus. Mososaurus. Icthyosaurus,' he said.

'Hm.' Standing in the silted road, Alan shrugged. 'Three very good reasons to favour shanks's pony.'

'Speaking of which,' Jan said, placing her medikit beside Julia on the wall, 'how's the leg?'

'Still kicking. Can I have a drink?'

'If you can hold a canteen and roll up your trouser leg at the same time.'

As Jan carefully unwrapped the bandage she had placed around the wound, Benton passed Julia the canteen. She gulped thirstily at the water, choked, recovered, splashed a little onto her hands and rubbed some of the day's accumulated grime from her face. She re-capped the canteen and handed it back to Benton. 'Cheers.'

Jan examined the wound. 'That hurt?'

'Ow! Just a bit, yes.'

Jan took a fresh bandage and rebound the wound in silence.

Julia stared pointedly at her. 'And?'

Jan held out a tube of pills. 'Take two now, two in a couple of hours. You've picked up a bit of an infection.'

Julia flexed her leg and winced. 'Is *that* what it is?'

'I expect it'll be a bit stiff for a while. Try to keep the weight off it if you can.'

'Oh, that'll be easy. Alan can carry me.'

Alan laughed.

'And you can wipe that lecherous grin off your face, as quick as you like!'

Alan mugged terribly. 'Ooh, sorry, lovey.' He winked at Ace. 'It's purely platonic between us, honestly.'

Smiling, Ace stood up on the wall, her feet set firmly apart for balance on the crumbling concrete. She peered downriver. A quarter of a mile away the muddy brown stripe was bisected by a thick line of cream and ochre. 'I'm going to check out the bridge.' Without waiting for a reply, Ace set off beside the river at a brisk walk.

Despite her frown, Alan insisted on helping Julia from the wall, and the pair set off after Ace.

As Benton turned to follow, Jan placed one hand on his arm. 'Sterilize the canteen thoroughly before you use it again. Better still, just throw it away.'

Benton stared at Jan. She turned with a sympathetic glance and began to walk down river, Rod close behind.

After a moment, Benton unhitched the canteen and lobbed it over the wall. Immediately the surface of the river bubbled with the activity of some underwater predator, the bobbing canteen vanished and another bow-wave appeared, heading out into midriver. 'Good luck to you, mate,' he said bitterly. 'I hope you choke on it.'

He began to walk after the others.

Close up, Westminster Bridge was as overgrown as the rest of London.

As she began to walk out onto the bridge, Ace peered over the edge and down at the overgrown ramparts and slowly crumbling columns which formed the superstructure of the bridge. 'Just goes to show,' she whispered to herself, 'no-one gets away with it in the long run.'

'Gets away with what?'

Ace turned as Julia and Alan joined her. 'Anything. Everything.' She touched the crumbling stonework. 'Depressing, isn't it?'

'And I thought you were into this world,' Alan said gently.

'Anyone can make a mistake.' Ace moved slowly along the bridge, trying to peer through the undergrowth to the far bank of the river and south London beyond.

Alan watched her go and then walked back to where Julia was leaning heavily on the edge of the bridge. 'You alright?'

Peering out across the moody stretch of river towards the far bank, Julia felt the touch of Alan's hand on her shoulder and tensed involuntarily.

'Sorry. Worried about the leg?'

'Some whopping great dog takes a munch out of it, you expect it to hurt,' she said brusquely. 'Got the canteen?'

'Benton's got it.'

Julia swore.

'Thirsty?'

'*I just want a drink, that's all*!'

'Okay, okay. Don't bite my head off. I'll check with Ace, perhaps she's got a flask in her satchel.' Alan wound his way through the undergrowth, and found Ace staring towards the south bank.

'Do you have any water in your satchel? Julia says she wants a – '

'I'm fine. Really.' Julia had come after him, and now stood a few yards away. She was swaying slightly and it looked to Alan as though her face was flushed.

'Are you sure? I thought – '

'*I said I'm fine*!'

Alan sighed, worried and irritated in equal measures. 'Come on then, the others'll be on the bridge by now. They'll be wondering where we are.'

He walked back towards the north bank. Julia's hand on his arm stopped him. 'I'm sorry, I don't know what I was thinking of.' She paused as a gust of wind brushed her face, bringing with it the ripe smell of the river. 'I . . . uh – ' Her eyes suddenly bulged in alarm and she began to choke. 'Alan . . .' She slumped to her knees, her hands flapping uselessly around her throat. Her lips began to turn blue.

Alan closed the distance between them, unsure of what to do. What was the matter with her? Had she swallowed something? Was –

Ace dashed forward. 'Clear her throat! She's choking!'

But the convulsion lasted no more than a few seconds. By the time Alan had fallen to his knees beside her and loosened the clothing from her neck, Julia's spasm had passed. Her colour began to return as she sucked in great, shuddering breaths of air.

'Are you okay? Julia! Are you okay?'

She managed a nod.

Alan's heart hammered in his chest. 'For Chrissakes! Give me a little warning next time, alright?'

Unable to speak, Julia flung her arms around him, pressing her face against his neck. He stroked the back of her head gently. It's okay,' he murmured. 'It's okay . . .'

'I'll get the others.' Ace ran off.

Julia pulled away slightly from Alan, gazed into his eyes as if searching for something.

'I . . .' he said, uncertainly.

She stood, carefully. 'It's okay, Alan. I know the signs as well as anyone. Mutated rabies. Once the symptoms are displayed, there's no cure.' She slammed a fist into the road. 'Bastard dogs!'

They crossed the rest of the bridge in silence.

Some time that year, fire had gutted St Thomas's Hospital and County Hall, wreaking havoc at the south end of the bridge. After struggling over the burned piles of rubble, they'd found the south bank was choked with new foliage and young trees competing for the sunlight, and the going became even slower. But Ace came away with a sandwich box full of charcoal scrapings, which she tucked carefully into her satchel.

They continued walking.

Before long, as much fed up with the quiet as the morbid silence, Ace used a couple of bricks to punch out the window of a chemist shop.

'I've only got the one smartbomb, and I don't want to waste it,' she explained to Benton, stepping across the sill of the chemist. 'But if Guys is locked up, we'll need a way in, won't we?'

Nobody bothered to argue with her. She shrugged, weighing some bags of household chemicals thoughtfully in her hands, before dumping them into her satchel.

'I still need potassium nitrate and some steel tubing,' she called out through the shattered window. 'So if anyone sees a florist or a DIY store, let me know.'

She ran to catch up, satchel swinging at her shoulders.

Beyond County Hall they were able to traverse the elevated walkways along the south bank and make better time. Hungerford Bridge had vanished into the river but the Royal Festival Hall still remained more or less intact. Ace had always considered this part of the south bank to be a bit of an eyesore, and was surprised at how well it had prevailed against the jungle.

Beyond the Festival Hall the footing grew softer and wetter as they left the concrete walkways and regained ground level. The reason for the damp ground soon became clear. Weakened by excessive tidal activity, Waterloo Bridge had subsided into the river until all that remained were two or three stumps of dissolving brick and rusting steel. Part of the south bank had gone with it, producing extensive flooding of the adjoining areas.

Fortunately Benton was able to lead them away from the river at this point. Crossing the roundabout at Tennyson Way, they'd trudged along first Stamford Street and then Southwark Street, Benton and Ace slashing at the dense foliage with a couple of long knives the Sergeant produced from his backpack, Julia and Rod following, Jan and Alan bringing up the rear.

Every so often Ace would disappear on little side trips of her own, to explore the wreckage of one shop or another, foraging for the things she needed to complete her bizarre 'shopping list'.

Under normal conditions Ace would have been able to walk the mile and a half to their destination in about twenty minutes; today it took them more than three hours. By the time they stood in the forecourt of London Bridge Station, staring up at the tower block that was Guys, they were all exhausted, irritable, soaked with sweat and itching from insect bites. Julia had suffered another laryngeal spasm when she'd tried to drink, and Ace sported an angry rash on her arms, neck and one side of her face where the older woman had knocked her into a thicket of nettle trees when Ace had tried to restrain her so that Jan could administer her medication. It hadn't helped Ace's temper that she had seen only one dock-leaf plant before reaching Guys. She'd eyed the tiny leaves disdainfully, mentally comparing them to the size of the nettles

118

into which she'd fallen. 'Typical,' she'd muttered in disgust, before ripping up the plant wholesale and heading off after the others, shredding leaves and applying them to her face and neck as she did so.

Now she sat, as exhausted and irritable as the others, and ran a professional eye across their destination. The new part of the hospital stretched thirteen stories above them. Across a small side street, the older, more baroque buildings lay beyond an iron-railinged car park. Sunlight caught the side of the hospital facing them and turned it into a chiaroscuro of light and darkness, jagged and dazzling where glass remained to reflect the sun's rays from between the relentless growth of vegetation.

Jan said, 'The equipment we'll need will be in the tower block.'

'Better start looking for a way in, then,' offered Alan. 'I'll go if you like. How you doing, Julia? Feel up to a little stroll?'

'I wouldn't advise it,' Jan interjected. 'Right now Julia could probably do with the rest.'

Julia stood with an irritable frown. 'I'll be the one to decide what I do and where I go, thank you,' she said coldly.

'Fine!' Jan said angrily. 'I'm only the doctor here.'

'Thanks, Jan.' Benton nodded. 'Your advice is appreciated.'

'You're welcome!'

Alan and Julia quickly circled the building and reported back.

'They must have been under seige here,' said Julia. 'The whole place is locked up tighter than a bank vault. And from the inside.'

'All the ground-floor doors and windows are secured by steel mesh and the bottom thirty feet of the fire escape is missing, so the only way to reach the higher floors is via the beanstalk there.' Alan jerked his thumb towards the growth of trees and vines enveloping the lower half of the building. 'I suppose I could give it a go, but . . .'

Benton shook his head. 'Even if we could all get up

119

high enough to force a window, we'd still have to get the equipment out of the building afterwards.'

'Fair point,' said Julia. 'Looks like it'll have to be the main doors then.'

'But how?' Rod wanted to know. 'We don't have wire-cutters or anything else capable of cutting mesh as thick as – '

'Leave it to the expert,' Ace interrupted. She tipped the contents of her satchel onto the ground in front of her.

'What are you doing?' asked Rod, fascinated.

'You'll see,' she replied with a smile.

Twenty minutes passed before Ace was able to demonstrate what she called the art of home *un*improvement. Tucking three pieces of chemical-packed steel tubing into the wire mesh sealing off the front doors, she lit the fuses and ran back to where the others crouched behind the concrete enclosure leading to London Bridge Underground Station. 'Cover your ears,' she yelled as she ducked down. 'It might be a bit – '

The bombs exploded. There was a tremendous crash followed by a prolonged screeching and jabbering from the jungle as great numbers of animals scattered in fear. Chunks of concrete, glass and burning wood tore past them to lie smoking in the road or catch against the vegetation smothering the station walls.

Almost before the blast wave had subsided, Ace was on her feet, staring towards the site of the explosion. Her hair and clothes were full of smoke and concrete chips whipped up by the blast; her eyes shone with exuberance.

'Just like old times,' she whispered, then added in a louder voice, 'Come on you lot. What are you waiting for, Christmas?' She began to run towards the hospital, stamping out tiny fires as she went.

There was no trace of wire mesh within twenty feet of the entrance. Both the wide doors had disintegrated, as had several feet of the surrounding tiled embrasure. Fortunately the concrete lintel above the entrance had survived the blast. Ace climbed nimbly across the pile of rubble which now partly blocked the entrance.

Benton ran to join her and they entered the foyer together.

The sun was just peeping over the tree-capped buildings on the opposite side of the road as Benton called back to the others that he thought it was safe for them to follow him and Ace in. The light slanted straight in through the main entrance and illuminated the foyer with a dusty, yellowish glow. Particles of smoke and pollen hung suspended in the flickering beams which edged around the others as they, too, scrambled across the rubble and into the building.

The foyer was long and narrow, running back into the building until swallowed by shadows. A line of widely spaced concrete columns running down the middle of the foyer supported a high ceiling. To their right, a large reception window was let into one wall beside a doorway. About twenty feet away, a few plastic chairs were ranged against one wall opposite a set of lift doors and the entrance to a wide staircase.

They stood beside the window to reception. Peering in through the window, Ace could see a desk on which rested three telephones, the dust-coated remains of a set of file drawers and a typewriter. Sliding aside the glass, Ace idly reached in and poked at the typewriter with a finger. A little puff of dust erupted into the air as the key stuck fast in the down position. 'What next?' she asked.

A large board hung crookedly from one of the supporting pillars close to reception. Jan walked across to it, rubbed the dust from one corner and grinned excitedly.

'It's a floor plan. If we use this, finding the equipment and supplies we need will be easy.' She ripped the board from the pillar, wiped it clear of grime and placed it on the floor.

'Look here, Rod,' she said quickly. 'Take Julia and check out the drug cupboards. The nearest ward is on the third floor. We're looking for antibiotics. Bactrim or Claforan, anything in powder form. Make sure it's sealed, though. Flagyl is no good. We'll be carting enough fluids back as it is, without more.'

'Right.'

'I'll check out the refrigerators for saline, dextrose and Hartmann's solution. Sergeant, would you come with me please? I may need some help if the door seals have rotted, or if the fridge itself has rusted up.'

Benton nodded. 'Is that everything?'

'No. We'll need two drips stands, plus giving sets for each stand and as many cannula needles and venflons as you can find. Make sure the tubes haven't rotted; if we put air into Jo's veins by accident she'll die for sure.' She thought for a moment. 'I'm going to check the theatres for surgical equipment and anaesthetics as well while we're here. We've precious little back at the Complex.'

Benton checked his watch. 'How much time will all this take?'

'An hour, maybe two.'

'No time like the present, then, is there?' Benton led the way to the stairs. In moments, Ace and Alan were alone in the foyer.

'Taking all this gear back with us is going to be a pain.' Ace caught Alan's eye. 'We're going to need transport. A car, maybe even a small van. We could check the car park. Sort something out.'

Alan thought for a moment. 'Benton won't like it.'

Ace shrugged. 'He can always walk back to the Complex.'

Alan peered narrowly at Ace, unsure if she was serious or not.

'Besides,' she added, 'It's better than sitting on our backsides here for the next couple of hours.'

'Now that I can't disagree with.'

'Come on then.' Ace climbed over the rubble blocking the foyer and emerged into the late afternoon sunlight. Slowly, they crossed the cracked tarmac towards the older part of the hospital.

When they reached the high railings around the car park, Ace took a short steel bar from her satchel and snapped the chain which had been holding the main gate closed. A couple of cars, including a Ford Cortina estate stood before them. Ace led the way towards the Cortina.

Alan said warningly, 'Watch out for predators.'

'Don't worry, I'm watching.' Ace kicked the car in frustration. All its tyres were quite flat, rotted with age. She moved on to another car. Every one was the same. She prised open the boot of the nearest car, hefted the spare wheel out of the boot and bounced it thoughtfully. 'This one seems okay.' She walked back and popped the bonnet on the Cortina. 'Come on. Let's check the engine. If it looks like a possible, we'll grab some of the spare wheels of the other cars, okay?'

'Er, sure. But what about the batteries? And petrol? Nobody's used these cars for twenty years. It's bound to have evaporated by now. And the fuel hoses are bound to have rotted – '

'First things first.' Ace stuck her head into the engine compartment of the Cortina. 'Right then,' she said indistinctly. 'I don't think there's too much wrong with this. You're right about the hoses though. It's definitely going to need some new ones.'

'What do you want to do, cannibalize tubing from the other cars?'

'No. It'll probably be easier to find some in a medical store somewhere in the hospital. I reckon it'll have lasted better in there as well. Tell you what: you go and have a sniff around for tubing; I've got a few modifications to make here, and then we'll be ready to rock and roll.'

'Hm.' Alan shrugged resignedly, picked up Ace's crowbar and began to walk towards the older part of the hospital.

Ace didn't watch him go; she was already head and shoulders inside the Cortina's engine compartment.

The main doors were chained shut, but Alan found a small side door a couple of hundred yards away which didn't look quite so well secured. He was right. Two minutes' exertion with the crowbar had the door open, the lock hanging free and useless. Alan eased the door open a fraction of an inch and peered inside. He was taking no chances. Just because he hadn't been able to find another way into the building, didn't mean someone – or something – else hadn't.

He let his eyes adjust to the darkness. Just ahead of him, a stairway ran steeply downwards. A turn in the staircase placed the end out of sight. Alan realized he'd found the entrance to the basement. A thin scattering of coal dust on the steps confirmed his deduction. Long ago, fuel would have been carried through here to the boiler rooms.

Propping the door wide open to allow as much light as possible to filter down the staircase, Alan started down the steps, his feet crunching on the thin layer of coal dust. He gripped the crowbar very tightly with one hand. With the other he scratched idly at his ear.

Julia shivered. Together with Rod she'd climbed as far as the tenth floor. The whole hospital seemed to have about it the air of a mausoleum. They had seen no bodies; the ward beds were empty, the sheets and pillows falling apart. Everything was caked in a thick layer of dust. And on every ward the story had been the same: the drugs cupboard had been looted, bags split, boxes burst, the contents spilled across the floor, mixed together and spoiled.

The tenth floor was no exception.

Rod thumped the broken wooden door in frustration. 'It's the same as all the others,' he said angrily. 'Whoever it was seemed to want the morphine. They threw everything else aside to get at that.'

'Why? The hospital was sealed up tight when Alan and I checked. Looters wouldn't have bothered to do that, would they?'

'Perhaps they wanted to preserve their supply, come back and finish the job later.'

Julia shook her head. 'What now?'

'We go on. There's a couple more wards; we could get lucky.'

With Rod close behind, Julia retraced her steps through the ward to the main staircase and began to climb towards the eleventh floor.

That was where they found the people.

A group of fifty or so skeletons were huddled together at one end of the closest ward. The skeletons were of different sizes; obviously this had been a mixed group, adults and children together. The skeletons were wrapped in the dusty remains of clothing: mainly pyjamas by the look of it, she thought with a shudder. They'd been patients. Some were huddled together, as if in their last moments they'd been hugging, either for warmth or comfort.

Rod picked up a nearby instrument tray. It was full of syringes. Several empty glass bottles with rubber stoppers lay on a table nearby. He picked up one of the bottles and wiped dust from the label. 'Now we know where the morphine went.'

'Christ.' Julia gazed at a tiny skeleton wrapped in the disintegrating remains of a nightdress and huddled upon the lap of a larger skeleton. She wondered if, placed in a similar position, she would have the courage to take the action these people had taken.

She swallowed hard, felt her throat spasm, choked.

Rod hurried closer. 'Are you okay?'

'For heaven's sake, Rod, stop fussing, I'm okay!' Julia scratched irritably at one ear. 'Now let's find the blasted drugs and get the hell out of here. Alright?'

Benton stacked a second plastic box full of medical supplies in the foyer and was about to go back to the theatre where Jan was filling a third, when he paused. There was a tickling sensation deep within his ears ... and he felt sick, as if he were seasick ...

Abruptly he ran back towards the staircase.

'Jan!' he yelled. 'Rod! Julia! Get back here now!' His words spiralled up the stone staircase in lazy echoes, dampened by the dust. 'Do you hear me? Now!'

Voices came faintly to him.

And from outside, a sound. One he hadn't heard in years.

With a tremendous shout, Benton clambered across the pile of rubble partly blocking the hospital entrance and charged across the side road separating the two parts of the hospital. He ran into the car park. Facing him was a Ford Cortina estate, with mismatched wheels and raised bonnet. Ace's head and shoulders had vanished into the engine compartment.

The engine was running.

Alan, standing nearby, came up to Benton with a tremendous grin. 'Great, isn't it? Don't ask me how she got it running, but – '

Benton pushed past Alan and grabbed hold of Ace's shoulders, yanking her back from the engine compartment and round to face him. 'You idiot! What the hell do you think you're – '

That was as far as Benton got. Startled at his unexpected approach, Ace grabbed hold of the Sergeant's arm without looking and threw him easily across her shoulder. He landed heavily on the ground, cracking his head against the car as he fell.

Only when she saw who it was, did Ace help him to his feet. 'Don't ever try to sneak up on me again,' she said warningly. 'I don't mind, but my reflexes have a hard time dealing with it.'

'The engine!' Benton gasped. 'Stop the engine!'

'Stop it?' Ace said angrily. 'I've only just got it going!'

'They'll detect it!'

'Who?'

'Can't you tell? The reps, that's who! The Silurians!'

Benton pointed over the hospital. From the south east came a noise, a vast hammering, like the thudding of pistons in a gigantic engine. Then, slipping like a vast mottled ghost from a low bank of cloud, came a huge, dark, oval shape. The flapping of leathery wings whirred through the skies of London as other, angular shapes detached themselves from the sides of the larger object and swooped towards the ground. The shapes were pterosaurs, each carrying a Silurian pilot, outriders to the half-mile long airship they accompanied.

'It's a military task force,' Benton's voice hammered at her itching ears. 'And you've led them right to us!'

The attack began in silence.

Then came the continuous thrumming of the airship's

engines and a nervous jabbering from the animals in the surrounding jungle. Then a leathery flapping sound, as two Silurian hunters left the main convoy on pterosaurs and angled down across the skies of London.

Ace watched the black shapes draw nearer with a mixture of horror and fascination. There was a spider-like inevitability about their movements. Somehow she knew that once they saw her, they would never give up chasing her until she lay dead at their feet.

She switched off the engine.

The hunters swept closer. In moments they were no longer silhouetted against the sky, but were painted by sunlight in their natural colours. Grey-blue for the pterosaurs, mottled green-brown for their riders, with sparks of ominous red that probed amongst the trees and animals for prey.

At first it seemed that the hunters might not have seen them, or detected the sound of the Cortina's engine; that they might continue on their low flight across London. But then Ace's hopes were dashed: with a screech, the hunters swept in an arc which put them within landing distance of the car park.

'They've seen us!'

'Hide!' Alan gasped.

'Too late!' Benton sank to his knees, hands worrying at his head and the terrible itch growing within.

Ace turned to run, a horrible, unaccustomed fear pounding in her mind, her heart fluttering as if she'd just sprinted a mile. Her legs tangled and she almost fell. A shout of defiance started in her, but by the time it came out it was little more than the frightened whimper of a small child.

A wind brushed aside her hair as the first of the hunters passed by. His eyes glowed with cool malice.

Ace felt daggers of pain sink into her mind. She screamed as darkness edged her vision.

The sound of a gunshot rang out above the sound of the hunters.

Benton.

Ace saw a flood of crimson blossom from the body of

the trailing pterosaur. Instantly the great winged animal folded and plunged to the ground, bringing the hunter with it, landing on a car halfway across the car park and crushing it.

The first hunter reined in his mount and swooped away.

Benton weaved across the car park towards the smashed car and the still thrashing pterosaur. He held his gun out before him in trembling fingers like a talisman. 'Ace,' he whispered hoarsely as he passed her. 'Back me up.'

Ace shook her head, unable to produce a clear thought. 'You'll never kill that thing, it's huge.'

'Not that. The rep. Can't you feel it? *It's still alive.*'

Benton ran on, and Ace staggered after him. From the corner of one eye she saw Alan face down on the concrete, partly hidden by a patch of high grass, jerking as if in a fit. Ace started towards him, stopped, remembering Benton's demand, spun in confusion. She turned her gaze forward. Benton seemed to have vanished. That wasn't right, surely; he'd been there only a second before because she remembered –

Ace stood quite still, suddenly mesmerized. Something moved amongst the wreckage of the car. Something mottled green and angular. Something that hissed quietly in anger, or pain. Something she could sense over and above the noisy screeching of the injured pterosaur.

A hunter rose jerkily from the wreckage of the car to stand, bloody but defiant, before the pterosaur. His primary eyes were filled with rage and pain.

The third began to glow.

Ace felt daggers of pain stab again at her brain. She felt her limbs begin to shake with muscular spasms.

'Wait!' she gasped. 'Why must you . . . always . . . kill . . .'

The hunter hesitated. He appeared to consider Ace's words.

The light of his third eye dimmed.

The daggers withdrew from her mind.

She was about to speak when Benton lurched from behind a car and shot the Silurian in the face.

A hideous screech from the air above them heralded the approach of the other hunter.

Julia, Rod and Jan crouched together in the foyer of the tower block, using the rubble and shadows to mask their presence from prying eyes. Julia felt her fists clench as she watched Benton make the shot. The outcome was in no doubt, even from this distance. The shot rang clearly, all echoes absorbed by the vegetation clothing the hospital. A puff of crimson erupted from the back of the Silurian's fluted skull as he toppled heavily backwards into the ruins of the car.

The other Silurian guided his pterosaur around and swooped low across the car park. Distance did nothing to diminish the angry light in his eye.

Ace and Benton fell as they ran for the Cortina. Julia did not realize as yet that the engine had been made to work, and assumed they were merely trying to find some cover. In any case they fell before they were able to climb inside, and lay writhing upon the ground, hands clamped to their heads. She shuddered as their agonized screams came to her across the car park. 'We've got to help them!'

She started forward but Jan held her back.

'Don't be an idiot, they'd kill you as soon as look at you!'

Rod added softly, 'We must stay here, Julia. Someone has to get the medical supplies back to the Complex.'

'But Alan's out there!' Julia wrenched herself free of Jan's grasp and began to scramble across the rubble blocking the entrance.

'Rod, help me stop her!'

But then Julia stopped of her own accord, and both Jan and Rod saw why. As the hunter swooped low across the car park, the injured pterosaur lifted itself into the air with a squeal of pain, great wings flapping wearily.

Collision was inevitable.

As the two great winged reptiles smacked together, the Silurian's concentration was broken. All three tumbled to the ground, the pterosaurs screaming horribly amid the sound of snapping bones and tearing wings.

Regaining the use of his senses, Benton scrambled to his feet, brandishing his gun wildly and yelling aloud with fear and panic.

Julia, her paralysis of surprise broken, scrambled across the rubble and ran across the side street towards the car park. Jan and Rod saw there was nothing now to do but grab what supplies they could and follow.

As they ran, another shot rang out.

By the time the three had reached the car, the hideous itching sensation within their minds had eased slightly.

Benton was doubled over beside a second Silurian body, struggling to regain his breath.

The sound of giant engines continued to pound across London. Looking upwards, they were able to see the huge airship drive swiftly through the air. Its passage stirred trees on top of the highest ruins. Moisture dripped in steady white trails from its belly. One side of it was made shining bronze by the light of the setting sun, while the other was steeped in grey shadows which stretched out horizontally for miles through the pink, scudding clouds. Both flanks of the craft bristled with flight racks: perches for an army of pterosaurs.

Julia pressed one hand to her throat and swallowed painfully. A hot flush ran through her, part fear, part fever. Her stomach muscles cramped. With an effort she controlled her fear until the spasm passed. She spied Alan lying amid tall grass some distance away and moved unsteadily towards him. At that moment, one of the ptero-saurs half glided, half hopped between them, squealing piteously, one wing trailing shattered upon the ground, one still frantically beating the air. There was no way around the creature; to approach it was to risk being beaten senseless by that fearsome wing.

As she stood indecisively, there was an electrical crackle behind her. The Cortina's engine coughed and began to run.

Turning, she saw Benton behind the wheel, edging the car forwards and back, getting the feel of the gears.

'The medical supplies,' he yelled as he brought the car to a halt. 'Load them in, quick!'

Jan and Rod began to pile the boxes they had carried with them into the back of the vehicle.

Jan called out to her: 'Julia, the drip stands! And the clear fluids! They're still in the foyer; we can't leave without them.'

'What about Alan?' she cried desperately.

Benton stuck his head out of the Cortina's side window. 'Get the supplies, Julia! There'll be more reps here any minute!'

With a last look back past the flapping monstrosity concealing her friend, Julia turned and ran as fast as she could back to the tower block, scrambled across the rubble and grabbed the medical supplies. By the time she'd staggered back across the rubble, the Cortina was in the side road only a few yards away, the engine chugging alarmingly.

'Quick, get in!'

'What about Alan? And Ace – '

'Shut up and do what I tell you! Look!' Benton pointed back across the old hospital. The angular shapes of pterosaurs could be seen detaching from their flight racks along the flanks of the airship. 'We've got to get out of here! Now!'

Jan and Rod grabbed the medical supplies and pulled Julia, still protesting, into the car. Benton slammed it into gear and sent them charging across the forecourt and out into the streets now thick with shadows.

Behind them, angular silhouettes grew into the shapes of four pterosaurs and riders. They swooped down from the sky, dropped out of the sunlight and fell into the shadow cast by the Earth as the sun slipped beneath the horizon.

Their eyes were lamps in the darkness, hunting.

Ace sat up, nursing a blinding headache, and a fifteen-foot pterosaur wing nearly took her head off.

She dived back onto the ground and rolled swiftly away from the squealing reptile. Her satchel was still slung across her shoulder and it rubbed agonizingly against the

131

stitches in her back. Somehow, she resisted the urge to swear.

From the relative safety of a Vauxhall Cavalier, she peered around the car park. The Cortina was missing, as was Benton. But where were the others? Had they been taken or killed by the Silurians? Or had they abandoned her as well? Ace felt a momentary anger flare inside her, but shrugged it off. I've got my own itinerary, she thought. Well, the Doctor's itinerary, anyway.

As she peered around, Ace caught sight of a pair of legs sticking out of a patch of tall grass. Benton? Or Alan? She sighed. Some days it was just one thing after another.

Dodging the injured pterosaur, she ran across the car park and knelt beside the body. It was Alan. He was unconscious, but still breathing more or less normally. She grabbed him, hoisted him over her shoulder and ran towards the hospital. She found the doorway Alan had opened earlier and made her way down into the basement, then up a second flight of stairs into the main part of the hospital.

The first door she came to was marked:

Research Block
Authorized Personnel Only

Feeling like a bit player in a bad B-movie, Ace kicked open the door and carried Alan into the room. It was deep and wide, a cage for shadows, the tall windows thick with grime. Ace swept a laboratory bench clear of equipment and dumped Alan onto it. Setting down her satchel she smoothed back her hair and retied it.

When her eyes had become more accustomed to the darkness, she examined the room. Long benches covered with experimental equipment ran parallel to the outside wall, which had a long row of tall, narrow windows set into it. At the far end of the room were two large wooden cabinets containing laboratory glassware and a water cooler. Most of the glassware was cracked and the cooler was empty, ringed with a faintly glowing green scum. Beside the left-hand cabinet was an open door. When she

132

moved closer, Ace saw that the door opened onto a small room full of microscopes. Another door in the far wall led to what was obviously an office. She walked through and looked around. There were two solid wooden desks strewn with mouldy paperwork, pens, and a scalpel. A pinboard held postcards. A 1973 calendar hung on one wall depicting characters from a soap opera that Ace could just barely remember. Dust coloured everything a uniform grey.

There was a box of slides on one desk with a notepad resting beside it. Ace brushed aside enough of the dust to be able to make out some of the words.

An investigation into the methods of propagation, symptoms and possible methods of treatment of Baccilus mammalia.

Following this was a thick wad of pages filled with a spidery handwriting which Ace couldn't easily read. Rolling the pages carefully into a tube, she stuck them in her jacket pocket. Maybe the Doctor would be able to make sense of them later.

Ace turned to leave the room and noticed a similar notepad on another desk. She picked it up to read, and as she did so a photograph slipped out from its pages. The photograph showed a middle-aged man holding a child and sitting on a garden swing. Behind the swing was a very normal looking rosebush. The sky in the photograph was a brilliant blue. Both man and child were grinning and pulling faces at the camera. She put both photograph and pad down, saddened beyond words. Then, on a sudden impulse, she picked up the photograph again.

There was a groan from the other room as Alan stirred and tried to sit up. Ace darted back through the connecting room and slipped her arm underneath his shoulder, easing him upright.

'How's the head?'

Alan winced in pain. 'I have a head? Hell, I thought I was evolving into a new life form: just call me the living bruise.'

Ace frowned. 'Did you see what happened to the others?'

133

'No. I remember...' Alan took a breath. 'Well, I remember the hunters coming. The reps. And then... Well, there was Benton creating merry hell about your starting the car, and then – I don't get it. You mean to tell me they've gone and left us here?'

Ace nodded grimly. 'Looks like it.'

Alan rubbed his eyes tiredly. 'That's no joke, is it?'

'We'll be fine.'

'Really?'

'Trust me, I'm a soldier.' Ace saw that Alan was staring at the photograph she held. 'I found it through there.' She gestured towards the far end of the room. 'They were doing research. Trying to find out what started the Nightmare.'

Alan took the picture from her. 'Lovely kid.'

Ace sighed. 'How did it happen? Why did we give up so easily? Let ourselves be taken over like this? Let ourselves be hunted, killed, dominated like, like animals?'

'You assume there was a choice.'

'Of course I assume there was a choice! There's always a choice.'

'It was so long ago. It was just...' Alan shook his head in slow remembrance. '... so long ago.'

Ace felt anger stir within her. 'You don't know, do you?' she said accusingly. 'You can't remember.' She paused, smoothed back her hair. 'I'm sorry. I'm just shaken up. It's probably this race memory thing.'

'Join the club.' Alan handed Ace back the photograph. She stuffed it into her satchel, along with the research paper she'd found.

'Well,' Alan continued sombrely, 'what do you want to do now?'

'Right at the moment, there's only one thing we can –' Ace paused. She lifted one hand to the side of her head.

'Ace?'

Ace swallowed. 'They're coming back.'

She ran to the nearest window and rubbed her sleeve in a circle across the cracked and grimy glass. Peering through she could dimly make out the shape of the ptero-saur. It was still now, and almost silent, one broken wing draped across the car she had hidden in, its belly pulsing infrequently. She gazed up. High in the air, two angular shapes were circling the hospital. Her gaze was caught by a third shape, this one at ground level: the smashed car into which the Silurian Benton had shot had fallen.

'They'll find them,' she said suddenly. 'The Silurians Benton killed. They'll see the bullet holes and they'll come after us.'

Alan struggled from the desk. 'We've got to get the bodies out of sight. Then the others might think they've moved away on foot and look for them somewhere else.'

'Yeah. Yeah, that's good.' Ace turned and immediately walked into one of the lab benches. She rubbed her ear viciously. 'I wish this itching would – I wish I could just *concentrate*!' She shook her head and carefully skirted the bench. 'Never mind. Let's go.'

The car park lay deep in shadows and it took a few moments to spot the place where the bodies lay. Once they had ascertained the positions, Ace said, 'I'll get the one Benton shot. You get the other.'

'Okay.'

'But be careful. And try not to be seen.'

Alan crept off into the darkness.

Using the stationary cars for cover, Ace moved across the car park to the car which the first pterosaur had landed on. The Silurian lay in the wreckage, exactly as she last remembered him. Surprisingly little blood soaked the bent metal on which he lay. His face was twisted in an expression she thought might have been surprise. There was a small black-edged hole in the bridge of his nose. The back of his head was gone.

A whisper of sound from above warned her the hunters were coming back for a second look at the hospital grounds. She crouched in the shadows beside the car. Minutes passed. She began to study the Silurian's body. Hesitantly, she reached out to touch the pebbly skin of one arm. The flesh was cold. She shivered. Risking a quick glance upwards, Ace saw the sky was clear. She stooped to pick the body up, surprised at how light it was, as if something were missing in death. She shivered, then realized that because of his ancestry, his bones were probably far less dense than her own.

Hoisting the body across her shoulder she ran lightly back to the basement doorway. Alan was waiting for her just inside, his burden draped across the top steps.

'Thought you'd got bored with my company,' he whispered.

'What, a nice bruise – I mean bloke – like you?' Ace smiled in the darkness. 'Come on, let's get these little beauties out of sight.'

As they began to move the bodies, there was a sudden rush of air across the car park.

'They've seen us! They're landing!'

'No.' Ace tried with all her strength to fight off the sudden dizziness she felt. 'We know they can link. Perhaps they're tracing the bodies by telepathy.'

Alan squeezed his eyes shut and tried to concentrate. 'Even though they're dead? But how – '

'I don't know how! Come on. We'll have to . . . have to destroy the bodies, somehow. Destroy them completely.'

Ace waited for Alan to drag the first body out of sight, then shouldered her own burden and staggered dizzily down the steps to the basement.

Behind her she fancied she could hear leathery footsteps crossing the car park.

'Alan,' she whispered into the darkness. 'The door!'

'Too late!' came the hissed reply.

Footsteps slithered through the grass outside the doorway.

Ace muttered something under her breath.

'Do what?' Alan said.

'Nothing. Come on, I've got an idea.'

'Where are we – '

'Boiler room. We'll incinerate the bodies. Move it!'

The door to the boiler room was locked, but Ace went through it as if it were thin air. She dumped the body she carried and looked around. The room was low-ceilinged, long and narrow, filled with a maze of pipework and ducting. At one end a heavy cylindrical construction loomed like a squat metallic spider. Thick pipes led from it into the walls. A large metal hatch was positioned centrally in the front end. A stack of coal lay ten feet or so from the boiler, a shovel stuck upright in it.

Alan dumped his body beside the one Ace had carried. 'It'll be stone cold, Ace. How are we going to start it up before they find us?'

Ace grinned in the darkness. 'That's what God invented Molotov cocktails for. I'll just – ' Ace stopped, then swore. 'My satchel! I left it in the research block. It's got all my stuff in it. Stupid! Alan, get that hatch open, shovel some coal in and dump the bodies inside. I'll be back.'

Before Alan could reply, Ace had run from the boiler room.

Her dizziness increased as she edged quietly back through the basement to the stairs which led to the ground floor of the hospital. The hunters must be really close. Perhaps even inside the –

She froze. From the outside staircase at the far end of the basement came a faint hissing. And the soft padding of footsteps. Ace groped in her pocket and withdrew the smartbomb. She began to whisper commands to it, pausing only as the Doctor's words echoed in her mind.

Save it for a rainy day . . .

Killing these Silurians would accomplish nothing except to bring more pursuit upon them. No. She had to – oh, this damnable *itching*, she couldn't *think* – had to convince them their companions weren't here.

Ace whispered commands to the bomb. She opened her palm and it glided silently away into the darkness.

The footsteps approached.

Ace crouched frozen at the foot of the stairs, shivering with an almost uncontrollable panic.

Now she could hear the soft hissing of breath as the hunters drew near. She could see the dim light from their third eyes, looming in the darkness. Her muscles began to spasm. Her foot nudged a dusty lump of coal which rolled a few inches to stop with a faint sound against the foot of the stairs.

The eyes swung towards her.

Faint thudding sounds and a crash came from the car park.

Ace shuddered with relief as the eyes swung away, vanishing into the fainter darkness of the staircase leading outside, tracking the noise to its source.

There was a faint sigh of displaced air. She reached out and the smartbomb dropped into her palm. She deactivated it as she ran silently up the stairs to the ground floor of the hospital.

The research block was in darkness, as she had left it. Grabbing her satchel, Ace risked a quick glance out of the window she'd wiped clean earlier. The Silurians were in plain sight, their eyes glowing in the darkness. They were investigating the car which she had programmed the smartbomb to bang against a couple of times. She smiled. Sometimes the old Spacefleet strategy briefings paid off.

Ace ran back to the basement stairs, slipped down them like a ghost and re-entered the boiler room.

Alan was shovelling coal into the boiler. The Silurian bodies were nowhere in sight.

'Have you . . .?'

Alan nodded. 'They're inside. Coal too. You got your stuff?'

'Yeah.' Ace grabbed some items from her satchel, poured, tamped, added a short fuse, lit it and dumped the mixture into the boiler.

There was a soft *whoomph* from inside as the mixture ignited. The pipes began to rattle as water was pumped through them.

Alan leaned against the wall and breathed a sigh of relief. 'And not before time. I was starting to get dizzy with all the exertions.' He uttered a short laugh. 'On second thought it was probably the effect of those other Silurians. The ones following us.'

Ace stared at Alan. 'Did you say dizzy?'

'Yeah. Ears itching, disorientation, the full works. Couple of minutes ago, just before you got back.'

'But I lured those Silurians outside. They shouldn't have affected you that much.'

'Did though. Especially when I was loading the bodies into the – ' He broke off suddenly.

Her mind reeling in horror, Ace dashed to the boiler and wrenched open the cover plate. Flame washed up towards her, fed by the sudden rush of air. 'No!' Her face reddened with the heat. She felt Alan grab at her shoulders, wrenching her away from the fire.

'Ace, calm down!'

'No! Let me go! I have to see whether – '

'It's the race memory! You're being affected – '

Alan cried out in pain as Ace rabbit punched him in the solar plexus then ran back to the cover plate and thrust her face right up to the opening. Her skin began to blister. She felt her hair scorch. Was that a movement she'd seen in there? An arm reaching out to her? Was the Silurian still –

The side of her head exploded with pain as Alan lashed out with the coal shovel. He slammed the cover plate shut as Ace spun away. More flame washed against it as the coal began to burn.

'What are you playing at, you almost killed yourself!'

Ace staggered, lifted her hand to her head, sat heavily on the floor looking stupidly at the blood coating her fingers. 'You don't understand,' she said slowly. 'You couldn't have felt anything like as strong a reaction as you said from the other Silurians, they were too far away.' Her voice began to shake. 'The one we put in there was alive; wounded, unconscious, but alive.' Her eyes glazed with memories. 'I could have saved her if I'd known.'

'Ace, I . . .' he began sympathetically.

Abruptly Ace's face lost all expression. 'Forget it,' she said. 'That all happened a long time ago.'

Alan stared at her in some concern. 'Are you – '

Once again she cut him off, this time by raising a hand. *Listen.* She began to rub her ear even as he felt a deep-rooted itching begin once again within his own. 'They must have heard the boiler start up,' she said. 'They're coming back.'

Benton attempted to lose the aerial pursuit by driving

through the maze of tiny roads which wound through a series of narrow brick tunnels underneath the tracks behind London Bridge station.

He shuddered as he felt the Silurians draw closer, circling above them, tracking them. It was all a horrible game to them. But he wouldn't give in! Not if he had to kill every rep between here and – '

'Benton, watch the road! *Watch the road*!' Rod's warning shout came a fraction of a second too late. His mind on what he might do and not what he was doing, Benton had steered the car too close to one of the crumbling brick archways. Now the wing caught on a steel construction, a maintenance gantry stacked against the wall. The wing crumpled, the driver's side front tyre burst and the car smashed into the wall. Benton screamed as the windscreen shattered in his face. The quarterlight window and surrounding door frame were pushed inwards, crushing his right arm against his chest. The car scraped sparks from the wall, bounced across the tunnel and up the narrow kerb, hit the steps leading to a maintenance archway, spun, rolled and finally came to rest on its passenger side, jammed lengthwise across the tunnel.

A moment passed in silence.

Hanging sideways in his seat, Benton shook his head. Stupid! Pain shot up his neck. Not broken. Whiplash? His right arm and ribs ached abominably. His face was covered in blood from a hundred tiny glass cuts. He tried to move his legs. No problems there, at least.

'Out!' His voice was a hoarse croak, his throat taut with shock.

At the sound of his voice, there was movement in the car.

Jan slid sideways in the back seat and kicked out the door on the driver's side. She climbed out and dragged Rod from the car. With Benton kicking from the inside, they managed to wrench open the driver's door. Benton staggered from the car into the backwash of light spilling from a single flickering indicator. His feet crunched on broken glass and crumbling brick. Moisture dripped from the roof. The air was humid, full of the smells of damp earth and rank vegetation. He looked up as sounds echoed dimly overhead: claws scrabbling on steel rails. Pterosaurs, he thought grimly. Landing on the tracks above the tunnel.

There was a groan from inside the car.

'Julia!' Jan moved back towards the car and leaned in through the driver's door. 'Take my hand. Can you get out?'

'I . . . I can't move. Legs . . . trapped.'

Jan swore.

Benton groped in his backpack and handed Jan his torch. She crouched down beside the shattered windscreen and shone it inside the car. 'Julia. Can you hear me?'

'Cold . . . legs . . . cold . . .'

Benton moved back along the tunnel and leaned against the damp wall. He felt a cold draft chill his own legs. He turned. Outlined in the flickering yellow indicator light was a regular patch of shadow darker than the rest of the wall. A maintenance archway. He peered into it. Weed-choked stone steps led upwards. He supposed they emerged onto the tracks above. He looked for a hint of sky or stars, but the upper part of the staircase was overrun with vegetation. He was about to turn away when he felt the familiar itching in his ears increase. Sounds came from behind the vegetation: footsteps.

'Hurry it up back there,' he called. 'We've got company.'

Jan didn't bother to turn her head. 'Julia's trapped here. Her legs are probably broken and she could be bleeding internally.'

Benton checked the magazine on his pistol. He groped in his backpack; it contained no ammunition. 'I've got one round left. I can hear two sets of footsteps, maybe more. Make your choice, doctor.'

He shook his head. The itching sensation was getting bad now.

Julia gasped. Jan put her head closer. 'What was that?'

'I said, get the medical gear and go! I've got bloody rabies, I'm dying anyway!'

'We can't do that.'

'Will you *please* just . . .' Her voice faded. '. . . off!'

'But we can't just – '

'Yes we can.' Benton staggered back from the archway. 'Julia's made her decision. Now grab the medical supplies and get going before I shoot you myself!' He pressed both hands to his head in pain.

'Shit. *Shit.*' Jan ran her hands through her hair. 'Rod, grab the clear fluids and the antibiotics. If you can get the venflon sets, get them. We'll have to leave the rest.' She thumped the car furiously, 'Shit!'

Rod climbed on top of the car, jumped down inside and began to pass packages out to Jan.

Benton moved back down the tunnel to the archway. The footsteps were louder now. He could hear the undergrowth at the top of the staircase being wrenched aside.

'Get a move on!' he hissed.

The itching in his mind went up another notch.

Footsteps sounded on the stairs.

Rod threw the last box out to Jan, climbed out and jumped down beside her.

'That's it, we're clear.'

Benton ran back along the tunnel. 'They're on the staircase.' He swayed dizzily, shook his head in a vain effort to clear it. Jan and Rod weren't in much better condition. 'The car. Climb over the car. Move it! Back down the tunnel!'

Rod climbed over the car. Jan slung the boxes to him, then followed.

Julia groaned as the car rocked on its side. Benton crouched beside the shattered windscreen. He gazed in at her. The left side of her face was a mass of bruises and cuts, and her left eye was puffed closed where she'd banged her head when the car had tipped over. Her left jacket sleeve was soaked in blood. From the waist down his view was restricted by the dashboard, but a slow trickle of blood oozed from beneath the car to mingle with the petrol already pooling there.

He swore softly.

Incredibly, she grinned. 'Doesn't seem to be ... my lucky day ... does it?'

Benton swore again.

Footsteps sounded from the archway behind them.

'Gun.'

'What?'

Julia held out her good arm with an effort. '*Gun.*'

He held the gun out to her. 'There's only one round.'

Her eyes held him. 'It's all . . . I . . . need.' She took the gun.

There was nothing more to say. Fighting the dizziness and disorientation all the way, Benton clambered over the car and dropped to the ground, trying to ignore Julia's gasp of pain as the wreck shifted under his weight.

He lay still for a moment, his face pressed into the damp concrete of the tunnel floor. On the other side of the car, the patient footsteps stopped. A flicker of crimson reflected from the walls.

A ragged cry of pain was torn from Julia's lips. '*Run!*'

Benton rose and staggered into the darkness. Behind him there came a single gunshot and a wash of golden flame which picked him up and hurled him out of the tunnel and thirty yards along the road.

The roof of the tunnel blew out with an enormous crash, sending a mass of debris rising on a plume of fire far into the night.

Later the same evening the Doctor gazed upwards from the top of the fortress. Anchored to a mooring tower by several thick cables was a huge Silurian airship.

'I must admit, Chtorba, when you travel, you travel in some style.' The Doctor lifted one hand to hold his hat in place, while pointing with his umbrella. 'Von Zeppelin would have been green with envy.'

Chtorba urged the Doctor towards the base of the mooring tower. 'Military action has not been necessary for more than a decade,' he said. 'It almost seems like an overreaction, under the circumstances.'

The Doctor stared blankly at his companion. 'Military?' he said sharply. 'Action? Action against whom, may I ask?'

Chtorba was silent. His third eye was dark, his face flushed with a bluish tinge which the Doctor took to be embarrassment.

'No, don't answer that,' the Doctor continued bitterly. 'You're going to attack the humans, aren't you?' Angrily, he slammed the point of his umbrella into the surface of the fortress, sending tiny chips of ice-green crystal spraying outwards. 'I thought you were made of better stuff than this, Chtorba. You're a scientist! A teacher! The future rests with people like you! How can you justify the promotion of violence?'

Was that a hint of anger shining dimly in Chtorba's third eye? 'How would your Brigadier justify it?'

'That's no argument! Your species is not under threat from the humans. The Brigadier's position is completely different.'

'I think not. If your home had been overrun with destructive vermin, what would you do?'

'The question is irrelevant! Vermin are not intelligent, and they can't communicate.' The Doctor spread his hands beseechingly. 'Talk to them, Chtorba. Help them see things from your point of view. Educate them in the areas of their deficiency, by all means, but by all that's sensible, don't wipe them out as if they were no more than a plague of mice.' His voice hardened. 'You know, when I helped you escape from the Complex, I hoped it would promote understanding. Not start the Nightmare all over again.'

'Understanding is not an issue. I understand perfectly what would happen were the humans allowed to run out of control.' They reached the base of the mooring tower. Chtorba dilated an archway without touching it. 'And it would be very easy to say the matter is out of my hands; that I am no longer responsible for the consequences of my actions. That I am acting *under orders*.' He ushered the Doctor onto an elevator platform and glanced towards a sensor plinth mounted to one side. The archway irised shut behind them and the platform began to rise towards the waiting airship. 'Unfortunately, or perhaps fortunately, that is not the case.'

'Then what is the case, Chtorba? Have you and the other Silurians suddenly developed a passion for genocide? Have you forgotten what peace can be like?' The

144

Doctor's voice fell. 'Don't let your creativity, your passion, your *heart* be used for war.'

Chtorba thought for a moment and then said quietly, 'You must look to the actions of your friend the Brigadier for the answers to your questions. My choice is made.'

Above them, the airship loomed larger and larger. They transferred from the elevator platform to an opening in the boarding tube, and began to move along it. A few minutes later the cables detached from the mooring tower, the great engines started up and the airship began to move south.

The Brigadier held the hypodermic syringe to Jo Grant's neck and wondered bleakly if he was about to become a murderer.

He'd stood here, frozen with indecision for several minutes now, having dismissed the duty nurse monitoring Jo's condition. The nurse had offered no argument, leaving the Brigadier alone in the ward.

Outside the sickbay, preparations for the coming battle progressed smoothly; there were few enough of them, he knew. Few enough for twenty years' worth of planning. But what could he do? He could only respond to a situation – to a world – now beyond his control. He could only follow his orders.

Now his eyes were drawn to the face of the woman in bed before him. Behind closed lids, her eyes jerked in REM sleep. What must she be thinking, feeling, dreaming? Did she know what had happened to her? What she had become at the whim of those who hunted her?

The Brigadier put down the syringe on the pillow beside Jo's head. He traced the outline of her cheek with one finger. The skin was hot with fever. Ice bags had been packed around her body in an attempt to reduce her temperature, but the Brigadier knew her condition was worsening despite all the doctors could do to prevent it.

He touched her hair. Once it had been fair and fine. Now, though brushed, it was coarse and rough, like her skin. Abruptly, he pulled away his fingers. He didn't know this woman. Yet if what the Doctor had said was true, he should do. Or rather, would have done. They would have worked together. Maybe even become friends. Instead, here they were: she dying of internal injuries caused by a Silurian hunt and he responsible for not only her safety but everyone's.

And she was the key to that safety.

His face hardening, he picked up the syringe once more and placed it against Jo's neck.

Behind him, someone cleared their throat. 'I hope you didn't forget to sterilize the needle. You can pick up all sorts of diseases from dirty needles, you know.'

The Brigadier turned. Meredith and the duty nurse were standing just behind him. 'There's no need for sarcasm, doctor,' said the Brigadier angrily.

'Perhaps a little common sense then? You know what will happen if you administer that injection?'

'Jo may recover enough to tell us where the other half of the book she carried is.'

'And she may die!' Now Meredith's calmness began to evaporate. 'Let me tell you some statistics, Brigadier, since you seem so interested in numbers. The number of people who have recovered from deep coma via the use of stimulant drugs, for example.'

'Doctor Meredith, I'm afraid I really don't have time for – '

'Then I suggest you make time!' Meredith said sharply. 'The number is zero, Brigadier. It's not even a calculated risk. You may stimulate her metabolism and speed up her rate of deterioration, but that's all.'

'You don't know what's at stake. I must take the risk.'

'There is no risk! The outcome is a certainty.'

'The knowledge this woman holds may mean life for all of us.'

'And almost certain death for her.'

'She's dying anyway!'

'And we're not, is that it? Sometimes, Brigadier, I wonder what drives you so hard. In case it's slipped your notice, we are dying. Our world is dying. Half a book can make no possible difference.'

'Oh but it can, Doctor Meredith. It can.'

Before Meredith could react, the Brigadier turned and administered the injection. At once Meredith closed the distance between them, but the Brigadier lashed out with one hand and sent the little man spinning into a corner. He scrambled to his feet, his face suffused with rage. 'You damned military idiot!' he yelled furiously. 'You arrogant, irresponsible, prioritizing bas – '

'That's enough!' the Brigadier snapped viciously. He turned, pointing at Meredith with his swagger stick. 'The choice is made.'

Meredith rubbed his chin with the back of his hand. 'I hope you're right. Otherwise, may hell damn you for a murderer, Brigadier.' He sucked in a breath and tried to control his anger. 'Now get out of my way. I have to monitor Jo's condition. Unless you want her to die before you get your precious information, that is.'

Reluctantly, the Brigadier stepped back a pace. 'How long will it be before I can question her?'

Meredith rounded on the Brigadier with an angry look. 'You assume so much. Look what she's gone through these past twenty years. I would say she's lucky to be alive. You've said yourself most of the people out there don't even have the survival rating of animals. Even if the injection works, there's no guarantee she'd be able to string two words together, let alone a coherent sentence.'

The Brigadier said nothing.

'Aha! Is that light I see dawning across a troubled brow?'

'For God's sake!'

'Oh go away, Brigadier. Go away. I'll call you when . . . if anything happens.'

The Brigadier wandered across the ward, his face carefully neutral. He paced. He thought about scuffing his feet impatiently, but didn't. He studied the tiny minutiae of life in the sickbay: the nightlights, an abandoned jumper draped across the duty nurse's chair, the silly pictures one or two of the children had scribbled, which hung on the walls in the office. It was the pictures more than anything which strengthened his resolve.

He became aware the nurse was staring at him.

'It's the children I'm doing it all for,' he said quietly. 'All I want is for them to be able to grow up in a world that's safe for them. And by God I'll make it safe for them, any way I know how.' He locked eyes with the nurse. 'Is that so wrong?'

The nurse looked away, grabbed his jumper from the back of the chair and began to pull it over his head.

The Brigadier found himself staring at the jumper. 'Doctor Meredith, what happened to Jo's clothes?'

'They were too filthy to reuse. I expect they were dumped with the rest of the rubbish, to be burned.'

'Has the rubbish been burned this week?'

'How should I know? I'm a doctor, not a dustman.'

'I'll be back, doctor. I'll be back.' The Brigadier ran from sickbay. Meredith opened his mouth to say something, but his attention was caught by an irregularity in the steady beeping of a heart monitor beside Jo's bed.

The nurse immediately joined him by the bed. 'Starting to look a bit unstable, isn't she?'

'I think you're right. Pulse, – breathing rate, – I don't like this, she could go into VF any time. What are the batteries like on the defibrillator?'

'Enough for one, maybe two jolts. More than that . . .' The nurse shrugged. 'You know how long the recharge time is.'

'In that case, you'd better get a message to Admin, tell them to stop all unnecessary usage for a while. We'll need the power here to charge the defibrillator.'

'Right.'

'And find me a couple more nurses, will you?'

'Sure. And the Brigadier? Should I tell him?'

'Can you honestly see him doing anything other than get in the way?'

The nurse grinned tightly, turned, and ran towards the office.

When Cheddar had been a thriving tourist centre, Gough's had been one of the more attractive caves. Now it was a refuse chamber holding a small hill of rubbish, a pyramid of industrial-sized black plastic dustbins waiting for their weekly trip out into the world for their contents to be burned or buried far away from the Complex.

The floor of the cave was slippery with moisture, the air thick with the smell of disinfectant. The Brigadier picked his way carefully towards the stacks of bins. Each bin had a date label attached to it by a loop of wire. The Brigadier began to check the dates on the nearest bins.

A calendar, he thought. I'm checking a calendar of human refuse.

The bin with the date of Jo's and the Doctor's arrival at the Complex was in the second layer. The Brigadier began to wrench aside the large dustbins in his eagerness to reach the bin he sought. The lid sprang off one bin as it tipped from the pile. He managed to dodge most of the rubish which spilled out, but slipped on the damp floor. He rose, angrily brushing at his uniform, trying to remove the stains, but succeeding only in smearing them more deeply into the material.

His face burning with embarrassment, the Brigadier reached for the bin labelled with the correct date.

The lights in the cave went out.

Jan and Rod stood together and looked back at the smashed remains of the railway arch, shining orange in the flickering light of fires still burning on the tracks above. Boxes of medical supplies, all they had managed to salvage before the explosion, lay at their feet. Burning rubble lay all around, blinking eyes in the darkness. Smoke drifted through the night, a deeper black layered on ochre clouds.

Rod whispered something.

Jan turned to him questioningly.

'At least we looked.'

Jan wiped her face with her sleeve. 'No point in hanging about.'

'And transport?'

'We might find some horses on the way back to the Complex.'

'We're not going back for Ace and Alan then?'

'Do you honestly think they're still alive?'

Rod shook his head sadly, glancing at the pile of rubble

where the archway had been. 'But then, that'll be all of us one day.'

Jan picked up a box and shoved it into his arms. 'Probably best not to dwell on it.'

'Whatever.' Rod shurgged and hefted the box. 'You're the boss.'

Flushed with anger and clutching a filthy set of clothes, the Brigadier rushed into sickbay. Meredith and a small team of nurses were clustered around Jo's bed. The covers had been stripped from it and various pieces of machinery had been wheeled closer, among them the defibrillation unit. Liz Shaw was standing a short distance away, staring at the floor, an expression of sad resignation on her face.

Sparing Liz no more than a quick glance, the Brigadier marched up to the group and tapped Meredith on the shoulder. 'I was to be informed of any developments in Jo's condition,' he said angrily.

Meredith turned, a weary look on his face. The Brigadier caught a glimpse of the still, pale form on the bed behind him. On the other side of the bed, one of the nurses began to pack away the defibrillation unit.

Meredith glanced down at the Brigadier's soiled uniform, and the filthy rags he carried. 'Been playing in the rubbish, have we, Brigadier? I hope you found what you wanted.'

Gently, almost reverently, he pulled a sheet across Jo's face.

Benton woke from the dark of unconsciousness to the deeper blackness of night. He struggled to move. Something he couldn't identify was holding him fast. He struggled harder and was rewarded with the sound of shifting rubble. At once the blackness was shot through with long streaks of fire streaming upwards into the night. Benton struggled to his feet, pushing aside more rubble, then immediately sank to his knees as the muscles in his legs gave out. He shuffled into a sitting position and tried to remember what had happened.

150

The car. The crash. The hunters.

He wiped a hand across his face, was surprised to find it slick with blood. He wiped the hand on his jacket.

He became aware his ears were ringing painfully.

The gun. The explosion.

Julia!

Benton put his head in his hands, overwhelmed by shock and sadness. Tears cut runnels in the grime coating his face.

After several minutes passed and he hadn't fainted from lack of blood, he tried again to stand. He fell almost immediately. Selecting a slightly less ambitious objective, he ran his hands over his limbs and chest. There was a sharp pain in his ribs when he moved his right arm. He plucked up courage to run his fingers across his face, skull and neck. There was pain, quite a lot of it actually, but no more than you might expect after having been blown up. In fact he was relieved to discover that apart from some heavy bruising and a few superficial burns, his upper body was pretty much intact. His uniform seemed to have absorbed the brunt of the explosion. He began to giggle; *doesn't look like I'll be wearing these clothes to any more dress parades.*

The giggles continued. After a few minutes he tried to stop but found he couldn't. After another few minutes he realized he could hear his own laughter. And the sound of burning. And something else.

Close by in the flame-shot darkness, someone was talking.

He felt around him, grabbed his backpack and began to rummage frantically inside it. As he fumbled with the R/T unit, a tinny voice, attenuated by distance and old circuitry, issued forth:

'*Greyhound to Trap One, Greyhound to Trap One. Do you read me? I repeat, do you read me? Benton! Are you there, man? Over!*'

Rod paused as he picked his way carefully along the debris. 'You hear that?' he asked Jan.

Across the rubble came the sound of movement. And voices.

Benton switched off the R/T. He looked up as footsteps approached him.

'I thought all radio transmissions were forbidden,' Jan's voice came out of the darkness, 'for fear of discovery?'

Benton stowed away the R/T. 'The situation's changed.'

Rod helped Benton to his feet. 'What do you mean?'

'We have another mission objective.'

'I thought our objective was to help Jo.'

Benton licked his lips.

Jan's eyes narrowed in anger. 'That damn fool Brigadier of yours! What's he done now?'

'That information is not within my purview.'

'Not within your purview?' Jan whispered incredulously. 'We're talking about a human life!'

'Yes, well, that's as may be. But the Brigadier's orders are that you'll accompany me to Whitehall and help me find the mission objective. Only then will we proceed back to the Complex. By staying together we improve our chances of survival.'

Rod glanced sideways at Jan, taking in her furious expression. 'I wouldn't necessarily bank on that, if I were you.'

Benton stared wearily at the ground. 'What are you saying?'

'You haven't told me what we're supposed to be looking for yet. Until you do, Jo's health remains my number-one priority.'

'I'm afraid that information must remain classified until we reach Whitehall.'

'Then I'm afraid – '

'No, doctor, I'm afraid you'll do exactly as I say.' Benton reached for his gun, forgetting the holster was now empty.

'No gun, eh?' Rod observed. 'So that's what happened in there.'

Benton opened his mouth, then closed it again without speaking.

With a disgusted look, Jan began to walk way. Rod

152

glanced at her and then back at Benton. 'I'd say you were on your own now, mate.' He paused. 'I'd wish you good luck, if I thought you deserved it.' He turned and walked away.

Benton stared after them until the darkness swallowed them up.

Ace heard an explosion, outside but not too far away. The blast rattled windows in their frames. Dust sprayed into the air and hung in thick, choking clouds.

At the sound, the soft padding footsteps patiently tracking them through the darkness of the hospital hesitated. Stopped. Then after a short pause began to slowly recede.

Ace's breathing began to ease. The coloured blobs edging her vision started to disappear.

Dust began to settle once again in the hospital.

She felt Alan jump beside her, startled, as the pterosaurs began to climb up the side of the building, sharp claws sinking into the soft brick, in some places punching through the glass of windows. The noise of this seemed to go on forever. Then there was a series of scraping sounds as the reptiles launched into the air, then silence. Soon afterwards, the horrible itching in her ears began to fade.

Alan reached out to Ace in the darkness. She found his touch oddly comforting. 'What do you suppose that explosion was?' he asked.

'I think you know that as well as I do.'

'I suppose.' After a minute, he added softly. 'We have to try to get back to the Complex.'

'That's not for me. The situation's changed.'

'What do you mean?'

'You could say – I have another mission objective.'

Despite his misgivings, the Doctor could not help but be impressed by the quality of the technology around him. A few minutes earlier he'd stepped from a hatchway which Chtorba dilated for him – again without touching it – and had found himself on the bridge of the airship.

Situated at the centre of the main gondola, slung

beneath the first third of the lift body, the bridge was split-level and expansive, with panoramic armoured windows giving a wide view of the moonlit terrain over which they flew. The upper ring was circular, with monolithic consoles manned by silhouetted figures. Beneath this, and bridged by three wide ramps, was a shallow well in which the command console and tactical layouts were positioned. Set in the well between the ramps were three curved windows, facing directly towards the ground. Everything had the characteristic look and feel of Silurian technology: dark and disturbing, with the nacreous glow from control systems lighting the shadows and glimmering from the crystal surfaces, giving the whole place an almost subterranean quality.

Status information, in the form of quiet, fluting whistles, filled the air, adding to the organic quality of the place.

The Doctor looked around curiously, taking a few hesitant steps in different directions, like a child in a museum who, though fascinated by the exhibits, is completely unable to decide which way to explore first. Eventually he simply stood quite still and let his eyes drink in the wealth of visual information available to him.

He turned to Chtorba. 'I assumed you would lock me away in a cell, somewhere I couldn't make any trouble.'

'The military Commander here wished to meet with you. Her name is Chtaachtl. She holds a rank in our army equivalent to that of your friend the Brigadier.'

'Oh good, someone in authority at last. Someone who might have a little common sense. Lead on, my dear Chtorba. Lead on!'

In the lab, Liz Shaw sat at the bench containing the Doctor's breadboard rig, frustrated and angry because she still hadn't managed to fit the last component in place. While she was concentrating, the lab door opened to admit a harassed looking soldier.

'Yes, what is it?' Liz said irritably.

'The Brigadier has ordered a stage two evacuation,' the soldier told her. 'All personnel are to go to the deep shelters.'

Liz sighed. 'It's nothing personal,' she said quietly, 'but sod off, will you? I've got a lot of work to do.'

Liz returned her attention to the breadboard rig. Ignored, the soldier stared at the back of her head for a moment, stuck his tongue out, then shrugged and quietly withdrew.

The Doctor stared up into the glistening eyes and mobile face of the Silurian who towered over him. He doffed his hat politely.

Chtaachtl wrinkled her nose in disgust.

I don't care what it says it is, Chtorba, it smells like a mam. What do you want me to do with it?

The Doctor smiled and cleared his throat modestly. 'Well, you could always listen to what I have to say. You may find the idea of peace isn't quite as threatening, or terrifying, as you think.'

Be silent, animal! Chtorba, you did not tell me it could link.

'It seemed obvious.'

Chtaachtl's face creased in surprise. *You speak in front of it. We should destroy these vermin, not defer to them.*

'The Doctor is not an animal, Chtaachtl. He does not behave like the other humans. He helped me escape.'

Was that a glimmer of irritation he saw in Chtorba's third eye? Anger, even? The Doctor smiled inwardly.

'At the very least he deserves our –'

The mam deserves nothing! Chtaachtl paused, her breath hissing angrily. *And you should not presume to speak for it!*

Now Chtorba's third eye did glow, an angry scarlet. The Doctor noticed a tiny muscular twitch along one side of his jaw. His voice deepened. 'And you, Chtaachtl, should not be so presumptuous. We both know who has the friendship of the Leader, do we not?'

Enough! Chtaachtl turned her back on the Silurian teacher. She gestured towards the Doctor and made a gentle fluting sound. At once, the personnel manning the bridge turned to look at the Doctor. *Observe this mam,* she continued, *this blight upon our planet, and tell me, what would you have done with it?*

The Doctor was aware of a multilayering of thoughts and communications symbols from the other Silurians. 'You're making a big mistake, Chtaachtl,' he said beseechingly. 'I can –'

The Silurian Commander went on, *you see, it threatens us! You sense its fear, its blind, unreasoning hatred of us. I repeat: what should be done with it?*

The layers of thought began to take on a more definite pattern.

That's right! It should be killed, as all mammals shall be killed. To preserve the peace of our world.

The Doctor shook his head. The beginnings of a disarming grin were spreading across his face when Chtaachtl concentrated on him through her third eye. He felt an invisible fist reach into his mind and *squeeze*.

He shrieked with pain.

Darkness came swiftly.

The Brigadier sat stiffly at his desk, his swagger stick and a fully loaded automatic pistol beside him on the blotter. He was listing points for the army Captain sitting opposite him.

'Now then, Wood, I want all military personnel issued with machine guns. Decentralize the ammunition stores; issue ammunition with the guns. Grenades, Tear gas and lysergic agents are to be used on my order only. Make sure there are sufficient gas masks to go round. I don't want the men gassing each other.'

'Sir.' Wood used a wax pencil to make a note on a plastic tablet he carried with him.

'Right, now what about the assault team?'

'They're in position at the top of the gorge.'

'Good. Have them maintain position. They are not to break cover until my order. Precise co-ordination is essential, is that understood?'

'Absolutely, sir.'

'Right then.' The Brigadier ticked points off on his fingers. 'All family members and children have been moved to the deep shelters. Deployment of troops is satisfactory. Deployment of arms and ammunition is satisfactory. R/T checks are satisfactory. I'll take charge of the anti-aircraft gun myself.'

'With respect, Brigadier, don't you think you'd be better placed here? As you said, – to co-ordinate the defence?'

'I was never one to sit behind a desk when something needed shooting. I see no reason to change the habit of a lifetime now, eh, Captain?' The Brigadier grinned.

'Er, yes, sir. Quite,' Wood said tactfully.

'Well, come on man, show a bit of backbone,' the Brigadier roared with sudden good humour. 'You're acting as if it's the end of the world!' He leaned forward and added in a conspiratorial whisper, 'To tell you the truth, I'm quite looking forward to it!'

Crouching amongst the dimly glowing ferns at the top of the gorge, Billy Wilson heard it first. A faint, hideous screeching, echoing with distance, underlaid by the disturbing vibration of massive engines. A sound he'd heard in nightmares all his adult life.

Then the airship glided into view over the hills. Clothed in silver moonlight, it was staggeringly huge. Human technology had never built anything like this. The screeching and the pounding of engines grew to almost unbearable proportions. To his left and right, Billy heard other members of the assault team moaning with pain. He imagined them clamping their hands to their ears and eyes, trying to block out the vast bulk of the airship.

It approached, slowly, implacably, growing larger and larger, and then larger still. Billy was forced to keep reassessing its size. After ten minutes had passed the ship slid in front of the moon and the upper half-mile of the gorge was plunged into shadow. After twenty minutes had passed, a quarter of the starlit sky was obscured.

When twenty-five minutes had passed the pounding of the engines ceased abruptly and the airship became motionless, hanging centrally across the gorge. Bill felt as if he could reach out to touch the hundreds of pearl and green lights glimmering across its dark belly, even though he knew the lowest part of the ship was still five hundred feet above them.

When thirty minutes had passed the flanks of the airship began to writhe, quicksilver in the moonlight. Droplets began to detach and fall.

'It's melting!' a voice said nervously to Billy's left.

An answering voice hissed: 'Shut up, Prescott!'

Then the screaming increased, along with the leathery flapping of wings in the darkness.

Pterosaurs.

Billy ground his teeth and gripped his machine gun tightly. Already his mind was beginning to spin. One or two Silurians were hard enough to cope with – the combined effect of hundreds, maybe more, both in the airship and piloting the pterosaurs, was almost unbearable. What must it be like for the other soldiers, down there, in the gorge?

There came a distant gunshot and a voice roared, 'No, you fool, hold your fire! *Hold your fire!*'

The distant shooting continued, tiny sparks rising upwards through the darkness towards the leviathan.

Lee Wood stood with his back to the moon and shot a Silurian hunter as she skimmed past on the back of a pterosaur. There was a thin hiss as the rider slumped in her harness before being borne back up into the sky by the now directionless pterosaur.

Wood looked around quickly, checking for other targets. It wasn't easy in the eerie half-light beneath the airship. Further down the gorge, the corralled horses were beginning to panic. Nearby, there was a sudden chilling scream. Wood turned in time to see a soldier fall to his knees, gun forgotten, hands clasped to his head. The soldier collapsed to lay writhing upon the ground. Wood ran towards him. By the time he reached him, the other man had stopped moving, his face frozen in a rictus of agony, his muscles tense as steel cables.

Wood scowled, grabbed the soldier's gun and straightened. Sparks, like embers from a fire, drifted through the air towards him. Wood realized he was seeing the terrible glow of the Silurians' third eyes. There was a gust of wind as a pterosaur swooped out of the night. Wood felt daggers of pain sink into his mind. He spun, firing from the hip, but missed his target. In another moment the pterosaur had banked around in a long arc, bringing its pilot back for another pass.

Seeing double, Wood tried to sight along the barrel of his gun as the Silurian swept closer. No matter how hard he tried, the images refused to synchronize in his mind. He loosed two shots into the darkness before the pain hit him again and smashed him into the ground, where he began to dig into the mud, trying to burrow to safety as the Silurian swept overhead. His screams were lost in the darkness and the hysterical chatter of automatic-weapons fire.

His mind dissolving under the onslaught of the Silurian's hatred, Wood was dimly aware of a gush of flame which turned both the pterosaur and pilot into shuddering torches. Wood struggled to his feet as the pair crashed to the ground; a wide swathe of undergrowth began to burn fiercely.

Wood felt strong hands guide him upright. 'You okay sir?' The UNIT soldier who helped him wore a napalm unit strapped to her back.

'Just give me my damn gun,' Wood mumbled.

'It's down there in the mud, sir. Whoops. Have to dash.' The flame-thrower erupted again, burning a nightmare vision of Silurians and soldiers locked in deathly combat into his brain.

Wood pulled out his R/T unit. 'Trap Two to Greyhound. Trap Two to Greyhound. Are you receiving me, over?'

'*Greyhound receiving. Lethbridge-Stewart here, Wood. What's the situation? Over.*'

'Tell Miss Shaw to hurry up with the gadget, Brigadier, they're taking us apart! We need an edge. Over.'

'*Understood. What about the airship? What's it doing? Over.*'

Wood stared upwards past the floating sparks of the Silurians to the great hulking shape looming above. 'It doesn't appear to be – wait! Wait, it's moving! It's coming down! Relay instructions. I say again, relay instructions. Over.'

'*Hang on, Wood, I'm coming out with the anti-aircraft gun. Over and out.*'

The Doctor awoke to a whispered imperative and the sensation of someone gripping his shoulders and shaking him. He groaned, blinked and finally opened his eyes, utterly amazed to find Bernice staring down at him.

'Some days, Doctor,' she said dryly, 'you do naught but impress.'

'Some days, Bernice, you do the same. I thought I'd lost you.'

'Ah, well, that was then.'

'I see.' The Doctor sat up and looked around. He was sitting on a padded crystal slab in a long, narrow room. The only light source was a dim glow from a corridor beyond the single door, which stood ajar at the far end of the room. There was a body lying just inside the doorway.

'Bernice,' he said sternly, 'sometimes I think you're quite as bad as Ace.'

'Yes, well, if I'd left it to you, you'd still be off in the land of nod.'

The Doctor rubbed his head ruefully. 'How did you get here? Do the Silurians know you're here? Why are you – '

Bernice held a finger up to her lips and smiled. 'Makes a change for you not to know all the answers, doesn't it?'

'Hm.' The Doctor jumped abruptly to his feet and twirled his umbrella, flipped it a couple of inches into the air and caught it again point first, still spinning, on the end of his right index finger.

Bernice frowned. 'My father used to be able to do that with a football.'

'It helps me to think. How long have I been unconscious?'

'A couple of hours.'

'I wonder,' mused the Doctor, 'how close we are to the gorge.'

A sudden violent explosion ripped through one wall. The Doctor and Bernice were blown off their feet, sliding

160

the full length of the room to fetch up against, respectively, the door and the Silurian Bernice had rendered unconscious. Smoke and flame washed in through the hole in the wall, followed by a blast of freezing air. Faintly, they could hear the sound of screaming and the thrashing of wings.

'Ah,' said the Doctor, retrieving his hat from the unconscious Silurian's face and placing it firmly back on his own head. 'Quite close, then.'

The airship drifted lower, bringing psionic amplifiers to bear on the gorge itself. The Silurian gunners projected their anger into the rock and under their onslaught it began to crumble.

Inside the caves the noise of distant screaming was a disturbing backdrop to the more frightening sound of splitting rock. The medical staff, already inundated with more injured soldiers than they could effectively treat, were pelted with boulders as the cave systems began to collapse. In the deep shelters the children were wailing in panic and fear. Nurses did not dare sedate even the worst cases; if a total evacuation was called for, the children could never be moved. One, a tiny, fair-haired little boy, gazed around him in fear, refusing to be calmed. Eventually he ran from the shelter altogether, back into the upper levels of the Complex.

'Right-o, Corporal. Move out!'

The anti-aircraft gun crept forward on the half-track, nosing out from beneath its camouflaged position at one end of the gorge. The Brigadier was strapped in the firing seat, with a soldier as loader beside him. Twelve high-explosive shells were uncrated beside the gun. Driving the half-track was a corporal named Vess.

The Brigadier ordered another round chambered, took careful bearing through the sighting mechanism, and fired. A thousand feet above, an explosion rippled along the superstructure of the airship.

The Brigadier resisted an impulse to cheer.

Twenty or thirty pterosaurs fell dead or concussed from

their flight racks. The dead pterosaurs hit the ground amid the sound of cracking bones and tearing wings. The one or two which were only stunned recovered swiftly, arcing up and away into the night, clear of the battle.

By now the screams and gunfire seemed to have taken on a chilling life of their own.

The airship glided slowly lower, engines idling.

The Brigadier ordered another round chambered and shook his fist at the leviathan. 'Come and take your medicine you damn . . . *bullies!*' he roared, unaware of the tears streaming down his face.

The soldier touched him on the arm in concern. 'Brigadier . . .'

The Brigadier shrugged off the touch. 'Get away from me, man! What's the matter with you? Not showing sympathy for the damn reps now, are you?'

'No, sir.'

'Well then! Show some backbone! Chamber another round!'

'Already in the breech, sir.'

'Good!' The Brigadier slammed home the trigger. The gun roared and the half-track rocked. The round spun away into the night, missing the airship completely.

Through his tears and the terrible itching in his mind, the Brigadier found a distant thought coming to his attention. 'Liz,' he said in an agonized whisper. '*Liz!*'

'Hey, you've got a puzzle!'

Liz turned in surprise at the sound of the voice. Behind her was a small fair-haired little boy.

'How on earth did you get here?'

'I ran away.'

'From the deep shelters?'

The little boy nodded solemnly.

'What's your name?'

'Tom-o.'

'Well you better come and sit up here with me, Tom-o. But you must be quiet. I've got a terribly important piece of work to finish.'

'I can see that. It's a puzzle.'

162

Liz smiled sadly. 'Yes, I suppose you could say that.'

Tom-o reached out for the last component, which Liz held in her hand. Her first impulse was to take it away, tell the kid to get lost, to go away and leave her alone. Something made her stop. Something in the kid's eyes.

He reached out for the component and Liz gave it to him.

On the highest point of the gorge, Billy Wilson gripped his machine gun tightly and resisted the overwhelming impulse to leap, firing wildly, into the battle. A pterosaur arced overhead, to land with a dry pattering of claws further down the ridge. There was a scream, but no gunfire. Footsteps approached him through the foliage.

Tom-o held the device up to the breadboard rig, searching for the key that would lock them together. There was a loud explosion somewhere nearby. The ground shook. Small pebbles and bits of rock fell from the upper part of the cave. One piece smashed into the far bench, destroying the small centrifuge.

The Brigadier punched the release and shrugged off the safety straps attached to the gunner's seat. A minute earlier the soldier had run screaming into the night; now the Brigadier had to load the ammunition himself. He dropped to his knees beside the gun, grabbed a shell, tried to chamber it, found he needed both hands for the job, dropped the shell, opened the breech and scrabbled for the shell again.

He rose, hands empty, as the hot tongue of a flame-thrower licked out into the darkness. The flame illuminated both the thrashing figures of soldiers firing indiscriminately into the night, and the patiently advancing force of Silurians, dropping one by one from the sky to move like shadows through the undergrowth. There was another blast of flame and a hissing scream. The explosion lit up the side of the half-track, showing both the position of the fallen shell, and that of the Silurian hunter which stood, third eye beginning to glow furiously, not ten feet from him.

Through all the chaos, Tom-o's concentration never wavered. He held the component nearer and nearer. Squinted with one eye as he moved it, rotated, touched it to the larger device, here, here . . . *here*.

The device fitted neatly into place.

The breadboard rig began to hum.

Liz grinned as she felt the itching and the pain fade from her mind. 'Of course, it was so obvious! Why didn't I see it. Tom-o, you're a genius!'

He looked up at Liz and smiled. 'S'easy!'

The smile turned to a look of horror as the ceiling above them split open. Liz looked up as a mass of rocks, concrete lintels, and plumbing began to fall out of the roof space towards them. Without thinking, she scooped him into her arms and ran towards the doors of the lab. Dumping the child, she turned back for the breadboard rig, just in time to see a rock the size of her head fall directly onto it, smashing it beyond all hope of repair.

'*No!*'

The room was obscured by a choking cloud of dust.

The itch in her mind began to come back.

The Brigadier felt the daggers of pain withdraw from his mind. The face of the Silurian lay beside him in the mud. The Brigadier blinked in surprise. How had he got here, on the ground? Why was he trying to dig a hole and not fighting the enemy?

He struggled to his feet. The Silurian stayed down, a bullet hole between his eyes. The Brigadier noticed Corporal Vess lying face down in the mud a few feet away. Her limbs were contorted in death, but she still held her gun.

Unable to help the Corporal, the Brigadier picked up a shell, chambered it, aimed and fired in record time. Fire bloomed along the airship's main gondola. Debris fell out of the darkness and wrought more chaos on the ground.

He managed to fire two more rounds before the daggers returned to his mind.

As he collapsed beside the body of the dead Silurian, he gasped an order into his R/T unit. 'Greyhound to Trap Three, stand by! I say again: stand by!'

He struggled to his feet and chambered another shell.

Bernice followed the Doctor along a darkly crystalline corridor. 'Where are you going?'

The Doctor paused to allow another explosion to die away, the light filtering through the corridor walls and enabling her to see the neutral expression on his face. 'I have to get to the bridge.'

'You're joking! We've got to get out of here!'

'No.'

'They'll kill you!'

'They didn't kill you, did they?'

Bernice didn't reply.

'Anyway, I have to risk it. I don't think the humans know anything about the time-stream distortion or my own death; the Silurians might.'

'I'm coming with you then.'

'No. I want you to get down to the ground and keep an eye on one Brigadier Alastair Lethbridge-Stewart. He's planning something – I'm not sure what it is, but it could prevent me from finding out what I need to know about the other matters.'

Bernice scowled. 'This time-stream distortion, does it have anything to do with what happened to me in the TARDIS?'

'No time, Benny,' said the Doctor hurriedly. 'We'll discuss it later – if everything goes according to plan.'

'And if it doesn't?'

'Ask me an easy one.'

She shrugged. 'See you later then.' She turned, stopped at a call from the Doctor.

'How are you going to get down?'

She grinned. 'A girl likes to keep some secrets.'

Another explosion drove smoke and flame along the corridor.

Chaos ruled on the ground. Soldiers broke rank and ran or tried to burrow into the undergrowth as their ammunition ran out. Only a very few kept their heads enough to ration their ammunition. They fought a rearguard action against the Silurians, who had now landed in force.

Staggering out of the Complex, Liz felt her intelligence and civilization slipping away into a haze of paranoia. Grabbing a gun from a dead soldier, she began to fire indiscriminately into the darkness. The livid spark of a third eye loomed out of the shadows, and Liz felt a fist clench in her mind. She fired, pumping rounds into the Silurian long after it was dead. She staggered between burning undergrowth, crying out, eyes streaming with tears, falling to her knees with a scream of anguish when she couldn't work out whether the dead UNIT soldier in front of her had been killed by a Silurian or by bullets from her own gun.

The Brigadier caught a glimpse of Liz as he loaded and fired the anti-aircraft gun. 'Miss Shaw! What happened to the Doctor's machine?'

She aimed her gun at him and fired. Amazed, the Brigadier ducked as a bullet ricocheted from the half-track. She fired again but, apparently, she'd exhausted her supply of ammunition.

Ignoring Liz, the Brigadier loaded his last shell. By now the airship was no more than several hundred feet above the gorge. The cool green arc of the bridge was outlined clearly in the shadows. The Brigadier laughed aloud at the stupidity of a soldier who provided him with a perfectly illuminated target.

He fired. The shell tore through the wing of a banking pterosaur, shot up through the air and blasted a glowing crater in the underside of the gondola, close to the bridge.

The Brigadier ran from the half-track as the pterosaur smashed into it. Dragging his R/T unit from his pocket, he screamed: 'Greyhound to Trap Three, activate! I say again: *activate!*'

Billy Wilson heard the order to launch. He dragged aside the camouflage tarpaulins from the unpowered microlight glider, whipped away the chocks, and launched himself through the trees. Behind him, the cold grey eyes of a dead Silurian stared up at the smoke-filled night sky.

Billy arced out into the cold air above the gorge. His wild yell of ecstasy echoed from crag to crag. He saw nothing but the leviathan.

When the Doctor entered the bridge it was illuminated by harsh flashes of light. The sound of screams and explosions was deafening.

Engage psionic amplifiers! Chtaachtl almost vocalized her orders in her rage. *Gunners to target area directly below with maximum force!*

'Excuse me,' said the Doctor politely. 'I wonder if we might find a few minutes' quality time for a little chat?'

Chtaachtl spun at the sound of his voice. The Doctor doffed his hat politely. He was about to speak when an explosion blasted one of the wide curving windows in the command well into a thousand crystal pieces which fell glittering into the darkness.

Chtaachtl's eyes narrowed with hatred. Before the Doctor could defend himself, the Silurian brought her third eye to bear, focusing all her rage upon him.

'On the other hand, perhaps I'll just call back when you're less busy!' The Doctor turned to run, felt daggers of pain enter his mind, slipped and fell from the ramp, towards the shattered window and the ground far below.

Bernice ran along corridor after corridor, entered a lift and was carried through the upper regions of the airship to the port forward pilots' gallery. Here a freezing wind whipped in past the open racks on which the pterosaurs hung, rocking her back and forcing her to grab hold of the superstructure to stop herself being blown out of the gallery altogether. The airship shuddered with another explosion.

Something must have hit something a bit vital, she thought. Then: I'm a bit vital. Hope the next one doesn't hit me!

Flame *slooshed* along the outside of the pilots' gallery.

The screeching of the pterosaurs increased. Some detached, panicking despite their link with the Silurian pilots. One fell, a burning torch in the darkness, smashing into the ground in a flurry of sparks and burning flesh.

The wind whipped smoke and flame into the gallery. Bernice doubled over, coughing and choking, lost her grip on the superstructure and was swept towards the racks, and the open sky beyond. Desperately, she reached out for a handhold and grabbed the nearest thing she could – a Silurian pilot. In the heat of the moment Bernice could not say who was most surprised. In any event, they both stumbled towards the edge of the gallery and tumbled over the lip.

Bernice screamed as she fell, then gasped painfully as the air was driven from her lungs by her impact with one of the lower perches. She'd only fallen ten feet, but it seemed like a mile. She grabbed hold of the stanchion and looked around for the Silurian; he was nowhere to be seen, above or below.

She rocked her head to shake it clear of her hair, which the wind had whipped into her face, and found herself nose to beak with a pterosaur, hanging upside down from the nearest perch. Its cold, grey eyes regarded her incuriously.

'Ahhh . . .' said Bernice. 'Nice boy. Good boy. Er . . .'

The pterosaur yawned. Its jaws were more than a yard long and filled with sharp, vicious-looking teeth.

She blinked rapidly.

'Want to go walkies? I mean, fly-ies?'

The reptile blinked and stirred, the wind seeming not to affect it at all. It stretched its wings lazily. Grief, she thought. It's bigger than a small shuttle!

'Hah!' she continued nervously. 'Of course you do. Now then, lets see. Hope you don't mind an unscheduled passenger.'

Her eyes streaming with tears, Bernice managed to make out the leather harness strapped to the pterosaur's body. Squeezing her eyes shut in a quick prayer, she swung her feet upwards, let go with her hands and flew through space.

'Yes!' Bernice found herself clinging the right way up to the pterosaur's back. It stirred and adjusted itself under the additional weight. 'Well, what are you waiting for? Giddyup!' Bernice kicked her heels into the flanks of the reptile. It uttered an abrasive shriek and detached from its perch. Bernice's heart lurched into her mouth. The pterosaur scooped air into its wings and levelled out. Bernice tightened her grip as she felt herself sliding backwards.

Now, she thought, if I could just see where the hell I was going . . .

Feeling the worst part of her escape was over, Bernice began gingerly to turn, keeping a tight grip on the harness.

Ahh, she thought, that's more –

With a shriek and a great crash, the pterosaur flew straight into a microlight glider.

'What the hell was that!'

Gill Lewis, the Assault Team Leader, whipped her head around but whatever it was had already passed. Billy Wilson's microlight was gone. Lewis returned her attention to the bulk of the leviathan before her.

Angling upwards, she pulled a grenade from her belt and threw it into the port forward pilots' gallery. She banked, coming in for a landing as the debris of the superstructure fell away into the night.

Eight more gliders followed her in.

The Brigadier ducked as a screeching mass which seemed to be composed of pterosaur, pilot, microlight glider and soldier whirled over his head and smashed into a copse of trees to his left.

To his right there was an angry hiss. The soldier he'd seen earlier wielding the flame-thrower was frantically trying to rekindle the pilot light on the nozzle. Dark silhouettes moved towards her, red sparks glowing. Even as the brigadier ran towards her, the soldier fell, hands clutching at her head, the canisters on her back exploding with a dull boom.

The Brigadier stumbled backwards and fell over a body.

By the time he regained his footing, the burning napalm had set light to the surrounding foliage and the fires were spreading. Taking a machine gun from the dead soldier, he marched towards the nearest of the silhouetted figures.

Gill Lewis blew open the portals in front of them and led the eight remaining members of the task force onto the bridge. The Silurians leaped towards them with unbelievable speed. To her left, Kevin Barker died where he stood, falling motionless to the floor. Prescott already had her gun out and was firing wildly into the bridge. Lewis wished Billy were with them. She turned to fire at the advancing Silurians but the nearest was already upon her, his eyes wide with hatred, his breath sweet and cold in her face.

Clutching his umbrella, which he'd managed to hook across a length of superstructure as he fell through the window, the Doctor hung above thin air and a lethal fall to the ground hundreds of feet below.

As his hands slowly slipped further down the shaft of his umbrella, towards the point, he was aware of a sharp humming sound from nearby. Engines pulsed aggressively in the darkness, and he realized a smaller airship had detached itself from the larger vessel. An escape vehicle? Chtaachtl's escape vessel?

The smaller ship was passing by, almost directly beneath him.

The Doctor began to swing his legs, rocking backwards and forwards. With a great heave of his body, he jack-knifed into space.

Long seconds passed, then he landed on the upper surface of a lifting body. He breathed a sigh of relief.

Then his umbrella fell onto his head, causing him to lose his balance. Arms windmilling madly, the Doctor began to slide across the lifting body, towards the open air beyond.

On the ground the battle continued. The moon came out once more as the airship drifted away across the gorge.

Lacking support or guidance, the Silurians on the ground began to withdraw into the jungle.

The Brigadier holstered his gun and ordered the conservation of ammunition.

A figure stumbled wearily out of the darkness. It was Lee Wood, his face black with smoke and mud, blood soaking one side of his uniform. 'Looks like . . . looks like they're withdrawing, sir.'

'Yes, Captain. We seem to have won this round.'

The Brigadier became aware of someone sobbing behind him. He turned to see Liz Shaw kneeling in the mud, cradling the still form of a small, fair-haired child in her arms.

'Tom-o.' She looked up as the Brigadier moved towards her. 'He must have followed me out.'

The child's eyes were fixed open and staring, one pupil larger than the other. There was a bruise the size of an apple on the side of his head; his hair was matted with blood.

Unaware of his own tears, the Brigadier reached out to close the boy's eyes.

'I only did it for the children,' he whispered, but nobody heard.

PART FOUR

ISOMORPHIC

Unaware of the fighting which had taken place in Cheddar, Ace and Alan had walked for several hours before bedding down for the night in the remains of the sailing ship *Cutty Sark*, still in its dry dock in Greenwich. It was miles out of their way, but was apparently the only place at which they stood even a vague chance of crossing the river.

Alan had spent an uneasy couple of hours trying to sleep, but found himself worrying about Julia. This together with the noises which drifted through the night kept him awake. Ace had had no trouble falling into a light but immediate sleep, apparently unaffected by the strangeness of her surroundings.

Dawn came in a welter of animal noises and a harsh downpouring of rain. The rain slammed into the upper parts of the ship, percolating through the shattered deckplates and streaming into the separate cabins in which they had spent the night.

Ace woke when Alan's voice echoed out of the depths of the ship. 'A well placed property with a glorious river view and all mod cons.'

'If by that you mean a shower in every room, I'd have to agree.' Ace rubbed sleep from her eyes and climbed to her feet, stretching before fully remembering the stitches in her back. She grimaced with pain. Sloshing through a fast growing pool of water she left her cabin and found Alan cooking breakfast over a small fire he had kindled in a trough of bricks in what had once been the wardroom.

When the rain stopped they emerged from the ship into a damp, pungent world and examined their surroundings.

Looking back at the ship, Ace could see a mass of vines hanging from the sagging masts like bizarre organic rigging. The bulk of the ship was obscured by greenery, with only the very tip of the figurehead emerging to point somewhat sombrely towards the grey torrent of the river, and the domed entrance to the pedestrian subway which crossed beneath it. Behind the ship, on the side facing away from the river, the baroque complexes of the old naval headquarters and the National Maritime Museum were overrun with greenery which blended into the expanse of Greenwich Park, rising steeply up the hill towards Blackheath. Looming silently from the early mist clothing the jungle at the very top of the hill a pale oval stood out against the sky. The Greenwich Observatory.

'Well,' Ace said, refocusing her attention on their immediate surroundings. 'What do you reckon?'

Wringing moisture from his jacket, Alan laughed. 'I reckon it's a rum do when the ships are wetter on the inside than the out.'

Ace frowned. 'I meant about the tunnel. Do you think we'll be able to use it to cross beneath the river?'

Alan shrugged. 'Only one way to find out.'

Nodding thoughtfully, Ace walked towards the tunnel entrance. Alan spread his jacket on a nearby wall to dry in the sun, then ran to join her. Together, they circled the low building, which was cylindrical, brick-walled and topped by a cracked glass dome. There were two entrances, one wide, barred by the cagework of a lift entrance, the other narrower, opening onto a spiral staircase. The staircase wound around the lift shaft, down into the darkness. Somewhere down there Ace could hear the sound of dripping water.

'Great,' she muttered.

They descended the stairwell cautiously; although rust had eaten away at the girders of the lift shaft, the concrete steps still held relatively firmly. Thankful for small mercies, Ace lead the way into the darkness, testing each step for its integrity before entrusting her full weight to it.

The sound of sloshing water grew louder as they descended. The walls and steps became slick with moisture. About halfway down, the stairwell began to show signs of lichen infestation. The lichen glowed with a cool, pastel light.

During a brief pause to allow her eyes to readjust to the light levels, Ace sensed Alan's presence close behind her. 'Don't get too close. Our combined weights might be too much for the staircase.'

'Sure. Just don't get any ideas about running the four minute mile down here, huh?'

Ace grinned to herself. 'I didn't know you cared.'

'Ha ha.'

Ace stopped. 'I wouldn't laugh too soon.'

At her feet, the bottom of the stairwell vanished into a scummy pool of water.

Despite her warning, Alan came closer. 'That's that then.'

Ace ventured a step or two further down the stairwell. 'I don't know. Hang on a minute while I check round the corner.' Holding onto one of the more secure-looking girders for support, Ace leaned out and peered around the lift shaft.

'Be careful, Ace.'

'I'm being careful, Alan,' she replied sharply.

'Yeah, well. Good. I just wanted to be sure – '

'Forget it. Anyway, we may be okay. I think I can see the top of the tunnel.'

'Yeah?'

'Yeah. Wait here, will you? I'll check it out.' Handing Alan her satchel and jacket, Ace descended the staircase until the water was up to her knees. She hesitated, then continued. The water level rose to her waist, and then her chest. When the level of the water had reached her neck she turned with a grin. 'That's it. the stairs have stopped. I'm on level flooring.' Suddenly her grin turned to an expression of alarm. 'Alan – ' She slipped, arms windmilling for balance, and her head vanished beneath the water.

'Ace!' Without thinking, Alan charged down the staircase and dived into the water. As he too vanished beneath the surface his arms and head hit something soft and yielding. Whatever it was lashed out at him with tremendous force. Dazed, he fought for the surface, emerged coughing and spluttering, spitting foul-tasting water from his mouth. He stared around himself frantically. 'Ace! *Ace!*'

Ace's head broke the surface beside him. She too spat water from her mouth.

'Ace, get out of the water! There's something in here with us! I whacked it a good one, but it could come back at any moment.'

'I know, you idiot. It was me.'

'Huh?' Alan stared at her in astonishment, his heart racing.

'Alan,' Ace said patiently, 'the bottom of the tunnel is covered with slime, or mud, or something. I lost my footing, that's all. You dived in like a right hero and swam straight into me.'

Alan blinked, wiped a hand across his face, glad Ace could not see his embarrassment. 'What a cretin.'

Ace touched his cheek. 'You okay? Where did I hit you?'

'Nowhere serious.'

Ace smiled. 'In the head, then.'

Despite himself, Alan began to laugh. 'No monsters ... There were no ... monsters.'

'Only the one masquerading as your brain.' Ace regarded Alan coolly, then leaned forward and planted a light kiss on his cheek. 'But that's in case there had been.'

In the sudden quiet, Alan began to mumble in embarrassment.

'Don't panic; that's a thank you, not an offer.' Ace splashed away into the darkness. 'Come on, hero. Yeuchh,' she added as Alan splashed after her into the tunnel. 'I don't know what you guys wear for aftershave in this world, but it tastes disgusting.'

The Cheddar Gorge was pocked with the smoking remains of fires and littered with bodies. Not all the bodies were dead.

Cradling Tom-o in her arms, Liz stumbled back into the Complex. The corridors and rooms of the cave system were at least half destroyed. A chasm had opened right through the residential quarters; the main passage was impassable; falls of rock and shattered masonry blocked many others. At one junction, she saw a bloodless human hand projecting from the rubble. Moans of pain echoed along the corridors and through the many chambers of the Complex.

Circling the areas of worst damage, Liz came finally to the sickbay. It was a mess. The ceiling had collapsed, blocking one end of the ward completely. Two beds were buried in the pile of rock and earth. At least twenty people lay on hastily rigged pallets on the concrete floor. The wooden partitioning separating the office section had burst apart; orderlies were sweeping aside what wreckage they could. Nurses tended to the prone figures. Even as Liz watched, the head nurse pulled a sheet over the face of one victim. He turned, rose as she stumbled forward. 'Easy, Liz. Let me have the boy now.'

Liz looked around as the nurse took Tom-o from her. 'Where's Sam?'

The nurse cast a quick look back at the pile of rubble. 'At least it was quick.' He turned his attention to the child. 'Liz?'

'Oh? Er yes, I know. Tom-o's dead. I just thought I'd better, you know . . . I thought it was best if . . .'

The nurse nodded. 'I understand. You can leave him with me now.'

'Thank you.' Liz turned away and wandered out of the sickbay.

The nurse called out after her. 'Liz? perhaps you'd better . . .'

Liz didn't hear the rest. She wandered out of the sickbay and through the corridors of the Complex. She could hear the thump of great engines pulse through the rock; the assault team must have recovered the Silurian airship and were steering it back. Soon she would have more work than she could cope with. She thought about making her way to the laboratory, but then reconsidered: the last thing she wanted was a confrontation with the Brigadier, but that was the first place he would go to look for her when he heard those engines. Liz changed her direction, circled back around the residential quarters and from there to the entrance to the Complex. She needed some time alone.

Out in the gorge, the half-track was still buried under the dead pterosaur; Captain Wood was overseeing a small team who were trying to winch the carcass off so they could loot the wreck for spares. The stink of the carcass was appalling. The operation was hampered by a number of small scavenging dinosaurs which frequently left the cover of the surrounding jungle to peck and claw at the corpse.

As Liz walked past, one soldier fired a couple of rounds. A feathered coelophysis fell dead; the other reptiles fought over the fresh corpse before returning their attention to the dead pterosaur.

Wood put his hand on the soldier's arm as the man lifted his gun for a second volley. 'Don't waste your ammunition.'

The soldier holstered his gun. 'You're right,' he said disgustedly. 'Anyway, we ought to let the little buggers eat the damn thing. Save us a load of work.'

Wood laughed. 'No such luck, I'm afraid. Anyway, the quicker we get this thing off, the quicker we can get on with salvaging the half-track and the gun, okay?'

The soldier nodded.

'Right then, let's get on with it.'

Liz walked on. A short distance away, one of the many cleanup details was moving slowly through the undergrowth, extinguishing fires and dragging bodies out into the open for disposal. They were examining the wreckage of a microlight glider – which had apparently collided with a pterosaur and crashed into a small grove of trees – when one of the soldiers gave a sudden shout. 'Hey! Someone call a medic, I've got a live one!'

Liz hurried over. 'I should hope so,' she heard a woman mutter in a woozy, somewhat irritated voice. 'Only life can hurt this much.'

The soldier helped her clear of the wreckage. As she struggled to her feet, someone else stirred not far away. At once the soldier moved across to the newcomer, leaving Liz to support the woman.

'Now take it easy. What's your name?'

'Bernice Summerfield. Professor Bernice Summerfield.' Bernice shrugged off Liz's touch. 'And I'm fine. No thanks to bloody Icarus there.'

She gestured to where the soldier was helping Billy up. He clambered out of the wreckage and stood, swaying unsteadily, hands clamped to the sides of his head.

Bernice fixed him with a cool, if somewhat unsteady, gaze. 'Headache, huh? Serves you right. Where in hell did you learn to drive that thing, anyway, an aerial demolition derby?'

Billy didn't answer, merely winced and looked around, as if for the source of a loud, piercing sound. Unused to being ignored, Bernice took an angry step towards him, slipped and sat down unexpectedly in the messy remains of the dead pterosaur.

'Oh great,' she said disgustedly.

She was about to continue when the pulsing sound of engines echoing along the gorge suddenly faded, and a vast shadow slipped quietly across them. Bernice looked up at the leviathan hanging above them and sighed. 'Didn't I just leave that party?'

Liz's eyes narrowed, all tiredness suddenly forgotten. She looked first at Bernice, then across to Billy, the crashed microlight and the dead pterosaur, constructing a worrying scenario in her mind.

'Did you come out of the airship?' she asked.

Bernice winked. 'Got it in one, toots. D'you wanna see my passport?'

Beyond the gondola's observation gallery the day was clear and bright with a swollen sun glowing pinkly through effervescent clouds. Above him, the Doctor sensed the bulk of the airship, glinting pale bronze in the sunlight. Beside him, clawed fingers grasping the handrail and muscular legs braced apart for balance, was Chtorba. Chtaachtl was in the airship's control room, navigating a course south across Europe on the first leg of the journey towards Africa.

The Doctor placed his hand beside Chtorba's on the

rail. The skin of his wrist was bruised in a pattern which precisely matched the spread of fingers on the reptile's hand. The Doctor looked sideways at Chtorba. 'I would have fallen. Why did you save me?'

Chtorba hissed gently, and his lips twitched in what might have been a smile. 'Now it is my turn to be enigmatic.'

'There's more to you than meets the eye, Chtorba.' When the Silurian made no reply, the Doctor tapped thoughtfully on the rail with his umbrella, then hung it on the rail. 'You don't really mean that, do you?'

'Let us just say, one good turn deserves another.'

The Doctor shrugged. 'A human saying.'

'Studying humans is part of my work.'

'Indeed? And what have your studies shown you?'

'That very seldom is there "more to a human than meets the eye".'

The Doctor looked back out of the window. 'You know, it's astounding how much the world has changed in so short a time.'

'Indeed?'

'Why certainly. Herds of diplodocus and brontosaurus hunted by carnivores across France. Woolly mammoth ambling through the dwindling snows of the Pennines, inevitably doomed to a second extinction. Ichthyosaurs and plesiosaurs gliding through the Mediterranean Sea like soft-edged cloudshadows on the water. Pterosaurs filling the sky with harsh, whining calls, their leathery bodies silhouetted in the light of a hotter sun.' The Doctor paused for breath.

Chtorba used the hesitation to interject, 'One of the first things our anthropologists found when they began to study human culture was a monumental body of work known collectively, I believe, as *literature*. Your impression of our world was very . . . evocative.'

'But don't give up the day job, right?' The Doctor grinned. 'Tell me, Chtorba, as a teacher, what is the Silurian equivalent of human literature?'

'I am surprised you think there should be one.' Chtorba considered. He dilated the window without touching it, allowing a fresh breeze to ripple into the gondola. 'Humans have paper and tools for marking it; we have our minds. The direct communication of ideas, unpolluted by the mediums of transmission, is more accurate, more stimulating and more . . . I think you would use the word *attractive*.'

'I see.'

Chtorba thought silently for a moment. 'I believe you are trying to postulate a common ground between ourselves and the humans.'

The Doctor nodded modestly. He was about to speak when a small flying reptile suddenly glided in through the open window, alighting on the handrail between them.

Chtorba placed his hand palm-up on the rail. The rhamphorhynchus studied it with beady eyes, then hopped a little closer.

'Such theories of common ground between reptiles and mammals have been proposed before. Personally, I do not believe any such common ground exists.'

'Really?' The Doctor extended his hand and made a soft *chck chck chck* sound between his teeth. The rhamphorhynchus edged sideways across the rail and nuzzled its long bony beak into the Doctor's palm.

Chtorba looked on in frank amazement.

The Doctor winked as the reptile hopped easily onto his forearm. 'Perhaps there's more to us mammals than meets the eye after all, hmm?'

Ace and Alan were moving cautiously through the remains of Perivale. Pushing through a growth of palms which would have been at home in the Bahamas on her own world, Ace led the way into the street where Manisha's family had lived.

They were both silent until they reach Manisha's house. At the threshold of the garden Ace hesitated. The gate had rotted. There was a giant patch of elephant grass which, as kids, she and Manisha used to play in. The patch was now sixty feet high and extended halfway down the street.

Alan reached out to touch Ace comfortingly on the

shoulder, saw the expression on her face, hesitated, then drew back his hand. Ace turned and gave him a small smile.

'Fourteen,' she said softly.

'House number?'

Ace shook her head. 'That's how old she was when they firebombed her house.'

'Jesus.'

Ace began to walk slowly up the overgrown pathway. 'She didn't die at once. I saw her when they brought her out. She looked at me, Alan.' Ace shuddered. 'She couldn't even scream.' She took a deep breath, continued, 'I was never part of the solution, you see. So in a way you could say it was my fault.'

Alan said softly. 'What, because you're white? Because you weren't there to stop it? Ace, you know it doesn't work like that. You can't be responsible for every maniac in the world.'

'Yes but if I was, Alan, if everybody was ...' Ace shrugged, wiped her hand across her face, surprised when her hand came away wet. 'You're right, of course, it's not my fault. I've been telling myself that for years. Unfortunately, I've never been the easiest person in the world to convince that I'm wrong.' She paused. 'Manisha died in casualty. There were respiratory complications. She breathed in flame.' Ace licked her lips. 'She couldn't even scream.'

The doorway was blocked by a palm which shared a trunk with a mutated orange tree. The mutant tree wound up the side of the house, sending fruit-laden branches to explore every crack and window.

Ace looked up at the tree and hesitated.

'Are you sure you want to do this?' Alan asked with some concern.

'Yeah, I'm sure. And no, I don't want to do it.' Ace straightened her shoulders. 'Come on.'

She forced her way past the tree and reached out to open the porch door, which folded away like wet cardboard at her touch. The front door of the house was revealed, soiled, mouldy, with cracked glass falling from warped panels. The name plate Manisha had carved for the door in art class was missing. Of course, Ace thought, in this world the Nightmare would have happened before Manisha ever had a chance to go to school.

There were no burn marks on any part of the porch, or the door.

Ace reached out to touch the door, placed her hand flat against the sill beside the lock and pushed. The wood splintered easily, puffing into dust. The door swung open.

Beyond the doorway, the house was in darkness. And there was a musty smell. Damp, and decay.

Ace led the way cautiously into the house. The floorboards were gone. Only dust was left of the interior passageways. Most of the joists were still in place, but they looked very fragile. Ace stepped carefully between them, on the concrete foundatios of the house, moving through the ground floor from room to room.

The house was all but finished; Ace thought it was probably only the tree growing up its front wall which kept it from collapsing altogether. Weeds choked the water taps and sink drains. Piles of scabby fabric marked the tombs of furniture and curtains. Interior panelling was like balsawood. A patch of scorched, peeling wallpaper related the demise of the living-room television.

There was a skeleton huddled in a pile of fabric in front of the charcoal-filled hearth in the living room. There were teeth marks on the thigh bone, and the left shin and arm of the skeleton were shattered. Ace shuddered. Was this Manisha's mother? Her father? Her sister Kosi? Ace blocked the thought that it might actually be Manisha from her mind altogether. Fate couldn't be that cruel.

Sensing her thoughts, Alan tried to guide Ace away from the body. Shaking off his hand, she turned away. 'Nobody gets away with it.' She crossed the room to where a mirror hung above the fireplace and stared at her reflection. A face filled with guilt stared back at her. And something else. Scrawled on the mirror in dust-furred lipstick was a message.

'Alan!' With mounting excitement, Ace carefully blew

dust away from the glass, until she could read the message there.

' "Kosi. I've gone to the City Farm." ' Ace turned to Alan, 'There's a date. And a signature – Manisha.' Ace suddenly threw back her head and gave a yell of pure delight. 'She's alive!'

Jan swung herself down from her horse and stared around with horror. She and Rod had arrived at the gorge some twenty minutes earlier. They'd been met by a military force and escorted to the entrance to the Complex. This had not been unexpected. What was unexpected – and horrifying – was the carnage they had passed on the way. Dead bodies. Smashed equipment. Dead Silurians. Scavenging dinosaurs tearing at the corpses. The stench of charred flesh and cordite.

The aftermath of battle.

Speechless, she and Rod had begun to unload the medical equipment as soon as they reached the main entrance to the Complex. As they worked, the Brigadier walked stiffly out to meet them. His uniform was straight but still covered in a slurry of mud, blood and excrement. His face was expressionless; there was no word of welcome on his lips.

'Orderlies will take the supplies to sickbay. I want you to go there immediately and take charge. There are heavy casualties.'

'Casualties? Take charge? What happened here? Where's Sam?'

'I'm afraid he's dead.'

'Dead? But – '

'There's no time for explanations. Lives depend on you.'

Jan rounded on the Brigadier with an angry glare. 'Brigadier, sometimes you assume too much!'

The Brigadier's expression hardened. 'Where is Sergeant Benton?'

Jan's mouth twisted in disgust. 'How the hell should I know? Or care? He's off on some damn-fool priority mission. Something I expect you'll know more about than either of us.'

186

'I need to know his ETA.'

'And I need to know how Jo is,' Jan said pointedly. 'So if you'll excuse us?'

The Brigadier pursed his lips.

'She *is* still alive?'

The Brigadier was silent.

Jan turned away, her face suffused with hatred and disgust.

'You don't understand.' Was that a hint of desperation in his voice? 'This is war. We must have an edge.'

'So go tell Liz Shaw to build you another Meccano doodad, okay? In the meantime leave me alone. I've got a job to do!'

The Brigadier looked thoughtfully at Jan for a moment, then turned abruptly. Shoving his swagger stick under his arm, he strode back into the Complex.

The City Farm was half an acre of intensely cultivated land sheltered between and partly within the crumbled ruins of high-rise blocks. The entrance was located beneath a brick railway arch; the track formed a curving boundary to the site. The woman guarding the barbed-wire fence across the arch made them empty out their pockets and Ace's satchel, examining the contents and assuring herself that neither Ace nor Alan were looters before opening the gate and waving them through.

When they were inside the fence, the guard stepped up to them and smiled apologetically. Her voice held a pleasant Welsh lilt.

'Sorry about that. Can't be too careful these days. I'm Nan Davis. I'm co-director here.' She smiled at Alan's expression. 'This is a sort of communal workplace. Everyone takes a turn on gate duty.'

Alan took the offered hand. 'Alan Tomson. This is Ace. We're – '

'We're here looking for a friend of mine. Manisha Purkayastha. I think she may have come here.'

Nan smiled. 'Manisha again, eh? She gets all the waifs and strays. Hang on a minute and I'll sort something out.'

Nan was on the point of asking a passing farm worker

to watch the gate when Ace suddenly caught sight of another, almost familiar, figure a hundred or so yards away across some allotments. The woman was dressed in cut-off denims, wellington boots and an old jacket. Her hair was cropped short. She was wiry and muscular.

Without another word, Ace shouldered her satchel and sprinted across the intervening distance. Just before she reached the figure, she slowed. 'Manisha?'

The figure turned. 'I'm afraid you've got the wrong Purkayastha.' She broke off, staring at Ace, first uncertainly, and then fearfully. 'It can't be you,' she said.

'Kosi?' Ace said hesitantly. 'Where's Manisha?'

Kosi pointed dumbly over into a corner formed by the junction of two long sheds, where a young woman dressed in shorts and galoshes was mucking out some pigs. Grinning hugely, Ace stumbled in the direction of Kosi's pointing finger.

The woman didn't notice her arrival. Once more Ace hesitated, suddenly scared. She watched the play of muscles in the woman's arms as she worked. Her hair was piled up and pinned. She wasn't as thin as Ace remembered. She was stronger, her movements more confident. She wasn't a teenager anymore; she seemed older than Ace herself. Ace tried to work out in her head if she really was older now, figuring her own relative time spent with the Doctor against normal time on Earth. Her mind, normally sharp and incisive, became filled with a whirling jamboree of numbers.

The woman became aware someone was watching her. She put down her bucket and mop, turned and caught sight of Ace. Her initial blank look was slowly replaced by an expression of shock, even fear. She tried to speak, but at first all she could manage was a sort of strangled gurgle.

Ace held out a trembling hand. For a moment she saw a Manisha whose skin was split and charred, whose hair was gone; a fourteen-year-old girl who glared accusingly at Ace through agonized tears. Then she was simply normal again, though the tears remained.

Ace reached out to hug Manisha. The other woman drew back suspiciously. Ace immediately froze.

They stood there like that for what seemed to Ace like an age, each staring at the other, neither one willing to make the first move.

Benton gritted his teeth and tightened a makeshift tourniquet around his right arm. Beside him, a deinonychus coughed blood before falling to lie still, a length of narrow drainpipe shoved through its chest. Placing his boot on the animal's carcass, Benton pulled loose the pipe, then used it to force open the mesh on a nearby sporting goods shop. He took a couple of guns and some ammunition from an interior display.

The sun was sinking over the ruins of Whitehall as he left the shop. The heat was sweltering. Insects buzzed around the wounds on his arm and face. Wearily, he slapped them away.

Shooting away the lock on another window mesh, Benton looted a nearby off-licence, grabbed a bottle of brandy, poured a liberal dose of alcohol over his wounds, ripped up his other shirt sleeve and bandaged those he could reach. The pain as the alcohol hit the wounds was excruciating; it shocked him back into full wakefulness. He sucked in a shuddering breath, lifted the bottle to his lips, hesitated, then lowered it slowly without drinking.

Recorking the bottle for medicinal use, he slipped it into his backpack. As he did this, his hand touched the portion of the damaged book he'd found, exactly where the Brigadier had said it would be, in the battered briefcase in the stairwell in Whitehall. He took the book out and looked at it. A5 sized. Twenty dog-eared pages. Damp, rotting, the columns of figures only just legible.

Thrusting the book into his pack, Benton staggered to the nearest car and tried to get it started. No luck. He tried the next. No luck there, either. He looked around for a horse. Something. Anything.

There was nothing.

He began to walk.

Bernice walked from the shadow of the Silurian airship, now moored halfway up the gorge. She found Billy Wilson at one end of a long line of dead bodies laid out for disposal, raking the gory remains of the previous night's violence into ditches and burying them. All along the gorge other clean-up details were doing the same thing.

The corral was a mass of churned mud, blood, pieces of animal flesh and shattered lumps of wooden fence. Small scavenging dinosaurs lurked at the periphery of the corral, as they did all along the gorge, waiting for the chance to dart forward and steal a mouthful of carrion. The surviving horses had been put out to pasture; Bernice wondered if their natural ability to select healthy fodder might not eventually give them the edge over their human masters in evolutionary terms.

Bernice scowled. Jan had treated her for her wounds, but she had hell's own headache. She'd wandered around the Complex, helping where she could, before being collared by an army Captain, who'd promptly stuck her on clean-up duty. Now, a couple of hours later, Bernice was beginning to regret her impulse to help. Already the carcasses were beginning to stink. Other people helping out wore masks to block some of the smell, and she wondered how Billy managed without.

'Hey it's Mister Suicide. How are you doing, Billy? Caused any good accidents lately?'

There was no response. Another worker caught Bernice's eye and tapped her ear. Catching on, Bernice touched Billy on the shoulder. He turned, startled.

Bernice smiled. 'How are you?'

'You'll have to speak up.' His Glaswegian accent was as thick as the smell in which he worked, and he spoke far too loudly for the quiet of the morning. 'It's the voices, you know?'

'Voices?'

'Did they no tell you I hear voices?'

'Someone may have said something.'

'You what?'

'I said, "Someone may have said something"!'

'Oh aye.' Billy leaned on his rake. 'So what do you want then?'

Bernice sighed. 'Are you alright? From last night?'

'Oh, yeah.'

'You were a bit of a maniac in that microlight, you know.'

Billy suddenly stood up and looked directly into Bernice's eyes. She was startled by the intensity of his gaze. 'You came out of that ship, didn't you? Riding a pterosaur like the damn reps, weren't you?'

'Yes, but –'

'What were you doing on a rep warship? Why were you there? How come you ain't mad, like me? Are you trying to trick us? What's going on?'

Bernice backed away from the sudden blast of anger. Billy stepped closer, the rake held threateningly in front of him. 'Well?'

The woman who'd tapped her ear earlier interposed herself between Bernice and Billy. 'That's enough, Billy! Pull yourself together. You're no use to us like this, you know that.'

Billy shifted his gaze to the newcomer. 'I know, but I'm angry!'

Bernice raised her hands placatingly. 'It's okay. Thanks,' she said to the woman. 'Billy's got a fair point.'

'Your funeral, chum.' The woman shrugged, returning to her work.

Billy turned back to Bernice. 'I get angry a lot, don't I?'

'You have to learn to control it.'

'Yeah well, I can't can I! Sometimes I just . . . just *can't*.'

Bernice felt something stir inside herself, something she hadn't felt for years: the need to support, to teach. 'I know.' She picked up a rake. 'You want to hear about my adventures on the Silurian ship?'

Billy snapped. 'It's not a children's story, okay? Don't patronize me. What are you trying to do, patronize me, or what? Don't *do that.*'

Bernice shook her head. 'I'm sorry.' She hesitated. 'Sometimes it's as hard for us as it is for you.' She leaned on her rake and puffed out her cheeks. 'But that's no excuse. Look, let's say this: you stay calm and I'll cut the crap. How's that sound?'

Billy's face lit up in a sudden, charming and utterly unnerving grin. 'Bet your lunch you can't keep it up.'

Bernice grinned. 'I'll take that bet.'

There were about fifty people who worked on the City Farm. Most had repaired or converted rooms within the surrounding tower blocks to live in. Alan and Ace were introduced to a handful when Nan invited them, Manisha and Kosi to dine that evening; most notably her husband, Geoffrey, a tall fellow with glasses and a constant, faint grin.

The meal took place in a room that was a bizarre mixture of old and new. The Davis's had taken one of the more structurally sound bungalows nearby, cleared it of vegetation and filled it with furniture from the original farmhouse. Dinner consisted of a simple meat stew, dumplings and vegetables, served from a great black cauldron onto a vast acreage of table. The dinner service was bone china. Alan wondered how they'd managed to keep it intact for so long.

'The food'll not be fussy, mind,' said Nan modestly, as they sat down to eat.

Geoff grinned. 'You can bet if my Nan's got anything to do with it the protein count will be nominal, there'll be the right amount of vitamins and the nutritional value will be bang on.'

'Geoff! Honestly, one Nobel Prize and you think you know it all.'

Geoff tucked into his stew with gusto. 'I know this much, love, it tastes delicious! So tell me,' he continued, mumbling through a second huge mouthful of food, 'how do you come to know our Manisha?'

Alan noticed Ace glance at the other woman. 'Well, we were best friends for a while . . .' She tailed off, sounding a bit nervous. That wasn't much like her, Alan thought, and smiled. It made a nice change.

'Now don't be so nosy,' admonished Nan severely. 'I

reckon Ace and Manisha will have a few years' worth of catching up to do yet.'

Geoff shrugged, jamming another forkful of stew into his mouth.

Alan said, 'You've got an efficient system here. It must be a good place to live.'

Nan laughed. 'Bless you, lad, but the Farm's more than just a farm. Oh, we managed to get certain animals with natural immunity to breed true for food stock, and our fields seldom lie fallow. But there's more here than that.'

Geoff added, 'After dinner I'll show you around the labs.' Alan was amazed. 'Labs?'

'In addition to making the finest stew this side of Cardiff, Nan is the most creative biochemist I've ever worked with.' He grinned. 'Sharp as a new pin and twice as pretty, that's my Nan.'

Alan nodded agreeably.

Ace glanced curiously at Manisha, but it was Kosi who answered her unspoken question. 'Part of our work here is to understand the disease and its effects on mammalian life.'

Manisha said, 'It's important work, but difficult for a number of reasons, not the least of which is that word is spreading to the looters and lowlifes that here's a ready-made source of food.' After a quick look at Ace, she added, 'I wonder if you'd all excuse us?'

Nan nodded quickly. After the women had left the room, there was a short silence. 'Hence the low profile and guards, I suppose?' said Alan at length. 'Because of the looters and lowlifes, I mean.'

Nan placed her cutlery by her plate and eased herself back in her chair. 'Most of the animals are young. The older ones seem to die off quite suddenly. Nobody knows why. And in plants the production and use of ATP in the photosynthetic process is becoming more unusual every year, with the result that certain fruit trees glow in the dark, from the excess unutilized phosphor in the plant.'

Geoff said softly, 'We're rather afraid the whole ecology of the Earth may well become totally unviable in the not too distant future.'

'It's a terrifying thought. We use the Farm to study the problem as best we can, but research and experimentation are no easy things to do when you're trying to stay hidden from the Silurians.'

'Have you thought about a military liaison?' Alan pushed his plate away with a smile of thanks. 'Protection for yourselves would be better, and I'm sure the Brigadier would be open to any ideas you might have about improving humanity's chances of survival.'

Geoff's response was immediate: 'We get by here, Alan. A military presence would only bring us to the attention of the Silurians. Besides – ' He broke off at a glance from Nan. 'Well, it's just not our way, d'you see?'

Seeing that Alan was about to argue in favour of common sense, Nan said, 'Thank you, Alan. It's a kind offer. We'll think on it. In the meantime, who's going to do the washing up?'

As Manisha led the way from the bungalow, the sounds of evening were beginning. High above, a rhamphorhynchus banked, screamed and dived for prey. The sun was slipping down in the sky, and the largest of the tower blocks cast a jagged shadow across the allotments, small fields and animal pens. Several hundred yards away a bank of earth shored with timbers rose to enclose the eastern part of the Farm in a curved wall. Ace could just make out the red glint of rusty metal on top.

'The tracks,' Manisha said. 'Remember how we used to pretend the trains were still running, Dorothy?'

Ace shifted uncomfortably at the use of her old name.

'Mum told me I went on a train once, when I was about two, but I don't remember.' She laughed. 'So we used to pretend. The stupid things you do when you're a kid, huh?'

Ace hesitated. 'So, look, Manisha. What do you do here? Geoff mentioned laboratories.' She smiled. 'I bet you're a botanist. Or a biologist, you always did like that at school. Yes . . .' She nodded confirmation of her own flight of fancy. 'My old friend, a biologist, helping to rebuild civilization.'

194

'Nothing so romantic, I'm afraid.' Manisha shrugged. 'The truth is, that sort of work is more in Kosi's line. She was gifted with all the brains in our family, I reckon.'

'But what about you, then? What do you do here?'

'Oh, you know. Some driving. A little of this and that. Muck out the pigs, sow the seeds, check the pollen count and the average rainfall. We have a Stevenson screen here, from before the Nightmare.' She hesitated. 'The work's not creative but it has its own rewards.'

Ace was silent.

'Why don't I show you?' Without waiting for a reply, Manisha led the way towards the highest of the tower blocks, entered a concrete stairwell and began to climb. Ace followed. At the very top of the staircase a metal door opened onto the roof of the block. Part of it had been cleared to provide room for a few basic meteorological experiments. A cold wind whipped her hair into her face, disturbing the vegetation woven into camouflage nets above their heads.

Manisha led the way to the edge of the building. Beyond was a view of London Ace would rather not have seen. Jungle. Shattered buildings. Empty windows. Burned cars. The view faded as the last edge of the setting sun thinned and vanished beyond the horizon.

Manisha said, 'That's what we're fighting against, each of us in our own way.' She reached out to touch Ace's shoulder, but she pulled away, still silent. Manisha looked at her with some concern. 'I know it's been a long time for us. But don't be guilty of putting me on a pedestal. I'm no-one special.'

Ace turned away. 'No,' she said. 'Of course you're not.'

As the airship drew nearer the equator, the Doctor was astounded by the amount of activity. Airships of all sizes appeared more frequently, their bronze lifting bodies and crystal gondolas flashing in the sunlight. Every so often great beams of light, like searchlights, swept through the clouds, and where that happened there were vast atmospheric upheavals which were quickly controlled and modulated.

The Doctor remarked on this activity to Chtorba.

'There has been much research in the area of meteorology over the years,' Chtorba explained. 'Sufficient to enable the establishing and control of windows in the atmospheric blanket.'

The Doctor grabbed hold of the information and leaped ahead with it. 'Manipulation of air density enables the focusing of sunlight through the windows. In this way the greenhouse effect can be selectively enhanced in order to change the climate where it's not suited to reptile life. I see ...' The Doctor stopped speaking, aware that Chtorba was studying him closely.

'You seem well informed about our culture,' said Chtorba.

The Doctor smiled modestly. 'I had a ... good general education.'

Chtorba's third eye glimmered humorously. 'I think you have an unparalleled education.'

'How do you control the resultant weather upheavals?' the Doctor asked curiously. 'Ah, of course, the gravitron installation on the moon.'

Chtorba refused to be deflected. The glimmer in his third eye strengthened and the Doctor felt the faint stirrings of an alien presence in his mind. 'I don't suppose now would be a good time to mention the *invasion of privacy* rule?'

'That is a human rule, Doctor.' Chtorba withdrew his presence from the Doctor's mind. 'I now believe you are anything but human.'

The Doctor raised his hands. 'Okay, guv'nor, it's a fair cop,' he said in an atrocious cockney accent. Assuming his own, softer voice, he added, 'The vital question is, does it change anything?'

Whatever reply Chtorba would have made was interrupted as he received a linked message from Chtaachtl in the control room. His third eye glowed briefly, and he said, 'The airship is nearing Kilimanjaro. Our capital city is located beyond, on the shores of Tethys.'

'Tethys?'

'You would know it as the Indian Ocean.'

'I see. You change many things to suit yourselves, don't you?'

'That is the nature of intelligent species.'

'I see. Your leader liked a room with a sea view, and so he's terraforming the Sahara Desert.'

'The desert is being turned back into rainforest. We are merely repairing the damage which occured during our long hibernation.'

The Doctor looked out of the airship, down at the ground. 'And the lakes? Victoria and Tanganyika? They're being enlarged, aren't they? Connected? Your Leader likes to swim?'

Ignoring the Doctor's sarcasm, Chtorba said. 'The lakes are to become inland fisheries. More of our people are being revived all the time from shelters all over the world. Would you have them starve?'

The Doctor frowned. 'No, Chtorba, of course not. I'm sorry.' He hesitated, then continued, 'You know, I am sure there's some part of me that abhors change. I don't know,' he mused, 'perhaps it's because change in my species is so traumatic.'

Chtorba studied the Doctor with renewed interest. 'Tell me about yourself, Doctor.'

The Doctor smiled inwardly. If anything was going to win over Chtorba to his way of thinking it would be gentle, subtle persuasion.

And if all else failed, there was always Ace.

Ace said, 'There's something I have to know. You said I was dead . . .'

'Yeah.' Manisha felt the intensity of Ace's gaze on her.

'Well,' Ace said, 'what are you waiting for? Tell me!'

Manisha looked out over the spectral remains of London, the darkness upon darkness of shattered buildings, empty windows, wasted lives. She squared her shoulders.

'You were seventeen . . .' she began.

Ace listened and the night crept slowly on. The moon

rose. At some point during the catalogue of horrors Manisha listed for her, Ace was aware of walking to the very edge of the rooftop and settling herself down with her legs dangling over the edge. Eighteen floors below a line of crumbling garages beckoned; Ace ignored them. The night air blew alternately cool and warm around her, ruffling her clothes and brushing her face with eerie night sounds carried for miles across the city. As Manisha described her death, Ace stared up past the camouflage nets to the sky. Through a break in the clouds, she could see the stars forming the sword of Orion. She smiled at the appropriateness of the constellation. For a moment she tried to pretend none of what was happening to her here was real. That her world was the real one. Then she thought how Manisha might feel about that. For her this world was the real one and Ace's the fantasy.

Ace abruptly shook her head. In fact both worlds were real, or at least had the potential to be real. And she was living in this one now. And in this world she had things to do.

' – not listening, are you?'

'Huh?'

'I said: "You're not listening, are you?" '

Ace jumped up to her feet, ran along the edge of the building and dropped lightly back onto the roof. 'I am sorry, Manisha. Tell you what, can we continue with this tomorrow?'

Manisha shrugged. 'Sure,' she said coolly.

'It's just that I've got a lot on my mind.'

'I can see that.'

Ace smiled. 'Thanks.' Impulsively she reached out to hug Manisha. 'It's really good to see you again.'

'Yeah,' Manisha said, but her voice lacked conviction.

The largest cave to remain intact within the Complex was the play area assigned to the school. More than a hundred people were gathered in the cave. Most stood, though some had found seating on the activity frames the younger children normally played on. Some packing crates had been placed at one end of the cave to form an impromptu stage. Standing on the crates were the Brigadier, Captain Wood and a priest. The Brigadier was reading the last rites for those killed in the previous night's violence.

From her place near the middle of the gathering, Liz Shaw listened carefully to his words. They were clipped, his sentences short, but there was a kind of poetry there, if you listened for it. The eulogy washed over her, but it brought no comfort; the image of little Tom-o's blood-soaked face was imprinted on her mind, too recent to be ameliorated by mere words.

And then the Brigadier's speech was interrupted.

'*Lethbridge-Stewart, you're a bloody hypocrite!*'

The Brigadier fell silent as the words rang out. A wave of surprise passed from person to person. Gradually a gap opened in the crowd around the speaker. Liz peered into the gap and saw Jan Martin, red-faced with anger, staring towards the makeshift stage.

Oddly, it was the priest who recovered first from his surprise. 'Doctor – Miss Martin – if I might just be permitted to interject – '

'Oh shut up, you self-effacing idiot! I repeat, Brigadier: how can you stand up there and talk about those who gave their lives so bloody nobly and so heroically when *you yourself are a murderer!*'

'Doctor, I'm afraid – '

'So you damn well ought to be! I was afraid too, every minute I was in London, risking my life to save a woman you killed.'

'I was about to say that now is neither the time nor place for this discussion. If you would care to join me afterwards – '

'Join you? To be perfectly frank I'd rather sleep with a snake.'

Liz noticed that one or two soldiers were unobtrusively forcing their way through the crowd towards Jan. One tried to ease her aside. Liz held her ground. 'What are you doing?' she said in a loud voice.

At her words, Jan turned and saw what was happening.

'Can't you bear the truth, Brigadier?' she said quickly, turning her back on the soldiers.

On the stage, the Brigadier appeared to be in pain. He lifted one hand to the side of his head. 'I'm afraid –' He paused. 'Afraid . . .'

Liz watched as Jan forced her way to the front of the stage. 'What's the matter, Brigadier? Don't you think the end justifies the means any more? Don't you think the sacrifice of Jo Grant was a necessary one, in this time of war?'

The Brigadier blinked. 'It was a matter of life and death . . .'

'Oh, you bet it was. My life, my death, if I didn't help Sergeant Benton in his new mission objective. Your mission objective. Brigadier, if he'd had a gun I am quite sure he would have used it on me had I not obeyed. And for what? Well, I don't know actually, because he wouldn't tell me. Wouldn't tell me why I was supposed to delay bringing medical aid to a dying woman. I wonder if he even really knew himself? Does anyone here, Brigadier?' Jan glanced quickly at the crowd, which was silent and still. Even the soldiers had stopped moving. 'Don't you think we have a right to know that you are willing to make a value judgement balancing the lives of any one of us against a predetermined greater good?'

Liz moved a little closer to the stage. The Brigadier was gathering himself for a reply. She had never seen him looking so vulnerable.

Before the Brigadier could continue, Jan spoke again. 'Cohlberg's theory of moral development tells us there are six levels of morality, Brigadier. Most of these levels proceed from the assumption that any actions one makes benefit individuals or subgroups of society. But the sixth level is different. To attain it, one must perceive in oneself the ability to look beyond the moment, beyond observable actions, beyond even one's own death. To attain the sixth level of morality it is necessary to believe that you are acting for the good of the entire species, and that your actions will bring benefit beyond any actual observations you yourself are capable of making.' Jan paused. 'Adolf Hitler was such a man, Brigadier. I believe you are another.'

The Brigadier straightened, and Liz saw in him for the first time the tired man that he really was. 'It is true,' he said, 'that I have received orders I believe essential to the survival of humanity. It is also true that I administered a drug to Jo Grant, which may have brought about her death, in pursuit of those orders.'

A soft sigh of surprise and fear swept around the cave.

'And I am sorry to have to say that I am still acting under those orders and will continue to do so until the moment of my own death. And that, regretfully, I am bound not to reveal what they are.'

Jan said quietly, 'You look scared, Brigadier. Do your hands shake? Do you forget things more than you used to?'

To Liz's astonishment, a look of absolute fear suddenly crossed the Brigadier's face.

'I see you do.' She raised her voice. 'In my capacity as Medical Supervisor of this Complex I no longer judge you to be medically or ethically fit to command. I also – '

Jan broke off as there was a sudden commotion at the rear of the cave. All heads turned as Sergeant Benton staggered in, bloody and exhausted, one arm in a sling, his uniform slashed and covered with charcoal and mud. He struggled to the stage and clambered stiffly onto it, refusing all offers of help. With a glance at Jan he staggered up to the Brigadier and pressed a small package into his hands.

'Mission . . . accomplished . . . sir.'

He tried to salute but his arm wouldn't work. His eyes closed suddenly. Jan was forced to catch him as he fell, lowering him gently to the stage. When she looked up there was a new light glowing in the Brigadier's eyes. A feverish light; that of an obsession fulfilled.

'Tell me, doctor,' he said, his voice strengthening with every word. 'Can you provide medical evidence to substantiate your claim?'

Jan stood, uncertainly. 'I am the medical authority here. My opinion is evidence. Tests can be performed later to determine the extent of your disability.'

'I see.' The Brigadier's voice has reached its normal

level and exceeded it, booming out into the cave and rolling like thunder. 'And so you are determined to remove me from command òn the grounds of mental disability, when I, for my part, have just secured the one, absolutely definite way in which we can rid ourselves and our planet of the Silurian menace?' He smiled. 'I'll take your tests, doctor. And I'll pass them. And then we'll see what we'll see.'

Incredibly, he smiled. 'You see,' he boomed genially, 'you'll just have to trust me on this one.'

Liz felt a sudden creeping feeling inch slowly up her spine. She turned away, uncertain how to interpret the feeling. As she did, she caught sight of Bernice Summerfield standing next to Billy Wilson at the back of the crowd. She was staring intently at the stage, observing the Brigadier closely, as if she were trying to absorb every bit of information about him that she could.

Ace turned at the sound of soft footsteps behind her on the roof. 'Manisha?'

'Afraid not.'

'Alan.'

'Hi'

Ace nodded. She looked back over the necropolis.

Alan moved closer. But not too close, she noticed.

'Manisha's not quite what you expected, is she?' he asked softly.

Ace turned, trying to put her confusion of feelings into words. 'I just ... waited. So long. And now ...'

'She's not the girl you remember?'

'No. She's not. But that shouldn't annoy me, should it?'

'Not unless she's a raging loony or just killed your pet poodle.'

Ace thought hard. 'Do you think we would have grown apart if Manisha hadn't died?'

Alan smiled. 'What makes you so sure you've grown apart?'

'It's obvious! I mean: her life, her work, the whole thing is – '

'Just take a little time, Ace. Get to know her again

before making any snap judgements. You may find you have grown apart. Then again, you may be surprised.'

Ace moved closer to Alan.

'Then again,' he said very softly, 'I may be surprised.'

'I don't follow.'

'Little change of subject there.'

'Ah.'

Alan remained quiet. Ace leaned closer. Then, very deliberately, placed both arms around Alan's neck and kissed him.

After a couple of minutes she stepped away.

Alan straightened his clothing self-consciously. 'I'm blushing like a schoolboy.'

'Daft sod.' Ace kicked absently at the low wall running around the roof. 'You want to know something?'

'What's that?'

'I closed my eyes. It's the first time I ever did that.'

Alan touched her cheek, very gently. 'That's to do with trust.'

'Yes, I know.' Ace also spoke softly. 'It's not something I've been too good at in the past.'

'Is that so?'

'Yeah.' Ace turned into the circle of his arms. 'So, you want to practise?' She looked expectantly at him.

Alan held her gaze for a moment before looking away; just a small flickering of eyes in the darkness but enough for her. 'Ace, it's not that I don't like you or anything, it's just . . .' He sighed. 'And it was nice, it's just that – well, it's lots of reasons really. I had a kid, you know; not so long ago as a matter of fact. She was about your age when she was killed. That sort of complicates things.'

'And there's Julia.'

'Yeah. There's Julia. I don't even know if she's alive or not.'

'I'm sorry, but you never said.'

'Yes, well, I never really had the opportunity, did I?'

'I suppose not.' Ace sighed. 'Benny wouldn't have missed that one. She's good at the old body-language game.'

'Benny? Who's that?'

'Someone I wish I'd got on better with. Hey, listen. We can still be friends, can't we?' She stuck out her hand; this time Alan took it.

They turned away from the dark city and went inside.

After breakfast next morning, Ace stared dubiously at the Range Rover standing in the farmyard and wondered if she might not have made a mistake in asking the Davises for help after all.

Converted to run on methane generated from a bin full of fertilizer in the luggage compartment, the Rover looked as if it had leaped straight from the drawing board of some insane film maker with an obsession with disaster movies. A bulldozer blade was welded to the front, while a swing winch and lifting tackle were clamped to the back. The sub-frame and chassis had been strengthened and weighted by having lengths of steel rail welded to them. More rails curved up the sides and across the roof of the vehicle, forming a protective cage. The wheel arches had been ripped out to allow four large tractor wheels to be fitted, each of which stuck out a good twelve inches from the body. Four spare wheels and tyres were bolted to the cage, two to each side. There were no doors. Ace was surprised to see seats. A pair of furry dice hung from the steel rail above the windscreen.

'We call it Ivor the Engine.' Geoff Davis thumped the bonnet proudly. 'And don't you dare laugh. We had it up to fifteen MPH yesterday, slipstreaming a cyclist.'

'You mean *I* had it up to fifteen MPH,' said Manisha. 'Everyone knows you can't drive, Geoff. There's no need to be embarrassed.'

Ace nodded. 'I'm sure we can rely on . . . Ivor.'

'It'll get you where you want to go alright.' Manisha tipped a final bucket of fertilizer into the fuel tank and clamped the lid shut. 'All we need to know now is where that is.'

Ace pulled a map from her satchel and unfolded it. 'Here,' she said, tapping a place on the map. 'UNIT HQ. London. The Doctor wanted me to get something from there for him.'

Geoff looked up from where he was checking the tyre pressure on the nearside front tyre. 'What's that then?'

'Something he thinks will help achieve peace between us and the Silurians.'

'No way,' Manisha placed the fuel bucket neatly to one side and walked around the Rover to where Ace and Alan were standing. 'Humans and Silurians will never work together.'

Ace stared narrowly at the other woman. 'So what do you want to do then, bomb them?'

Manisha looked faintly hurt. 'There's no need to be so angry, Ace. A lot of people think the same way as I do.'

'I'm sure they do,' Ace looked away.

Sensing an argument brewing between the two women, Alan asked, 'What do we do with this bit of gear when we've got it then? Take it back to the Doctor?'

Ace popped the bonnet on the Rover and buried her head in the engine compartment. 'We're taking it to the Research Centre at Wenley Moor. That's where this all started.' She closed the bonnet, favouring Manisha with a chilly glance. 'And if I have my way that's where it's going to end, as well.'

Re-entering the observation gallery after several hours rest, Chtorba noticed the Doctor was still staring out of the open window. Apparently he hadn't slept at all during the long flight across Africa. Now, as the airship began its approach to the Capital, the mammal seemed even more animated than usual, running from one side of the gallery to the other, peering out of the windows, oohing and aahing with a combination of curiosity and delight.

The heat was sweltering by now. The temperature was up several degrees and a patchy mist obscured the ground. Harsh sunlight reflected back from the mist.

Watching curiously, Chtorba saw the Doctor inhale, testing the air flowing in through the windows. Chtorba also inhaled, relishing the additional moisture in the air. Not quite as hot or damp as he remembered from the time before his long hiberation, but so much better than England.

Chtorba was pleased the Doctor seemed impressed with this evidence of his people's ability to alter their environment.

'We must be close to the Capital,' the Doctor said at length.

As if to emphasize his words, the snowy ramparts of Kilimanjaro became suddenly visible, rising through the mist and glittering in the clear air above the heat haze. A number of bronze ovals, tiny with distance, drifted across the lower slopes: food gatherers, harvesting the scattered herds of elephant and mammoth.

'You know, Chtorba, I'd like to thank you,' said the Doctor. 'This trip has been absolutely fascinating. I bet even Jules Verne couldn't have imagined a voyage so chock-full of wonders.'

Chtorba found himself puzzled. 'The average human would find the changes we have made in their world disturbing, even frightening.'

'Well, perhaps they'd have reason to. I have a somewhat different perspective.' He shrugged. 'And a different reason altogether for being here.'

'Ah yes. One strongly associated with my escape, no doubt.'

The Doctor smiled enigmatically. 'You could say that.'

Chtorba found his curiosity about this creature growing. Forgetting the explanations he would soon have to give the Leader regarding the fate of his son, Chtorba began to formulate the questions and procedures he would use to discover more about this mysterious mammal. His contemplation was interrupted when thermals began to rock the airship. They were circling the mountain.

Chtorba peered out of the window as the air drifting in grew suddenly colder. Layer after snowy layer of mountainside peeled away until the view beyond was totally unobstructed. Beyond, the land sloped away through drifting shreds of mist to the Taita hills, shelving beyond them for a hundred miles towards the ocean.

Spanning the entire distance was a bronze and crystal wonderland.

Ophidian.

The Capital of Earth.

UNIT HQ had been part of the War Office in Whitehall. Ironically, Ace found that to get there they had to retrace their journey of the last two days, albeit from a different starting point.

Judicious use of a fertilizer cocktail removed the pile of rubble blocking the entrance to the basement garage; from there it was all stairs to the third floor and the wreckage of the Doctor's laboratory.

Ace was first in through the double doors. She took in the room in a single glance: an eclectic mix of the contemporary, the hopelessly out of date, and the downright strange.

A blackboard was covered with odd diagrams in different coloured chalk; wall maps depicted various regions of the Earth. One was labelled 'Atlantis'. Three benches were crammed full of electronic equipment and glassware. Along the left-hand wall ran a fourth bench containing various brass dishes, scales, a microscope, an orrery made entirely of blue crystal and brass, a television (broken), a sandwich toaster (empty), a bag of sherbert (mouldy), and what looked like several (possibly genuine) Tibetan religious artifacts.

But what Ace most wanted to see was jammed into one corner, cloaked in shadows, paint peeling quietly in the darkness.

The doors clacked behind Ace as the others followed her into the laboratory.

'That's it,' she said, pointing into the shadowy corner.

'A police box?' Alan shook his head. 'Forgetting the obvious questions for a moment, we'll never move it; those things were made of concrete you know. It must weigh half a tonne at least.'

'No,' said Ace smugly, 'the last thing this is made of is concrete.'

'Next thing, you'll be telling me it's papier-mâché.'

'One better than that: it's isomorphically mass-degenerated.'

'Right.' Alan grinned in complete incomprehension.

Geoff moved closer to the police box. 'Isomorphic. "One to one correspondence between elements of two or more sets." It's a mathematical term.'

'Yep.' Ace nodded. 'When the Doctor died, the TARDIS underwent an internal shutdown. It'll be light enough for us to carry it.'

'Oh I see,' said Alan. 'You mean it's shrunk.'

'Didn't I just say that?' Ace frowned. 'Sorry. I've obviously been hanging around the Doctor too much lately.'

For the Doctor, the spectacle of Ophidian was no less intense that it had been for Chtorba. An image taken directly from minds of architectural genius, the city had been fashioned and built without the need for either plans or tools. It was a thing of beauty, of cathedral spires and glistening domes. It sang, a triumph of concept unsullied by any medium of communication. But more than that, there was a warmth to it, a welcome apparent even from this distance. Even its placing was interesting, an echo of the human theory that sentient life had first developed on the African plains.

Gazing seaward, the Doctor could see that the section of coast between the rivers Tana and Rungwe had shifted inland. The islands of Pemba and Zanzibar were almost gone, submerged until only a tiny agglomeration of barren, rocky islets remained. Closer, beneath the mist, he could make out the swirling shapes of new forests emerging from vast dunes of soil, their growth accelerated almost beyond reckoning. Dark, lumbering shapes moved amongst the trees, while the smaller, faster shapes of predators circled the herds.

The city itself was huge, stretching right across the Taita Hills towards the coast, covering nearly a hundred miles to the east and twice that distance north towards where Mombasa had been before the sea level rose. Airships hovered above it in their hundreds, legacy of the huge technological centres the Silurians had buried deep in the

208

crust of the Earth. Parks and gardens abounded, multilevel, ramped, helical; the Doctor was reminded of designs he'd first seen in Alexandria, nearly two thousand years before.

The similarities to human design were almost as fascinating as the differences.

Pointing with his umbrella, the Doctor drew Chtorba's attention to an irregularity in the city. One which grew as they approached, from a point to a dome to a towering construct both audacious and breathtaking in its design. Parks surrounded the structure, together with ornamental pools, the whole forming a gigantic wheel with the main building positioned at the central hub.

'The Royal Palace,' said Chtorba proudly.

'In that case,' said the Doctor, with a completely straight face, 'take me to your leader, Earthling.'

It took an hour to manoeuvre the police box down into the garage and hoist it onto the back of the Rover. In the last stages of collapse, the building's integrity had not been improved by the ealier use of explosives to excavate the garage entrance. Passage floors sagged alarmingly under the combined weight of TARDIS and people. One actually collapsed only seconds after they had crossed it, sending a mass of debris crashing into and through the lower floors. The creaking and groaning of stressed timbers followed them to the only safe way down: the concrete staircase of a fire escape.

Once the TARDIS was secured on the back of the Rover, Manisha let in the clutch and gently eased the vehicle through the garage towards the ramp leading up to street level. Ace, Geoff and Alan moved ahead of the vehicle, clearing some of the more manageable bits of rubble from its path.

A trickle of concrete dust drifted to land on Ace's hair. She spun at the touch, exchanging looks with the others as an alarming creaking sound echoed through the sub-basement.

Geoff looked around nervously. 'I think we'd better hurry it – '

A chunk of masonry detached from the roof and fell towards him, trailing electrical conduiting. Ace grabbed Geoff and hurled him unceremoniously from the path of the rubble as the garage roof, unable to sustain the weight of the building above, began to cave in.

'Get in the Rover,' she yelled. 'Manisha! Drive!'

They scrambled in and Manisha sent the vehicle hurtling towards the exit ramp, heedless of potential damage to the wheels or axles. The Rover jerked and shuddered, bouncing Ace in her seat, once almost throwing her clear. Only Alan's arm around her waist saved her from being hurled back into the hail of debris smashing to the ground behind them.

Manisha dropped the Rover down into first and the engine roared. They hit the ramp doing twenty miles per hour. The steel cagework struck sparks from the concrete walls as she sent the Rover spinning upwards, lumps of steel and masonry falling to burst on the rails and bonnet, showering them with shrapnel of concrete chips as they burst at last into the midmorning sunlight.

As, behind them, the building collapsed with a roar like a live thing denied its prey.

The Rover skidded twenty yards up the road before Manisha applied the brakes, bringing the vehicle to a stop. Instantly, she was out of the vehicle, her face and arms bloodied from tiny cuts, her hair in a wild disarray. She glared around at dead London, her face a mask of fear and pain. 'There has to be a better way to live than this!'

Ace knew the feral intimacy of real war and so had the answer.

'Peace,' she said with utter conviction. 'It's the only way.'

Bernice was quite happy with her association with Billy and the status it brought her as resident nonentity. It meant she could go more or less where she wanted in the Complex; as long as she was careful enough to make it look as if she had every reason to be there, everyone else was too busy to ask her business.

I'm a spy, plain and simple, she told herself. But at least I'm working for the good guys.

During the course of the previous day, Billy had shown her around much of the cave system. As badly damaged as it was, the place had the complexity of some insect-based cultures she had studied during her years as an archaeologist, although without the associated high level of sophistication. All in all, she thought, the Complex probably hadn't been a very nice place to live; even now she got the feeling most people were simply making do until the order came to evacuate. Already some of the more determined families had left, able to foresee a future in which the cave system would become untenable, packing their meagre belongings into plastic panniers and simply walking out of the main entrance. Nobody had stopped them, though guards had been placed on the food, clothing and medical stores; when they left, they did so with precious little except the will to survive.

For most it would not be enough.

Saddened by her train of throught, Bernice had tried to sleep in one of the makeshift dormitories and, failing, had risen to drift at random through the Complex, absorbing a sense of the place, turning over in her mind the events of the past days. The apparent destruction of the TARDIS, her incarceration by the Silurians and subsequent release, her reunion with the Doctor, and his new instructions. To watch, to listen. To learn all she could and, she assumed, to act on value judgements derived from her observations.

But to act how? To do what? Her conversation with the Doctor had been so brief. So imprecise. Did he want her to act in a particular way? How could he without first knowing the things he wanted her to find out? Well, he knew her, probably better than she really liked, if she was honest. He knew how *she* would act. Maybe he was trusting her to be true to herself. To follow her nose. It would be just like him to second guess her.

Deep in thought, she came to an area where plastic ropes painted with luminous colours delineated an area where subsidence made occupation impossible. She stopped then and, as an exercise, calculated the tonnage of rock in the limestone hills above them, balanced the result against the force required to cause so much damage and whistled softly. The Silurians had a fair degree of psi-ability, she knew, but to be able to amplify it to the degree she observed here, to focus it, and project it, the technology was staggering.

She almost wished she'd stayed aboard the airship.

She sighed, leaned against the wall of the passage, pressed her forehead against the rock. Beyond the plastic ropes, a chasm split the passage vertically, as if the hill had been riven by a gigantic blade. The channel was narrow, but it was an indication of how dangerous the area was. A cool breeze sighed out of the crack in fitful gusts. Somwhere it must connect to the outside. As if to confirm her supposition, she detected a freshness in the breeze, a hint of earth and pollen, a nuance of rain. And something else.

The sound of voices.

Ducking under the ropes, she edged closer to the blackness. The crack must be acting like a whispering gallery, bringing voices to her from who knew how far away. She strained to filter coherent sound from the susurration of the wind, imagining a lovers' quarrel, or the worried conversation of a family deciding whether to stay in or leave the Complex.

What she finally heard made her eyes narrow thoughtfully: voices raised in anger. Two she didn't recognize, one masculine, a deep baritone, an authority figure. This Brigadier whom the Doctor had asked her to watch? The other man she did not recognize either. The woman she did: Liz Shaw, who'd helped her from the wreck of the crashed microlight and who later had kept silent about her theory regarding Bernice's sudden emergence from the Silurian airship.

'You mean to say you interrupted my research on the airship – research which, I might add, you deem of the utmost importance to the continued survival of humanity – and drag me here to ask me whether or not I can build a radio transmitter for you? A radio transmiter,

Brigadier! I think your sense of values has become some-what warped.'

'Miss Shaw, I assure you, my sense of values has never been more finely honed.'

'But who would you contact with this radio transmitter? Who on Earth has the means to receive such a signal and the wherewithal to act upon its instructions? I'll tell you, shall I? No-one. The Earth is dead, Brigadier, we are the last. When we go, everything ends.' There was a long pause. 'I almost hope it happens sooner rather than later.'

Now the third voice added, 'Come on, Liz, you can't mean that. Not after all we've been through.'

'All we've been through, Sergeant? Like Jo's murder, you mean? Like the assault on this Complex? Like the obsession you both have with this blasted book of yours? As if that'll solve anything.'

The Brigadier spoke again. 'What will solve everything is a belief that mankind will overcome its aggressors. That – '

'That right will triumph over evil? That God's on our side? That the truth will out? B-movie bullshit, Brigadier, and you know it. Alright, I'll fix Sergeant Benton's R/T unit since yours was damaged in the assault. And boost the signal strength the way you wanted. But I am absolutely positive of one thing: I'm not going to lay my hands on a single screwdriver and nor will any of my staff until I know what's going on around here!'

There was a long pause. Bernice scrunched closer to the crack.

'Very well, Miss Shaw. The plan is to reactivate the Silurian airship. Then it, and its two remaining ancillary ships, will be mobilized for simultaneous attack on the Silurian capital city.'

Bernice detected a note of horror in Liz's voice. 'No wonder you wanted me to work so hard to understand the Silurian technology.'

'Correct, Miss Shaw. Using the psionic amplifiers, trained operators will be able to control large groups of dinosaurs the way the reps can. Perhaps even more efficiently, if we're lucky. Think of it: diplodocus; brontosaurus; seismosaurus; ultrasaurus. Great herds of them moving at our command; thousands, millions of tonnes, a living army to trample the reps back into the mud. Their own weapon used against them!' He sighed. 'And the children. At last the children can live in a world that's fit for them to grow up in.'

'My God.' Horror, pity and disgust all mingled together in Liz's voice. 'Jan was right, you are mad.'

'On the contrary, Miss Shaw. I am the world's best hope.'

'There has to be a better way than this!'

The Brigadier's next words had Bernice reaching for her hip flask, and a stiff pick-me-up.

'War,' he said with utter conviction. 'It's the only way.'

Manisha drove the Rover up the M1 at a steady speed, only occasionally having to leave the cracked blacktop to skirt accident sites or areas of thick vegetation.

She had tried several times during the journey to start a conversation with Ace, but her friend didn't seem to be in the mood for catching up on old times. The best she'd been able to get from the other woman had been a terse series of laconic comments on the effect of violence and the many causes which lay at its roots.

After an hour Manisha let the conversation drop, unaccountably disturbed. Ace was no longer the girl she remembered, even beyond the effects of the Nightmare. When she'd know Ace before, she'd been a little rough around the edges but essentially a warm individual. Now, though she was sure that centre of warmth and kindness still existed, it seemed to be covered by a thick shell of disillusionment, arrogance, black humour. Manisha recalled a day when Ace had brought her sister a whole bunch of comics she'd dug out of the ruins of a shop. She had spent half an hour desperately trying to convince both herself and Kosi she was too old for them, only to sit down with them eventually, and read just as many as they did, and laugh the loudest of all of them. Somehow Manisha couldn't imagine this new Ace laughing at anything less important than a badly assembled gun. This new

Ace scared her. More than that, Ace confused her, for she seemed quite happy with her new persona.

Behind her, Ace pulled the map out of her satchel and unfolded it, batting the corners back against the breeze whistling through the open cagework of the Rover.

'We should reach the turn off soon,' Manisha told her.

'If we were to cut across country it'd be even quicker.'

'True.' Geoff sat up in the front passenger seat. 'You know I'm really looking forward to having a good mooch around this research centre of yours. We might find some useful equipment to take back to our labs.' He thought for a moment. 'You mentioned a cyclotron?'

'I did. But you'll never move it.'

'I know, and we wouldn't have the power to run it anyway. No, what I'm after is some of the ancilliary gear that would go with such a device. Our own labs are running short of equipment, and it'll be a nice surprise for – '

The rest of Geoff's sentence was lost in a scream of pain.

Manisha wrenched the wheel to one side as pain stabbed into her own mind. Her muscles spasmed as the Rover spun, toppled, rolled, the screech of rending metal mingling with screams to form a frenzy of sound which beat viciously at her ears. Vaguely, Manisha remembered taking her hands off the wheel to cover her ears, and that must have been when the Rover flipped off the tarmac altogether, coming to rest upside down jammed firmly into a wall of palm trees.

The stabbing pain in her mind increased, then faded abruptly, to be replaced with a sickening dizziness and itching. She thought she heard a distant sigh of pain and effort.

She caught hold of a curved metal rail and hauled herself, upside down, from the wreckage. Rocks and bits of metal dug painfully into her body as she dropped to lay panting on the ground. She shut her eyes, aware that something warm and wet was dripping into her face. There was a metallic, salty taste as the fluid ran into her mouth.

Blood.

215

She was also vaguely aware of yelling voices, a gunshot, a vicious reptilian hissing.

She struggled to open her eyes, finally managing the task to find herself looking up through the warped cage-work of the Rover to the source of the warm fluid trickling onto her. There was something there, a pale oval jammed at a crazy angle between the steel rails that ran beside the shattered windscreen. She thought the shape looked like a face, a human face, but that couldn't be right because it was all twisted up and parts of it seemed to be . . .

Manisha began to scream when she realized the reason the face looked strange was because she could see jagged reflections of parts of it in the bloody shards of glass sticking out of the pale flesh.

The Brigadier sat at his desk, his swagger stick beside him on the blotter. He turned the R/T unit over in his hands.

On the other side of the desk, Benton saluted, turned to leave.

'Actually, would you mind staying, Sergeant?' The Brigadier flicked a switch on the R/T. The dead sound of an empty carrier wave came from the little speaker. The Brigadier knew he could take this box anywhere, to the highest mountain, the farthest shore, and never receive so much as a bleep generated by anything other than a storm or sunspot activity. The thing was an icon of the new Earth; an Earth the Silurians had made, one he was determined to win back from them.

Actually, he thought, that wasn't strictly true. If he used the correct code sequence he would receive a reply of sorts. Not one transmittable over the frequencies scanned by this unit, but it would contain a potent message, nonetheless. Potent, and quite lethal.

The Brigadier took out the watch Doris had given him all those years ago. The watch hands were still, frozen at a certain time. The date on the watch bore no relation to the day on which it had stopped. Together the numbers formed a code sequence he hadn't thought of in nearly two decades. One he had not dared to record anywhere except here, where it could be interpreted by no-one except himself.

He activated the unit. 'Greyhound to Sea Dog. Over.'

There was the hiss of an open carrier wave.

The Brigadier read out the time and date from his watch.

'Meeting will take place as arranged. Do not acknowledge this transmission. Greyhound, over and out.'

Benton shuffled uneasily from foot to foot. 'You could still call it off, Brigadier.'

The Brigadier stood, abruptly, his back ramrod straight.

'Deserting the sinking ship, are we, Benton?'

Benton snapped to attention. 'No, sir!'

'Good ... good. You and Captain Wood are the only two men I'd trust to lead the assault force.'

'Thank you, sir.'

'You may have cause to regret that thanks soon enough. But no matter. Is the half-track drivable?'

'I'm afraid not, sir. It was too badly damaged in the battle.'

'I see. What about horses?'

'The men are rounding some up.'

'Excellent. I am about to make a short journey. I'll brief you on the rest of the plan when I return. That will be all, Sergeant.'

'Sir!' Benton saluted and left the office.

The Brigadier crossed to his safe, took out the two halves of the book, slipped them into his pocket, closed the safe, locked it, and picked up his swagger stick. As an afterthought he set his watch to the correct time and date. He left his office winding it thoughtfully.

From her hiding place in the passage, where she and Billy had been listening to the entire conversation, Bernice watched him go.

It all happened so fast. Ace remembered the dizziness, and the sudden incredible pain deep within her mind. She remembered grabbing Alan and throwing him from the Rover, jumping clear herself seconds before it smashed through the motorway crash barrier and buried itself in a wall of palm trees thirty yards away.

Almost immediately the pain vanished from her mind, although the disorientation remained. She struggled to her feet, trying to make sense of the images which swirled around her like fog: the Rover, upside down, warped, erupting with steam and lathered with blood. Manisha, face up on the ground, screaming. Glass falling in glittering torrents from the windscreen to lie all around her. Further away there were sounds. Hissing speech. The pattering of reptile footsteps. Ace groped for her satchel. It was gone, swept away in the crash. She was digging in her pocket for her smartbomb when the gunshot came. Following the shot there was a hissing screech and a ragged scream of pain. Ace finally shook off the effects of the crash sufficiently to make sense of the scene before her.

Alan was kneeling on the ground, thrashing from side to side with his arms wrapped around his head as if to ward off invisible blows. What she could see of his face was contorted; he was trying to draw breath and scream at the same time.

Standing before him, third eye glowing brightly, was a Silurian.

Ace blinked. Her eyes skittered away from the figure. It was only with a tremendous effort that she was able to refocus on the tableau.

She went a little crazy when she saw the blood seeping from Alan's eyes, ears and nose, running along his arms and dripping from his elbows onto the ground. Grabbing a lump of rock from the ground she leaped at the Silurian. The reptile spun instantly and fixed her with his killing gaze, but the momentum of her charge carried her forward and together they tumbled to the ground.

The Silurian was fast. He twisted as they fell, landing on top of Ace with bone-crushing force. Ace felt the breath go out of her in a great *whoosh*, and darkness came edging in. With the darkness came madness. This close to an adult Silurian the race fear was utterly over-

218

whelming. All Ace's experience was forgotten, swept away in a storm of fear, anger, mindless violence.

– get you bastard I'll get you I'll get you I'll –

The Silurian hissed in agony as Ace grabbed hold of his broken arm, wrenching and twisting it with all her strength as she felt the bones grate together.

His third eye began to glow. Ace head-butted him.

He rolled away and Ace followed, kicking, punching, scratching, biting; yelling triumphantly as she heard the snap of bones in his arm, rising to kick again, to slip, to fall in a rain of blood as the wound in her back betrayed her. To close her eyes as the Silurian loomed above her, to yell defiantly as she felt the pain lance again into her mind. To gasp as the pain faded at the sound of a blow.

She stared around herself as the dizziness faded; spat cold, bitter-tasting blood from her mouth at what she saw.

The Silurian lay twitching on the ground, unconscious, blood streaming from a scalp wound. Manisha stood over him, shaking with reaction. Blood, sweat and tears mingled on her arms and face and drenched her shirt. Clenched in one hand was a spanner from the Rover's tool kit. A short distance away Alan lay on the ground, bathed in sweat, his face a bloody mask, his muscles convulsing in agony. Tiny animal noises came from him as he writhed from side to side.

Unable to find the strength to stand, Ace crawled over to him.

'Dear God, what's it done to you?'

Alan's mouth struggled to form words. 'Huh ... huh ... *hurts*.'

Ace's hands fluttered across Alan's face, stomach, chest. 'Where?' she said urgently.

'Every ... bloody ... where.' Alan writhed in pain.

'Christ, Alan, lie still, where's your common sense!' Ace cried angrily. 'I'll get the medical kit – I – there'll be drugs, splints, I'll ...' She tailed off.

Alan shook his head. 'No good ...'

He struggled to move again, flopping his arm across his chest, immediately wracked by convulsions.

'Ace!' Manisha knelt beside her but Ace didn't look up.

Alan jerked his hand, tapping at her knee. She looked down. He was still holding the gun. He tried to lift it to her hands, failed, pressed it weakly into her lap.

'What are you doing?'

'You know I'm ... dying,' he gasped. 'Telekinesis. All smashed up inside. Make it quick for me.'

Ace brushed tears of pain from Alan's face. 'Are you sure?'

'Remember what I said about ...' Alan struggled to get the words out. 'About being friends? About trust?'

'I remember.'

'I'm trusting you now, Ace.' Alan's head flopped as he tried to look into her eyes, failed, dropped back to the ground. With the last of his strength he sought her hand, took it, pressed it to the gun in her lap. 'Trusting you ... nuh ... now ...' His voice tailed off into a moan of pain.

Ace moved to bring the barrel close beside Alan's head. With her other hand she reached out to clasp his. His shaking fingers closed around hers hard enough to bruise. His eyes closed in pain, opened again, beseeching. His breath rasped from between his lips; too strong, not strong enough.

She remembered his kiss. The way he'd tasted, smelt. The play of muscles in his chest and arms as they'd hugged. *Only friends.*

Screaming a name, she pulled the trigger.

The sounds ripped into the afternoon, refused to fade.

Name, shot, shot, name.

Not Alan's.

The Doctor's.

Her voice held no grief but, instead, a blinding fury.

The Doctor looked curiously out across one curved arc of the Palace Gardens. Landscapers had placed a low rank of almost genetically pure weeping willows along the bank of a huge ornamental pool, in which an infant mosasaur was badgering a shoal of more normal-looking fish. Beyond the willows a curved line of cycads swayed delicately beneath the hot tropical sun. The Palace itself rose beyond the cycads, the colour of its lower ramparts washed out by distance. To either side were sections of transplanted savannah, in which a pride of lions competed with a pair of baryonyx for the privilege of hunting antelope and giraffe. Beneath his feet the transporter belt which had carried him and Chtorba from the mooring tower hummed quietly, coloured a dull yellow ochre to blend in with the grassland. It wound through the undergrowth, lifting to cross the crescent-shaped pool, passing through the trees and vanishing in the direction of the Palace.

The Silurian Leader was waiting for them on a raised stone parapet overlooking the pool, feeding live fish from a bucket to the infant mosasaur. When they were thirty feet from him, the transporter belt slowed and Chtorba ushered the Doctor off and onto the stone parapet. The Leader turned slowly from his contemplation of the pool, put down the bucket, and began to walk towards them.

He stopped a few yards from the Doctor.

Even from a distance his presence had been overpowering, almost intimidating. Close up, the effect was enhanced. The Doctor could make out more details in the face and body. The deeply etched pebbling around the eyes and neck lent character to the face, the heavy veins running through his almost translucent aquamarine skin pulsed with a determined flow of blood. Tiny pearls had been implanted into the reptile's fluted crest, a vanity the Doctor assumed was associated with advanced age. The pearls formed a ring around his third eye, currently open in startled recognition.

The Doctor doffed his hat as the Silurian closed the distance between them. He managed to hide almost completely the sudden terrible fear he felt at the Leader's approach. 'Hello, Morka,' he said calmly. 'It's been a long time.'

'Time passes faster for us than for mammals,' said Morka in a voice which, although soft, carried easily through the hot, still air.

'I am sorry.'

'There is no need. Our lives are as full as any you have known.'

'Of course.'

'You may not believe me, Doctor,' Morka continued, 'but it is very good to see you again. In my experience, fate does not often provide for second chances or lost opportunities.' His lips curved in a passable smile. 'Or regrets.' The smile faded. 'Killing you was probably the worst mistake of my entire life.'

Ace levelled the gun at the back of the Silurian's head. Her finger twitched on the trigger. Her hand shook like a junkie's in terminal withdrawal.

'Ace,' Manisha said warningly.

Ignoring her friend, Ace knelt beside the prone reptile, placing the gun barrel against the highest fluting of his domed skull. Her left arm encircled his shoulders, easing him into a sitting position.

'Ace, what are you doing?'

'I want him awake. I want him to know what I'm going to do. Alan was my friend.'

'No.'

An expression of pure hatred came over her face. She whirled, her arm pointing towards Manisha, the gun levelling at her chest. 'Don't tell me what I can and can't do!' she hissed.

Manisha froze.

Ace felt movement. In her arms the Silurian was beginning to stir. She placed the gun against the back of his skull. Cocked the safety catch. 'Wake up, sweetheart, wake up.' She murmured the words like a mantra, slapping the reptile's face gently in time to the rhythm.

She felt the stirrings of an alien presence in her mind.

The Silurian opened his primary eyes.

He struggled weakly; Ace held him firm.

The third eye blinked, opened, began to glow.

'Goodbye,' she whispered.

And squeezed the trigger.

The spanner that knocked the gun from her hand as she fired came near to breaking her wrist. She stared in amazement at Manisha as the bullet whined away into the afternoon. The gun fell to lie on the ground between them.

'Don't you understand!' said Manisha as she picked the gun up and aimed it at Ace. 'Don't you understand anything?'

Ace began to shake. 'The gun. Give me the gun. Give it to me!'

'*That's the way all this began!*'

When Ace spoke there was a catch in her voice. 'Intellectually I have to admit you're right.' She slammed a fist into the Silurian's face, rocking his head on his shoulders, knocking him out cold with a single blow. 'Emotionally, though, it's a different thing entirely.'

There was an awkward silence.

'Look,' said Manisha eventually, 'it's been a bad time. I don't want to argue any more.' She hesitated. 'Do you want your gun back?'

Ace ignored the offered weapon. 'You keep it.' She looked down at the unconscious Silurian with a half self-conscious, half embarrassed frown. 'You might feel safer that way.'

Manisha frowned, but kept the gun.

While the Silurian was unconscious, Ace used the Rover's winch to hoist the vehicle back onto the road. The TARDIS had been flung clear during the crash and was lying on its side. It looked undamaged. Ace decided to leave it where it was for the time being. There would be plenty of time to set it upright when she'd retrieved the key. Hoisting the Silurian into the back of the vehicle and securing him there was easy. Removing Geoff's body from the cab wasn't. Already insects were coming to investigate the interesting new smells.

While Manisha checked the Rover to see if it was drivable, Ace took the fuel shovel and dug two graves.

When the bodies had been buried, Manisha scattered a handful of dirt over each one. 'Do you want to say anything?'

'I never eulogize,' said Ace. 'Alan knew what I thought of him; Geoff – well, I never really formed an opinion.'

She looked up. 'How's the Rover?'

Manisha shook her head. 'How can you be so – ' She caught herself. 'The drive shaft has sheared.'

Ace walked over to the Rover and patted its dented bonnet. 'Poor Ivor. At least he got us this far.' She scouted the clearing and retrieved her satchel.

'I suppose we walk, yeah?' asked Manisha.

Ace nodded. 'That way.' She pointed.

'What do we do with him?' Manisha nodded towards the Silurian Ace had chained to the inside of the Rover.

'Hmmmm,' Ace mused. 'I see what you mean. Handbag or shoes. Tough decision, huh?'

Manisha carefully kept her expression neutral.

'Perhaps we'd better just leave him here to guard the TARDIS.'

As she followed Manisha from the clearing, Ace threw a last look at the two graves.

Clear air and good landings, love. Wherever the hell you are.

Imorkal struggled into wakefulness. He could not move. He was bound! Chained! How dare they!

He raged against the chains until completely exhausted. Then, with no other recourse available to him, he began to think.

If the mammals had entered the research centre they might gain access to the cave system and beyond, the shelter his own people had built. He could not allow that.

Opening his third eye, Imorkal cast tentatively about him with his inner senses. The effort was extremely painful. He rested for a moment, gathering his thoughts, then, without moving, began delicately to explore the inside of the padlock which secured his chains.

Ace forced open the blockhouse doors and stared into the frustratingly empty lift shaft. If they wanted to get into the Research Centre they'd have to climb down the ladder set into the wall and break in through the top of the elevator car.

Before that was the lift shaft.

Five hundred feet, straight down.

Manisha stared nervously into the shaft. 'I'm not sure I really want to go down there. Especially not without knowing why.'

Ace stared impatiently at her friend. 'We need the key. The TARDIS key. From the Doctor's body.'

Manisha shook her head. 'But it was the Doctor who – '

'Look, I've been through all this with Alan. The fact of the matter is, with the TARDIS dead, the key, which is also isomorphic in function, will have become neutral. Any telepathically authorized user will be able to bond with it, gain access to the TARDIS and – ' She broke off. Manisha was looking at her as if she were mad. 'Oh sod it,' she said impatiently. 'Come if you're coming.' She started to climb.

An hour later she was still climbing.

By the time she dropped onto the top of the elevator car, Ace was exhausted and gasping for breath: too long without seeing action.

There was another thump beside her in the darkness. Manisha.

'Hey, it's spannergirl.'

Manisha huffed impatiently. 'Shall we just get on with it?'

'Yeah.' Ace grabbed hold of the emergency hatch set into the roof and wrenched it off. She jumped down into the elevator.

'What about the lift doors?'

Ace pulled her crowbar from her satchel and winked.

The Research Centre was freezing cold and thick with dust. The only light came from torches Nan had given them as they'd left the Farm. As they walked out of the elevator and into a long corridor lined with closed doors, they passed the mouldy remains of two lab technicians' white coats. Ace imagined them shoving the button for the elevator and waiting, frantic with impatience, for its arrival. She wondered what they had been running from. Further along the corridor was her answer: another set of musty clothes, this one containing a skeleton. The skeleton held a pistol in one claw-like hand.

The cold had frozen the smell of decay in place.

Her breath steaming in front of her, Ace said, 'Now all we've got to do is find the Doctor's body.'

'Where do we start?'

Ace fished in her pocket and pulled out a crumpled Mars wrapper. A map had been hastily scribbled on the blank side in the Doctor's multicoloured biro. 'He didn't know where he was when he died. I suppose the Cyclotron room is as good a place as any to start.'

If the Doctor had expected to be taken into the Palace and chained up in some dungeon cell he was mistaken. Instead, Chtorba had been dismissed after a short linked conversation. Now the Doctor and Morka were walking slowly through the Palace gardens. It was all quite disturbingly amiable.

Morka halted at the edge of a grove of redwoods when he noticed the approach of a duckbill and rider. He signalled the rider to approach. The Doctor's interest increased when he saw it was Chtaachtl who dismounted and approached them.

'Leader,' said the Silurian airship captain without preamble. 'I must protest at the treatment of this mammal.' She pointed at the Doctor, who doffed his hat politely.

'Indeed?' Was that a hint of danger in Morka's voice? 'Having extended every courtesy to the Doctor, I would be very interested to know in which way you find my behaviour deficient.'

'You misunderstand. I do not say that you treat the animal badly, but instead, too well.'

'Oh? You feel I should emulate your own behaviour when attacking the humans?'

'With respect, Leader, my actions were sanctioned by the Council for Operations – '

'Who acted improperly and without my authorization! The fool Icthar has aged even less well than I have. I begin to think his mind is on the verge of total collapse.'

'I do not understand, Leader. There was a time when Icthar and yourself were in very firm agreement regarding what should be done about the threat posed by the humans.'

'Threat? There is no threat. If Icthar had two *shnizz* of common sense he would be able to see that. Instead, he chooses to remain inflexible and thus his strategies are both excessively violent and a waste of resources better devoted to the revival our people.'

'With respect, Leader, I disagree! The humans themselves display more violence every year. Now the conjectures concerning a last military stronghold have proved true. The humans have organized resistance! Our warship was taken, my command overthrown!'

'Hmm. I wonder just how much of your careful justification is due to embarrassment at strategic incompetence.'

'I protest! My command decisions were never in question. The aggression of the humans prompted – '

' – prompted incompetence, sloppy behaviour and sloppier thinking! Perhaps there was once a threat from the humans, but that was a direct response to violence of our own – of my own – and in any case the time for violence has passed.'

'But, Leader, their aggression is ingrained in their nature. They cannot help but display violence towards us.'

'Of course it is, Chtaachtl. And it is fear that provokes the aggression. Fear of us.' Morka paused, chest heaving wearily. 'Fear I have taken steps to eliminate.'

The Doctor pricked up his ears and faded quietly into the background. Something interesting was coming.

'Steps, Leader? The Council know nothing of any steps.'

'Of course they do not! My work was carried out in secret on a human which you very obligingly carried back to the zone of operations for me in your own airship. Oh, completely unaware, of course,' he added with a stiff little smile. 'So I am sure there will be no court martial involved.'

'It was Bernice, wasn't it?' whispered the Doctor suddenly. A terrible fear was building inside him and he was unable to remain silent. 'What have you done to her?'

Visions of Major Barker filled his mind. Poor, xenophobic Major Barker who had been captured by Morka twenty years ago, at the time of the Doctor's first encounter with the Silurians, and who had been infected with a terrible virus which would have wiped out most of humanity if the Doctor himself had not –

He froze. 'That's it,' he said softly. 'That's the nexus point where the real and parallel Earths diverged. The *Nightmare*.'

He lifted his hands to his temples as if to ward off a great pain. Both Morka and Chtaachtl turned to study him.

He met their gaze with one of his own, one he felt scarcely concealed his own terrible realization. 'You've infected her, haven't you? Just like Major Baker,' he continued, his voice gradually getting louder, angrier. 'She never did say what happened to her here, but it's obvious now: infect her with a viral plague and pack her off back to England. Then there was no need to worry if your attack on the humans failed – the virus would do your dirty work for you!' By now the Doctor's voice had reached a peak of anger. 'I should have guessed. You did it once, of course you can do it again. A new breed, a different strain. What is it this time, Morka? An Alzheimer's mutation? Fast acting Parkinson's disease? Or something cheap and nasty of your own? Something that affects the neural system, hits intelligence where it can't defend itself? By all the powers that rule this universe, Morka – you had a chance to make peace with the humans! You had a *chance*.' The Doctor leaned back against the rough bark of a redwood, unable to speak any more.

Chtaachtl gazed at Morka with renewed interest. 'Is this true, Leader? The plan is audacious, but one to be admired – '

Morka gestured angrily, his third eye glimmering with impatience. 'Be silent, you militaristic idiot. You are both wrong.' He turned to face the Doctor. 'Of course your friend Professor Summerfield was infected. But not with a plague. With a viral serum isolated from her brain once she had been cured of her own race fear. When the infection spreads, the root cause of all aggression between our people will be eliminated. The time for violence has ended! Communication is the way to peace, and I will see peace between us before my time on this world is done, or I will see nothing at all!' Morka swayed wearily. 'If you think I have learned nothing in the last twenty years, Doctor, you have done me a grave injustice.'

The Doctor approached Morka. 'I rather think I have. Please accept my apologies.'

'Accepted. And now perhaps – '

But Chtaachtl hadn't finished. 'You . . . fool. You *have* learned nothing. You *don't* understand. The humans have captured our technology. With no race fear to impede them they will soon learn its secrets. Human nature is not the same as Silurian nature. Their *instinct* is to kill, and you have taken away the one barrier to that instinct, the one advantage we had over them.'

As Chtaachtl spoke, Morka's expression changed, suffusing with a terrible realization. He turned to the Doctor, who sighed. 'Under the circumstances, and having observed the humans, I'm afraid Chtaachtl may be right.'

'May be? Of course I am right!' Chtaachtl almost spat her last words out. 'When their attack comes it will be more ruthless than we have ever known and it will be fuelled by our own technology.' Her voice rose scathingly. 'Old One, your arrogance has killed us all!'

That night at the Royal Portbury Docks at Avonmouth, the Brigadier reined in his horse alongside the rusting skeleton of a cargo ship. He dismounted and walked along the docks to a clear berth. As he walked he stared around him at the ruined sheds and rusting cranes all overgrown with vegetation. If everything went according to plan, much of this could be reclaimed, renewed, rebuilt. Civilization would start all over again. His only regret was that he would almost certainly not live to see it. Actually, he thought, that wasn't his only regret. He missed the Doctor. The old Doctor. The white haired chap, and before him, the little clown-like fellow. Jaunty pair of characters, the both of him. Full of life and optimism and hope. All the Brigadier's own hope seemed to vanish with the life of his old friend. And this new Doctor, well he was different. He had a darkness about him, a disturbing ambiguity. The Brigadier was not at all sure he could be trusted.

He walked slowly on, his boots splashing in puddles, squelching in patches of weed which the high tide regularly deposited on the surface of the docks. A hundred yards behind him, Bernice and Billy climbed quietly off their own horses. Tethering the animals, they crept forward and hid behind a dock crane. The Brigadier checked his watch. Bernice frowned. Now why on Earth would he come all the way out here just to –

Billy grabbed her arm and pointed silently. The water in the docks was bubbling in the moonlight. She peered closer, and at that moment the moon slipped out from behind a bank of dark cloud. The water in the docks heaved and surged. A massive shape broke the surface. It had a curiously regular double row of scabbed wounds along its back, behind its square and inflexible dorsal fin. Bernice realized she wasn't looking at an aquatic dinosaur at all. 'It's a submarine,' she whispered in amazement.

Water cascaded, shining in the moonlight, from the spine of the vessel. When most of it had drained away the Brigadier clambered stiffly onto the deck, then climbed the recessed ladder to the top of the conning tower. A hatch was flung open and a gangling man with thinning hair dressed in a general's uniform climbed out to meet him.

General Hobson greeted the Brigadier with a warm smile. He took the package from him, unwrapped it and examined the book.

The words *Computer Control Related Missile Launch Protocol Manual* were embossed on the mouldy cover. He opened the book and riffled the pages gently. 'The value of this book is beyond measuring,' he said quietly, almost reverently.

'I know that, sir,' the Brigadier replied equally quietly.

Hobson looked up. 'And the second objective?'

The Brigadier dug in his pocket and pulled out a three cassette pack of assorted classical music.

'Excellent, Lethbridge Stewart,' said Hobson. 'With men like you on our side the reps will never know what hit 'em. Now, you're quite sure you can carry out the diversionary tactics as planned?'

The Brigadier nodded.

'Sorry I can't take you down here with me, old boy, but I need the right man for the job upstairs. I'm sure you understand.'

'Of course, sir. I understand completely.'

'Good,' Hobson descended the interior of the conning tower, began to close the hatch, then on a whim flipped through the collection of cassettes. His face lit up with pleasure. He selected one and held it up to the Brigadier. 'Schubert's *Unfinished*. Appropriate music to end the so-called Silurian World with, eh Lethbridge-Stewart?'

'Absolutely, sir.' The Brigadier turned and climbed off the submarine and back onto the docks. He made a point of watching the submarine submerge. He knew he would never see it again. As he began to untie his horse, he became aware of a steady nickering sound coming from nearby. Leaving the animal, he drew his pistol and crept off into the darkness to investigate. What he found made him think deeply for a moment, before staring back at the docks.

Tethered to a crane in front of him were two more horses.

Although the Brigadier searched for more than an hour he could find no sign of any riders.

He gazed thoughtfully back at the water glimmering in the moonlight. He pulled out his R/T unit.

PART FIVE

GROUND ZERO

On the savannah a lion yawned, sunning itself lazily in the grass as a baryonyx stalked and killed an antelope less than fifty yards away.

From the morning room of the Palace, Morka also watched the event, and wondered if the making of his world had been worth the sacrifice of so many lives.

On the other side of the incubator containing Morka's second egg, the Doctor leaned casually on his umbrella. Morka felt a rush of interest from the mammal. The Doctor turned away from the window view. 'The lion won't attack the baryonyx because it's learned the reptile will leave most of the antelope to rot,' said the Doctor. 'And the baryonyx won't attack the lion because it knows it could never defeat the whole pride.'

'A model of evolution,' agreed Morka. 'Cooperation, not competition.'

'Everybody wins.'

'Except the antelope.' Morka felt the rush of interest from the Doctor change to curiosity.

'Is that how you see yourself, Morka?' the Doctor asked.

'As a victim?' Morka tried to fathom the Doctor's intent. 'No. I am more powerful than the strongest hunting beast.'

'Ah yes, because of your intelligence; the intellect as opposed to the instinct to kill.' The Doctor returned his gaze to the view from the window. 'Then again, intelligence brings its own problems, doesn't it? Responsibility, for example.' He paused. 'Guilt.'

Morka shrugged. All three eyes blinked slowly.

'You said you regret your actions of two decades ago.' The Doctor turned and walked into the centre of the room. His voice rose, echoing slightly despite the various woven tapestries adorning the distant walls. 'Suppose I were to give you the chance to relive the moments of those decisions. Would you change them?'

Morka turned swiftly. 'You don't have that power.'

'I'm rather afraid I do.' Morka was surprised to hear a change in the Doctor's voice. No longer confident and bright, it held darker undertones. His skin blushed azure at the thought the Doctor had planted in his mind.

'You are talking about creating a pivotal point from which alternative realities may spring,' he said. 'As a philosophical concept it is absorbing, if flawed. It would, of course, result in chaos: the creation of an alternative Earth, perhaps an infinite number of parallel sub-universes.' He shook his head in emulation of the mammal's gesture of negation. 'An impossibility. I am here. The Earth is ours. What is real, is real. The universe contains only a finite amount of matter and energy, and that – '

' – must remain where it's supposed to.' The Doctor nodded in agreement. 'It would mean the end of your civilization, of course. Possibly your own death; we live in a conservative universe. But on the plus side . . .'

'There would be peace.' Morka turned away, allowing a glimmer of the feelings he had so carefully controlled over the years to emerge. 'An end to the violence, an end to the guilt . . .' He turned back to the Doctor. 'You can offer me this?'

The Doctor nodded. 'There are rules, but I can break them. If I'm prepared to take the risk – and pay the price.'

Morka sighed, his breath hissing through trembling lips. 'You offer me something I cannot refuse.'

Though still dark, the Doctor's manner became brisk. 'Then I suggest – '

'But I must,' Morka interrupted, his voice holding a note of finality. 'I cannot accept your offer.'

The Doctor frowned. 'I could force you.' He said the words slowly, thoughtfully, as if trying out the idea for the first time.

Morka hissed in amusement. 'My choice was made a long time ago.'

'Indeed.'

'The most I can do now is learn from the results of my actions.' He tried to determine the Doctor's emotional state. The results were uncomfortably vague. 'The way to peace is forward, not back.'

The Doctor stared down at the crystal mozaic forming the floor and twirled his umbrella in a thoughtful figure of eight. He was silent for a long time. 'You know, Morka,' he said eventually, 'as old as I am, I may just have learned something very important.'

'The ability to learn is the most important gift of all.'

The Doctor suddenly smiled. 'Sometimes I forget how fast most species mature. It seems only yesterday that we were locked in irreversible conflict.'

Morka felt another of the sudden flushes colour his face. 'I was a child and did not know it. A child with the power of a Leader.'

The Doctor continued, 'And now you've outgrown the impetuous violence of youth. Okdel would be proud of you, of your ability to learn. Morka, now you are a Leader with the strength to perceive things as a child would.'

Morka recognized the envy in the Doctor's voice and nodded. 'If any of what you say about me is true, it is you I must thank for it.'

'Oh?' The Doctor twirled his umbrella curiously. 'How so?'

Morka considered.

'Open your mind to me,' he said at length. 'We will link. And I will show you.'

The Cyclotron room was as cold and empty as the rest of the base. Hulking machinery crouched in the shadows all around them. Even the doorway was a short passage beneath an archway made through the main accelerator torus. Their footsteps echoed dully, softened into flatness by the dust which coated every surface.

Ace looked around, scanning for signs of life. Seeing nothing, she moved across the room to a wide set of glass sliding doors set in another archway in the far wall.

Manisha followed her. One of the doors was shattered,

a set of clothes containing a skeleton draped across the jagged edges. Old blood mixed with dusty fragments of glass on the floor. An image of Geoff Davis's dead body looming over her in the wrecked Rover suddenly filled her mind; the glass sticking out of his face was as real in her memory as the glass which had sliced this set of clothes to ribbons. Manisha swallowed hard.

Stepping over the broken glass and body, Ace referred to her map. 'This must be the lab.' She opened the intact door and Manisha followed her down a short flight of steps into the room beyond.

Manisha could see at once that the lab had once been lavishly equipped. Banks of computer cabinets lined the walls, behind long administration desks. A line of five incubators stood on a long bench. Several more benches were filled to overflowing with glassware and microscopes. Stacks of used culture plates filled every flat surface. Most were filled with a dull powder, which she presumed was all that remained of the dead cultures. The room stank of decay.

Manisha moved slowly into the room, her eye caught by an incongruous sight: to her left a large tunnel had been drilled, no *melted*, straight through the far wall.

She called to Ace, who was examining drawers full of computer tapes at the far end of the room. Ace slid the drawer shut and together the two women moved towards the hole. About six feet high, the tunnel angled upwards through the floor and wall, slicing through a computer cabinet and part of a lab bench. Where the tunnel's circumference had intersected with glassware, the part of the glassware within the perimeter had simply vanished. A large microscope had lost a shallow curved section from the main optic tube and slide holder. The edges were fused as smoothly as if the microscope had been designed that way. Manisha ran her finger along the edge of the microscope. To her surprise, the metal flaked away at her touch.

Ace examined some of the surrounding stonework. It was dry and powdery, crumbling between her fingers, all molecular adhesion gone.

'No human technology could have done this,' she observed simply. She pulled away some of the powdery rubble which had fallen from the surrounding wall. Behind the wall was bare rock. The tunnel led directly into the depths of the hill.

'This must be where they got in.'

Manisha shone her torch into the hole. 'What do you reckon?'

Ace turned suddenly and went back to the body jammed through the glass door. She flipped the paper-light skeleton over and read aloud from the name tag stitched to the left-hand breast pocket. 'Lawrence, K. Director of Research.' She shook her head, walked back to the tunnel. 'Looks like they took the Doctor through here.'

'So we go on?'

'We go on.'

They moved into the tunnel. It was long and narrow, opening into a cold, damp cavern. Slowly dripping moisture from the roof collected in pools and runnels along their path. Stalagmites and other limestone formations rose to block their way, while stalactites descended to pen them in. One deceptively delicate-looking formation had drawn blood when Ace accidentally banged her head against it ducking through a narrow fissure. Now she had a splitting headache in addition to her worries about ever finding either the entrance to the Silurian shelter or the Doctor's body.

'Do you think we're going the right way?' Manisha voiced a worry that Ace refused to acknowledge in herself.

'I'll let you know when we get there.'

'It's just that there seem to be an awful lot of branching passages around.'

'I know.'

'Well, it's just that I thought, you know, maybe we should – '

'No need.' Ace's voice was calm and full of assurance. 'I think we've found the front door.'

The door was thirty feet wide and higher than their torch beams could penetrate in the darkness.

Manisha ran her hand lightly across the door. 'How do we open it? Your explosives?'

'No. The smartbomb would bring the roof in on top of us. Besides . . .' Ace frowned. 'There ought to be another way.' She began to cast about with her torch. 'That's funny.' Ace shone her torch on a nearby column of limestone.

'It's just a stalagmite.'

'Then why isn't it wet?' Ace ran her fingers lightly over the formation. Behind them, the door irised open with a gentle sigh of displaced air. 'Answer: because it isn't a real stalagmite.'

Manisha eyed the opening suspiciously. 'There's no way I'm going in there first,' she said with absolute conviction.

Ace shrugged and led the way through the opening. She moved cautiously, testing the air in front of her for a hint of a foreign smell, sweat, anything that would give away a potential aggressor. There was nothing. The passage ahead was empty.

'Well,' she said slowly, 'it seems quiet enough.'

A dim green light began to shine from the walls.

'You were saying?' Manisha looked around nervously.

'It must be an automatic system, triggered by our presence here.'

'What, you mean body heat or something?'

'Yeah, probably.'

'But Silurians have a different body temperature to us. Surely the system would be set to detect them, not a human presence?'

Ace nodded. 'Good point, Batman.' She looked around in the dim green light. They were standing at the end of a wide, smooth, tunnel. The walls, floor and ceiling were formed of ribbed sheets of sea-green crystal. Long grilles set low in the walls provided footing for a green moss. The moss glowed, providing the tunnel with its source of illumination. She moved forward.

'Ace?' Manisha hurried to join her after a nervous glance back into the cavern. 'I think I saw something moving back there.'

'Yeah?' Ace increased her speed. 'Better hope it can't run as fast as us then.'

'Ace, this is no time for jokes!'

'Get a hold of yourself then!' Ace snapped impatiently, adding, 'This place bothers me just as much as it does you. But it's dead, Manisha. Dead! And we have to find the Doctor's body. Now come on.'

She led the way deeper into the shelter. Manisha followed with obvious reluctance, after a last look back into the cavern.

'Can't we just work out how to close the –'

'No!' Ace was almost as surprised as Manisha at the note of anger in her own voice. 'We'd be trapped in here then, if we needed to ...' ... *make a fast getaway*, she added to herself. But she didn't speak the words aloud: she had her hands full coping with the Doctor's imperative without turning Manisha into a nervous wreck as well. Shouldering her satchel, Ace kept moving forward. In a few more moments she came to an intersection of passageways. As she looked down each, Ace could see the green-on-green flicker of glowing moss on crystal walls. There seemed to be no structure to the layout of the passages. They seemed merely to join and divide at random, or at least in some pattern she couldn't identify, a pattern that tantalized her, teased her with a definite familiarity yet eluded her with frustrating ease. Ace stood quite still at the intersection, peering this way then that, frozen with indecision. If only she could work out the best way to go! Time was bearing down on them and the last thing they wanted was –

'You are here,' said Manisha suddenly.

'What?!' Ace jumped, startled at the sound of her voice.

Manisha eyed her nervously. 'That's what we need. You know, one of those signs saying "You are here," with a big arrow pointing to the street the loos are in.'

Ace drew in a shuddering breath. Her heart was pounding in her chest. What had she been thinking, doing? 'I could have stood here forever,' she said wonderingly. 'Trying to decide which way to go.'

'It's this place,' Manisha whispered. 'It gets into your head. Screws you up.'

'And then some,' Ace agreed. She looked at the walls. The floor. Finally at Manisha. She blinked. 'Have you got a headache?'

'Yeah,' said Manisha after a moment's thought.

Ace shook her head. 'Well, there's no aspirin here.' She looked either way down the passages. 'What were we doing?'

'Looking for something.' Manisha hesitated. 'No . . . I know. Looking for some*one*.'

'Yeah! That's right, the Doctor's body.' Ace looked around. 'Now, all we've got to do is decide which way to go . . .'

After a minute, Ace turned to find Manisha staring at her with an expression very close to terror. Her breath came fast and shallow. 'I was doing it again, wasn't I?' she whispered.

Manisha nodded silently.

Ace shook her head. 'This is ridiculous. They're just passages! Nothing can be that alien!' She strode off down a passage leading to the left.

'Ace, wait! Don't you think we'd better –'

'No I don't, and I wish you'd stop saying we should!' Ace snapped angrily.

Manisha ran to catch Ace up. 'Well, sorry, it's just that –'

'Look. I've just about had it up to here with your whingeing, okay? If you're not up for this, naff off!'

'But I only –'

'Will you *please shut up!*'

'But I –'

Ace whirled and grabbed Manisha by the throat with both hands. She lifted her clear of the ground and hurled her against the nearest wall, turning away contemptuously as Manisha slumped to the floor.

'Ace! What –'

'Get away from me, I hate you! I hate you!'

Shaking her head Manisha struggled to her feet. 'Ace, what –'

Ace turned, stepped closer to the other woman and rabbit punched her in the solar plexus. As the air whooshed out of Manisha's lungs, Ace grabbed her again by the throat, straight-armed her off the floor and began to pound her head methodically against the wall.

'Ace -!' Manisha gasped. 'What are you – what – Ace – '

She kicked feebly, but her feet found no purchase on the slick crystal wall. She tried to speak but the pressure on her throat was overpowering. She found herself staring right at Ace, and what she saw there made her go cold with fear.

Ace wore an expression of quiet concentration, as if reading an interesting book.

Manisha brought her hands up to Ace's arms. They were corded with muscle, the fingers biting agonizingly into Manisha's neck. Her hands tried to grip, failed, slid around Ace's shoulders. She could feel the wound there open as her back tensed. Blood began to soak her shirt.

She found the strength to gasp, 'Ace – you – going – kill me – '

The walls of her throat closed and she began to choke. Ace's eyes were fixed at a point some inches behind her own. She felt her head smash against the wall. Once. Twice. Three times.

She started to lose consciousness.

The wall opened up.

The pressure on her throat eased and she found herself falling.

Somehow she managed to find the strength to twist as they fell, a tangled mass of limbs and clothing, landing on her knees on Ace's chest and driving the breath from the other woman with a cry of pain. She toppled forwards and fell across Ace, her head whipping down uncontrollably to hit the floor, the movement continuing so that the two women rolled apart, Manisha moaning, clutching at her throat, Ace gasping for breath, her face grey and clammy with pain.

Eventually Manisha recovered enough to struggle into a sitting position. She stared guardedly at Ace, who gazed back, her eyes filled with sudden realization. 'Manisha . . .'

'Don't say it, okay!' Manisha snapped. She began to add something, bit the words off angrily, 'Just don't say anything.'

Her face flushed with shame, almost relishing the sharp pain of a fractured rib, Ace hauled herself to her feet.

Unable to meet Manisha's gaze, she stared around the room. The chamber they were in was vaulted, its ceiling lost in emerald shadows. A number of tall, narrow pens ringed the chamber, the horizontal bars made of the same glassy substance as the walls. There were skeletons in the pens. They were stretched out on the ground or pressed up against the bars in attitudes of pain and terror.

But these were almost peripheral to Ace. Her gaze had been caught by the central pen. One holding a skeleton taller than the rest, with two extra ribs, draped in the remains of a frilly white shirt and dark cloak, long trousers and spats.

It was the Doctor's body.

They came for him in the early hours of the morning, on the thirteenth day of the Nightmare. They took him from his laboratory, sealing the fate of Homo sapiens as easily and efficiently as they sealed the chasm they had opened in the solid rock of the Derbyshire hillside. Then they took him down into the hot, damp reaches of the Earth, to their new home, and there they chained him to a metal pillar behind a barrier of glass. He remained there for nine days without food or water. A quarter of a mile above him, friends first searched and then died, horribly, and the Earth itself convulsed at the touch of the engineered virus unleashed upon it by his captors.

On the morning of the tenth day of his incarceration, the Leader came to him. He watched for a long time, his three eyes observing the mammal's suffering dispassionately.

Weak from starvation and moisture deprivation, the Doctor mumbled through cracked lips, 'It's still not too late, you know. The madness can still end. Let me speak to Okdel. Morka, please! In the name of humanity!'

'Okdel is dead.' The words were flat, the intonation mini-

mal, but the emotion was there. '*I killed him. I am Leader of the Silurian race now.*'

The Doctor gasped, '*Then the choice is yours.*'

'*Yes.*' Morka's voice was cold and harsh. '*And humanity's time is at an end.*'

Then the new Leader of planet Earth glared at this warm-blooded animal who had struggled so hard and so nearly cost his people its rightful existence, and in the cold light of his gaze was embodied every bit of hatred, disgust and, yes, even pity, he could summon up for the mammalian form of life.

The Doctor felt an invisible fist reach out to close around his mind. The fist began to squeeze. He had a single moment to anticipate extinction, a last brief memory of Morka's cold, sweet breath as his face loomed closer and closer, like the Little Planet which had precipitated the whole tragic misunderstanding so long ago . . .

And then he died.

Morka's cheeks trembled and his face distorted in what the mammal would have called a smile. Gradually the rage in his third eye faded, to be replaced with satisfaction.

The Doctor stood quite straight, his face perfectly composed. His hands were open at his sides. The only sign that betrayed his inner turmoil was the loud clatter as his umbrella fell to the floor.

It bounced once, rolled and lay still.

Morka thought the mammal had taken the linked memory of his own death very well, all things considered.

'I think of that moment often,' he said slowly. 'Every time I may be rushing an important decision.'

The Doctor blinked rapidly several times. He bent to retrieve his umbrella slowly, as if movement would bring back to his body the pain still fresh in his mind.

Morka continued, 'I expect you've noticed the function of *crying* in mammals. I sometimes wish I could cry.'

'As an apology, I've . . . heard better,' the Doctor gasped. 'But . . . thank you anyway.'

Morka felt the presence of Chtaachtl outside the room. He dilated the door and she entered. She took in the scene at a glance, her eyes, her senses, missing none of the nuances.

Nodding to Morka, she directed her words at the Doctor.

'Well, mammal,' she said with deliberate malice. 'Military Liaison Icthar has recommended you be studied in some detail.'

'Dissected, you mean,' the Doctor answered weakly.

'Icthar feels there may be much we can learn from examination of your body processes.' She hesitated. 'Is it true you are an alien? That you can change your appearance?'

The Doctor shrugged. 'Morka recognized me. Why not ask him?'

'Morka is old. His perceptions are flawed.'

'And yours are not, I take it? Link with me, Chtaachtl. Examine me and you will see I have two hearts and a lower body temperature than the average human.'

'Link with you? Humans – mammals – cannot link.'

'Then let me prove otherwise!'

'You cannot prove anything. The actions of an intelligent species can be observed and mimicked. The only true test of intelligence is the demonstration of creative thinking. Are you able to demonstrate such thinking?'

The Doctor was about to reply when Morka spoke. 'The Doctor is not answerable to you or to Icthar. He is my guest at the Palace and will remain so until I decide otherwise.

Chtaachtl's cheeks trembled. Her third eye glimmered with anger. 'I hear you, Old One. But the time will come when actions, not words, will determine the destiny of the mammals.'

'And our own destiny, I suspect.' Morka turned to gaze out of the window at the Palace gardens. His weary posture, the set of his shoulders, the dull gleam of his third eye before he turned, all these things told their own story. 'There will – there *must* – be peace!'

The Doctor did not have to see Morka's face to know his inner feelings. There was anger in his voice, desperate anger, but no conviction.

The Doctor suddenly experienced a conviction of his own, a premonition, almost: there will be violence here, he thought. And death on a scale perhaps impossible to comprehend.

The idea came into his head that despite, or perhaps *because* of everything he could do, this world was doomed, and uncounted millions doomed with it.

And how far would the repercussions spread? he wondered. And who would carry the blame?

Ace moved closer to the cage, hypnotized by its single, motionless occupant. She had witnessed death on a monumental scale. She had experienced war, seen its horrors, had taken life herself. Still, there was something about this tableau that wrenched at her; that demanded her attention; that defied her to look away. This was *death*; an end to life. This one single place and time, here and now, would forever be the moment when Ace knew that death was far more than simple *killing*. That the repercussions of death reached out after you forever, and touched you, and *changed* you, and that there was no escaping them, ever. To see the fists of the skeleton grasping the cage bars as if in a last defiant plea, to know that, once, knotted ligaments had held the bones in place, and that the flesh covering them had once been alive with sensations, was a thought more terrifying to Ace than anything she'd ever thought she'd been afraid of before. She found herself imagining the realization in the Doctor's eyes, the moment of understanding, and then the long moment of nothing at all . . . and she staggered forward and grasped the bars of the cage herself, struggling just to keep her balance, her body a mirror to the corpse on the other side of the bars.

She suddenly realized she was no longer angry with the Doctor.

She felt the sensation of arms around her, of warmth in the chill cold of the long-abandoned shelter. 'Manisha,' she whispered. 'I . . .'

'Just don't go all bloody standoffish on me,' the other

woman said sharply. 'Everyone needs to be held sometime.'

'I . . . yeah.' Uneasily, Ace pulled herself clear of Manisha's arms and looked back at the cage. She had a job to do.

Pooled on the floor, like a dinosaur's gizzard stones beneath its skeleton, were a few items which had weathered the years better than the Doctor's body.

A fob watch on a long chain, its shiny surface tarnished by damp. A yoyo. A slim silver cylinder with an adjustable head which she realized from his earlier description of it was the Doctor's sonic screwdriver. A couple of vacuum-formed valves. A 1957 half-a-crown. Three marbles. A key ring with four keys attached to it.

Ace scratched her ear.

There was also a separate length of chain with a single key moulded into the clasp.

Ace reached through the cage bars for the objects. Her hands closed over them when she heard Manisha scream.

Ace whirled, her mind burning with sudden pain, entangled her arm in the bars, lost her balance and fell against the cage, shuddering as she felt something give way in her arm. The Doctor's skeleton collapsed into a cloud of choking dust, closely followed by the skeletons in the other cages.

Ace gasped, momentarily blinded. She tried to get to her feet, reaching out with her hand for leverage. Sickening waves of pain surged through her shoulder and she realized her arm was broken.

Blinking dust and tears from her eyes, Ace saw the flat scarlet glare of Imorkal's third eye as he transfixed Manisha with the killing force.

Her scream was that of an animal; there were no words, just a shuddering outpouring of pain which could find no other release. She collapsed and Imorkal adjusted his gaze to track her falling body.

With the wrong hand, Ace reached in her pocket for the smartbomb.

– *rainydayacesaveitfora* –

A red glare rushed through her mind, backwash from

the killing force. Her head felt as if it would explode. As if from a long way away she heard Manisha scream that her eyes were bleeding they were *bleeding* and why didn't someone –

Ace's fingers closed about the smartbomb.

Imorkal swung his head to target Ace. His third eye glowed fiercely through the choking dust.

She grabbed the tiny sphere.

'Targetreptilianbipedaldistancesixmetresproximitydet-posEXECUTE!'

The smartbomb blurred towards Imorkal.

He reached out and caught it.

ItsadudibuiltadudibuiltafraggingDUD –

Imorkal turned the smartbomb over in his hands, study-ing the smooth shell and tiny, blinking LED. His face stretched in an expression even Ace recognized as con-temptuous. He dropped the tiny device to the floor and dismissed it from his mind. He gazed at Ace and prepared to dismiss her similarly. Ace shut her eyes. Blood trickled from her ears; she felt as though scalding needles were being jammed through them into her brain. This is it, she thought. It's all been for nothing after all.

Then Manisha screamed again and Ace had a sudden overwhelming picture in her mind: of a younger girl screaming from an ambulance stretcher. Of dazzling light as the backdraft blew out the front wall of her house. Of screaming her own impotence as slow flame crept *down* the side of the building, an animal thing, gloating as it brought her the stench of her dying friend . . .

Ace wanted to hit the fire, to hurt it, to hurl her rage and hatred at it, blast it into oblivion.

Her muscles began to spasm, her heart stuttered.

With every ounce of strength she could muster, Ace clenched her fist around the sonic screwdriver she had retrieved from beneath the Doctor's body, aimed it at the flat glare of the Silurian's third eye and randomly triggered a number of different settings.

Imorkal screamed.

Half a world away, Morka convulsed.

The Doctor looked at him in alarm. 'What's wrong?'

Morka ignored him, dropping to his knees as Chtaachtl approached, her face flushed blue, her third eye glowing worriedly.

The Doctor said, 'What are you doing to him!'

Chtaachtl whirled angrily on the Doctor. '*I?* I do nothing!'

'Chtaachtl, I don't understand.'

'Understand this then!' Chtaachtl spat contemptuously. Her third eye glowed brightly and the Doctor felt an image swell to fill his mind. He gasped as the sunlit morning room vanished and –

– he was in a crystal chamber. Dust filled the room. Slatted bars hung suspended in the gloom. There were monsters in here with him, monsters who had killed his protector and teacher, and attacked him. There was blinding pain in his body. Monsters lurched towards him. One fell at the touch of his mind, but the other had picked up a tool and was pointing it at him. He felt an agony of dissolution rush through every limb, felt his mind collapse under the impact of pain upon pain upon –

The Doctor staggered, fell to the floor of the morning room, his body the mindless mirror of another's death. He felt blackness creep in around his vision. Fighting against it he struggled into a sitting position. 'Wait. I know Ace. She'd never kill in cold blood.'

Chtaachtl snapped her head around to gaze at the Doctor. 'You know this creature?'

The Doctor fought to regain his strength. 'Of course I do; she'd never kill anyone in cold blood. She wouldn't even know how to pick a lock with my sonic screwdriver, let alone – '

'The weapon is yours?'

'It's not a weapon, it's just a *tool*.'

Chtaachtl strode to where the Doctor was struggling to rise. 'Then the blame is yours also.'

Her third eye glowed angrily. The Doctor gave a shuddering scream and collapsed back onto the floor. Chtaachtl focused her full anger on the Doctor – then stopped.

Icthar would relish the chance to examine him – while he was still alive.

Summoning an attendant, Chtaachtl had the mammal's body removed. As the attendant left, Chtaachtl turned to find Morka beside the incubator containing his second egg. His hands were placed flat against the translucent crystal casing. He was trembling violently, the veins beneath his skin risen, his cheeks flushed deepest blue.

Chtaachtl stood some distance from him and linked.

Morka needed no images to understand her feelings. *You blame me.*

Of course I blame you! You chose his teachers, his weaponsmaster. You allowed him to admire you, to emulate you. You even told him of the decision you made so long ago: the Nightmare and its consequences for the humans.

I did it to show him I was wrong!

But he was too young to understand! Chtaachtl turned away, trembling.

Morka took her hand and placed it against the glass of the incubator, covered it with his own. *Here is the future now.*

Chtaachtl flushed angrily and wrenched her hand away. *What do you say of peace between our species now?*

Morka was silent.

What do you say!

Still Morka said nothing.

It is your job to ensure the future for the children.

Morka shook his head. 'I know.' He spoke the words quietly, wondering if Chtaachtl really understood the depths of grief and guilt in him, how hard the words were for him to say. 'But the best way to do that is to make peace between our species.'

Chtaachtl hissed contemptuously. 'Of course I understand how difficult if is for you. You feel guilty and so wish to prove yourself worthy of your own self-respect. Your use of the mammal language proves it.' She turned. 'If you cannot ensure the future of the children then others who are stronger will!'

Morka reached out to Chtaachtl, but she turned away

and closed her mind to him. Body rigid with anger, she left the morning room.

Morka stayed by the incubator, reaching out with his mind to soothe the developing intellect of his unborn child.

And outside the morning room, Chtaachtl marched angrily to the Palace Operations Centre. Bursting in she directed a linked command to the Chief of Operations.

Give me control of an opening in the atmospheric blanket over the country the humans call England. And do it quickly! The humans who killed the Leader's son must pay for his death with their own.

'Blimey, it's hot isn't it?'

'An hour ago you were wishing for sunlight,' Ace said.

'Yeah well, that was then.'

The trek from the caves had been quicker than Ace had expected. From the shelter entrance a wide passage led more or less directly to the main cave lower on the hillside. The sunlight had been dazzling as they'd stumbled onto the moor; it wasn't any cooler now, half an hour later. If anything it seemed to be getting hotter.

Ace peered up at the sun. Sweat slipped into her eyes and made them sting. Without thinking she lifted her hand to wipe her face. She gasped as the movement sent waves of agony pulsing along her broken arm. 'Something tells me we'd better get a move on.'

Manisha nodded eagerly. 'Back to the police box?'

'The TARDIS, yeah. Come on. I think it must be this way.' Ace began to fight her way through the undergrowth, using her good arm as a club to beat back the foliage.

Above them, the air rippled in the sun's heat.

By the time they had walked for another twenty minutes the temperature had risen to the point where breathing was difficult.

'Something's going on here,' gasped Manisha.

'Too . . . right!' Ace groped in her pocket for the TARDIS key, slipped the chain around her neck like a necklace for safe-keeping. 'Feels like an atmospheric change. Smell the ozone?'

'Yes, I do. That's going to be a problem if we can't find the TARDIS. Ozone is a poison in sufficient quantity.'

'Great.' Ace shouldered her bag and forged on through the undergrowth, trying to ignore the scalding pain in her shoulder where the buckles had burned through her shirt to bare skin.

Suddenly she shouted: 'We're here! Come on!' She staggered across the little clearing to the wrecked Rover and the reassuringly familiar shape of the TARDIS lying on its side beside the vehicle.

'Al*right!*' She fetched up against the base of the TARDIS, dropped her bag, fished the key on its length of chain from around her neck. Gasping, she staggered around the police box, hunting for the door.

It faced towards the ground.

She couldn't get in.

Ace gazed at the sun. It rippled in the hot air. She ran a hand across her brow, astonished to find the skin there peeling. Sunburn?

'Manisha, come on! We've got to turn the TARDIS over!' There was no reply. Ace turned to see Manisha had collapsed on the other side of the clearing. She ran back to her, tried to lift her, couldn't manage the job with only one arm. She knelt beside her friend, slapped her face. 'Come on! Wake up! Manisha, don't do this to me now! Not now!'

Manisha stirred, groaned, blinked a couple of times and then collapsed back to the ground unconscious. 'No!' All around the clearing, the vegetation was beginning to curl away from the sun.

Ace stumbled to her feet and ran back to the TARDIS. She grasped the edge and began to push with all her strength, trying to tip the device over to allow her to get at the door. 'Come on, come *on!*' The TARDIS tilted, balanced precariously on one edge – then slipped in the dry and crumbling earth, falling back onto the door.

Ace swore; her voice was a ragged croak.

Air molecules shivered wildly in the heat.

Ace grabbed the TARDIS and *heaved*.

Leaves crackled and blackened. Her shirt began to

smoulder. The pain in her broken arm was unbelievable. She realized she was yelling, screaming at the TARDIS to tilt, to tip, to fall, dammit, *fall!*

And then it did.

Ace shoved the key into the lock and twisted. The door fell inwards. Ace was about to crawl inside when she remembered Manisha. She looked around. The other woman hadn't moved. Her shirt was blackening in the heat.

'Not again. Not this time! I won't let you burn again!'

She staggered across the clearing, grabbed hold of Manisha's belt, began to drag her back across the smouldering ground.

Behind her a ginkgo burst into flame. The flame spread rapidly, racing along the side of the clearing. Sparks and smoke exploded into the air. The earth began to burn beneath her feet.

Then she was at the TARDIS, scrambling to push Manisha into the cramped space within, struggling desperately to follow her inside.

She jammed the key into a slot in the console. She felt the TARDIS connect with her mind, drawing information from it, changing her as she changed it.

She reached for the emergency dematerialization switch.

Outside, the clearing dissolved into flame, then even the flame was extinguished as a vast pulse of energy shot down from the sky, vaporizing the crashed Rover as easily as the trees, removing the top foot of soil from the entire acreage of Wenley Moor and fusing the rock beneath into glowing slag.

SSBN HMS *Revenge* cut a smooth furrow through the cold waters of the Atlantic. The submarine's hull was jet black, alive with a constant vibration; it moved forward at a steady ten knots.

Inside the vessel, General Frank Hobson walked unsteadily along the main B deck companionway, opened the watertight hatch to the bridge and stepped through. He was very careful to make sure the hatch was closed properly behind him. He hated being at sea, hated the motion, the *inconstancy* of all that water. He longed for the brief times spent ashore during periods when the submarine was being serviced in the old naval pen on the coast of south Wales. Those times had been few and far between in the last twenty years. Still, he thought with a slow smile. All that was going to change, and very soon now. Lethbridge-Stewart had come up trumps, reliable old military bulldog that he was. If everything went according to plan, Hobson would ensure the Brigadier received a posthumous purple cross. Possibly even a monument. He was the last of a rare breed. A true hero.

The bridge was long and narrow, lined with banks of equipment, and smelling faintly of disinfectant. Banks of computers, navigational equipment, radio, sonar and radar spreads, and torpedo launch and guidance controls branched off to either side of a central companionway, forming small alcoves in which ratings sat. In a more open area towards the centre of the bridge, three thick metal columns ran from deck to ceiling: these were the periscope housings. A clean-cut man in his late forties stood beside them. This was Robin Ridgway, Captain of the *Revenge*. Ridgway turned, saluting as Hobson came closer.

'We're all ready to start the test run, General,' he said. 'if you have your key . . .?'

'Of course.' Hobson fished inside his shirt and pulled a tiny key on a length of chain from around his neck. Ridgway did the same. Then both men crossed to a small metal safe on one side of the bridge. The safe was secured by two locks.

Back at the far end of the bridge, the locking wheel of the hatch Hobson had been so careful to close turned slowly, and the hatch itself eased open an inch. There was a dim glitter at the crack, as if someone were peering through.

On the other side of the hatch, Bernice suppressed a shiver of fear as she watched the two men unlock the safe. Then Ridgway reached inside and withdrew a slim book. The same book she had seen the Brigadier pass to Hobson before she and Billy had sneaked aboard through the aft escape hatch.

Beside her Bernice could hear Billy breathing quietly. 'If we hang around here much longer we're going to get caught,' he hissed urgently.

Bernice nodded. 'Billy, we're on a submarine; they don't exactly build these places with stowaways in mind. We were lucky the bloke who opened the hatch for us wasn't expecting to see a woman.' She sucked her bruised knuckles and grinned. 'You're right though: we're going to get caught eventually. But if we can find out what they're up to beforehand, then we stand a better chance of stopping them, don't we?'

Billy frowned. He was peering back up the companionway. 'There's someone coming!'

Bernice thought quickly. 'It's okay,' she said. 'I've got a plan . . .'

On the bridge Ridgway ran his fingers across the cover of the book. 'Prepare to input firing codes,' he told the weapons officer.

'Aye, sir.'

He opened the book carefully and began to read out columns of numbers. As he reached the end of each, the weapons officer entered them into the computer, where they were transmitted to the main launch control system in the missile tube bay, further aft.

Ridgway hesitated when he found a cup of coffee pressed into his hands. 'Thanks,' he said, 'uh . . .'

'Billy,' said Billy, pulling his cap further down over his eyes. It was just as well the cap was a bit too big for him; the rating he'd knocked out, and whom Bernice was guarding, hadn't exactly been a small man.

Ridgway nodded his thanks and sipped his coffee.

Billy peered over his shoulder at the book of codes.

Hobson moved closer, took a cup of coffee from the tray Billy held. 'That'll be all, mister,' he said.

Billy nodded and began to sidle away.

The weapons officer said, 'Missile room confirms input of control codes, sir.'

Ridgway nodded. 'Begin systems check.'

'Aye, sir.'

Billy moved further back through the bridge. He set down the tray of coffee cups and was about to leave the bridge when the hatch opened from the other side. A rating dressed in shorts and a singlet pushed Bernice onto the bridge and stepped through after her. Bernice glanced at Billy and shrugged helplessly. Billy looked around quickly, trying to find somewhere to hide. There was nowhere.

The rating pointed at him. 'There he is! Stowaway!' he yelled. He pushed Bernice forward and she cannoned into Billy. In the confusion Billy had time to whisper a few words to Bernice, but she didn't have a chance to speak before Hobson and Ridgway turned to see what the commotion was.

Hobson was holding a gun.

Bernice froze, signalled Billy to do the same. She took in the book, the keys, the open safe with a single glance. 'You're going to attack the Silurians, aren't you?' she said. 'With nuclear weapons!' Her voice rose in horror. 'You're going to start a war!'

Hobson's voice remained calm and even. 'On the contrary, Miss Summerfield. I'm going to – finally – end one.'

'How the hell to you know my name?'

'A radio message from the Brigadier. He found your horses tethered at the docks. We've known you were on board for some hours now. There was no way you could escape, so we thought we'd play you along a little, find out what you were up to.'

Bernice swore.

Hobson smiled politely.

She was about to swear again when a rating manning the sonar station interrupted. 'Sir, I have a new contact: bearing zero six four. Speed twenty-five knots. Contact designated: tango-seven-niner.'

Hobson's smile faded.

Ridgway crossed to the sonar spread and leaned over the panel. 'Tell me about it, Charlie.'

The sonar operator fine-tuned some controls and

pressed his headphones a little tighter against his ears. 'It's an unusual signal, buried in surface clutter. And . . . I have some thermal layer reflectivity also . . . but there's no reactor noise that I can hear. And definitely no cavitation.'

'Could it be one of the big aquatic dinosaurs? We've seen kronosaurs up to eighty feet long.'

'Uh . . . I don't think so, sir, no. I'd hear the movement of water across its skin.'

'Very well. Start your track.'

'Start track, aye.' Charlie hit a command sequence and the noise was recorded. The sonar continued to blip gently.

Casting a wary glance at Bernice, Hobson also crossed to the sonar station. 'Will you confirm a hostile contact?'

Charlie looked up. 'Contact confirmed, General. I think we have another bogey.'

Ridgway said, 'Helm: all stop. Let's hope it hasn't heard us.'

'Helm answering: all stop, aye.'

'Sir.' It was Charlie again. 'Contact changing heading to one-niner-seven. Speed now thirty knots. I think they've acquired us, sir.'

'Helm: come right to zero-five-niner. Speed ten knots.'

'Coming right, speed ten knots, aye.'

While still keeping his gun aimed at Bernice, Hobson leaned towards Ridgway and said in a quiet voice, 'We have to submerge. We're a sitting duck on the surface.'

Ridgway answered sharply, 'You know how dangerous that is.'

'We have no choice.'

'The hull may not be able to take the strain!'

'Captain – do as I say! If we can put a few thermal layers between ourselves and this bogey we may lose him. Otherwise . . .'

Ridgway scowled. After a moment's thought, he said, 'Stand by to flood tanks.'

'Standing by.'

Charlie said, 'Sir, range to contact now five hundred yards. Bearing one-niner-five and closing. He's definitely tracking us.'

'Alright.' Ridgway began to bark orders in a steady stream. 'Helm: submerge. Come right to zero-five-zero. Down five degrees. But gently. Tactical: load and lock two Tigerfish. Wait for my order to fire.'

'Helm answering: submerge, down five degrees, speed three knots.'

'Tactical answering: port torpedo room signals aye.'

Bernice looked around in alarm as the hull began to creak gently. Nobody else seemed to notice. Or at least to respond. She wondered if they all could have gone mad.

'What's our depth?' asked Ridgway.

'Passing three hundred.'

'Good. Level off. How are we doing, Charlie?'

'Range to contact now four hundred. Contact is still tracking.'

'Helm: come right full rudder. Tactical: stand by to fire one.'

Hobson said urgently: 'If we destroy that contact the Silurians will know we're here.'

'I can't help that. You know what will happen if we come within range of their weapons.'

'They'll melt a hole right through us just like they did the *Resolution* and all the other SSBNs.'

'Damn right they will.'

'Sir, range to contact now two hundred. Speed increasing to . . . forty knots.'

'Tactical, sir: they'll be within firing range in seconds.'

'Fire one! Helm come left to zero-seven-five. Speed: ten knots.'

'Fire one, aye!'

'Zero-seven-five, aye. She won't make ten knots submerged, Captain.'

'Best speed then!'

'Aye, sir. Speed now five knots.'

Bernice grabbed hold of the periscope housing as the deck began to shake.

'Sir,' said Charlie. 'Torpedoes away and running true.' Suddenly he stiffened, one hand rising to his headphones.

'Sir, the bogey has altered its signature! I think they're preparing to fire – '

There was a tremendous concussion. The submarine shook wildly, then tilted downwards. Bernice heard the sound of water rushing across the hull and boiling into steam. She lost her grip on the ladder and fell sideways into Hobson. Both of them went flying.

' – helm: full left – '
' – hydraulic failure! Planes not – '
' – our depth! Watch – '
' – got a fire over here – '
' – to environment systems! Repeat: fire control to – '
' – our depth, I said – '
' – passing five hundred – '
' – the hull will never – '

There was no time to think. The air was full of smoke and flame. A panel exploded above her head, showering her with burning sparks. Ignoring the pain, she grabbed for Hobson's gun arm. She expected resistance, but the General was pathetically weak. He struggled to aim the gun at her but she was able to wrench it from his grasp easily.

' – up ten degrees – '
' – planes still not responding – '
' – lighten her up! Lighten her – '
' – eight hundred – '
' – them all! Blow everything – '
' – all blown, sir – '
' – vent tanks inside – '
' – vented! Vents shut – '

Peripherally she was aware of Billy running interference for her. A rating collapsed with a painful sigh as Billy's fists blurred into his face. Then the gun was aimed, not at Hobson but at Ridgway.

' – we've got her back again. I think – '
' – planes now responding – '
' – going to make it. I think we're going to – '

'If you've got any sense,' Bernice hissed, panting, 'you'll tell them all to return to their stations.'

The ratings froze. In the sudden quiet, Bernice could

260

hear very clearly the creaking sound of stressed hull plates. The rating she had kicked to the deck stirred and groaned. Somewhere behind her was the sound of fire extinguishers.

'Billy – help him up.'

As Billy moved to comply, Ridgway watched Bernice narrowly. 'If you've got any sense you'll realize that firing the gun in here will undoubtedly damage some important system, perhaps even puncture the hull. We could all die.'

Bernice hesitated, cocked the pistol, smiled. 'Give me the book.'

Ridgway shook his head. 'You know I can't do that.'

Bernice frowned impatiently. 'You can't believe him!' She jerked the gun towards Hobson. Before she could continue, the General took his chance and grabbed her arm. Her finger closed reflexively over the trigger. A bullet whined off the deck as Billy swung a fist into the side of Hobson's head. Charlie yelled as the bullet pierced his arm and continued on to blast a chunk from the sonar spread. Dark glass fragments showered the rating as he fell to the floor. Bernice flinched away from the explosion and suddenly everyone was moving.

Hobson was on his knees, clutching his head. Billy was wrestling with two ratings in the confined space of the navigation well. Bernice suddenly found the rating whose clothes Billy had stolen had leaped to attack her. She swung around but as she did so Ridgway knocked the gun from her hand. She kicked the rating hard on the knee and jumped over him as he fell.

'Billy! Let's go!'

Billy cracked the heads of two ratings together and ran after her, only to trip over the kneeling form of General Hobson. In that moment the rating she had kicked scooped the gun from where she'd dropped it, flopped over on his side and fired after her. The bullet took Billy in the neck as he fell. Ridgway's shout to hold fire was drowned in the sound of the gunshot and the explosion as the bullet passed through Billy to damage the environment controls.

Bernice ran backwards, tripped on the hatch coaming and fell through. Scrambling to her feet, she could see that the confined space of the companionway was now working to her advantage. Ridgway was taking the gun from the rating, and nobody else could get past. Then her gaze fell to where Billy was lying on the deck, blood soaking his collar. With a grim expression she slammed the hatch and spun the wheel, jamming it in place with a spanner she grabbed from a wall-mounted tool kit nearby. Then she turned, landed a sharp right hook on the chin of a rating who was staring at her with open-mouthed astonishment and took off along the corridor. The rating hit the deck, mouth still agape with surprise. He stayed down.

In the bridge, Hobson struggled to his feet, panting, heart hammering in his chest. A tingling sensation ran down his left arm and he winced. A rating helped him to his feet and he nodded gratefully.

He looked around. The stowaway, Billy, was lying on the deck, his face resting in a puddle of his own blood. The rating Bernice had kicked was groaning and clutching his knee as he struggled upright.

Ridgway slipped the safety on the gun. 'All personnel return to your stations. I want a damage report in ten minutes. Lieutenant Mitchell, see if you can get the hatch open, then send some men after her. Navigation, when damage has been assessed continue on course at best speed.'

He turned to see Hobson watching him intently. He gestured with the book he still held. 'Don't worry. It's quite safe.'

Hobson sighed with relief. 'Thank heavens.'

'So, what do we do now?'

Hobson shrugged. 'What else can we do? Continue with the dry run when the damage has been assessed, and try to catch that . . . woman.'

Mitchell called, 'The hatch is open.'

'Get after her then. And get Harry up here. Tell him Darnell's broken his knee.'

'Sir!'

Bernice ran aft into a room filled with banks of computers and then through another hatch leading to a long chamber containing twin rows of thick, red-painted cylinders. The cylinders reached from floor to ceiling. Each was inset with a circular inspection hatch. As she dogged the hatch behind her, Bernice was aware of running footsteps from somewhere in the chamber. She turned in time to see a rating level a gun at her. She dived to the ground as he fired. The bullet tore through her left bicep, leaving a track of scalding pain and blood. She rolled clumsily behind the nearest cylinder. At once she heard the rating's footsteps as he approached. Gasping with pain from her wound, Bernice tried to still her breathing. She slipped around the cylinder, timing her movements to keep her on the opposite side to the rating. As she moved, a painted sign on the cylinder caught her eye: the trisected circle of radiation hazard warning.

She thought: I really don't need this.

There was a sound from the other side of the cylinder. The scuff of rubber-soled shoes on metal deck plates.

Bernice flattened herself against the cylinder as the rating came into view, gun arm first. Then she grabbed his wrist with her good hand. He yelled with surprise. Using all the force she could muster, Bernice swung herself inside his gun arm, grabbed, twisted – and the rating flew over her shoulder and crashed headfirst into a cylinder in the next row. The gun flew from his hand and landed with a clatter on the deck. The rating slumped, unconscious, leaning against the cylinder.

Bernice grabbed at her wounded arm and stifled a yell of agony. After a moment she regained her breath, picked up the gun, and pointed it – rather unnecessarily, as it turned out – at the rating.

He did not move.

'Well what do you know,' she mumbled indistinctly. 'It actually worked.'

She struggled to control her breathing. Her arm felt as if acid had been poured over it. Her sleeve was soaked with blood, and so was her other hand, where she had grabbed at the wound; the gun she held was also covered in it. She knew she would have to control the bleeding even though the wound was only superficial. But first she had to check out the missile chamber. It all looked pretty automated. With any luck her snoring friend would have been the only rating on duty here.

Keeping the gun levelled, Bernice walked cautiously through the chamber. Halfway down the chamber there was a circular hatch set into the floor. The hatch was open. Bernice listened at the coaming. There was no sound of conversation or footsteps. No pushing of buttons or rattling of clipboards. Cautiously she stuck her head through the hatch. The chamber was empty. She climbed down the metal ladder. The red cylinders continued down into this deck. She found each cylinder had a grey metal cabinet bolted to its base. The cabinets were all locked. Each was stencilled with a hazard warning sign, and with the words: *cold gas launch firing key*. Forward, there was a bank of grey metal cabinets labelled: *launch control*. Beyond was a bulkhead fitted with a hatch similar to the one through which she had entered the deck above. Quickly she closed and locked it. Then she climbed the ladder back into the upper chamber and continued aft, locking the hatch there. With any luck she was now completely sealed off.

She walked unsteadily back to the unconscious rating. He had not moved. Ripping her shirt sleeve off, Bernice tied it round her arm as a makeshift dressing. Then she wiped the blood from her hands on the rating's uniform. Then she sat wearily on the floor with her back to one of the cylinders and tried to decide what to do next.

After a minute or two had passed she heard someone banging on the forward hatch. There was the sound of distant voices calling, but the words were indistinct, muffled by distance and by a metal bulkhead. Bernice jerked, realized she had closed her eyes. She opened them and found herself looking at the rating. He had opened his eyes and was obviously assessing the possibility of regaining the gun from her.

Bernice jerked the gun up and aimed it at him. 'It's here if you want it.'

The rating made no move.

What the hell do I do now? she thought. Aloud, she asked, 'What's your name?'

'Wallace. Tom Wallace.'

'Yeah, Tom. I'm Bernice. I'm sorry about your head. I bet it hurts like hell, right?'

'No worse than your arm.'

'Yeah.' Bernice gave a short laugh. She waved the gun. 'Well, Tom Wallace. I'm afraid I'm going to have to ask you for a little favour.'

Tom remained silent.

Bernice levelled the gun at his head. 'I did ask nicely.'

'Go to hell.'

Bernice lowered the gun until it was pointing at Tom's lap. 'Sure you don't want to reconsider?'

Tom swallowed hard. 'Okay, okay! Don't shoot! What do you want?'

Bernice smiled thinly. She realized she had decided what she had to do.

'I want you to show me how to arm and detonate a missile.'

The Brigadier walked slowly onto the bridge of the Silurian airship. He looked around himself curiously. This was the first chance he'd had to inspect the captured leviathan. The bridge was teeming with technicians, all studying the various control systems and reporting their findings to Liz, who was herself examining the central systems ranged around the command well.

She looked up as he approached. 'Brigadier.'

He nodded. 'How are things going?'

Liz straightened up, rubbing her back. 'Very much better than I expected, actually. Apparently, for some reason I can't explain, our race fear of Silurian technology seems to be diminishing.'

The Brigadier frowned.

Liz smiled. 'Surely you must have noticed it yourself.'

'Now you come to mention it, yes.'

'Well, it's working to our advantage. The analysts I've had working on the motive and attack systems are really coming up trumps. I think with a couple more weeks' work we could modify them for use by UNIT personnel.'

'I'm afraid "a couple more weeks" are completely out of the question,' the Brigadier said flatly. 'You have eight hours.'

Liz gaped. 'That's insane! We'll never do it.'

'My thinking on this is very clear: there is no alternative except destruction. You have priority call on any resources or manpower from the Complex.' The Brigadier sighed. He seemed to collapse internally. 'Make it work, Liz,' he whispered. 'Not for me. For the children.'

Liz bit her lip and did not reply.

'I've locked out the bridge computers. Which missile do you want to arm?'

Bernice glared at Tom and levelled the gun. 'Just arm any of them!'

Tom began to input commands into the fire-control computer. 'You realize you're quite mad, don't you? If you detonate a missile in the sub we'll all die.'

'One nuclear bomb can ruin your whole day, right?' She smiled dryly as Tom turned away in disgust. 'Your General Hobson wants to start a war that would probably wipe out all life on this planet.'

'We're just taking back what's ours.'

'That's what the Silurians said.' Bernice shook her head. 'Why can't any of you see the big picture? As an archaeologist, I've seen the remains of more dead cultures than you've had ice lollies!'

'Yeah, and we're going to be one of them unless we do something about it.'

'Ever thought about negotiation?'

'Frankly no.'

'Maybe I should let you kill yourselves.' Bernice sighed. 'Trouble with that is the Silurians would die as well.'

Tom glanced at her scornfully. He didn't need to speak for Bernice to know what he was thinking. 'And before you say anything, don't. Just get on with the programming.' She gestured once more with the gun, and for a few minutes more the only sound to break the silence was

266

the clicking of Tom's fingers on the keyboard. Then he input a final command. The lights in the fire-control room suddenly turned red. A radiation alert siren blared loudly.

'That's it,' Tom said over the sound of the siren.

'How do I know you're not lying?'

'See that red light there on the missile ready check display?'

'Yes?'

'That means I'm not lying.'

Bernice studied Tom for a moment. Satisfied, she gestured with the gun. 'How do I detonate it?'

Tom pointed to a glass flap covering an absurdly clichéd looking large red button. 'Just hit that and you can kiss your arse goodbye.'

Bernice smiled humourlessly. 'Why thank you for that gem of wisdom, Thomas.' Her voice hardened. 'Now get me the bridge on the intercom.'

The intercom was already bleeping for attention.

'This is Ridgway. Our systems monitor tells us we have a "go" situation on missile oh-eight. What the hell are you playing at down there, mister?'

Tom pressed the *speak* button. 'Fire control, aye. We've got what you might call a situation here, Captain.'

Bernice pushed Tom aside and spoke loudly into the intercom. 'This is Professor Bernice Summerfield. I'm afraid I have some rather bad news for you.'

'You're not kidding, lady! Do you know what you've done?'

'I've armed a missile and I'll detonate it unless I have your assurance that we will return to England immediately and remove the firing cores from all missiles.'

Now Hobson's voice came over the intercom. *'Miss Summerfield, by performing this action you have become a traitor to your own species. I cannot allow your threats to jeopardize my mission.'*

'Your mission is to start a war! It's genocide! Don't you think the Silurians will fight back with everything they've got?'

'A sufficiently well-planned pre-emptive strike will ensure

total obliteration of main centres of Silurian population. We will succeed.'

'You cannot succeed!'

'My plan has been two decades in the making. It cannot fail.'

'You're mad! The Silurians are civilized, intelligent people who want to make peace. I can't let you start a war with them.'

'You'll be killing yourself as well if you push that switch.'

'Do you think I don't know that?' Bernice's finger tightened angrily on the gun's trigger as she swung it to cover Tom. 'Back off! I have to do this. If you had an inkling of the bigger picture you'd agree with me.'

Tom sucked in a deep breath. 'That's exactly the rationalization General Hobson uses.'

'General Hobson is insane!'

'I rest my case.'

'Get out of my way!'

'This isn't going to happen!'

There were running footsteps. Suddenly the room was filled with ratings.

Bernice thought: a hatch, I missed a bloody –

And: they were just keeping me talking while –

'Give me the gun!'

Tom made a grab for the pistol and Bernice swung it against the side of his head. He groaned and sank to the floor. Ratings leaped towards her from the aft part of the chamber. Bernice flung the gun at the nearest. He ducked, pulled a gun, aimed it at Bernice.

'I have orders to shoot to kill!'

'But I'm going to die anyway, so you see, I can't let you stop me now!' Bernice turned, screaming as the first bullet tore into her chest, coughing blood as she flipped back the glass flap and slammed her fist down on the red button.

I can't let you stop me now.

The red light turned green.

DETONATION: POSITIVE.

Circling the Palace operations room was a ring of huge, free-floating mind-screens, each flanked by control systems. The room lighting was a subterranean dim green, but the light from the screens was generated by hot daylight; the screens showed views at various places in the city. Technicians stood at regular points around the room, monitoring the screens and operating systems. The fluting sound of information exchange was present, as always. Standing to one side, Morka found himself oddly comforted by the soothing, almost musical quality of the sound.

He looked into the command well where the city director would normally have sat. Chtaachtl sat there now. Her eyes were fixed on a large monitor screen directly in front of her.

The screen showed a murky, grey-green light: water. An object slid through the murk. Morka recognized the subtle curves of one of his people's deep-sea craft and realized the scene he was experiencing was made up of memories drawn from the mind of a crew member – one of the sea dwellers.

He thought: why was that Silurian in the water?

Without turning, Chtaachtl linked. *Watch!*

Another shape came into view, long, thin, an angry wake of turbulence thrashing at one end, propelling it forward. *Torpedo.* Morka shuddered. The thing was ugly. Human. He started to speak again, but was interrupted by a bright flash as the second object struck the Silurian craft. The craft vanished and the screen was suddenly full of sinking wreckage. The picture shuddered as the crew member who was experiencing the scene was overcome by the pressure wave. Morka puffed out his cheeks, hissing with pain that was just as real as the other Silurian's.

Now Chtaachtl turned to stare accusingly at Morka. *You have just seen the destruction of one of our deep-sea craft by a human vessel.*

That is impossible! There are no more human vessels capable of such an act. They were all destroyed!

You are wrong, Morka. If you doubt me you have only to link! The mind-screens are now showing images in real time.

Morka returned his attention to the screen.

The images flickered as the Silurian hovered on the

brink of unconsciousness. The pressure wave rocked the sinking debris, swirling it into a storm of jagged chunks. Through the mess of wreckage a new shape could be seen. Cylindrical, like the torpedo but vastly bigger. The shape drove through the wreckage, batting it aside like weed. The images began to shudder now, and Morka realized the Silurian in the water had recovered slightly and was trying to swim away from the huge object bearing down on him. Morka blinked each eye in turn, aware that the whole of the operations room was transfixed by the scene.

The swimming Silurian was struck by the huge prow of the vessel.

Morka shuddered with pain and the scene rolled sharply –

– as he was dragged along the side of the vessel, caught in its powerful wake. Water swirled through his gills, cloying, dense. He could feel the bubbles in the liquid as he struggled to extract the oxygen he needed to breathe. But the effort was too much. He was being smashed repeatedly into the hull of the craft. He tried to swim clear, but his arm caught on a metal fin which tilted as he touched it. He shrieked soundlessly as the arm snapped and he was whirled away, back along the side of the vessel. Now the water was clouded with blood from his arm as well as wreckage from his craft. He felt his outer eyelids blink involuntarily to shield his eyes from the worst of the debris. He thumped once more into the great metal hull of the craft, rolled along it, felt it taper beneath him, felt himself drift clear. He opened his eyes with relief, then let loose an ultrasonic scream of fear when he realized he was being dragged towards the driving mechanism of the –

Morka hissed with pain as all coherent thought vanished in a churning whirlpool of agony. He sank to his knees, gasping for breath, aware that more than one member of the operations room staff had done the same, unable to tell if the pulsing sound he heard was the terrified pumping of the dying Silurian's heart or the relentless noise of propellers driving the human warship forward through the cold water.

The screen gradually went blank. The pain began to

fade. Morka struggled to his feet, aware that every mind was focused on him.

Chtaachtl was the first to link. *The humans have started a war.*

Morka shuddered and closed his eyes against the guilt which threatened to overwhelm him. This had to end! Somehow this madness had to end. *What do you want me to do?*

The road to Trident began at a church fête.

Ridgway glanced around the bridge of the submarine and felt the world was closing in around him. He'd been a lieutenant before the Nightmare happened. Just a lieutenant. Oh, he'd agreed in principle with the concept of a nuclear deterrent. Believed that sufficient strength in wise enough hands would maintain the knife-edge balance of peace. Had even been proud of his part in that peace. Now he was a captain, not by promotion, but of necessity; twenty years older aand twenty years wiser. With hindsight he could see how precarious the balance had been, even in the best years. Could see how the construction of HMS *Revenge* and her four sister ships to carry Poseidon missiles with MIRV warheads had been the thin end of the wedge. Trident was on the drawing board; the nuclear deterrent would have come of age.

He thought: we were due to clock out even before the Nightmare. Right from the moment William Bourne drafted the first designs for a submersible warship in 1578; and earlier, from the moment the idea had been generated within Bourne's mind.

The road to Trident began at a church fête.

'Robin.' The urgent, weary voice belonged to General Hobson.

Ridgway came back to the present with a start. 'General?'

'Now that the panic is over, I suggest we resume the missile test sequence.' He paused. 'It wouldn't do for us to throw a load of wet squibs at the reps, now would it?'

'I agree.' Ridgway smiled thinly. 'Except for number eight, I presume.'

'Ah yes, except for the fortunate number eight. Fortunate for us, that is.'

Ridgway found the callous edge to Hobson's voice oddly out of character. Despite his resolve, his mind filled with images of the woman – Bernice, he reminded himself, her name had been Bernice – sprawled across the fire-control computers, coughing blood, hammering weakly at the launch control. How could she know that the fissile material for missile number eight had deteriorated years ago, and had been jettisoned along with all its chemical fuel?

'You know,' he began hesitantly. 'I'm not so sure this is a –'

Hobson's voice was like a savage bite. 'You're not going to let me down, are you, Robin?'

Ridgway chewed on his lower lip.

'If it's any consolation. I will take full responsibility for our actions here today,' said Hobson.

Responsibility to whom? Ridgway thought.

Hobson must have read his mind. 'To the future, m'boy. The future.'

The Brigadier gazed out of the airship at the African savannah rolling past far below. Despite being weary to his bones, the Brigadier found the experience of flying exhilarating after so long living underground. The air smelled so damn good.

Beside him, Liz Shaw gripped the observation gallery handrail and shook her hair out of her face.

The Brigadier glanced at Liz. 'Bracing, isn't it?'

Liz's expression hardened. Unlike the Brigadier, she was not uplifted by the sight of vast herds of dinosaurs moving along the ground in the wake of the airship.

'As good a day as any to commit genocide,' she said.

Lieutenant Tony Mitchell knocked once and entered the Captain's cabin. 'The missile test sequence is complete.'

'And?'

'You want the bad news or the bad news? It comes in special easy-to-grasp packages for the hard of thinking.'

Ridgway smiled. 'Tell you what, hit me with the bad news.'

'Well, from a total of fifteen missiles, not counting number eight, three aren't going to fire, and two more might not reach the target if they did. That leaves us with a thundering grand total of eleven missiles, or thirty-three MIRVs in go condition.'

'More than enough to wipe out the Silurian's cities, even if they are all as big as Wales.' He considered. 'So what's the bad news?'

'Well, the bullet Jonesey put through that Summerfield woman knocked out the inertial guidance system. We've lost all current location coordinates. Without knowing where we are we can't supply the missile guidance system with a target.'

Ridgway swore. 'That is a problem. How long to fix it?'

'I'm not sure it can be fixed, the gyros are shot. And anyway, we still wouldn't know where we were without sailing to a fixed reference point and returning to launch position.'

'There's no time for that. Lethbridge-Stewart is already en route.' Ridgway considered. 'We'll wait until nightfall and take a fix by the stars.'

'If it's not cloudy.'

'If it's not cloudy,' Ridgway agreed. He drummed his fingertips lightly against the desk. 'How are the other repairs going?'

'Sonar control transferred to the backup system, so that's okay. The other stuff . . .' He shrugged. 'Some of the lads are slapping Band-aids on the worst bits now.'

'And the hull?'

'Intact.' Mitchell uttered a short laugh. 'Though I wouldn't plan on diving for pearls in the near future.'

'Hm. What time's sundown tonight?'

Mitchell glanced at his watch. 'According to the almanac, four hours seven minutes from now.'

'I see. Well. Thanks, Tony.'

'Sure. You want me to tell the General?'

'No.' Ridgway sighed tiredly. 'That's the Captain's privilege.'

Mitchell nodded, saluted, turned smartly and left the cabin.

No sooner had the door closed behind him than the intercom bleeped. '*Bridge to Captain.*'

Ridgway thumbed the transmit toggle. 'Captain aye. What's cooking?'

'*Sonar reports multiple images sir. More than a hundred! They're all around us!*'

Ridgway swore. 'Don't let them do anything until I get there!'

He left the cabin at a dead run.

Darkness.

A pounding headache.

The Doctor stirred groggily. He opened his eyes. The darkness was shot through with streaks of murky green. Underwater? No: respiratory bypass not in effect. Where then?

The Doctor tried to turn his head, found he had only a limited movement. Restraints? He shook his arms. There were weights at his wrists. He heard the *clink* of metal on glass.

Chained to a crystal pillar somewhere in the dark. On ice until Icthar decided what to do with him.

Oh no, he thought. Can't have that.

He began to contract the muscles in his hands.

Something smashed against the hull with a reverberating clang.

Ridgway burst onto the bridge as the collision alarm sounded. Unprepared for the shock, ratings had fallen over amid a flurry of loose trash. Pens, paper, clipboards and coffee cups flew across the deck.

'Sonar: what the hell was that?'

'Sonar, aye. One of the blips just . . . just rammed us!'

'What?' Ridgway began to climb the metal ladder leading into the conning tower. 'Helm: put us on the surface! Now!'

A thin dribble of water ran down the conning tower as Ridgway pushed up the hatch and scrambled into the observation well. He stared around him blank-eyed with astonishment.

All around the sea was bubbling and frothing. A collection of aquatic dinosaurs surrounded the submarine, swimming on or just below the surface, some leaping clear like killer whales and slamming back with immense force. Some of them were more than fifty feet long. As he watched, one particularly large specimen, a kronosaurus, rammed its huge armoured head against the hull.

The submarine *lurched*.

Ridgway peered closer. There was something attached to the kronosaurus, straddling it just behind its huge head. A smaller fish? A remora? No . . . it didn't look much like any fish he'd ever seen.

In another moment Mitchell and Hobson had joined him, the older man clutching a pair of binoculars like a life-saver. 'Robin? What's going on here?'

Ridgway grabbed the binoculars and peered through them.

'Aquatic Silurians,' he said wonderingly, 'riding bloody aquatic dinosaurs.' He handed the binoculars back to Hobson. 'And they're trying to knock holes in the hull!'

The Brigadier walked into the airship's auxiliary bay. With him were Captain Wood and Sergeant Benton. The bay was several hundred yards long, open to the air. Filling the bay to two-thirds capacity were the slim shapes of the two remaining auxiliary airships. A crew of twenty stood to attention in a line beside each airship.

The Brigadier halted and turned to his companions. 'Well, gentlemen. It's time to go our separate ways.'

Benton looked as if he was about to say something.

'No speeches, Sergeant.'

Benton nodded.

The Brigadier shook each man warmly by the hand, then saluted smartly while Benton and Wood walked in opposite directions to the boarding ramps of the auxiliaries.

When both crews had boarded and the ramps had

retracted, the Brigadier brought his arm smartly down to his side, turned and marched stiffly from the bay.

Behind him, the airships lifted, gliding slowly towards the exit portals.

Ridgway grabbed the conning tower handrail as the sub shuddered again.

'How can they do that?' asked Hobson. 'Move the sub like that?'

Mitchell peered to starboard. 'They must be synchronizing their attack, hitting us below the water line.'

Ridgway nodded. 'If they crack the hull we've had it.'

Hobson looked around in alarm. 'Can they do that?'

'Twenty-five, thirty tonnes travelling at a couple of knots. You work it out.'

Mitchell scowled. 'They could probably do it even if the hull wasn't twenty years old.'

Hobson looked around nervously. 'Well, can't you . . . I don't know, torpedo them or something?'

'That's probably just what they want us to do. These dinosaurs are being directed to attack us.'

Hobson shuddered. 'Silurians?'

Mitchell swore. 'They're probably waiting for us to waste all our torpedoes blowing up the fish before moving into range themselves. Smart buggers.'

Hobson's voice took on a harder edge. 'Oh they're smart alright. We have to be smarter.'

A kronosaurus suddenly leaped completely clear of the water and landed on the deck forward of the conning tower.

The submarine shuddered. Ridgway lost his grip on the handrail, went spinning across the observation well to crash against the low wall on the other side. Through the ringing in his head he thought he heard a despairing scream and a faint splash. Ridgway scrambled to his feet and looked around. A great plume of spray shot into the air as the dinosaur slithered off into the water and sank quickly out of sight. Drenched, Hobson was scrabbling on the deck of the well. The conning-tower hatch fastening had snapped and the hatch had slammed shut on his arm. Mitchell was nowhere in sight.

'Tony!'

The submarine shuddered again. The blows were coming with terrible regularity. Dimly, Ridgway was aware of Hobson screaming, trying to lift the hatch one-handed from his arm.

'*Tony!*'

Ridgway staggered to port and stared down at the heaving sea. Nothing. He crossed to starboard, helped by a sudden lurch of the submarine in that direction. Still nothing.

He grabbed the hatch and lifted it clear of Hobson's arm. He stuck his head into the opening and yelled: 'Man overboard!'

Beside him, Hobson was scrambling to get down the hatch.

Ridgway groped for the life belt, knowing it was useless. If Mitchell was in the water he was dead. He threw the belt anyway.

In the Palace operations room, Chtaachtl was watching a mind-screen depicting the attack on the submarine when one of the operatives turned from another monitor station and signalled for her attention.

She linked impatiently. *Well?*

We have reports of a massive movement of animal life on the north-west city border.

Are these reports confirmed?

They are. Loss of property is considerable. The operative hesitated. *There have been . . . some deaths.*

Chtaachtl's body tensed in anger. *These animals. Are they reptile or mammal?*

Reptile.

Chtaachtl hissed. *Reptiles do not behave this way naturally. The humans have found a way to control them.*

The operative turned briefly to receive a new report. *Loss of life and property is mounting*, he sent urgently.

Then they must be stopped! We must protect our people!

277

The operative hestitated. *But human mind-emissions cannot be detected.*

I know that! Chtaachtl sent angrily. *Their minds are weak!* She paused thoughtfully. *Begin a search for the engine signature of my warship.*

At once.

And evacuate the areas of the city most heavily affected.

Evacuation is already underway.

Morka said softly, 'We could abandon the attack on the human submarine and direct our mind energies to deflecting the reptiles.'

Chtaachtl almost screamed: 'That is what they want us to do!' Recovering, she linked. *Without our energies to help them, our aquatic kin are powerless. We cannot abandon the attack on the human warship!*

If we do not, the reptiles will destroy our city.

But if we do, the warship will destroy our city with nuclear weapons!

Morka nodded. *This is true.*

Chtaachtl hissed angrily. *This is your doing, Morka!* She returned her attention to the mind-screen, wondering how long they could maintain the attack in the face of the new threat.

She summoned an aide.

Bring the Doctor here! She turned to Morka, a triumphant expression on her face. *We will force him to help us.*

And if he cannot?

I will kill him!

Ridgway fastened the heavy-weather rig around his waist and clipped the straps to the conning tower rail. He clicked on the intercom. 'Captain to bridge. Make revolutions for five knots. Course oh-seven-nine.'

'*Bridge, aye,*' came a tinny voice in response.

'Are the torpedoes loaded?'

'*Aye, Captain. We've programmed the on-board guidance system to hunt for Silurian vessel signatures.*'

'Good! Fire one!'

A thin white stream of bubbles emerged from the prow of the submarine and streaked away.

There was an enormous explosion. In the middle distance, a plume of water gushed into the air. Ridgway staggered as the submarine rocked, then hoisted Hobson's binoculars to his eyes.

'*Bridge to Captain. Did we score a hit, sir?*'

Ridgway sighed with disappointment. 'Negative. I can see blood; the dinosaurs are fighting over something. I think we hit one of them.'

'*The torpedo guidance system must be reacting to the animals as it would to countermeasures.*'

Ridgway swore.

A kronosaurus smashed itself into the hull.

'Captain to bridge: what's the situation down there?'

'*Not good, sir. Bulkhead seventeen sprang a leak, but we managed to patch it. The hull is going to go if we can't get clear soon.*'

'There's no chance of that, sailor. They're nose to tail up here – you could probably walk to the bloody mainland!'

Chtaachtl gestured impatiently to an aide.

Where is the Doctor?

We have just received news – the mammal has escaped from our detention centre. He is at large in the city.

He must be found!

Xukbahkn shivered with fright. He'd never seen any of the great reptiles this close. Normally they were used for excavating or transportation of loads too heavy or cumbersome for the city mind-builders to move. Now they were stampeding through a part of the city which only a year before they had helped to build.

Xukbahkn became aware that his mother had linked, was summoning him to the family transport.

I'm coming!

He turned to run. A diplodocus blocked his path. Xukbahkn stopped. The reptile had approached unheard in the chaos. He turned again. More of the giant creatures pressed close around him, smaller, faster animals darting between the giant legs of the larger ones. He could sense the panic from the creatures; it terrified him.

Xukbahkn! Where are you!

I'm here. I'm coming!

He turned once more, slipped nimbly between the flanks of two reptiles, ducked, rolled beneath the belly of a third, dodging huge, thudding legs as he ran. Behind him came an enormous crash as his family home was smashed aside like a toy.

Xukbahkn!

Xukbahkn was about to reply when he cannoned into another figure. A human figure. Xukbahkn stared at the mammal, trembling.

'Good afternoon!' beamed the Doctor. 'I wonder if you could direct me to the Palace. I seem to be – '

An ornithomimus ran between them. The Doctor dodged backwards. Xukbahkn yelped with surprise and backed away as well.

His mother linked again and her mind was swamped with fear.

It's alright, mother, I'm –

He screamed as the left hind foot of a camarasaurus knocked him to the ground and crushed his legs into the rubble of his home.

To port there was an explosion and three dinosaurs dissolved into flame. The spray from the explosion drenched Ridgway with a bloody froth.

From the rear of the submarine came a sudden grinding noise and the shearing of metal. He grabbed the intercom. 'Captain to bridge: what the hell's going on?'

'*Bridge aye: engineering reports the port drive shaft has sheared. One of the dinosaurs must have rammed the prop.*'

'Christ on a stick! And the hull?'

'*Not good, sir – another few minutes and we've had it.*'

Hobson pushed open the conning tower hatch and clambered out into the observation well. His arm had been splinted and bandaged. His eyes were shadows in a face grey with pain. 'Robin. It has to be now. We have to launch the missiles now.'

Ridgway was about to reply when a kronosaurus leaped from the water and crashed down onto the submarine aft of the conning tower, wrecking the hatch mechanisms of several launch tubes.

Circles within circles, the Silurian city glistened in the rays of the late afternoon sun. The beams slanted to lay dusty yellow spokes across the discs of buildings, on the spiral paths of rampways and parks gliding past beneath the airship.

And on the thousands of reptiles thundering through the streets.

Benton watched the animals trampling figures and buildings alike into a bloody wreckage and smiled harshly.

Rubbing a hand absently across his bandaged arm, he ordered the airship lower so he could direct the attack more efficiently.

He glanced upwards. Hundreds of black specks were rising from the city towards them. Pterosaurs. Beyond them he could see the faint bronze glitter of airships.

Benton's smile didn't falter.

He was the hunter now.

In the Palace operations room, the mind-screens were glowing with scenes of chaos and destruction. All over the city, buildings were collapsing as the giant reptiles trampled everything before them into rubble. The mental aura of pain was so great that both Chtaachtl and the operators were struggling to stay linked to their systems. In the flickering beams of light from the mind-screens, Morka was utterly still and silent. Of them all, only he was fully linked. Only he could really encompass the carnage being wreaked on Ophidian.

He turned to Chtaachtl. *We must stop our attack on the human submarine. Our city will be destroyed, our people killed.*

We cannot!

We have no choice!

Lee Wood tried not to scream as daggers of pain sank

281

into his mind. The auxiliary airship he commanded shuddered as the navigator slumped across the controls. Wood staggered clear of the command well and wrenched the man from the controls. He stared through the wide canopy and was horrified to see the sky thick with pterosaurs and their riders, tiny black shapes with the coal glint of red at their foreheads. His mind reeled with yet more pain.

The ship shuddered again. There were scrabbling sounds. Screams, echoing along the companionway leading to the observation gallery.

The gallery! It was open to the air! If the Silurians could land there . . .

He spun as the door to the bridge dilated, drawing his pistol as three Silurians stepped through the opening, firing even as the third eyes glared with hatred, emptying his clip as daggers of pain tore his mind apart.

'*Bridge to Captain!*' There was a note of amazement in Charlie's voice, as if he was unable to quite believe his own ears. '*The dinosaurs! They're moving away!*'

Ridgway was already on his way down the ladder from the conning tower, Hobson close behind. 'I saw. Can you get a fix on any controlling submersibles?'

'Yes, sir. Absolutely, sir! Six blips! Feeding co-ordinates to fire control now, sir!'

Ridgway said calmly, 'Fire control: load and lock six Tigerfish. Program on board sonar with signatures of target vessels. Fire one to six sequentially on my command.'

'Fire control, aye. Six 'fish loaded, locked and programmed.'

'Very well, mister: fire one to six sequentially.'

'Firing one to six, aye.'

The deck trembled.

'Helm: make best speed, bearing zero-niner-seven.'

'Helm, aye.'

Charlie turned in alarm. 'Captain! I'm picking up another signature! Closing fast from – '

Something smashed into the hull. The collision alarm rang. Ridgway was hurled across the deck as the submarine rocked. The air was full of smoke. He scrambled to his feet, choking, aware that the deck was tilted at a precarious angle.

' – pumps, start the – '
' – hatches! Seal off the bloody – '
' – not responding – '
' – no, seal them all – '

Christ, he thought. We're shipping water!

Benton shuddered, his mind reeling as auxiliary airship number one drove through a cloud of pterosaurs and riders. The sound of bodies thudding against the lift body, to fall dead or stunned towards the ground, filled him with savage pleasure.

The pilot turned suddenly. 'Sir, I think – '

The head of a forty-foot pterosaur smashed in through the pilot's canopy, showering the control system with lethal shards of crystal. Though the reptile was dead, there was movement; a Silurian began to climb in through the gap in the canopy, third eye glowing red. Benton felt his mind shrinking away from the sight. With an effort he caught himself. He drew his pistol, marched up to the creature and shot it cleanly through the head. It fell back out of the canopy and was whirled away by the slipstream.

'Detail!' roared Benton. 'Help me get this bird out of here!' He turned as UNIT soldiers leaped to comply. 'Where's the pilot?'

She was on the deck, still and silent, jagged shards of crystal projecting from her face, neck and chest.

The submarine rocked to the sound of another explosion.

' – to bridge, what the hell's going – '

Ridgway became aware Hobson was scrambling across the deck towards him, his feet sloshing through an inch of water.

There was another explosion. The submarine tilted even further.

Blood was smeared across Hobson's face. ' – the key. Take my – '

' – sonar: I have multiple blips, approaching from – '

' – helm: get us out of – '

' – to bridge: the starboard prop shaft just sheared – '

An explosion.

' – take the firing key!'

And another.

' – *sake, Robin, you have to launch now!*'

Benton drove the ship lower, scudding across the city. Gunners blasted chunks from the city as it passed. They fell, lost among the greater wreckage wrought by the trampling dinosaurs. Somewhere deep in his mind, Benton realized the damage his ship was causing was about the same as a bird might make pecking at the hide of an elephant. Except that if it pecked at the soft eye, and the brain beyond . . .

'Gunners, concentrate all weapons on the Palace. We're going in!'

More airships swept across the sky. Benton screamed as pain exploded through his mind. Fire bloomed in the lifting body. The command well shook as the structure began to come apart. Control systems exploded. Smoke filled the air, burning his eyes and lungs.

Tears streaming from his eyes, he screamed into the slipstream blasting in through the damaged canopy. 'You made an animal of me for twenty years! Never again! Do you hear me? *Never again!*'

He fell across the controls as flame blew the bridge apart.

The ship shook itself into glowing fragments less than a mile from the Palace. Burning debris rained down on the parklands, killing a baryonyx and three lions.

Ridgway stared at Hobson. The man's eyes were fixed, motionless. For a second Ridgway thought the older man was dead, but then his lips trembled. 'Don't let it all have been for nothing.'

Then Hobson slumped into the water. Blood poured from a massive head wound. His hand was stretched towards Ridgway. As he slumped, the fingers uncurled.

Lying within them was the second firing key.

The Brigadier glanced at his watch, calm amidst the scenes of battle. Half a mile away, Benton's airship was blasted into flaming ruin.

Beside him, Liz whispered, 'A present?'

'From my wife.'

Liz swallowed hard. 'There's something I have to tell you.'

'You didn't fit a unit to muffle the ship's drive signature as I asked. That's how the Silurians detected us.'

Liz looked puzzled. 'You knew? Why didn't you do anything?'

'Because it didn't matter.' The Brigadier consulted his watch. 'Because in something less than two minutes nothing any of us did or didn't do will matter.'

Liz stared at him. 'You mean, they were supposed to detect us?'

The Brigadier shrugged. 'We're just a diversion.'

Liz frowned. 'I don't understand.'

'We're at ground zero.'

Liz gasped with horror.

There was the sound of machine-gun fire. Beyond the canopy a pterosaur screeched and plummeted towards the ground. More pterosaurs swarmed outside the canopy and beyond them hovered the glistening bronze shapes of airships.

The Brigadier glanced at his watch. 'We're not important, Liz,' he said quietly. 'Only the children.'

'Sound abandon ship! All hands into the water!'

Clutching Hobson's key, Ridgway waded through knee-high water to the launch computer. He grabbed the sonar operator, whirled him around. 'Not you, Charlie.' He pressed Hobson's key into the operator's hand.

Charlie stared at him. 'I don't know if I can – '

'*We don't have any choice!*'

Chtaachtl linked with the systems operative. *Report on status of craft attacking human warship.*

Contact is lost. All ships are now presumed destroyed by the human torpedoes.

285

Chtaachtl drew in a shuddering breath. *Focus an atmospheric window on the human warship. It must be destroyed!*

At that moment the Doctor entered the operations room, a Silurian child clutched in his arms. 'No!' he yelled. 'You must talk to the humans! Negotiate for peace!'

Chtaachtl signalled to an operative. *Destroy that mammal!*

Ridgway choked. Steam was rising from the water to mix with the smoke in the air.

'Some of the hatches are jammed.'

'The missiles will blow them open when they fire!'

The water began to boil.

'How do we know that?'

'If they don't, it won't matter. Now do as I tell you!'

The hull began to glow.

'You must talk!' yelled the Doctor desperately. 'You must make peace. In the name of humanity!'

'Humanity's time is over,' Chtaachtl said, contemptuously. She glared angrily at the Doctor and her third eye began to glow.

'No,' said Morka. 'I can't let you make that mistake.' Focusing all his frustration and anger on Chtaachtl, he blasted her aside.

He linked with the operator. *Cancel the firing sequence!*

The operator turned despairingly. *It is too late!*

'I can't do it!'

'You must! I'm ordering it!'

Beneath Ridgway's feet, the hull of the submarine shuddered like a paper boat in a storm.

'– Now! Do it –'

Steel and glass and human flesh ran like meltwater.

But the missiles had been launched.

Calm among the chaos in the operations room, Morka turned to the Doctor. 'What can we do?'

The Doctor thought for a moment. 'Perhaps Ace –'

Morka shook his head. 'Chtaachtl killed your friend.'

'Then the combined telekinetic ability of all your people?'

'It will not work. The missiles have too much kinetic energy to stop. Deflecting them wouldn't be enough.'

'In that case, there is nothing we can do.'

'Then the Nightmare will begin all over again, and all my hopes and dreams, all the lessons we learned – all these were for nothing!'

Nothing. Morka's words echoed through Chtaachtl's mind as she gazed at the crushed child the Doctor had brought with him to the operations room. She crawled weakly across to the child and closed his eyes without touching them. 'Only the children . . .' she whispered, but nobody heard.

Beside Morka, the Doctor swiftly considered several plans, discarding them equally quickly. He began to pace. He stopped, began to speak, stopped, shook his head. It was impossible. Inconceivable. Despite his vast intelligence, his creativity and imagination, he was powerless, impotent before a simple mechanical law. He could do nothing except wait for death.

Like a human.

A tiny yellow raft bobbed up and down on the mid-Atlantic swell. Inside the raft, the naval surgeon gazed down at the woman with the punctured lung and wondered if either of them would live out the hour.

Two miles away, the ocean was split by multiple explosions. Poseidon missiles erupted from the surface. Harry was dazzled as the engines ignited, driving the missiles into the air. Less than a second later, the sky opened and a shaft of light drove down into the water, vaporizing it instantly. Harry yelled and turned away, one half of his face sun-burned an angry red. The water heaved again as SSBN HMS *Revenge* exploded into vapour.

Hobson, his music, his choices, all gone in an instant.

And the radio. And the medical supplies. And the food. And the water.

The raft rocked harder. Harry looked around and saw a thirty-foot high wall of sea water rushing towards them.

287

He heaved a desperate sigh. 'I swear, if I ever get out of this I'm going to give up the ruddy Navy.'

He put his arms around the woman and grabbed hold of the raft's safety lines.

The wave hit.

Ace coughed smoke from her lungs. Beside her Manisha lay on the floor of the console room. Her clothes were blackened, smoking. Ace smelt the odour of burned clothing and flesh. She struggled to her hands and knees, crawled across the tiny space to Manisha's head. She touched her cheeks. Her eyelids fluttered. Opened.

'Ace? What the hell did you put in my drink?'

Her eyes closed and her head fell back. But Ace heaved a sigh of relief. Manisha was alive.

Sensing the TARDIS trying to gain her attention, Ace turned her mind to other matters. She struggled to her feet, squashed into the space between the edge of the console and the blank wall. Facing her was the control surface containing the slot into which she had jammed the key and a big black box holding a single large red button. The button was jammed in the 'on' position.

'I did it then,' Ace said wonderingly. 'I launched the ship.'

She reached out to touch the key, intending to retrieve it for the Doctor. As she touched it, she felt a force flow through her. She gasped.

The interior space of the TARDIS began to unfold around her.

Rooms, corridors, passages, floors, all slid out of architectural hiding and locked together. Laboratories, living quarters, a swimming pool, cloisters, libraries, all unfolded like clever pieces of origami.

The walls receded, dimpling into their familiar roundelled form.

The dimness was shot through with iridescent colours. The colours flashed into a strong, even white light.

The hum of the engines strengthened and steadied.

The time rotor began to oscillate smoothly: a beating heart giving life to the renewed ship.

'Yes!' Ace clenched her fist, ignoring the pain of her sunburned skin. 'Absolutely genuinely unadulterated *yes!*'

Then she lowered her hand. 'But . . .' If she were to carry out the Doctor's instructions, the first thing she had to do was put the life of this reborn TARDIS at risk.

The Brigadier and Liz Shaw were ushered into the Palace morning room. The Brigadier had been relieved of his pistol and his swagger stick. Liz thought he looked rather lost without the stick. The warship was moored at the Palace tower; the rest of the crew remained inside it.

The Brigadier looked around suspiciously. The scene was not exactly what he'd expected. Instead of hordes of interrogating reps, third eyes blazing, he saw relatively few Silurians. The crystal edges of the room were softened by rich tapestries. An arched window allowed the cool red light of late afternoon to fill the room. In the middle of the room stood a tall, slightly stooped Silurian whose skin was mottled with age. Beside him was the Doctor; the new, suspicious model, the Brigadier was careful to remember.

'Brigadier Lethbridge-Stewart,' the Silurian said. 'Welcome to my Palace. Perhaps you'd like to see some part of it before it, and we, are destroyed by your missiles?'

The Brigadier licked his lips. 'You're in charge here?'

'I am the Leader of the Silurian race.'

The Brigadier reached for his gun; the holster was empty.

Liz's hand on his arm stopped his movement. 'It's too late for that now, Brigadier.'

'I'm afraid Miss Shaw is right!' said the Doctor in an overly perky voice. 'Just at this moment the last thing you need to complete your destiny as a race of killers is a gun.'

The Brigadier stared at the Doctor. 'I thought you would have left this planet by now.'

'No, indeed. I have . . . other plans.'

'Really?'

'Unfortunately, as Morka has observed, in about two minutes from now, those plans won't be worth a bent ha'penny. Unless, of course,' he added with a narrowing of his eyes, 'you have in your possession a radio code which will disarm the missiles before they detonate.'

The Brigadier laughed. 'Disarm them? How little you understand the nuclear mentality, Doctor. They are weapons of *war*. In war, there is no provision for a change of heart. Once launched, those missiles cannot be disarmed. They will detonate, I can assure you, precisely as planned.'

'Oh dear.'

Morga sagged. His eyes flickered to the incubator. The Brigadier followed his gaze. The incubator contained a large, mottled egg.

The Brigadier noticed his glance. 'Your child?'

Morka nodded.

'My sympathies.'

Morka hissed in anger. 'Do not speak to me of sympathy. There is no sympathy in you! In any human!'

The Doctor placed one hand on Morka's arm. 'Anger won't help you now.'

'Nothing can help us!'

Morka glared at the Brigadier. The Brigadier said nothing.

Liz moved across to the Doctor. 'You knew this would happen, didn't you? "Everyone dies, Liz," you said. You knew.'

The Doctor stared at his shoes. 'No, Liz. Believe it or not, I was generalizing.' He squared his shoulders. Lifted his umbrella, slipped the handle over his arm. Straightened his hat.

Beyond the window, over the burning city of Ophidian, vapour trails split the sky.

He took out his fob watch, flipped open the lid. 'It's time.'

The sun went out.

In the sudden darkness, the bright glare of missile tail fires came clearly across the city. One by one the columns of light tilted over and the missiles drove downwards.

They hit the ground, smashing into buildings, flattening

gardens that hadn't already been trampled by the vast mass of dinosaurs.

Liz flinched. She reached out for the Doctor but he was no longer beside her.

A minute passed.

There was no explosion.

Liz found she was still alive.

'What,' she said nervously, 'happened to the sun?'

The Brigadier made a sort of strangled gulping noise. 'Doctor? Where are you? What have you done to the missiles!'

The Doctor didn't reply. Liz heard him shuffling around the morning room, muttering. 'I'm sure it was supposed to be around here somewhere – ah ha!'

At the Doctor's triumphant exclamation, a thin crack of light appeared, as if from a small, square doorway. The thin wedge of light widened. It *was* a doorway. Beyond it was a roundelled corridor.

The Brigadier strode across the room, his shoes clicking on the crystal floor. 'Doctor? I demand to know what you've done to my missiles! Why you've materialized the TARDIS in the Palace wall!'

The Doctor hesitated at the threshold of the door, a dapper silhouette. 'I'm afraid you're wrong, Brigadier. The TARDIS hasn't materialized in the Palace. And as for the missiles, I haven't done anything to them – yet.'

'That door certainly wasn't there earlier,' said the Brigadier. 'And it looks very much like part of the TARDIS.'

The Doctor sighed. 'That's because it *is* part of the TARDIS. Now do please be quiet, old chap. I have some rather important business to attend to.'

The Brigadier spluttered in annoyance. The Doctor vanished into the corridor, calling Ace's name.

Ace heard the Doctor's voice and ran to meet him at the doors to the console room.

'Ah, there you are. Why did you take so long to do what I asked? The instructions were quite clear, weren't they?' He brushed past Ace and began to run around the console, checking read-outs.

Ace frowned in annoyance. ' "Hi, Ace. How are you? Not too badly hurt, I hope. Manisha? Oh she's fine, I took her to the sickbay. Thanks for fetching the TARDIS for me. How's your arm?" '

The Doctor looked up briefly. 'Stop pontificating and help me.'

'It might help if you told me what you were doing, instead of running around in ever decreasing circles like the Oozlum bird.'

The Doctor took off his hat and scratched his head. 'Oozlum?' he muttered. 'Now what planet . . . Oh never mind,' he dismissed the puzzle. 'There's no time.'

'You're right there.' Ace pointed to a large red light which was flashing on the console. 'That's been flashing ever since I reprogrammed the dimensional stabilizer.'

'Reprogrammed it? You shouldn't have had to do that.' He thought for a moment. 'Or been able to.'

'Yeah well, I did, didn't I?'

The Doctor poked a button. The red light continued to flash. He thumped his fist on the control board. The light went out.

'There you are. Perfect working order!'

'Oh yeah?'

At least twenty red lights began to flash on the console. 'Ah.'

Part of the console exploded violently.

'Um.'

Ace handed the Doctor a slim cylinder. 'Fire extinguisher,' she said. 'From the store room. I had a sneaking suspicion you might be needing it.'

The Doctor looked absently at the extinguisher and handed it back to Ace. He ran around the console and began to input commands into the main operating systems.

Ace shrugged, angling the extinguisher towards the fire. As she began to spray foam, there was another gush of flame, this time from a subsystem located on the far side of the console room. The TARDIS shook.

'Doctor? What's going on?'

The Doctor looked up briefly, pushed his hat back out

of his eyes, and said, 'It's very simple. The instructions I gave you caused the TARDIS to materialize around the entire planet.'

'What, you mean the whole Earth?'

'Of course I mean the whole Earth, now kindly don't interrupt. Because the inside of a working TARDIS is in a state of *temporal grace*, weapons won't function. That means the missiles won't explode. Now all I have to do is delete the sections of architecture containing the missiles and they will cease to exist. Then, allamy-gallamy-zoop! No missiles, no problem.'

Ace frowned. 'Except . . .' she said, pointing with the fire extinguisher to the burning environmental control system.

The Doctor nodded, hands racing over the console. 'Yes. Except, apparently, the TARDIS *isn't* working properly.'

'And I suppose that's my fault, is it?' Ace said.

The Doctor stared at her. She began to feel uncomfortable.

There was another explosion. The TARDIS shuddered.

In the Palace morning room the shock was amplified out of all proportion. Liz found herself flung to one side. She crashed against a wall and fell to the floor, grabbing a tapestry to try to keep her balance. The tapestry tore clear of its mountings and wrapped itself around her as she fell.

Morka stumbled to the floor. His hearing was no longer acute enough to hear the fabric of the Palace walls creak with stress – but nothing stopped him feeling the vibrations through his palms and knees, and through his third eye. He struggled to his feet, in time to watch with horror as the incubator containing his egg began to topple slowly towards the floor.

In the console room, Ace discarded the spent fire extinguisher and grabbed a fresh one. The room was full of smoke and sparks and choking foam. The Doctor was manipulating the controls so fast Ace couldn't see his hands move. The smoke whirled in tiny storms around his hands.

He was mumbling something she couldn't make out.

'Doctor! The ceiling's getting lower!'

'I know, Ace. The power expenditure necessary to keep the old girl at this size relative to a whole planet is practically inconceivable.'

'You mean this TARDIS is going to crack up too?'

'Not if I can help it, Ace. Not if I can help it!'

The Doctor suddenly leaped back from the console as a fountain of sparks erupted into the air.

'Oops.'

Ace hurried around to his side of the console. 'What's up now?'

'The architectural co-ordinate selector just exploded. I'll have to input the co-ordinates for missile deletion manually.'

'And if you get it wrong?'

The Doctor fixed her with a horribly honest gaze.

Equilibrium disturbed, the city rocked on its foundations. Buildings toppled, crushing thousands who had escaped the violence so far.

In the morning room of the Palace, the incubator surrendered to the inevitable pull of gravity. As it toppled, the Brigadier whirled and in one movement scooped the egg into his arms. He cradled it as the room shook around them.

Ten yards away, Morka clambered to his feet and stared at the Brigadier. 'You saved my son.'

The Brigadier's expression hardened. 'You were responsible for the death of my wife,' he said. 'The downfall of my society. The extinction of everything I have ever loved.'

Cradling the egg in one hand, he wiped the other across his face.

'Why shouldn't I destroy the one thing *you* love?'

'Come on, Doctor, I don't think the TARDIS has got much longer.'

'I'm calculating as fast as I can. One slip and you can wave goodbye to most of the eastern seaboard.'

Ace frowned. She was about to reply when the Doctor silently pointed to a distant subsystem. A second later, it exploded.

Ace rushed to extinguish the flames.

'If the console room's shrinking again, like last time . . .'

'I know, I know.'

'Then that must mean the TARDIS is dying.'

'Full marks, Ace,' the Doctor said in a strained voice.

'But if that happens – *what happens to the Earth?*'

'Ace, callous though it may seem to you, there is something infinitely more worrying to me than the fate of the Earth. You see, if this TARDIS collapses internally now, it will end up occupying the same space as the old TARDIS, the one in the tar pit. And then . . .' He shuddered. 'Time ram.'

'What's that when it's at home, then?'

'Something that makes the destruction of a planet look like a popped bubble gum.'

Ace's eyes glinted.

'And don't say *neat!*'

Morka stared furiously at the mammal. The human. The being for whom he had worked all his life to bring peace. His third eye began to glow with anger. No – with rage.

'I really wouldn't do that, if I were you,' the Brigadier said calmly.

Morka hissed gently. His cheeks trembled. The light in his third eye intensified.

The Brigadier held up the egg. 'The city is still shaking. I don't know how long I can keep my balance. I expect you could kill me, but then . . .' He shrugged. 'Do you think you could catch the egg before it hit the floor, even with telekinesis?'

Morka froze. 'What do you want?'

'I want you to feel anguish. Frustration. I want you to suffer as I and millions like me have suffered.'

'I sympathize – '

The Brigadier screamed, *'I don't want your sympathy! I want . . .'* He hesitated. 'I want your understanding. Understanding . . . of what it was like to be hunted. To be an animal. To die an animal, scrabbling in the mud. Fighting each other for the simple privilege of growing crops or digging for fresh water, or loving, or raising children.'

He stared at Morka, and his fingers trembled where they held the egg.

'Get down on your knees, you damn *animal*.'

Manisha staggered into the console room, ducking to avoid banging her head on the top of the door frame. She stared around her in amazement.

'Ace?'

She caught the fire extinguisher Ace threw at her.

'Come on, chum,' said Ace. 'Make yourself useful.'

Manisha pointed the extinguisher at a fire and triggered it.

Liz struggled clear of the tapestry and took in the scene in an instant. The Brigadier holding Morka's egg high above his head. The Silurian Leader on his knees before him. 'What do you think you're doing!' she yelled.

'No more than I must, Liz.'

'For the children?'

'Of course!'

'*Then look over there!*' Liz screamed, pointing to the corpse of the Silurian child lying on a pallet some yards away. 'And think about what you're holding!'

'The future!'

'*A child!*' Liz poured all the emotion she could into her words. 'Brigadier, that's a child in your hands. You're right: the future belongs to the children. But to *all* the children. Not just ours.'

The Doctor's hands blurred over the controls, set a final sequence of commands and poised, motionless, over the *function execute* switch. There was a fixed, distant look on his face.

Manisha threw aside her extinguisher. 'It's empty.'

Ace ducked to avoid the sinking ceiling. Something made her glance at the co-ordinate input selector. 'Doctor!'

He looked up.

'What have you done to the co-ordinates? They're inverted! You'll delete everything *except* the missiles! You'll destroy the planet – everything!'

The Doctor appeared to come to with a start. Giving Ace a sheepish smile, he reached out and spun a dial. The co-ordinates righted themselves.

Ace gave him a disparaging look.

The walls closed in, crushing them into the tiny space around the console.

The air was thinning. The fires began to die away. Ace gasped for breath.

'Doctor!'

'Somehow, I always thought there would be words for a situation like this.' He shrugged. 'Ah well, can't win 'em all.'

He pressed the switch.

One by one, throughout the cities, the warheads and the surrounding few feet of architecture began to vanish.

Ace and Manisha followed the Doctor into the Palace morning room. Both women were coughing, their eyes streaming with tears. Ace's arm was in agony. Manisha staggered because of her burned back. As they entered the room, Ace was amazed to see the Brigadier reach out a hand to a Silurian and pull him to his feet.

Liz crossed to them and supported Manisha as she sat, suddenly, with a surprised gasp.

She became aware something odd had appeared at the far end of the room: a bright yellow rubber raft. Water spilled from the raft and ran across the floor. In the raft were two figures, a man and a woman. Both figures were drenched; the woman was coughing blood.

'Benny!' Even as Ace ran towards her, there was another movement, this time by the window. An archae-opteryx, one of the world's earliest birds, flew in through the window. Though reptilian, the bird had feathers. It fluttered across the heads of Morka and the Brigadier as

The Brigadier offered him back his egg. Morka took it from him with trembling hands.

The Doctor held out his own hand. The archaeopteryx settled gently on it. The Doctor made cooing noises. He smiled.

Behind them the TARDIS doorway vanished noisily.

The sun came out.

EXTINCTION

The sun sank behind Kilimanjaro, momentarily gilding the snow-capped mountain with flame; a moment later there were only the stars to light the scarred city of Ophidian.

In the Palace gardens, Bernice sat on the curved wall of the fountain, studying its shape, the little chips of crystal glowing silver within its depths, like stars mirrored in the water.

She rubbed one hand across the side of her chest, level with her lung, and took a long swig from her hip flask.

A familiar reflection beside her own made her look up. She hadn't heard the Doctor approach.

'Fascinating architecture they have here, don't you think?' she said, somewhat blearily. 'To design without use of tools allows for a more unified concept and final construction than . . .' She tailed off. Took another drink. Stared pointedly at the Doctor as if daring him to comment.

The Doctor ignored the stare. 'I really thought you were gone, you know.'

'Yeah, well. You weren't the only one, upon occasion. Their regression therapy was prettyss . . .' Her voice slurred. 'Pretty scary.'

'I can imagine.'

'Can you?'

'Oh yes.'

'And as for that bloody submarine . . .' She took another swig. 'I never knew, what it was like . . . I . . . I would've done it, you know. Killed myself for an ideal.'

'That's scary too, isn't it?'

'Scary? Grief!' Bernice lifted the flask to her lips. 'I thought I was more cynical than that.'

'Fear is a mirror, Benny. It shows us ourselves.'

The Doctor reached out and gently took the flask from her. She made no move to stop him. He corked it, handed it back. Bernice took it from him, shrugged, shoved it in her back pocket. She trailed her hand through the water of the fountain. Dozens of tiny glowing fish rippled away, alarmed at her presence.

'Ace thinks I shouldn't do this,' she said, scooping water and allowing it to trickle back into the pool through her cupped fingers.

'Ace thinks a lot of things,' said the Doctor. 'She thinks she wants Manisha to travel with us in the TARDIS. She thinks she wants me to stop interfering in the situations we encounter.' He sighed. Leaned heavily on his umbrella. 'Do you know, Benny, I think she may be right.'

Benny tried to sit up straighter on the edge of the fountain.

'If that's true, I *do* need another drink.'

'Try coffee,' said the Doctor. 'There's some in the TARDIS.'

Ace found Manisha studying artifacts in the Museum of Silurian Culture situated in the north spoke of the Palace. Through wide, arched windows, she could see the dark expanse of grassland bordering the estate, and beyond that the edge of the city. Fires were still burning there. Smoke drifted slowly into the air, indigo clouds eclipsing the stars above that part of the city.

Manisha had her hand pressed to a transparent case. Inside it were a number of tiny, flute-like objects.

'I wonder what sort of music they would make,' she mused quietly.

Ace sighed. 'Flutey sort of music, I expect.'

Manisha turned. 'Yeah, probably.' She grinned. Held out her hand.

Ace studied the hand, the callused skin, the smooth muscle. 'You're not coming then?'

'The life of an intellectual isn't for me; there's enough adventure right here to go twice round and still leave some over for breakfast.'

300

Ace nodded. 'To tell you the truth, it's probably for the best.'

'Yeah.'

Manisha offered her hand again; this time Ace grasped it firmly.

'So long, space girl,' said Manisha.

'Don't let them grind you down.'

Manisha grinned. 'Would I?'

Ace squeezed Manisha's hand once more, hard enough to bruise, to make a lingering memory. Then she turned and walked back to the TARDIS.

Liz met the Doctor walking through the Palace gardens.

'I expect you'll be leaving, then,' said Liz as darkness closed in around them.

'I expect I will. I can't sort out all your problems for you, you know.' The Doctor smiled gently to take the sting out of his words. 'You have to help yourselves. Learn to work together with the Silurians.'

'That's something we're going to have to practise.'

The Doctor nodded. 'Especially the Brigadier, eh?'

Liz smiled. 'Especially the Brigadier.' She shrugged. 'He's in there now, you know, with Morka and Chtorba and Icthar. Negotiating. It's real House of Commons stuff.'

'Hm. The longest route between two points.'

'But what a world we'll be able to build, eh, Doctor?'

The Doctor smiled, a little distractedly. He pulled a slim packet from his pocket and handed it to Liz.

'What's this then, Peter Pan, fairy dust?'

'You could say that.'

Liz examined the packet, shook some of its contents onto the palm of her hand. 'Seeds?' she asked wonderingly. 'Flower seeds?'

'Bit of a mix-and-match selection, I'm afraid, but I'm sure with a little thought you can make that work to your advantage.'

Liz poured the seeds back into the packet. She looked up, studied the Doctor frankly. 'Do you really think we'll be okay?'

The Doctor pointed up at the sky. 'On my world we

used to have a saying,' he told her. 'You see all those stars? Each one of those represents a promise. All the time they shine the promise remains unbroken. When you look at them, Liz, think of me.'

Liz gazed upwards, captivated by the stars of this hemisphere. She stared at them for a moment, almost seeing them through the Doctor's eyes. When she looked back he was gone.

She hefted the packet of seeds, squared her shoulders and walked back into the Palace.

Into the future.

When the Brigadier entered the morning room, Morka was standing beside the repaired incubator.

Preliminary talks had ended an hour before; the UNIT personnel had been assigned guest quarters. Fortunately, only one or two of them still displayed signs of the race memory malaise, and they were being treated by Morka's physicians with a serum derived from Bernice Summerfield. The funeral for those who had died in battle was due to be held tomorrow, after which the rebuilding of the city would begin.

The Brigadier had found himself unable to sleep. Perhaps there was a lingering trace of paranoia there, he didn't know.

Morka turned as he approached. He remained silent, allowing the Brigadier to speak first. The Brigadier searched for a long time for the right words, in the end giving up. 'I had orders to kill you even before the Nightmare began,' he said quietly. 'Twenty years ago.'

Morka hissed, his cheeks puffing out. The Brigadier found the expression impossible to interpret.

'As an apology, I've heard better,' Morka said quietly. 'But the night moves on.'

The Brigadier raised one eyebrow. Then, realizing Morka wouldn't understand the gesture, said, 'I don't understand.'

'That is an admission.' Morka gestured through the broad windows. 'The future is coming, one that we've made by our choices of twenty years ago.'

He took the Brigadier's hand and placed it flat against the incubator. 'The responsibility for the future is ours.'

The Brigadier pressed his fingers against the transparent crystal surrounding the egg and, like the future, suddenly felt he could almost touch it.

'We have to make a better world for the children,' he said. 'If it's possible.'

Morka nodded. 'If it's possible.'

The Doctor entered the TARDIS, parked normally now, if a little unconventionally, in the middle of the Palace fountain.

Inside the console room, he found Ace and Benny sitting at either end of the Edwardian chaise longue. The two women were staring at each other; neither was speaking.

'Making up?' he asked ingenuously.

Ace scowled.

Benny huffed angrily, tried to sit up straighter on the couch, succeeded only in leaning a little further sideways. 'You said something about coffee?'

'Indeed I did.'

The Doctor opened one of the wall roundels and rummaged within. He fished out a Thermos flask. 'For emergencies,' he explained with a little grin. He unscrewed the cap and filled it from the flask. Bernice reached out for the cup. Took a sip. 'Ah,' she said with a disgusted expression. 'Vintage pre-Cambrian.'

The Doctor offered more coffee to Ace, who prudently shook her head. The Doctor set the flask down beside Bernice.

'So what happens now?' asked Ace.

The Doctor hovered around the console, looking, Ace thought, decidedly nervous. Then he looked up and there was that look of terrible honesty in his eyes again.

'The universe ends several billion years before it should, about ten million species which would have been born, aren't. Wars aren't fought which should be, peace that ought to develop never does, cosmic evolution is truncated. In short, chaos. Billions and billions and *billions* of lives eradicated.'

Bernice stopped with the plastic cup halfway to her lips. 'You've been drinking your own coffee.'

The Doctor scowled. 'Believe me, it's no joke.'

Ace felt a cold shiver rush through her mind. Fear? A lingering connection with the TARDIS? 'But how?' she asked. 'Why?'

There was anger in the Doctor's voice. 'Why don't you tell me?'

Ace shook her head. The Doctor's anger seemed to be directed at *her*. 'I don't understand.'

Benny put down the coffee. 'I think I do.'

Ace stared 'Go on then,' she urged.

Bernice sat up straighter. 'It's all to do with mass-energy, isn't it?' She looked at the Doctor. He nodded and she continued, 'This world never happened in the real universe.'

'I gathered that much when we first landed here!' Ace said impatiently.

'Well then. By changing the history of this planet, the rest of the universe is changed as well, ipso facto.'

'So?'

'Thus creating an alternative time-line. An alternative universe. A sub-universe.'

'But that's impossible, isn't it? There's only one universe.' Ace shivered; the chaos implied by Bernice's explanation scared the hell out of her. 'There's only a finite amount of mass and energy *in* the universe. If another one exists – '

' – the real one suffers accordingly.' The Doctor's voice was like thunder. 'And someone has been "mucking about with time," as you put it. Playing games with the universe; and with me, by making me think I was responsible.'

Bernice stood, all trace of her drunkenness gone. 'When did you catch on?'

'Morka allowed me to share his memory of the moment of my death in this time-line. A death that should never have happened, but which somehow happened anyway.'

304

He thought for a moment. 'Which some*one* caused to happen.'

'But not Morka?'

'Not Morka. Time Lords regenerate. Once Morka killed me I would just have regenerated. There would still have been an alternative time-line, although only a slightly different one. No. Someone ensured that Morka *could* kill me. *Someone* made provision for it.' His eyes glowed angrily. 'Someone is playing games with me. Someone is *meddling*.'

He turned angrily, his slight body hunched, rigid with tension. 'And the game's not over yet.'

Ace leaped to her feet. 'Right. Let's take this creep out.'

Bernice put one hand on Ace's shoulder. Ace looked at her. Benny did not move. 'That's not what he means,' she said.

'Then what . . .' Ace tailed off, realization dawning. 'That's what you were doing in the console room! You were going to time ram the other TARDIS – destroy this entire sub-universe.'

The Doctor turned. 'It was – still is – the only way of ensuring the real universe regains the mass-energy it needs to live out *its* allotted life span.'

Ace shuddered. 'And I stopped you.'

'I was as much responsible as you,' said the Doctor. 'We'd all spent time on this world. We'd known the people here, grown to like them. To love them a little, perhaps.'

Ace looked away.

'The game has been played already,' said the Doctor. 'It was designed to take advantage of my compassion, but we've all lost.'

Ace said, 'There must be something we can do.'

The Doctor looked at Ace and Bernice in turn. 'There is one move we can still make.'

Ace lifted her hand to her brow. 'You mean destruction. End the universe. Kill Manisha, Liz, Morka, the Brigadier . . . everyone.' She stared at the Doctor and her eyes flashed furiously. 'How can you do that?'

'How can I not?' he replied simply.

'They're people! We risked our lives for them. Don't tell me they have no future.'

'Ace, Ace . . . They never really existed. Except in someone else's game.'

'How can you see it as a game?' Ace shouted. 'They were real. Manisha was real. The scars in my back are real, the bullet in Benny's lung was real, the children were real, Alan was *real!*'

The Doctor reached out to Ace, but she struck his hand aside. 'Don't touch me.' She looked up at the Doctor, and he flinched from the disgust in her eyes. 'I thought I was getting to like you again.'

'Ace, wait, let me finish. I didn't mean – '

'Then what did you mean?'

'I can channel the energy from the time ram. Use it to allow this universe to wind down gracefully, while still returning to the real universe its allotted amount of energy. Manisha will live a full life. She will die naturally, before entropy takes everything. Everybody wins.'

'And what about the children?' Ace said harshly.

The Doctor licked his lips.

Ace opened her mouth to say something, hesitated, closed it again without speaking. She turned away in disgust.

Bernice took her arm. 'It's not like that and you know it.'

Ace pulled away from Bernice. 'Why don't you open your eyes? He's got you right where he wants you, you know that? Right where I used to be. You were going to kill yourself to make peace happen there. Why don't you think about how futile that gesture would have been.'

Ace turned to open the console room's inner door, realized it wasn't where it used to be, walked towards its new location.

'Ace.' The Doctor's voice was hard and grainy. 'Where are you going?'

'I'm going to my room.'

'Your room doesn't exist in this TARDIS.'

'I configured another one!' Ace paused at the threshold of the room. 'In Spacefleet the veterans always told you

306

not to get involved. Not to make it personal. I always thought they were talking rubbish. I was so sure.' She turned back to the Doctor. 'Thanks for teaching me I was wrong,' she said bitterly, and left.

The Doctor lowered his gaze.

After a minute, Bernice whispered, 'This time ram thing. It's pretty dangerous, right? We could be destroyed as well?'

'Oh yes.' The Doctor looked up. 'Yes indeed. Our opponent is a clever player. His ultimate objective has to be my extinction.'

Bernice considered. 'You know ...' She hesitated. 'I don't think Ace should be alone.'

The Doctor nodded. 'I understand. I'll see you both afterwards.'

'If it works.'

The Doctor held her gaze. 'If it works.'

Bernice was about to leave when something made her look back.

'Be careful, won't you, Benny?' said the Doctor. 'The old girl's a new ship now. There'll be places where she's still a little unsure of herself.'

'I'll watch it,' Bernice promised. She left the room.

Alone with his choice, the Doctor began to reprogram the console.

You win this round, whoever you are, he thought. *But watch the shadows. And don't slip for a moment. Because when you do, I'll be there, and I'll bring you to book. For Earth. For the children.*

He touched the function execute switch.

ACKNOWLEDGEMENTS

Letting Off Steam

A book only needs an author. A *good* book needs more. I like to think that this is a good book. If I'm right, this is due to unparalleled efforts on the part of the following people:

Doctors Jon and Alison Barnwell-Cooper (Neurological research, medical research, sweating, clammy flesh, distended organs and septicaemia.)

Paul Hinder (Mix-and-match biscuits, mix-and-match vegetation, a new car battery and some astoundingly useful proof-reading.)

Andrew Dymond (To whom more thanks are due than I could list in twenty books.)

Tim Keable (For some seriously ace work on some seriously ace illos.)

Mum and Dad (Endless support, stacks of bacon butties and lashings and lashings of ... er ... well, tea, actually.)

Michelle Drayton RGN RM (Ret.) ('Sick is when you use the handcuffs but you have a feather as well ...') (Medical research, Claforan, Flagyl, Venflons and making sure the little polystyrene ball goes up and down.) (Up and down in what? – J.)